ANAL PROBES SUCK ASS

ANAL PROBES SUCK ASS

UNLIKELY BOUNTYHUNTERS™ BOOK 2

MICHAEL TODD

DISRUPTIVE IMAGINATION

Copyright © 2021 LMBPN Publishing
Cover Art by Jake @ J Caleb Design
http://jcalebdesign.com / jcalebdesign@gmail.com
Cover copyright © LMBPN Publishing
A Michael Anderle Production

LMBPN Publishing
PMB 196, 2540 South Maryland Pkwy
Las Vegas, NV 89109

First US edition, June 2021
eBook ISBN: 978-1-64971-860-0
Print ISBN: 978-1-64971-861-7

THE ANAL PROBES SUCK ASS TEAM

Thanks to our Beta Team:
John Ashmore, Jim Caplan, Kelly O'Donnell, Rachel Beckford

JIT Readers
Deb Mader
Debi Sateren
Dave Hicks
Dorothy Lloyd
Peter Manis
Zacc Pelter
Jeff Goode
Jackey Hankard-Brodie
Paul Westman

Editor
Skyhunter Editing Team

DEDICATION

*To Family, Friends and
Those Who Love
to Read.
May We All Enjoy Grace
to Live the Life We Are
Called.*

— Michael

CHAPTER ONE

Gage was still groggy when they pushed him out of the car. Thankfully, the callous bastard driving the tan Cadillac DeVille had the courtesy to stop first rather than throw him out of a moving vehicle.

Even so, the one in the back kicked him in a part of his anatomy that was already sore, and he ended up on his hands and knees in the dirt. The car door slammed, and the two agents peeled out like thugs in a cheap gangster movie. Dust blew in Gage's face.

The last thing he remembered was walking down the street near his house to buy his siblings some dinner. He was about three blocks from Chipotle when the Cadillac pulled up, and the driver asked directions to the San Felipe de Neri Church. Gage thought it was odd that two guys in black suits and sunglasses were going to mass on Tuesday night, but he knew where the church was located and told them where to turn.

Then he saw a red flash. After that, no memories—except for the anal probe, which probably stuck in his brain simply because of the *enormous* size of the device they stuck in his ass—everything else was a blank. He wasn't even sure if it was the same day.

He stood and brushed himself off. The tail lights of the tan DeVille continued up the dirt road that went fifty miles into the desert away from Albuquerque. Only then did he realize he was going to have a long walk home.

"Assholes!" he yelled, flipping them off. "What is it with you guys and the anal probes? Some lube would be nice. And *dinner!*"

He pulled at the crotch of his jeans and lifted one leg.

"Perverts," he muttered angrily.

In the dimming twilight, he saw the driver roll down his window, stick out his arm and flip Gage the bird. He must have been a half-mile away.

Gage was dumbfounded. *How did they hear me?* There was no way. *Oh shit. They bugged me.*

He began walking back toward the distant, twinkling lights of town. *Silently.*

On the other end of the galaxy, at that exact moment—relatively speaking—John was doing some probing of his own. The notable difference was that John's was pleasant, unlike Gage's, and John's was oral, not anal.

Meehix was giving him a blow job on top of Mount Rushmore, specifically, on top of Abraham Lincoln's head. The location didn't strike him as strange at the moment. He was too busy enjoying the fact that he was finally

2

engaged in significant sexual activity with Meehix—her mouth, anyway.

Still, immediately afterward, he couldn't help but question *why* Meehix gave him head while atop Honest Abe's head. How did they even get there?

"Did you like that?" Meehix said as she stretched out next to him.

"Very much," he admitted.

Even Hannah never did it that good.

"I'm glad." She kissed him on the cheek. "Sorry about the next part."

She suddenly straddled him and bit a giant, bloody chunk of flesh out of his forearm.

John screamed.

"What happened?" Meehix said. "Are you all right?"

They were back on the ship. Honest Abe's hard head disappeared, revealing that they were both lying on the hard cabin floor. John was fully clothed, and Meehix was next to him wrapped in a blanket.

His arm was throbbing, and he saw that the *bite* was actually the *burn.* He had rolled over in his sleep and popped the giant blister. The wound was wet and gross. His jeans were also.

Why Mount Rushmore?

He vaguely remembered an old thriller on Netflix where some guy and his girlfriend were on top of the national monument with *Men In Black*-type characters chasing them, but he didn't recall a sex scene, only a train going into a tunnel.

I've got to get laid. This dry spell is for the birds.

That was it. *The Birds.* An old Alfred Hitchcock movie.

No, wait. That's not right. There were no birds on Abraham Lincoln's head in the movie I saw.

Meehix shook him.

"Hey! Snap out of it!" Now she sounded concerned.

"Sorry," he finally responded, making sure he kept his crotch covered with part of the blanket. "I just had the weirdest dream. You were in it."

"Really? What was I doing?"

"Um…just traditional Kdackan activities, like…*sightseeing*."

"Sightseeing on Kdack," she said sardonically. "That's how this whole mess got started."

She got up—with the blanket—and John grabbed it. She looked at him funny.

"I'm *cold*," he lied.

"I'm *naked*," she countered. She was about to yank the blanket away from him until she saw the laser burn on his arm.

"Oh my God, that looks awful." She sat back down next to him. "Your blister popped."

That's not the only thing that popped. How embarrassing. If Meehix knew my innermost thoughts, she'd think I was a sex fiend.

She looked his arm over. It didn't appear infected, but it would leave a nasty scar if they didn't get him a skin graft. She realized it was because of her that the injury happened and also why the blister popped.

"Sorry about the pheromones. I don't know what got me going like that. When you passed out, I figured you needed some sleep. I should have bandaged your burn first, but I…got distracted."

She remembered her pleasure toy. It was lying above them on the makeshift bed for all to see. She let him have the blanket, quickly slipped on some pants, and casually tossed a shirt over the toy.

How embarrassing. If John knew my innermost thoughts, he'd think I was a sex fiend.

"I've got to go to the bathroom," John said.

He stood with the blanket still around his waist and shuffled across the cabin to the alien toilet thing. While doing his business and using the blanket as a shield, he quickly took off his pants and put on some clean ones. He felt like a total perv.

While John answered the call of nature, Meehix snatched the pleasure toy and hid it in a storage compartment under the bed. She felt like a total perv.

"We should probably find a place to do a load of laundry and get some supplies," John said as he kicked his dirty clothes into the corner and turned back to Meehix. "Where are we anyway?"

"On our way to Nerth B space station, about midway into the third arm. It's an older station, but we should be able to eat, get cleaned up, and get Chuckie defrosted."

"Nerth B?" John repeated. "Why does that sound familiar?"

"Nerth B is where you go when you don't want a lot of questions. We should be able to get your burn fixed there too."

"Nerth B. Nerth B..." John kept repeating the name.

"What about it?" Meehix asked.

"I don't know." He sounded perplexed. "That name sounds so darn familiar."

Gage took a warm bath as soon as he got home. It was about eleven o'clock in the evening, and his backside felt a little better. He'd managed to convince a Lyft driver to pick him up in the desert, and he made it back in time to grab some food for his siblings and have a late dinner. He'd only been gone for about four hours, which was a relief since initially, he didn't know if he'd been away for days. His main concerns now were *why did these assholes kidnap me? And am I really bugged?* Maybe it was all government misinformation and the fact that they flipped him off a half-mile up the road after he called them perverts was a coincidence. Perhaps they *were* perverts, and the anal probing had nothing to do with a listening device. He wasn't going to the cops—that much was sure. What could they do? Give him a rape test? Regardless of their exact intentions, the guys that nabbed him had USSF connections. You'd think they'd know that planting a microphone in his colon was the worst possible place to listen from—especially after Chipotle.

He was in his bedroom flipping through streaming services on his flatscreen TV when an old movie came on. Some well-dressed guy was holding on to some well-dressed girl hanging over the edge of Mount Rushmore. He asked another well-dressed guy to help him. The other well-dressed guy stepped on the first one's hand to try and make him *and* the girl fall to their deaths.

"What a dick," Gage said.

The cops shot the bad well-dressed guy—with a *pistol* from about three hundred yards up Mount Rushmore, an unbelievable shot—and the bad well-dressed guy fell to his death. Then the guy holding the girl told her to hold on tight and pull herself up. She said, "I can't make it!" The next thing you knew, he pulled her onto a bed in a sleeper car on a train. The train went into a tunnel, and the title card said *The End.*

Hmmm. Gage tried to process the ending. *It's pretty obvious that there's an implied sexual innuendo. The well-dressed girl got rear-ended by the well-dressed guy in the sleeper car. What the heck am I watching, porn from the 1950s?*

He was about to look up the title on the menu when his computer *chirped* at him. He had a new email. He didn't recognize the address, and the sender attached a video link. Sometimes Draylop sent him information through unusual and untraceable IP addresses, but he was unsure of the source of this one. He checked it for viruses and any other sneakiness—found nothing suspicious—and played it.

The video was very grainy at first. There was no sound, just movement. Then it cleared up and looked like a space battle from a science fiction movie. It was the POV from a small ship shooting at another small ship over icy terrain. The fleeing ship zipped into a collapsing wall of ice. The following craft veered off, and Gage saw another one was also in pursuit. Then he heard a crackly radio voice.

"That should finish them," the pilot said confidently. "They flew right into the avalanche."

The pilot's words appeared at the bottom of the screen like subtitles and Gage realized that someone must have transcribed them to make all the crackly communications clear.

The two pursuing ships flew side-by-side for a moment then a laser blast came from behind.

"Oh shit!" the pilot yelled and flew evasively. The craft next to him was hit and went down. The remaining pilot engaged in a dogfight with the ship that made it through the avalanche. This went on for a while—like a silent flight training film—until the pilot got the other spaceship in his sights.

"You're finished." He locked on to fire.

Then there was a bright flash, and everything seemed to stop. The pilot was banging on his control panel and cursing. The other ship floated by, and Gage saw John and Meehix looking through the window.

"Holy shit!" Gage yelled. "That's Shippewa! That's Jojacko and Meehix!"

He didn't recognize their ship until he saw John and Meehix.

When was this taped? Who were the pilots attacking them? How and why did someone send this to him?

Gage watched in amazement as the video continued. John and Meehix saved the disabled pilot by pushing his craft into orbit around the icy moon they were fighting over. He realized it was one of Jupiter's moons when he saw the gas giant's swirling red eye.

Shippewa departed, and the video continued for a long time with not much happening. All Gage could see was the back of the pilot's head, the control panel, and the stars. He got bored and started scanning through the video, reading the subtitles as they popped up every once in a while.

The pilots talked back and forth about a distress signal. They'd sent one and were now waiting for rescue. The video dragged on for hours. Gage fast-forwarded some more until he saw the words *we're dead* flash on the screen. He stopped and went back.

"We're dead," one of the pilots said with finality. "They're not coming. I just got the word from my buddy in Control. They black-balled a rescue. It's been nice knowing you guys."

One of the pilots contacted his brother—they'd apparently been estranged for years—and told him he was sorry about something and asked him to remember him.

"Oh my God...they left them to die," Gage whispered.

The video ended.

Gage sat back in his gaming chair. *Are they still up there, floating around, dead and frozen? Could anyone see them through a telescope? Probably not.* He thought about John and Meehix. *Did they get away or are they dead too, blown up, dismembered, frozen, or all of the above?* There was no way to know.

He copied the video and saved it to an old crap computer he kept for storing sensitive materials. Then he went online and looked up the legal requirements to create a non-profit organization.

CHAPTER TWO

Several top USSP brass—including the chief of space operations, the lead intelligence officer, and the acquisitions manager—sat around an oversized, oblong, hardwood conference table in a red-carpeted room. The CSO was puffing away on an almost-consumed, twenty-dollar cigar and he didn't look happy.

Truth be told, no one in that room had *ever* seen him look pleased so it was difficult to tell sometimes whether he was baseline normal or ready to explode. If they had to put money on it, most would bet on *explode*. It was always the safer bet.

"We've reclassified thirteen new species based on the recent findings of the R&D department alone," the acquisitions manager read from an iPad on the table in front of him. "If we continue at this rate, we should have a galactic catalog similar to the more advanced races we're competing with."

"But we're still in the red!" the CSO blurted and coughed loudly. He grabbed some water in front of him, finished it, and ashed his cigar in the empty glass. Several people at the table casually covered their mouths with their hands. One even put on a mask. You could never be too careful about airborne viruses, and flu season was only a few weeks away.

"How do we have all these sales and new tech and still end up holding the shitty end of the stick?"

The AM adjusted his posture and dove into more facts and figures. The CSO never intimidated him, and he didn't care how much the senior officer barked, cursed, or threatened. The AM was banging the director's secretary so he had an indirect connection to the top dog's ear.

Also, he was a practicing Zen Buddhist. He knew inherently that all negative and positive inner feedback was merely an illusion so no one could intimidate him or make him feel small—or big, for that matter. He knew that, in reality, neither he nor the CSO existed in terms of Ego.

So in the big picture, what difference did these meetings or their outcome make? He often considered allowing his USSF commission to lapse, move to New Zealand and become a beach bum anyway.

"Well, sir—and please excuse my candidness, but *you asked*—part of the issue is the deep black ops projects that are kept off the books entirely. While a number of them have been highly lucrative, several have not, ultimately offsetting our legitimate bottom line.

"The problem with maintaining so many clandestine operations is that they still ultimately must be financed. When one or two tank horribly, the ripple effect translates into hard numbers that reflect poor profit margins.

"When you add in multiple levels of secrecy clearances

and excessive compartmentalization, that also hinders information-sharing between teams, affecting overall development and growth and therefore profits once again."

"All right, shut up—you're giving me a headache." The CSO rubbed his temples. "What about all the TV and movie licensing? Did that Fran Drescher religious thing ever gain any traction?"

"It did. We're bringing in quite a successful profit margin per episode of *The Nanny*. It only caught on with about an eighth of the inhabitants of Baralex XIV so far. As long as we don't start a Holy War between the Drescherites and the Kinsbons, we have a shot at converting a third of the planet and possibly some neighboring systems.

"However, the Galactic Bank is investigating us for 'religious manipulation of a sub-species.' Our lawyers don't anticipate it going any further than the Chuck Norris case we had three years ago."

"Damn, I wish we actually had a hand in that. We'd be up to our sinuses in money if we could've controlled *that* one."

"Hindsight's twenty-twenty. That said, we did lose the *Terminator* case and were fined ten million credits for setting back the emotional and mental development of a planet for at least two generations. However, that case is presently on appeal."

"Fucking Arnold," the CSO mumbled.

"On the other hand, there is good news regarding exportation of the TV show *The A-Team*, where no one dies regardless of how many shots they fire. It's doing very well in the second arm, and we hope to recoup most of the losses we took from *The Terminator* debacle."

"I love it when a plan comes together!" the CSO blurted, ala John "Hannibal" Smith. No one in the room understood the reference. Too young.

"Speaking of which—and this is the last item on my agenda." The AM tried to wind it up. He was supposed to meet the director's secretary for lunch five minutes ago.

"The bounty on John Jacobs and the Dolurulodan has become a problem. Not only do I feel that the initial payout was set far too high, but we've had three failed attempts to bring them in, two of which drew a lot of negative attention to us.

"The Dolurulodan Council is investigating an attack on Tagbedden Castle, and the Sector Twelve Lagud Police are pushing for an official inquiry into the death of a concierge at the Gallacher Spire. Both incidents were the direct result of inept bounty hunters attracted to the high payout.

"Some of our finance lawyers have also estimated that even if someone successfully bags them, it could affect our interest rates and draw down our reserves in the Galactic Bank. I have the memo from the legal department if you're interested."

The CSO was seething. Gretchen, his assistant, excused herself to retrieve his medication from the car. He should have taken it fifteen minutes ago. Actually, she wanted an excuse to get out of the boring meeting and have a cigarette. The meeting room was a "No Smoking" area, but try telling that to the CSO.

"That bluesy and her ass-licking boyfriend killed three of our best test pilots, and now they're running around the galaxy playing Bonnie and Clyde," the CSO snarled. "I want him *dead* and her *alive*. I deliberately ordered a high bounty to draw attention to the case and get them picked up sooner."

"It's drawing the wrong kind of attention," the AM dug in his heels, "and it will cost us an unreasonable amount of credits if they're caught and may prove more expensive in the long run than handling this ourselves. I'd like it on record that I oppose the use of bounty hunters in general, and I recommend canceling the Crec Alert immediately."

The room got as quiet as Orfon IX on a slow night. The CSO chewed an imaginary cigar.

"All right," the CSO said quietly. He knew when to stand down. You win some, you lose some, and as much as he hated to admit it, he knew that the AM only asked to be on record when he was on the winning side. "Cancel the bounty. *For now.*"

"Yes, sir," the AM said without an iota of smugness. Everything was an illusion anyway.

"Anybody else have anything?" the CSO barked.

The lead intelligence officer referenced a memo from the director indicating that Agent Stanley—who oversaw covert operations in the third arm—was handling the Crom Limean extraction ship protection scheme. The money transfer was DBO—deep black ops—and therefore didn't officially exist. They finished up the meeting by discussing how much new technology they should allow the normal world to enjoy for the next year—none—and adjourned for lunch.

Chuckie N wanted to hug Meehix, but he knew he'd pass right through her. Her hologram was standing in front of him in his little virtual room. He was anxious to get back to the real world, especially one where he and Meehixiheem were partners, at least in the business sense. If he could negotiate any intimate transactions along the way, that would be a bonus.

He was unsure of Meehixiheem's relationship with John. She had referred to him as "just some guy I met," but Chuckie had a feeling there was more to it. Regardless of that, Meehix was back in his life. He was almost out of prison and could meet and talk to her pretty much whenever he wanted—just no physical contact. *Yet.*

He figured he'd test the waters after he thawed out. If they seemed favorable, he would bring up the old offer he made to her. Hack into the big money, settle down in some outer-spiral paradise, and live happily ever after—only not get busted this time. That would be his pitch. However, it now appeared that *she* was pitching *him*.

"What do you think?" she asked excitedly, snapping him out of his romantic reverie.

"I don't know. How do we make money from a nonprofit organization? I mean, it's right in the title. *Nonprofit.*"

"John and I are licensed bounty hunters. We can bring in money that way. Besides, nonprofit doesn't mean we can't pay our way from any of the proceeds. We'll have operating expenses and other write-offs that can help sustain us. We might have to do a little of this and a little of that to make ends meet, but it's for a good cause."

"Yeah. Ending the slave trade. Very ambitious."

"Exactly."

"Sounds like a good way to make a lot of enemies."

"I guess."

"And get killed."

"Anything's better than being forced to do crossword puzzles for five hundred years…*right?*"

"That's not my point." Chuckie walked around the little table, sat on the edge, and looked up at her from his four-foot vantage point, which was now about three inches lower because he was sitting.

"I've uncovered a lot of dirt on a lot of institutions over the years, and I don't think you know what you're up against. You may as well try putting an end to supernovas or black holes. You're talking about big business in high places as well as a lot of dangerous personal exposure if you go public with this."

"That's why you're perfect for the job, Chuckie," she said sweetly. "You have all the skills to get us the information we need *and* to get us in and out of forbidden places."

She reached out to put her hand on his shoulder. It passed right through, but the intent was there.

In and out of forbidden places. If I weren't frozen right now, I'd sure be trying to get in and out of forbidden places on that body.

She continued, "The three of us together would be unstoppable."

Boner kill.

"Yeah, look, about that." Chuckie rebounded from his hard fantasies and bounced back into flaccid virtual reality. "How did you meet John anyway? You said something about him busting you out of a USSF base but—no offense to him or his species—he's a *Kdackan,* and they're not known for their honesty.

"I mean, aside from Chuck Norris—who might be a descendant of ancient Dwan DooVoo genetic manipulation but that's beside the point—Earthmen aren't trustworthy. How do you know you can trust *him?*"

I wish I had a galactic credit for every time this issue came up, she thought.

"I can't know," she admitted. "All I can do is judge him by what he does and John has proven by his actions that he's trustworthy. He saved my life more than once."

Chuckie looked at her as if to say, *that's it?* She got the feeling it wasn't the kind of answer he was looking for, and she felt compelled to add something else.

"I do know this," she said in all earnestness. "All you can do is all you can do. After that, you have to let go and trust that the universe knows what it's doing. Kind of like what you're doing right now, trusting us to get you out of prison."

"I don't know, Meehix. You sound like a Kinsbon mystic who's in over their head. I'm a hacker, a numbers guy. The odds of you pulling this off seem overwhelmingly *not* in your favor."

"Impossible odds, huh?"

"Yeah." He felt like he might be getting through to her. "You'd be fighting against powerful enemies."

"It *would* be dangerous, wouldn't it?" She moved closer to him.

"*Very.*"

"Overwhelming odds…" she almost whispered, step-ping into his personal space, "…danger…powerful enemies.

Sounds like a job for someone I find extremely attractive—and *manly.*"

She was so close to him that if she weren't a hologram, he'd be able to stick out his tongue and lick her lips.

"Maybe I need...*Chuck Norris?*" she said. She licked *her* lips and drove the last nail into his four-foot coffin. *"What would Chuck Norris do...*Chuckie N?"

She disappeared.

The hologram dissolved. Meehix was in the cabin with John and Ship. John was not pleased.

"Attractive and manly? Really? Chuck Norris is probably old enough to be your grandfather." John sounded incredulous as Meehix backed away from the projector.

"You shut up," she said sternly. "I'm trying to get Chuckie onboard, not date Chuck Norris."

"I didn't know whether to laugh or virtually punch Chuckie in his virtual mouth. He knows I can hear him, right? I might as well be sitting in the room with you two."

"I'm sure he knows, but he might have forgotten."

John folded his arms and stared at her. "You're quite the operator. Maybe the bigger question is, can *I* trust *you?*"

"Oh stop," she said virtuously. "This is exactly why I made you swear you wouldn't say a word. I know how a man thinks and don't act like you don't know too."

She's got me there, John admitted.

"**Sorry to interrupt,**" Ship interrupted, "**but I have an urgent message to relay to Meehixiheem from Chuckie N.**"

"Go ahead, Ship," Meehix said.

"**Are you sure I can repeat it with John in the room?**"

"Where am I gonna go, outer space? I've heard it all anyway," John said begrudgingly.

"Yes, Ship, John can hear it too. Please relay the message."

"**Chuckie says, 'Tell Meehixiheem that I've made a decision. I will join her cause and help in any way I can.'**"

"See?" Meehix smiled at John.

"Whoop-de-doo." John threw up his hands.

"**Please also tell her,**" Ship continued, "**that I've always loved her and that I always will. I am her slave in this life and the next, even if we successfully abolish slavery, and if given a chance, I will ravish her body and destroy that pussy like Chuck Norris did to the Viet Cong in** *Missing In Action*."

"I may have come on a little too strong," Meehix said innocently.

"**P.S.**" Ship continued, "**make sure John does not hear this message.**"

Great, John thought. *That's all I need. A four-foot Chuck Norris trying to bang my girlfriend while we're all stuck on the same ship saving the aliens. I love it when a plan comes together.*

The Nerth B space station looked completely different from L-222. It was a series of rusty-looking, giant metal cigars all in a row, connected by octagonal tubes running parallel with a bunch of satellite dishes and other sensing apparatus stuck all over the place. It reminded John more of a junkyard than a space station, and even though it was much smaller than L-222 it was still *enormous*, maybe five times as big as Manhattan on Earth.

They had to negotiate to get docking space. The port was all booked up with no available slips. Meehix haggled back and forth with the port manager. She wouldn't let John do it, firmly stating that he had made enough enemies for one week via his less-than-subtle tact and negotiating skills.

She finally got them in by agreeing to pay half the docking fee for another private craft scheduled to leave the next morning. Supposedly, the owner decided to depart immediately if John and Meehix split the bill. John thought the whole thing was a scam and that the port manager was pocketing the money, but Meehix simply pointed out, "I got us a slip, didn't I?" They parked without a hitch, and neither of them brought it up again.

Once docked, the next order of business was Chuckie. Although he was on John's shit list for professing his undying love for Meehix and revealing his hardcore sexual intentions, John was genuinely concerned for the little fucker's health. They'd arranged for a heavy lifting robot to meet them at the docking bay, which cost extra, of course, and when they were lowering the pod, John noticed fluid leaking from the bottom. The thing looked like it had been through World War III.

Thankfully, Meehix had done her homework. There was a high-tech medical company on the station called Radik-Ex that specialized in cryo repairs, rebuilds, and defrosts.

John discovered, to his surprise, that not every species in the galaxy had access to the Gates and that many still used cryogenics to traverse the vast distances of space. Most considered it old-school to travel that way, but hundreds of species without the means or the desire to travel inter-dimensionally still used it.

Radik-Ex seemed legit enough to know what they were doing but shady enough not to ask too many questions.

John and Meehix wheeled Chuckie into the establishment and delivered his tube into the eight capable hands of a bio-mechanoid tech named Munch. John saw—to his relief—that the "Property of Orfon IX Penitentiary" label on the front of the tube had burned away during their escape. If the authorities ever questioned Munch regarding the tube's origins, he and Radik-Ex had plausible deniability. As long as they received payment for the job, everyone should be happy.

"You know this stop is going to cost us about half of what we have left in our account," John said to Meehix as they walked down the giant hallway after dropping off Chuckie. They were back in their bounty hunting gear— full armor, guns, knives, etcetera. They figured that looking badass was the way to go on Nerth B.

If Nerth B were a part of town on Earth, it would be considered the wrong side of the tracks. Imagine if someone had converted an old airport into a giant biker bar, only in space, and filled it with aliens instead of Hell's Angels. That's kind of the vibe it exuded.

"The estimate for Chuckie is three to five thousand credits depending on complications," John read from the receipt Munch had given him. The mechanoid had printed it in English and Spanish, the only two Earth languages available on the station. Apparently, the USSF or some other Earth organization had a presence. "We might have to find another bounty job soon," he added.

"I'll scan the Crec Alerts tonight when we get a room." Meehix sounded unconcerned.

"If they *have* any rooms. This place is packed."

"Do you want to see about getting your arm fixed up?" She reminded him.

"I don't know." He'd noticed other humanoids with various scars and injuries from God-knew-what-kinds of encounters, especially the bounty hunters. It almost seemed like they collected scars like medals. And tattoos.

"I don't want to waste any more money. As long as it doesn't get infected, I might just leave it. It's good for a bounty hunter to have some battle scars." He looked at the bandage Meehix had applied before they left the ship. "Maybe I'll get a little skull tattoo on my other arm every time we get a kill."

"Are you serious?" Meehix was horrified. She couldn't tell if he was joking or acting stupid.

A haggard little alien that resembled Gollum from *The Lord of The Rings*—only with purple skin—ran up to John and began speaking in Spanish. John had heard enough Spanish at Gage's house to know it by how the little guy's lips moved, but his translator converted the dialect into English anyway.

"Hey, man," the Spanish-speaking alien said, "you *carrying?*"

"Carrying what?" John didn't know what he was talking about.

"He's not carrying," Meehix said rudely. "Now fuck off."

23

"You're from Earth, man. I know you got maple. I got cash."

"Maple?" John was perplexed.

"I told you to fuck off!" Meehix grabbed the little guy by the scruff of his purple neck and literally kicked his ass away from them.

"Be cool, bitch!" he yelled as he scampered off in the other direction.

"Fucking maple addicts," Meehix cursed.

"What's maple?" John asked.

"You know." She wiped her hands on her pants. The little purple bastard was sticky. "Maple syrup—from Earth."

"What about it?"

"That's what he was after."

"Why?"

"Because he's an addict. Maple syrup is a hard drug. Rots your brain and turns you into an idiot. It's a real problem in this part of the galaxy."

"Are you *serious?*" John laughed.

"It's not funny, John. It's one of the hardest drugs to kick. I had a niece who got hooked on the stuff and spent six months in rehab. She was never the same."

John had to bite his tongue to keep from laughing. *Maple syrup* was a hard drug in space? What was next? Freebasing *ketchup?*

"Have you heard of Mexico?" Meehix asked straight-faced.

"Uh...*yeah.* I live in *New Mexico,* remember? Gage has family in Mexico."

"The Mexican drug cartels worked out a deal with the

Crom Limeans. They're a race of four-armed arachnids with three-foot stingers on their butts. The cartels distill the syrup from the sugar maple trees, and the Crom Limeans smuggle it to the third arm. Very illegal stuff, very addictive. Stay away from it."

I'll have to remember that the next time I'm at the International House of Pancakes. John chuckled to himself.

"I didn't know there were maple trees in Mexico," he admitted.

"Giant forests of them. The Mexican cartels are trying to muscle in on the galactic drug trade. Judging by that little creep, they're succeeding."

"I should tell Gage to buy stock in Mexican maple syrup."

"Sure, if you want to be part of ruining millions of lives."

Meehix wasn't kidding. *He* was kidding, but she either didn't get the joke or didn't think it was funny. Strange how one man's breakfast condiment was another man's living hell.

I'll never look at a box of Eggo waffles the same.

"Maybe we should sell maple syrup. I know a grocery store in Albuquerque that has twelve-ounce bottles— Anderson's pure maple syrup. It's hardcore, man."

"Become drug dealers? Are you crazy?"

"I'm kidding!" John couldn't help himself. He knew he should shut up, but this was even crazier than the Chuck Norris stuff. "I can't take this seriously. I've been eating maple syrup since I was a little kid."

"That explains a few things," she said indignantly.

They continued walking around the station, looking for

25

a good place to eat. They found a diner not too far from where they berthed the ship.

John considered ordering pancakes and maple syrup but decided it would piss off Meehix and might even get him arrested. They ended up ordering a local dish that Meehix recommended. It looked like green spaghetti with fettuccini sauce on top and tasted pretty much as it looked. It wasn't bad.

He was about to comment on the food when he heard the words "Blavarian dreadnought captain" and "crazy bastard" from someone in a booth behind him. He perked up his ears but couldn't catch any more details of the conversation. The diner was a jumble of competing discussions, and he finally returned to theirs.

Meehix was trying to develop a practical way to combine smuggling, bounty hunting, and the save the aliens venture into one lucrative machine. John listened to her ideas, which he thought were a little weak, then offered a few of his own.

"What if we grab stuff out here—you know, rare or high tech—take it to Earth and sell it. Use that money to buy rare stuff on Earth and smuggle it back out here. Keep it going like a circle. While we're there, we see what's going on with the free the aliens cause, help Gage out, and come back out here to make more dough."

"I guess." Meehix picked at her food. "But I'm totally against maple smuggling."

He thought of something else.

"What if we found a way to bottle your pheromones? I bet we could make a killing selling your mojo juice on Earth. Instant orgasm in a bottle? It'd fly off the shelves!"

"Sounds charming. We could have giant barns where we milk Dolurulod females for their sexual excretions," she said sarcastically. "Will you get off this money kick and get back to the cause? The idea was to *end* slavery, not create a whole new market for slave labor."

Boy, I really do need to shut up. I'm stepping in it everywhere I go, and Meehix's mood is not improving. I guess we should quit talking about money and change the subject entirely.

He took another bite of food and thought of something he had meant to ask her for a long time. "So, where do your pheromones come from anyway?" he asked innocently. "I mean, from what part of your body?"

Meehix glared at him. "From my asshole...*asshole*," she said coldly.

Stepped in it again.

CHAPTER THREE

Proggetti, Jex, Crabbo, and Lazy Buff followed Sergeant Gist and the coroner into the morgue. Blue spheres floating near the ceiling provided dim lighting, and it was cold. There were at least five hundred storage drawers of varying shapes and sizes on one giant wall.

They walked to the humanoid section, and the coroner touched a button on a remote. A drawer gently slid open revealing a body covered in a silver sheet. The coroner removed the shroud.

"Oh, fuck me!" Lazy Buff yelled. Jex fell onto Lazy Buff's shoulder and sobbed. Crabbo put his hand over his mouth, and Proggetti bit his thumb.

"What did they do to his *face?*" Lazy Buff screamed.

Frelo Cocksman Raxmugg didn't look good. Not that he ever *did*, but compared to the way he looked before, he looked terrible now.

His nose was more or less inside out. Black, dried, coagulated blood filled his eye sockets. His entire face had turned into one repulsive bruise. It looked like a giant had grabbed him by the ankles and used his head to play polo.

"He suffered a serious contusion," the coroner said. "It's normal after such an injury for ecchymosis to spread through the facial tissues like that."

Lazy Buff grabbed the coroner by the collar.

"*Icky Moses?* Don't give me that fancy doctor lingo!"

Sergeant Gist grabbed Lazy's arms.

"Hey! Hey! Cool it, buddy!"

He backed off and Gist released him. The coroner was a little freaked out and moved away from the group. Lazy Buff adjusted his jacket.

"Relax, Lazy," Crabbo pleaded.

"Don't tell me to relax, Crabbo. I ain't relaxed. I'm the fuckin' complete opposite of relaxed right now."

"Guys!" Gist intervened again. "I know this is a difficult time; a lot of emotion. I see it all day, okay? I know what you're going through. I had a lady in here this morning whose husband got crushed to death by a shuttle. He was *mush.* She had to identify his body by a tattoo on his ass. That's the only part of him we could save. One ass cheek."

"Oh, geez." Jez gagged.

"Oh my God, that's terrible," Lazy Buff admitted.

"Awful thing," Proggetti added.

"What is life for?" Crabbo lamented.

"My point is, it could be worse. Even though this is terrible, we still have paperwork to sign. I'm sure you'd all like to get out of here as soon as possible."

"The sergeant's right." Crabbo declared. "Plus, the boss is waiting."

"True, very true," Lazy Buff agreed. He adjusted his

jacket again and patted Sergeant Gist on the shoulder. "I'm sorry, officer. I get emotional. This whole thing has got me wound tighter than a nun's you-know-what. I apologize, truly. Sorry about that, doc. No hard feelings."

The coroner didn't respond.

They signed short documents confirming that the deceased was in fact Frelo Cocksman Raxmugg, a.k.a Frelo Vikrellion, a.k.a. Frelo the Mooch, a.k.a., Baby B. In reality, the witness signing was more of a formality than a legal requirement. Frelo had already been identified through a DNA match with the Galactic Registry, as all beings were when they expired.

Truth be told, Sargent Gist did *not* require the widow of the guy killed by the shuttle to identify her husband by his severed ass cheek either. Gist figured, correctly, that it would be a good horror story to calm down the gangsters and put things in perspective.

"What's this?" Lazy Buff demanded and held up the short stack of papers Gist had handed to him.

"I told you. That's the police report."

"Yeah, I know that, but what's *this?*"

Lazy Buff pointed at several thick, black lines in the report.

"Those are redactions. We don't release the personal information of other involved parties."

"So...let me get this straight." Lazy Buff flexed his chest muscles and clenched his fist. "You're telling me that some weasel waxes Frelo like a dog in the street...and the police won't tell me who done it?"

Lazy was right in Gist's face. Gist put his hand on the butt of his gun.

"Yes." Gist said firmly. "It was a legal kill. As far as the station is concerned, we don't get involved with legal kills. I'm sorry about your friend, but that report is all I can give you."

Lazy Buff looked at Gist, then at the gun, then back at Gist.

"*Legal kill*, huh?" he said softly, staring right into Gist's eyes.

Gist didn't flinch.

"Okay," Lazy said, almost reverently. "How do we get Frelo Vikrellion back to our ship?"

The way he said Vikrellion—*that* gave Gist a chill.

An hour later, Lazy was on a direct hyper-bump call to Victor Vikrellion on Brakeb III.

"How is he?" Victor asked.

How is he? Lazy thought. *He's fuckin' dead! He's not good, Boss!*

Victor's question threw Lazy for a micro-second, but he recovered quickly. He knew what the boss meant. Victor was thinking of his wife, his children, and the extended family. Relatives would arrive from all over the galaxy for the funeral. The real question was, would it be an *open* casket or a *closed* casket?

"I ain't gonna sugar coat it, Boss. His face looks worse than Anto Anken's after he got worked over by the Crom Limeans. I wouldn't want nobody to see him like this. His arms ain't even on right."

"All right. Make sure he's boxed up on ice. Have Jez and

Proggetti bring him back. You stay there with Crabbo. It's time to find out who did this."

"Awww, we're gonna miss the wake." The food at a Vikrellion funeral was excellent.

"Are you fucking kidding me?" Victor screamed. "I'm asking you to find the bastards who murdered my baby brother, and you're worried about a *fucking wake?*"

Lazy ran his hands through his hair and shuffled his feet. "I'm sorry, Boss. I'm...I ain't thinkin' right. Frelo lyin' there...it got my head all screwed up. Forgive me."

"Okay, forget it. I'm a mess too. But you listen to me. It's all on you and Crabbo now. I don't care what it takes, you find out who did this, and you put two in the back of the head. You hear me? And if you have the right time and the right place, you rip their guts out, make them eat it, and take a picture...*you understand?*"

"I hear you, Boss. We'll take care of it."

Victor hung up.

An hour after that, Lazy and Crabbo sat in a bar on L-222 doing shots of Kinsbon Whiskey. So far, all they knew—at least according to the bartender—was that two bounty hunters, a big, male Kdackan and a hot female bluesy, had wasted poor Frelo. Nobody else they'd talked to had any information beyond that.

"Shit detail, huh," Crabbo muttered.

"I hate bounty hunters," Lazy replied. "Wannabe cops who are too dumb to get on the force."

Lazy slammed another whiskey and waved to the

bartender to bring another round. Behind him, a group of Blavarian military guys was also getting drunk and yukking it up. Lazy didn't care much for the noise, but he had respect for Blavarians.

Victor Vikrellion had connections with Blavarian families, often bringing them in on certain jobs as extra muscle. They liked to drink and party, most of them were loyal, and they were *all* into kinky sex. Lazy respected Blavarians.

He overheard them talking about a comrade recently killed in action.

"It won't be the same without him," one of the soldiers said.

"No, it won't. But he was a tough old bastard, and he always said he'd be ready for it when the day came. He went down fighting. What more can you say?"

"Salud!" they yelled and lifted their ale glasses.

"Salud!" Lazy shouted and lifted his shot glass.

At first, the Blavarians thought he might be making fun of them. They looked at each other like, *do we kill this guy?*

"Respect to your dead comrade," Lazy continued. "We lost someone too. That's why we're here. Salud to the dead."

They sensed that Lazy was legit and all raised their glasses again.

"Salud."

Crabbo leaned in. "Hey, Lazy. Let's not get beat up on our first day, huh? I mean, I can hold my own but the two of us against six Blavarians? We'll end up like the guy with the ass tattoo."

"Salud to poor Frelo." Lazy finished his seventh shot.

The Blavarians were soon laughing and engaged in their personal stories again.

"So get this," one of them was chuckling so hard he could barely tell it. "The guy is on speaker, and he tells Captain Prooshevekk to—and I quote—shove that dreadnought up your ass, suck on a plate of veonk spheres, and let a Quoteggian female bust a nut on your face...and eat it!"

"No fucking way!"

"What?"

"That's insane! The guy had to be crazy!"

They all went nuts with laughter and disbelief.

"What did Prooshevekk do?"

"What do you think he did? He reported it and got permission to hunt the guy down and execute him—after he ass-rapes him with a laser cannon. This guy is *toast*. They're saying it's the biggest breach of galactic hierarchical respect in Blavarian history. They're keeping the entire incident top secret, but one of the analysts I talked to said it could start an interstellar war if they find out what planet the guy's from."

"Damn. That dude's got balls like red giants!"

"Not for long."

They all laughed again.

"To the insane guy who told off Captain Prooshevekk!"

"Salud!"

Lazy Buff and Crabbo were listening.

"See? That's what we need." Lazy slurred his words, his eyes half-open.

"What?" Crabbo didn't understand.

"A guy like that. That nut who told off a Blavarian

dreadnought captain. More balls than brains. Fearless. Doesn't give a fuck about anything. He's my new hero. I want to meet *that* guy."

Gage's little sister Isabella kept opening the bedroom door and peeking in. Gage would wave her off with one hand, adjust his microphone with the other, and she would close the door again. When he started talking, she would repeat the game.

He was trying hard not to get pissed off and stay focused on what he was saying over the live podcast. He was multi-broadcasting on every platform he could think of, except Facebook. Gage *hated* Facebook. Too corporate. He currently had twenty-seven live viewers, which he thought was pretty amazing for the first episode of Save the Aliens.

"...and to be completely honest with you, I chickened out. Jojacko was the one who insisted we keep going and he kicked ass. Not only did he save the alien girl, but he got hold of one of the alien spaceships. I'm not making this up. I was on it. This was some real Bob Lazar shit. We even flew it to Hawaii and Mongolia."

Gage saw a comment from one of his live stream viewers. It read, "Did you take any pictures?"

Gage gulped.

Holy shit. I went through all of that and didn't take a single selfie? What was I thinking?

"Um..." Gage started to sweat a little. Isabella stuck her head in the door again. Gage turned and smacked his hand as in, *you're gonna get it!* She slammed the door and ran down the hall.

"SpunkJam814 just brought up a good point," Gage said. "He asked if I got any pictures. You know, in retrospect, I remember being so overwhelmed by what was going on that...honestly...I completely spaced it."

Three of his twenty-seven live viewers signed off.

"But look, just because I'm an idiot doesn't mean there isn't proof and it doesn't mean I won't get more proof in the future. In fact, I'm going to get some real evidence right this second if you'll bear with me. Hold on, don't leave the stream yet."

Gage started flipping through windows as fast as he could.

"Just one second..." he said. He found the local Albuquerque Channel 5 news website with Trey McSwirley.

"Check *this* out," Gage said confidently, scanning through the news videos. Where was it? It was there yesterday—the footage of John hovering over his house and blasting off with two jets in pursuit. *It was gone.* Not a trace. Like it had never even been posted.

"Um..." now Gage really was sweating. For a second, he even questioned his sanity.

Was there a video there yesterday or did I imagine it?

Two more viewers signed off. The Save the Aliens show was getting cringy.

"Wait! Wait!" Gage burst out, suddenly remembering. He searched again—this time on YouTube—for John's video address to his parents and the world in general. Last time Gage saw it, it had over a million views. He found the video.

Thank God.

He went to play it, but the YouTube window said, "Video removed: Terms of Use Violation."

"Oh no..." Gage whispered.

He lost another live viewer.

"I swear there was this great video of John *on the ship.* I mean, you could see the interior of the spaceship behind him. They even showed a clip of it on the news the other day. You can see where it was on YouTube, but now it's gone."

Three more viewers left.

"Wait! Wait! I've got one more! This one didn't make the news or get many hits. I don't know why because it's the best one of all. I guess it's because she didn't already have a channel, or maybe it was something to do with the tags or the algorithms or something. Hold on...this is the best one of all. *A real alien.* Her name is Meehixiheem, and she recorded this from *inside the secret USSF base.* Here it is!"

Video removed: Terms of Use Violation.

"Shit," Gage said.

He was down to twelve live viewers now, and little did Gage know, two of them were agents Bixby and Shaw—or as Gage now referred to them—the Butt Brothers. They sat in a McDonalds' drive-through in their tan Cadillac DeVille, giggling at Gage's dwindling viewership as they watched it drop on their laptop. It was one of those rare but special moments when they really enjoyed their job.

"Well..." Gage felt beaten in this round but not defeated. "I guess the Powers That Be shut down all the video evidence. *Almost all.*"

Shaw and Bixby straightened in their seats. Shaw told the girl at the drive-through window to shut up a minute.

"Make sure you come back and join me for my next live stream. I've got some *amazing* footage that'll blow your socks off. This is Gage Gonzales signing off for now. More to come in Part Two of Save the Aliens!"

He signed off.

"Make a note of that," Shaw said to Bixby as he paid for their Egg McMuffins.

Gage sat back in his gaming chair and looked at the old crap computer sticking out from under his bed. Should he show it without knowing its origins? The video didn't *look* fake, but maybe it was a setup.

If it was real, it thoroughly incriminated the USSF in the worst way—proof of them killing their men and attempting to kill John and Meehix, not to mention American pilots operating sophisticated alien technology. It was bigger than Watergate, Bob Lazar, and the Phoenix Lights put together.

"What have I gotten myself into? I'm getting another anal probe for sure."

Gage saw a container of Vaseline used for Toñito's diaper rash sitting on his dresser. He seriously considered putting it in his pocket—just in case.

"You'll have to sign for your slave as well, sir," the desk clerk of the Seboris Hostel informed John.

He eyed John's registration card with two long stalks that independently moved so he could easily see what John was writing. It even appeared that he could rotate the eyeballs at their ends and see the paperwork right side up.

"English, huh? You from Kdack? Been seeing more and more Kdackans out here lately. You USSF?" the clerk pried.

"No, and I wouldn't want to be either."

"Then why does your license say United States Space Force under the declaration?"

"Why do you ask so many questions?" John raised his voice. He was getting tired of Mr. Eyeballs and his nosiness. "I've heard that Nerth B is where you go when you *don't* want a lot of questions."

"Just curious. Trying to run a clean business. You know."

"Well, I'm trying to rent a room and questions make me want to spend my money elsewhere."

"Ha!" He laughed confidently. "Good luck getting a room somewhere else. If that Drellen mining ship hadn't canceled, we'd be booked clear through the holidays."

"Why'd they cancel?" John asked even though he was still miffed. He filled out the card as quickly as possible to get away from the intrusive guy and escape all the pointless small talk.

"Don't know for sure but it sounds like pirates to me. Lots of attacks in this quadrant although they usually go after big cargo ships. Haven't heard of anything small getting hit....*yet.*"

John pushed the card across the desk.

"And the slave portion, sir. That's what I was saying before. You have to fill out the back of the card for your slave. She's not allowed to do her registration."

Meehix acted like she didn't hear even though she did.

She walked casually to a wall in the lobby with a giant map of the quadrant plastered across it and pretended to be interested.

"Haven't you ever signed for a slave before?"

Now John was pissed. "Listen, buddy. She's a licensed bounty hunter, just like me. You see that sword on her back?"

"Yes, and you'll have to answer for it if she uses it."

Was this asshole looking for a fight? "If she uses it, it'll be on *you* when she slices off your snooping eye stalks!"

"Please fill out the card, sir." He was still smiling.

What the fuck? Is this some kind of alien cultural thing? Am I the asshole here?

John opted to ignore the guy and continue filling out the card. He didn't need to make any more enemies. He was already trying to shake the feeling of late that he was accumulating adversaries on an almost daily basis.

The words "Blavarian dreadnought captain" and "crazy bastard" that he overheard earlier in the diner kept coming back to him. Could they have been talking about *him*? He didn't want to ask Meehix about it because he was afraid of what she might say.

"Thank you, sir," the clerk said as John slid the completed card back to him. "I have you in a two-bedroom —B-17—on the second level. I see you have an Abyss Exchange account. Will we be putting the room on that card?"

It was pretty dingy compared to the Ho Hi Pollipicrucian on L-222. In fact, it was more like the exact opposite. *A Pollipicrucian would have a heart attack if he saw this place.*

John set down their new suitcases, which they had bought cheap at a pawn shop near the diner, and started taking off his gear. Meehix went into the bathroom and closed the door. John realized that she hadn't said much since they ate.

I guess Meehix hates me too.

He laid his gear on the floor next to the bed except for Layla9, his concussive blaster, which he put on one of the two end tables within easy reach. He hadn't asked Meehix, but he assumed he was sleeping in here and she was sleeping in the other room, as usual.

What difference does it make? I'm sleeping alone either way.

Then he heard Meehix in the bathroom. She was crying.

He went to the door. He was about to ask if she was okay when he caught a strong whiff of her stress pheromones. He immediately felt dizzy and frisky at the same time.

Oh shit.

He backed away from the door and looked around the room. There was nothing to cover his nose and mouth. He went to the window and flung open the curtains but forgot he was on a space station. Not only were they sealed shut, but they were fake—only clear plastic over a faded wall poster of a double sunset above a red ocean.

He took off his shirt, wrapped it around his head like a face mask, and went back to the bathroom door. He tapped on it lightly.

"Are you okay?" Through the shirt, it sounded more like, "ur yur oh-ay?"

"What?" Meehix answered. "Are you talking to me?"

"Yeth. Ur yur oh-ay?"

"I think there's something wrong with my translator," she said despondently. He heard her sniffling. It sounded like she was trying to compose herself. She opened the door.

"What…" She saw the shirt wrapped around his head and started to laugh. "What are you *doing?*"

"I wuth warried abouth youth but I did'nth wanth to half an orgathm an path out."

He could still smell suntan oil, and now it was making him feel drunk.

"I'm sorry."

She was half-laughing, half-crying. She pushed him away from the bathroom and into the other room, then unwrapped the shirt from his head and let it fall to the floor.

"Is it better in here?" She wiped a stray lock of hair from his forehead.

"Yeah, it's better. I was getting a little tipsy in there."

"I don't know what happened. I just got…*sad.* Sometimes I get overwhelmed. I mix up who I am now with who I was before. I'll think of something or someone from my old life, and I'll realize that they're gone…or that I'm gone…and it will never be the same again."

"I understand," John said. He did. He understood—or at least he thought he did. He'd had similar moments. Maybe not as intense and certainly not pheromone-laced like hers, but he'd had lost and lonely flashes, a kind of melancholy "naked and afraid in a world I never made" dive into the depths of existential despair.

"I think you're going to have to deal with me breaking down from time to time." She put her blue hands on his bare chest. "Can you put up with me?"

She looked him in the eyes with her horizontal pupils. Her cheeks were still wet.

"I don't think of it as putting up with you. I like being with you."

She smiled and guided him over to the bed. She gently laid him down on his back, climbed on top of him, and kissed him on the mouth.

Strawberry ice cream. Before he could say anything or even think another coherent thought, the little room turned into a tropical suntan oil-scented sauna, and everything went dark.

John was out like a happy light, and Meehix could see that he'd messed up another pair of pants. She snuggled up next to him. "Trust me," she said softly. "It was good for both of us."

John snored.

CHAPTER FOUR

John woke up alone the next morning. At least he thought it was morning.

One of the things he had learned—one of the very *few things* he had learned during his brief extraterrestrial travels so far—was that morning depended on which side of the ship you woke up on. Or in this case, Space Station Nerth B. The side facing the nearest sun was always day. The other side was always night.

He sensed, more than thought, that Nerth B was also on a fast rotation, alternating sunlight and starlight roughly every six hours. *No wonder the windows, if they existed at all, were generally darkened glass.*

He was nowhere close to being considered a physics major, but he did briefly wonder if the creatures on the station's outer rings had to take some type of Dramamine pills to help them while rotating faster than those closer to the center.

That led him to also ponder about the gravitational pull of the space stations. How much mass did their centers have to prevent everyone from bouncing around all willy-nilly? How much did he weigh on Space Station Nerth B?

A couple of revelations that he was all too familiar with brought him out of this unaccustomed brain revelry.

He was alone and felt like he had creamed his jeans, again! *Fuckin' Meehix!*

Had he fucked her?

No, he had not. He hadn't yet gotten within sniffing distance of her vaginal flap.

He thought he remembered her saying, *Trust me, it was good for both of us.* A sudden flashback lesson in Quoteggian female mating rituals crashed in, and John's hands immediately flew to his crotch in a panic. Everything felt like it was still in place, and when he brought his hands out from under the covers, they were sticky and white. Not dripping blood.

Sticky and white he knew how to deal with. Waking up alone was also something that he was used to. When he slowly rolled over, he found a piece of hotel stationery on the next pillow. It showed a crude drawing of a fork and what he took for a slice of bacon alongside something resembling a coffee cup.

Galactic earpiece translators might be good for spoken words, but they couldn't teach someone how to write in another language. Meehix's drawing was close enough. A sudden panic!

"Ship?" It was a few moments before the response came.

"Good morning, Dave."

WTF? "Ship, it's John! Who the fuck is Dave?"

"Too early in the morning for *2001* spaceship humor, I suppose?"

"Too early for anything other than to know that Meehix is safe somewhere sipping a Dolurulodan version of a latte!"

"Yes, she is safe. She is in a third-level café and is trying to find something that will pass for either a bagel or a donut to bring back to you."

John couldn't remember the last time he had let out a sigh so earnestly.

"Okay." Deep breath. "Tell her to take her time, but make sure that she gets her blue butt back safely to the room."

"Blue butt back. Nice use of alliteration, John."

"Great. If this bounty hunter gig doesn't work out, maybe I can get work as a poet."

"According to Kdackan history, poets usually die broke."

"Look, I have some laundry to do. If you talk to her, tell her…tell her…"

"Tell her what?" came Meehix's voice from his translator earpiece.

"Crap on a crutch, Meehix! Have you been listening this whole time?"

"You and Shippewa and I are linked, John. There are a few things about the translator that you aren't quite aware of yet."

He could almost see her weird-ass smile as she said that. *Damn, he missed that smile!*

"Okay, Meehixi-HEEM. Just as long as you're safe! I, umm, have some laundry that I have to do before we do anything else that requires me to go out in public."

He swore that he could see her smile as she answered, "I

47

understand. There is a washing unit in the bathroom. Use the gentle cycle. I'll be back soon. Oh, and remember that the translator is waterproof, so don't get too excited while showering because Ship and I will be listening."

The next sound that John heard through his earpiece seemed like a shared giggle between the Dolurulodan and the ship. It came in sounding like "snork-snork-schnuffle."

John found the washing unit easily enough. It was a two-door affair, one on the left, the other on the right. The operating instructions consisted of pictures but not in any particular order. Like most Kdackan males or males of any generic sentient species, he didn't bother carefully following the directions before pushing a button.

Behind the right-hand door came a fast whirring sound that lasted for all of thirty seconds, followed by a *beep*. After a quick leap backward, and a cautious step forward after the beep, John cautiously approached and opened the door on the right.

He remembered a brief glimpse of some pink panties that Meehix had tried on while shopping in Hawaii. What he pulled out from behind the door on the right were a few tattered shreds of something soft, pink, and now of no use for anything other than confetti.

Remembering his translator earpiece and that Meehix and Ship could hear anything he said out loud, he thought, *Whoops. Maybe I can blame it on the room-cleaning staff.*

"It's worth a try," he mumbled to himself.

"What's worth a try?" came Meehix's voice. "You're not thinking of doing anything stupid, are you?" She sounded worried.

"Nothing other than mixing darks and lights."

"Wash everything in cold, then dry on low."

When did spaceships learn how to do laundry? "Okee-dokee."

An hour later, when Meehix finally returned to the room, John was dressed in clean clothes. The recently washed laundry, what little there was, lay neatly packed in the suitcases and ready to go.

Meehix used the keycard and the door silently opened. As she stepped into the room, John greeted her by immediately pulling his stun-blaster on her. She barely managed not to spill his cup of drixly-mix and throw the brown bag of braddit-holes at his head as a means of self-defense.

The immediate sense of danger passed, and it didn't take her long to assess the situation. She eyed John's outfit. *"Bounty Hunter Unleashed?"*

"Huh?"

"It's a Chuck Norris film. Try to keep up."

She took in the whole room. John, dressed in his bounty hunter weapons-at-the-ready best, stood in front of a full-length mirror.

"You were practicing quick-draws." She couldn't resist a smile.

"Was not."

"Was too!"

She carefully set down the cup of drixly-mix and bag of braddit-holes on the nearest surface. Then she did one of those stretchy-rubber things with her right leg, wrapped it around his neck, and pulled him down on the floor on top of her.

"The hand is quicker than the eye. The leg is quicker than the hand."

Considering what the situation was, John could only nod in agreement, hoping that she would release him soon before he had another *release* of his own. They didn't have time to do another load of laundry.

She uncoiled her leg and rolled him off, cackle-laughing the whole time. A quick flash flitted through his brain: If Santa and Mrs. Claus ever had a baby girl, that laugh is what it would sound like when the girl-child was going through her terrible twos. Thanks to Gage and his siblings, John knew exactly how that would sound!

Please, God, John found himself praying to a God that his mother was convinced existed, *keep the Gonzalez brood safe.* "Ahmen," he said out loud.

"Who is Ahmen?" Meehix asked a while later, as he was finishing his last sip of drixly-mix with sugary pieces of braddit-holes still covering his lips. *Now is not the time for deep religious or philosophical debates.*

"Ummm, he's a friend of my mom's. Kinda like an uncle. The kind of uncle you don't wanna get on the bad side of."

"Oh. Like my Uncle Mohabbic. That is *one* guy you don't wanna piss off."

"Yeah. Some uncles are fun. Some uncles you don't wanna mess with."

Having wiped the last bit of sugary shit from his face and dressed in full bounty-hunter regalia, John couldn't resist standing in front of the mirror and admiring his badass self. Meehix was donning her gear. When done, she stood beside him, and they took each other in via their reflections.

"Does Chuck Norris have a wife?" Meehix wondered out loud.

"I dunno."

"I bet that if he does, no one calls her Mrs. Norris."

"Not if they wanna live to see tomorrow."

They twirled, drew their weapons at the mirror, and performed an almost perfect high five.

At the USSP headquarters, not to be confused with the USSF headquarters, the general thought to his own damned self, *Who needs bombs when acronyms are the ultimate weapons?*

While the United States Space Force was endeavoring to establish a galactic presence, they could count on the penny-pinchers in the U.S. Congress for only so much. That's where the USSP, the black ops division of the USSF, came in.

All the fancy-ass USSF ships that looked so impressive flew around for all to see. The USSP tried to keep all their flights off the radar, off the books, and as far under the table as possible.

The general hit his intercom. "Maddie? You can send in the Ass now."

The door *buzzed*. Susky hurried in as fast as someone six-foot-five could and immediately sat in front of the general's desk. The general was all of five-foot-four but had a custom-built desk on a slightly elevated platform and a custom-built chair that also helped to prop up his height.

All visitors sat on chairs that were three inches lower than the standard issue.

Susky was the brightest bean-counter they had and was the top alien species specialist, or ASS, hence his nickname.

"General," Susky began, after sitting in the lowered chair and finding his knees level with his ears, "I think I found something."

"Go on." While the general envied Susky's height and hated him for it, there was no one better at finding pennies in watermelon patches.

"Insurance," Susky squeaked out, his high-pitched voice not matching his stature. "It's all about the insurance."

"Listen to me carefully now, and answer using simple words that I won't have to try to dumb down for the suits."

Susky drew a deep breath. "We can insure cargo."

"My house can be too."

"But we can estimate your house's value because it's a defined commodity. It's tangible."

"No three-syllable words, please. I have to be able to sell this."

"Items loaded onto a ship are sent into space."

"Yeah, yeah. Done all the time. We ship shit. Sometimes we make a profit. Sometimes we don't. Que sera sera."

"But we always insure the contents according to their value, right?"

"With you so far."

Susky was having a hard time keeping his voice down and leaned closer. "We can ship anything. Grass clippings, dog poop, old VHS films from thrift stores. It doesn't matter!"

"Why doesn't it matter what we ship?"

Susky glanced first to his right, then to his left, and leaned even closer, lowering his voice until it was a whisper above the carpet.

"We can insure anything without any questions asked unless we insure it for over half a mil."

There was a moment's pause as the general rose from his seat, leaned his five-foot-four frame over the desk, and matched Susky's tone.

"Anything?"

"Anything."

"Up to half a mil?"

"Anything over that would raise questions."

The general slid back into his chair that helped him maintain his illusionary height advantage. "Let me get this straight. We ship shit?"

"Any kind of shit."

"And we insure it way above its value?"

"Uh-huh."

"Then what, pray that it gets space-raided or something?"

"That's where the Crom Limeans come in."

"Corona limes and friends?"

Susky allowed himself a long stretch while remaining in the chair and trying to keep the top of his head lower than the general's. He didn't want his height to overshadow him. The man did not take kindly to that happening.

"I came across an alien species called the Crom Limeans. They're what you might call galactic mercenaries."

"Anything for a dime, types?"

"Exactly! Insurance is high value-low value and risk

adjustable. So far, we've always shipped things and insured them for their *actual* estimated value."

Susky now had the general's complete attention because the man leaned forward over his desk as he saw where Susky was going.

"*Estimated* value." Susky nodded, and the general continued. "Who does the estimating?"

"That would be us."

The general leaned back, and Susky could see the wheels spinning as he did some calculations, which Susky knew wasn't his strong suit.

"So, you're telling me that we can ship anything we want and insure it for as much as *we* estimate its value to be?"

"Now you're getting it, sir."

"Up to five hundred thousand credits, without any questions asked."

"You got it! There are dozens of insurance companies looking to branch out into the galactic sphere. I mean, anything shipped is being shipped by the USSF."

"And what alien species is gonna be dumb enough to wanna fuck with the U.S. government?"

"Exactly!" Susky wanted to stand and start pacing to burn off some of his excitement but knew that wouldn't go over very well. "These insurance companies are lining up at the door because it seems like a win-win proposition to them. The USSF ships items and they always arrive intact, so they'll never have to pay off any claims."

"I'd like to get in on some of that action myself."

"So would I." Susky paused for a long moment. "But what if the *cargo* never made it to its destination?"

"Then the insurance companies would have to pay out. Is this where your Cro-magnons come in?"

"Crom Limeans."

"Whatever."

"Even with using hyper-dimensional Gates, the cargo ships still have to make an occasional stop or two."

"For what, potty breaks?"

"Something like that. That's when the Crom Limeans hit—and no worries about anyone getting hurt. The USSF shipping ships are intended for shipping only, and simple flying and loading-unloading crews operate them. They never carry any weapons more dangerous than a butter knife in their cafeterias."

"Then these Croms, can I just call them Croms?"

"Seems easiest for now, General."

"They do their space-pirates thing and steal the cargo."

"Bingo! If the cargo makes it to its destination, then it's 'let the buyer beware' of what they've purchased, but the buyer never pays anything until the shipment arrives."

"But if the shipment never arrives," Susky waited for the last cog to turn. "Then the insurance companies pay through the nose."

"And there are dozens of them already lining up to do just that."

The general leaned back and smiled. "Fifty bucks worth of useless shit, insured for half a million galactic credits. Remind me never to buy any stock in galactic shipping insurance companies."

In the Radik-ex waiting room on Nerth B, the overseeing thaw-technician, Munch, had decided that it was in his best interest to take an extended lunch break while waiting for Chuckie to thaw. *Waiting* being the operative term. He had an extra hundred credits burning a hole in his pocket thanks to Meehix's and John's petty cash fund.

John was bored out of his remaining wits and had left Meehix sitting there. She wasn't going anywhere until she made damn-well sure that the little wannabe Meehix-fucker Chuckie was thawed and safe. So he'd wandered a little through the hallways and found what passed for a vending machine.

He'd finagled his way into getting something resembling a creamsicle bar to drop. He'd taken an immediate bite off of the top. It was cold and had a coating of hard chocolate on the outside, with something creamy surrounding the stick.

He returned to the thawing room, still sucking on the creamsicle with a pleasant smile, and was met by Meehix, who had ratcheted up her tension level to "don't fuck with me" orange.

"What is that?"

"I dunno. I bought it down the hall."

Meehix and her emotions performed an immediate one-eighty as she took a seat, a deep breath, and a touch of her goofy-assed smile made an appearance.

"Ship, define what a Felaggan Impregnation Limb is."

"The appendage of a creature from the mostly frozen planet of Flipteen, sliced off at the height of its virility."

"Does it have a creamy center?"

"Yes, that would be its sperm."

John continued to enjoy his spermsicle as he gave Meehix a squinky-eye. He hoped it was galactically recognized.

It wasn't what his mom would call a side-eye. Anyone who'd ever had a mother of any planetary origin would recognize that. A side-eye could mean anything from "Do you expect me to buy that bullshit?" to "Oh, baby child. Do you plan to stick to that story and try it out on your father, or would you rather tell me the truth now?"

A squinky-eye was almost the same look but shared more among equals, as if to say, "Pull my finger once, shame on me. Pull it twice; shame on you."

"I no longer care what I eat," John butted in. "A delicacy for one species could be the equivalent of eating green baby crap off a shag carpet for another. So, if I'm about to put something known universally as being poisonous in my mouth, then please stop me! Otherwise, just let me enjoy the food and spare me the where, what, who, or what body part of whomever it came from!"

"Sorry that I ad-libbed there, Ship."

"No worries, Meehix. How'd I do with my Felaggan improv?"

"You did great! I think we almost had him there for a minute."

John heard the shared snork-snork-schnuffle laughter between Meehix and Ship.

"Are you two quite done?"

"Yes, John."

"No, Jojacko." came the simultaneous replies.

John couldn't help but emit a snork-snork-schnuffle of his own.

"There's a comedy club in Chicago where I think I can get youse guys booked as a duo, sight unseen, for a two-week gig."

"Youse guys?"

"How much does it pay?"

"Slaves don't get paid." The snork-snork-schnuffle vibe left the room faster than the air in a child's balloon when met with a needle.

"Gotcha!"

"That wasn't funny!"

"Well played, master." The *I Dream of Jeannie* theme song followed.

Damn, Ship did a whole lotta uploading in what seemed like such a short time. I wanna hang with this dude until I can figure out a way to get a few Long Island Ice Teas into his system. Just gotta remember to disconnect his power supply first because no one needs a drunk Shippewa flitting between galaxies.

"Are we ready to get serious now?"

"Being a slave is always serious to those in bondage."

John bowed his head and spread his arms wide. Meehix accepted the apology and approached for a hug. *Fucking pheromones!*

"Dammit, Meehix!" John backed away. "Does anything come out of your ass that smells like an actual fart?"

"Fart?"

"Yes! A pheromone fart that smells like something coming out of the ass the morning after dinner at Gage's house washed down with a six-pack of Coronas."

"That would be an unpleasant smell?"

"Oh yeah. Very unpleasant."

"Why would I want to release unpleasant pheromones?" She was serious.

"You've never even thought about it?" John took a step backward and motioned for her to do the same. Not quite sure what would happen if this went where he hoped it might, he snatched up a cushion from a chair and held it within smothering distance of his face as he tried to gather his thoughts.

"From my brief experience with you and your pheromones, and my friend Gage would back me up on this—"

"Gay-jaw?"

"The one and only...Look, or listen, carefully, Meehix. Your pheromone farts bring most men to their knees in ecstasy. "

"Kdackans, maybe. Other species aren't quite as susceptible, but that's their purpose. To bring pleasure."

"Yes! And trust me and my laundry, they're very effective." John couldn't resist a smile at the memory of what he'd experienced before he'd ultimately passed out every damn time she'd released one. "The thing is, the *question* is, can you control the smells? Make them come out as something unpleasant?"

John had a couple of reasons for asking this. Both were practical, but one might be needed sooner than the other. He reasoned that if Meehix could utilize her farts as a defense, she could send a room full of humans scurrying for the closest window.

The best defense is a good offense. If Meehix could turn her gas-blasts into something as offensive as her pleasure ones were pleasing, that could come in handy sometime in the future.

A brief thought flitted through his brain. If she could *channel* her farts and bottle the repellant ones, they could market it on Earth as Chanel No. 6. "Just one whiff will let you and your girlfriends enjoy a martini in peace."

He shook his head. Where was he going with this? *Right, Chuckie N.* As fond as he was of the little dude who he hadn't quite yet met, and in awe of his hacking skills as he was, *fuck, how do I phrase this to Meehix without sounding like a galactic-level jealous asshole?*

"Ship?"

"Yes, John?"

"I don't know what buttons to push. I need to talk with Meehix, just her and me, alone for a few minutes."

"Sure. How long do you need?"

"Four minutes, max."

Ship schnuckled. **"Hear you in five."**

"What the Eternal underloping star is this about?"

"Meehix," John had never been more earnest in his nineteen years of life and hoped that the woman he had fallen in love with—*yes, he'd fallen in love with the blue chick*—would hear him out. "I'm in way over my head here. A few days ago I was a master coder and a kickass king on worldwide online video games, all while living in my parents' basement.

"Now? I'm a galactic bounty hunter with a dead or alive price on my head, preferably dead. *And* you and me and Gay-jaw and maybe Chuckie N are going to try to free aliens from wherever they need freeing."

John drew a deep breath. He needed to get his right.

"What none of us needs is the complications of dealing with the about to be unfrozen Chuckie N, who has expressed his undying love for you! I know that you love him, but not in the way he wants to be loved by you."

"What do you need me to do?" Yes, she had heard what he'd said more than the way he'd said it.

"Fart at him when he thaws. Fart at him with an unpleasant smell."

"But I've never farted unpleasantly before, and I'll be so happy to see him again that I don't know what I will emit."

"Emit anything other than a waft of Lofian berries and Terragon chocolate!"

"Something a little less pleasant?"

"There ya go! Give him a nice scent that will smell like freedom after his confinement! Then dig deep, for your sake, and his sake, and for the sake of slaves everywhere, and give him a sniffer full of something unpleasant. Something that will turn him off you and help him to focus on what needs doing."

John saw her taking it all in. Then she smiled her weird crooked-face smile, and a smell enveloped the room. It was the scent of, John struggled for the word...

It was the smell of baby powder and little brothers and sisters laughing after changing the old diaper and wrapping a new one around a baby's now clean bottom. It was the odor of kids working up a sweat while playing under a hot summer sun. It was the scent of watermelon juices dribbling down your and your best friends' chins after you'd hacked into one and passed the pieces around. It was the smell of, of, *innocence!* The smell of an innocent child with no ulterior motives.

"Yes. Give him that scent!"

"If it works, can I also fart it at you?"

"Any time." *Damn, John, did you actually just say that? And mean it? Yes, John, I think I just did.*

John had enough time to hug Meehix and give her a French kiss that would make a Coxian blush before the five minutes were up and Ship came back.

"John and Meehix?"

"Yes, Ship?" an out-of-breath Meehix answered.

"Chuckie is thawed and needs to be released, pronto!"

Meehix and John didn't wait for Munch to return. She left an IOU on his desk and rushed in. They flipped every latch on his encasement box they could find. Chuckie's brain was fully functional, but after his confinement, what few muscles he'd had were basically useless. Meehix jammed a second-hand translator into Chuckie's ear.

John tossed him over his shoulder, and they ran.

"Ship?"

"Yes, Meehix."

"Drop the door. We're heading your way!"

"Put me down, you big Galoomfoamiac!"

"Shut up, munchkin!"

They ran through innumerable walkways, John and Chuckie trading insults all along the trek, until they were finally aboard Ship. Meehix hadn't even worked up a sweat, but her shaking gave her nerves away.

John *had* worked up a sweat. A year coding and playing online games in the basement had kept his mind sharp, but his earlier rugby playing muscles were screaming for mercy.

"How does it feel to be an oversized ape?"

"How does it feel to be an overstuffed piece of baggage?"

"Ship?" They all heard Meehix's voice. "Are we all safe for the moment?"

Ship raised the stairs and sealed them all inside. "**I believe that we are.**"

Meehix then turned her ass toward the miscreant boys and let out her strongest baby powder pheromone fart.

All struggling ceased as John laid Chuckie gently down on the floor, where they proceeded to roll and tumble over each other like a couple of playful puppies.

After a few too many "I love you man's," Meehix sighed and shrugged her perfect blue shoulders. *What have I wrought?*

CHAPTER FIVE

Lazy Buff and Crabbo were now in the middle of their fourth day sharing a room in the Hi-Flixum Hotel on Space Station L-222. Following Victor Vikrellion's orders —and who with half a functioning brain cell wouldn't, whether they were on his payroll or not?—they had remained behind. Jex and Progetti delivered what was left of Frelo's body back to his older brother's estate on Brabek III for a proper funeral.

"I tell ya, Laze," Crabbo muted the V-box, "and I never thought I'd hear myself saying this, but there's only so much porn a man can watch."

"Hear ya, Crabs." Lazy washed down another handful of Klik-mix with a swig of Brillian's Best. "Ya know, Frelo may have been Victor's little brother."

Crabbo hoisted his bottle of Brillian's. "And what a pain in the ass of a brother he was." They clinked bottles.

"But after all the times that you and me got sent," Lazy let out a belch, "system-hopping to get him outta whatever fix he found himself in, it felt like he was our little brother too. And it seemed like he'd finally found a home here."

Usually, watching rented porn charged to the room would be a distraction to conversation, but Lazy and Crabbo had learned that as long as the mute function was on, then talking while the movie played wasn't too hard. Lazy glanced at the screen and counted four bodies, seven breasts, three dicks, and one other appendage that he wasn't familiar with.

"True that." Crabbo agreed. "It's been what, three years since the last time we got sent to dig him outta whatever hole he'd dug for himself?"

"Flow & Glow Emporium on Jaylek 7."

"How many credits did that one cost Victor?"

Lazy didn't even have to pause to think before answering. "More than you and me will make in ten years on Brabek III."

"We shoulda been allowed to go back for the funeral."

"Yeah. We shoulda had a chance to pay our respects."

"And coulda lived for three days on the dinner spread alone. It's not that the food here sucks Slikionite vomit. It's just that it's so, so…"

"Generaleed?" Lazy suggested.

"Yeah." Crabbo reached out and snatched up a handful of Klik-mix from Lazy's bowl. "'Home cooking' is best on home planets, not in space station restaurants trying to duplicate a recipe they found on a galactic forum of 'favorite dishes guaranteed to please the masses longing for home.'"

Lazy got up and went to give his bladder a chance to drain some Brillian's.

"Oh, shit!" Crabbo heard Lazy shout from the bathroom.

"Got a good one goin' on in there?" Crabbo hollered back.

"No, no...*ouch!*"

"Need some help in there? 'Cause I'm the wrong one to ask!" Crabbo was laughing.

Lazy rushed out of the bathroom, zipping up his pants along the way, and started clearing off the shit-pile on their kitchenette's table.

"It's here. It's here. It's gotta be here!"

"Chill, Laze. Your Brillian's is empty, but we got lots more in the fridge."

"Turn off the V-box porn and crank up our D-player!"

Crabbo couldn't remember the last time he'd heard or seen Lazy in panic mode. So he hustled to what passed for a desk in their suite and fired up their portable D-player as Lazy tossed and dug through the mess on the kitchenette's table. Crabbo noted that Lazy wasn't shouting or even mumbling any words that might make a Quaquaan seaman blush. He was in a quiet panic.

"Got it!"

Lazy met Crabbo at the desk, carrying a thin white envelope that Lazy tore open with his teeth, not daring to risk damaging what was inside by using a knife to open it.

"Hold out your hands together and face up," Lazy commanded.

In his mind, Crabbo did a quick calculation of how many Brillian's they'd drained so far that day and lost count somewhere between thirteen and twenty-four. He held out his hands.

From out of the white envelope, a disc dropped into Crabbo's hands.

"Play it."

Crabbo did.

What played, was a crystal clear video.

"That's Frelo!" Lazy Buff slapped Crabbo's head. *Hard!*

"Shut the fuck up so we can watch this!"

The video had no sound, and the scenes jumped around in what seemed like chronological order.

Frelo at the bunghole table. Apparently on a hot streak, followed by a colossal cold streak. Followed by a big Kdackan dude pulling Frelo's hands behind him and slapping on some handcuffs, then tugging until Frelo's arms detached from his body.

There was a scene cut and Frelo was running, armless, being chased by a blue chick. The blue chick slung some ropes with weights attached and they caught and wrapped themselves around Frelo's legs. Frelo crashed face down... and that's where the video ended.

"What the—"

"Fuck!" Lazy completed the sentence

Crabbo leaned back from the screen. Lazy fetched two more Brillian's from the fridge, handed one to Crabbo, and collapsed into a chair with his.

"What we just watched," Lazy Buff tried to explain, "was a quick-splice of some camera footage from the Tri-2-Beatum Casino right here on L-222, with no *redacted* Official Report of a Legal Kill by bounty hunters' *paperwork* bullshit!

"But how'd we get it?"

"Between the porn and the Brillian's," Lazy was more

than happy to explain to his partner, "I managed to do some actual work." A quick, well deserved sip. "Frelo had been living in a house that Victor owns a few blocks from the casino for nearly three years, which is why we ain't been sent to track him down and bail him out lately."

Crabbo took this in and caught up as quickly as the Brillian's let him. "Lemme guess. Frelo was probably spending most of his time in the casino?"

Lazy nodded as Crabbo continued to work it out.

"So, any, umm, issues, that came up at the casino were handled *in house.*"

"That's my thought too."

"And his bankroll?"

"Mostly his own," Lazy mused. "Victor don't go for gambling unless it's in one of his casinos."

"And the Tri-2 isn't one of Victor's."

———

Lazy was still trying to put the pieces together himself. "But all of Frelo's legal difficulties were handled, paid for, and paid off by his older brother."

"Fuck-all." Crabbo gulped a swig and belched again. "Did I just say that out loud?"

"The fuck or the burp? Because I heard them both."

"The mouth fart... Excuse me."

"You're excused." Lazy held up a finger to indicate a pause and let out a traffic-stopping belch of his own.

"So Frelo and his...his..."

"Older brother?" Lazy prompted.

Crabbo took the prompt. "*Older brother,* had finally

figured out a way to keep the family name from being sullied too much while remaining loving brothers?"

"Loving brothers. Yeah, because all brothers love each other sooooo much."

They heard a *bleep-bleep*. It took a moment for it to register. Crabbo beat Lazy to the red button on the wall.

"Room 437." There was a short pause before Crabbo turned to Lazy. "Were you expecting a call from a realtor?"

"Put it on speaker."

"I'm trying to reach a Mister Buff?" came the disembodied female voice.

"Speaking."

"Mister Buff, this is Brezlew Anlin. I'm the realtor assigned to market and sell the house located at 726 Kanton Avenue."

"I'm not looking to buy or sell anything."

"I understand, sir," Miz Anlin continued, "but we received a hyper-bump call this morning from one," a brief pause as she confirmed her notes, "A Mister Victor Vikrel-lion? Do you know him?"

Lazy and Crabbo immediately set down their Brillian's.

"Yes. He's my employer."

"Good. Because he instructed me to contact you so that we can meet at the residence, give it a look-see and go from there."

Lazy motioned for Crabbo to find something to write with and on. Crabbo scurried and gave a thumbs-up.

"Okay. What was the address?"

"726 Kanton Avenue."

"When would you like to meet?"

"According to Mister Vikrellion, and I quote, yesterday would be best."

Crabbo had made himself busy locating the address and held up one finger.

"See ya there in an hour, Miss..."

"Anlin, but please, call me Brez. An hour from now would be fine."

"All right, Brez. An hour it is."

Lazy and Crabbo sent debris flying as they cleared off enough space to make a hyper-bump call of their own. Victor's face immediately came up on the screen.

"Progress report, if you please."

"Yes, Boss," Lazy began. "I called in a few of your favors and just this morning got a disc from the Tri-2 Casino's video surveillance cameras. Me and Crabbo ain't had time to track down any names yet, but Frelo's murderers' faces are clear, and we'll get them identified soon."

"And they are?"

"A blue chick, probably a Dolurulodan, and what appears to be a large Kdackan male."

"A Kdackan in a casino on L-222? Was he wearing a uniform?"

"No, sir. Looked like a large, out-of-shape tourist dressed up like he'd just come from one of those Pay & Play Soldier For A Day locations that are popping up all over."

"You're saying that amateurs murdered my little brother?"

"Seems like it."

"Find them and bring them in, alive! I will personally introduce them to the meaning of pain!"

"I'd like to get in on some of that action if you would allow me, sir?"

"I would allow. You're one of the best at that." Victor had a moment of distraction as something was going on off-screen but then returned his focus to the call.

"But *tracking* isn't one of your strong suits."

"No, sir. Pain and protection, yes. Tracking, not so much."

"Then find the best tracker out there. Not some *Crec Alert-chasing bounty hunter dimpweed!*"

"I think I know exactly who to put on it. He only goes by the name of Trexit and isn't easy to get hold of. We've used him twice before with good results."

"How much does he charge?"

"We're talking about Frelo here, Boss."

"Right." Victor's face went off-screen for a moment, and Lazy knew he was wiping away a tear. Victor returned. "Tell Trexit that I have a blank check waiting with his name on it."

"Will do." Lazy then went back to the second purpose of the call.

"I was also just contacted by a realtor."

"Right. Brezlinskew or something?"

"That's the gal. I'm meeting her at Frelo's old house in an hour. Any instructions?"

"Meet and greet and be done with it. I don't want any memories left to deal with from the location of Frelo's demise."

Lazy and Crabbo were left staring at a blank screen as the call disconnected. Lazy turned to Crabbo as he took in the mess in their hotel room.

"Crabs. I gotta go. Can you chat up a housecleaning staff and ask for a few bags off her cart? I don't wanna hafta leave an extra tip."

Crabbo looked around the room and sighed. "Our per diem only goes so far. You meet the realtor lady, and I'll take care of the dirty work."

The hotel where Lazy and Crabbo stayed was only a short distance away from the house at 726 Kanton Avenue. After donning proper attire, Lazy chose to walk it. After all the Brillian's, some fresh air would do him good.

Five minutes later, he was in front of the entrance to the Tri-2 Casino and paused. If he'd been wearing a hat, he would have taken it off as he paused and offered his silent respect to the place where Frelo had come to his undeserved end.

One block down, he turned right on Kanton Avenue and took it in.

These are houses?

These were nothing more than low-slung dwellings ten paces long in front and maybe twenty paces deep. Lazy followed the addresses for half a block and found a three-legged, two-armed, professionally dressed female carrying a Nipian knock-off briefcase, staring at what passed for a house at 726.

"Brez?" Lazy spoke as he approached. She turned.

"Mister Buff?"

"My friends call me Laze." They shook hands as they took in the block.

There were various signs on the front of each abode, stating, "Rent by month. Rent by week. Rent by day.

Hourly rents available on request." There were no signs on 726.

Lazy covered the distance between the walk and the door in three steps. Brez covered the same distance in nine, and they paused in front of the door.

"You have the key, I hope?" Lazy was nothing if not ever hopeful.

"Mister Vikrellion told me that the door is never locked."

Lazy could believe that. After a three-day gambling binge at the Tri-2, the last thing on Frelo's mind would be trying to find his house keys. He tried the knob, and the door creaked and swung open freely.

Lazy wished that it hadn't. What the opened door revealed was nothing more than an assault on both of their olfactory senses. They took a quick step back, or two, or six, depending on who did the stepping, to give the air a moment, or thirteen hundred and fifty-two moments... however many were necessary for the smell to dissipate!

Knowing that they would both eventually need to find some vapor-liquid capsules to stuff up their noses, they approached the door and risked a look inside.

Shit was piled over ankle-high on the floor, with a trampled-down path that they could only assume led to the bedroom and maybe a bathroom somewhere in the back.

Lazy looked down at his best pair of shoes he'd put on because he was on official business.

Brez looked down at her best three-footed matching heels because she had dressed for success.

Lazy closed the door. "How much to clean it?"

"Minimum? I'm guessing ten thousand credits."

"What can you sell it for?"

Brez glanced up and down the block. "Maybe twenty thousand."

Unlike Brez, Lazy knew who the actual owner was and that the owner wanted nothing to do with this property and anything else related to Space Station L-222. He closed the door and led Brez back toward the street.

"Here's the deal. Dig into your knockoff Nip briefcase and pull me up a contract to sign."

Brez did exactly that. She was new at this realtor gig. So new that she'd never even had a property to list or sell before.

"This morning, Victor Vikrellion enlisted you, right?"

She dug frantically through her briefcase and found her pad. "Yes, I think that was his name."

"Trust me, that's his name, and I am authorized to sign for him. So find whatever pad-work contract you need that will state that you and your realty firm now own the property at 726 Kanton Avenue."

Brez found a standard blank contract and frantically tried to fill in as many lines as she could. Lazy looked it over and signed at the bottom.

"You now own 726 Kanton Avenue. Do with it whatever the fuck you need to do to make any kind of a profit. But trust your life on this. You never want to see me or hear from Mr. Victor Vikrellion again. Is that clear?" With that, Lazy walked off and left her standing on the street.

Brez watched him tread away.

Real estate, she heard her mother's voice. *A young woman can never go wrong selling real estate.*

"Do we need to get you two a room?" Meehix butted in.

John and Chuckie paused from their bonding and took a good look at each other.

"Damn, John, you're so big! I've never had a big brother before!"

"Damn, Chuckie, you're so little! I've never had a little brother before!"

"Have either of you two *ever* had a brother before?"

John and Chuckie looked at each other. John let Chuckie answer.

"None that my mother ever told me about." John and Chuckie shared a perfect high five.

"May I suggest bunk beds?"

"I call dibs on the top bunk! I don't want an overgrown Kdackan to smother me in my sleep if the structural integrity of the bed fails in the middle of the night."

"Will you two please cut out the...the..."

"Bromance?" Ship suggested.

"Bromance? Okay, I can work with that." Meehix pointed to a corner. "Jojacko, you go stand there until I tell you otherwise." John was wise enough not to dare disobey.

Once John was safely ensconced in his corner, Meehix approached her childhood friend, who currently sat on the floor.

"Chuckie N. Permission to approach?"

"Permission granted."

Meehix rushed in and swept the little guy up off the floor and into her arms, baby powder pheromone farting as she held him in her arms and twirled.

"I love you, Momma." came Chuckie's muffled voice. Meehix realized that in her excitement to whirl and twirl, she'd clutched Chuckie in a way that snuggled his face right between her breasts. She let him loose, and he managed to land feet first.

"You are such a perv!"

"And mommas shouldn't have such perfect mammaries!"

She snatched him up again and twirled him.

John was staying in his corner, as commanded, watching. *Pheromones can only go so far, but dammit, I want in on the hugging the little fucker dance too.* So he rose, tracked their movements, and tapped Meehix's shoulder.

"May I cut in?"

Meehix set Chuckie down and held out her arms to continue the dance with her next partner. John scooped Chuckie up.

"What kind of dance shall we do?" John whispered into Chuckie's ear.

"Any dance that'll leave her and her perfect blue tits sitting alone, learning how it feels."

"And her perfect legs. Don't forget her perfect blue legs!"

"You go, bro! I'll follow your lead."

"I got an idea."

John set Chuckie down and turned to Meehix.

"You're gonna have to trust me on this. We need a few boxes that we can stack and something long and straight... one of your spear-type weapons."

"What the fuck are you babbling about?"

"I need something long and straight."

"I got your long and straight right here in my pants, bro."

"Can I be taken seriously for just one fucking moment?"

"I suspect that the answer to that question will be a no, John."

"Stay tuned, Ship! I'm gonna need your help in a few minutes!"

Chuckie made his way over to Meehix and stood by her side as they watched John rushing around like a madman.

"Meehix? In case I've forgotten to mention it, thank you for rescuing me! You have my undying devotion."

"I had that before you were busted, you little twerp."

"Bitchy times twelve when left out of a dance. Good to know."

Baby powder farts enveloped the air. "You were saying?"

"Yes, yes. I was about to say that you and I have at least one thing that will bond us together forever."

"Which is?"

"We both know that all Kdackans seem to have been born with an insanity gene."

"Except for Chuck Norris."

"Obviously! I've done some research, and rumor has it that Chuck isn't actually a Kdackan. I'm still tracking the info down,"

John's "Whoop, there it is!" interrupted Chuckie.

John had finished his scurrying. In the space they all shared, there were now six boxes from whatever cargo bay John had found them in. He'd stacked them, three on one side and three other boxes stacked four feet away. Meehix had bought a spear as she and John were choosing their weapons of choice a few days previously, and it formed a bar from one set of boxes to the other.

"Ship?"

"Yes, John?"

"Please tell me that you had the time back on Kdack 3a to upload some Chubby Checker!"

"Can you be more specific?"

"How low can you go?"

John remembered the challenge at Gage's various siblings' birthday parties. He could never win then and had no damn-sure chance of winning now, and that was the point!

Ship came through, as John knew he would. *Oh crap! Would Ship prefer a feminine pronoun when I think of him?* No time now for those contemplations because Ship came through once again, and Chubby Checker's *Limbo Rock* started playing.

John pointed at the spear spanning the distance between the boxes that he'd hastily set up.

"How low can you go?"

Meehix and Chuckie shared a *Yeap, Kdackan's share an insanity gene* glance.

It took a few moments as Chubby continued to sing in what John hoped Shippewa had set up as a loop. John pointed at the spear and demonstrated the dance's technique, knocking the shaft off with his knees before the rest of his six-foot-four frame got anywhere near it. He reset the makeshift bar and turned to the four-foot-nothing Chuckie and the way-too-limber blue chick.

"How low can you go?"

That's when the "We freed Chuckie" party finally started to rock!

"Well done, Ship," John tried to whisper. All lights did a quick off-on blink.

Message received.

Having dealt with the realtor and the issue at 726 Kanton Ave., Lazy Buff returned to his room at the Hi-Flixum. Crabbo had managed a fair amount of cleaning. Actually, *gathering* would be a more precise term. He'd piled up four large disposable bags inside the entrance.

"Crap, Crabs, you been busy."

"All in a day's work." Crabbo was back to watching porn, Brillian's in hand, and hit the mute button. Lazy hit the fridge and helped himself to a brew as he seated himself at the desk.

"Just be glad we're not the cleanup crew at 726."

"Frelo as messy as ever?"

"Birthed messy, lived messy, died messy."

Crabbo raised his bottle. "Gotta give him points for consistency."

Lazy matched his toast from the desk, then flipped open his Pad.

Lazy knew that the tracker known only as Trexit wasn't someone you could simply dial up and chat with. There was a process to getting in touch with him. Lazy found Trexit's BringItOn address and sent a note.

Trexit. Vic-Vik has another assignment for you. Please, at your earliest convenience, respond as soon as reasonably possible. –Lazy Buff

Lazy glanced at the new porn video that was playing. "What part of any being's anatomy is *that* thing?"

"I dunno. But I don't want it anywhere near me," came Crabbo's response. "Wanna help me carry the trash down to the disposal receptacle?"

"Can't do anything until I get a response from Trexit."

"That could take days."

"Yeah, I know. Looks like we may be stuck here a while longer. The reception here's good, and I don't wanna miss his response while we're traveling."

"And once he responds?"

"Then it's home, sweet Brakeb III, home."

"I'll Brillian's to that!"

The scene in the porno film did a jump-cut, and they both shut their eyes as quickly as possible before the image indelibly scorched into their brains.

"Did you see that?"

"Nope!"

"Neither did I!"

CHAPTER SIX

The limbo dancing ended with Meehix winning. How could she not? John knew that he was too tall and lunky.

That was why he'd chosen the song, so he could relax and watch Meehix and Chuckie go at it in a way that didn't offend anyone. Chuckie, whose height disadvantage in most situations should have given him an advantage getting under the bar, wasn't quite as limber.

They all sat on the floor, catching their collective breaths while sipping from cups that they'd refilled from Ship's onboard water supply.

"Your water tastes like Zellion piss, Ship."

"I've seen better dancing performed by the drones I watched after downloading the *Star Wars* movies from Kdack 3a."

Chuckie and John were sitting on the floor, their backs against a wall, with Meehix between them. Chuckie leaned forward and spoke to John. "I really thought her boobs would be a disadvantage for once."

John wanted to distract Chuckie from ruminating about Meehix's boobs as quickly as possible.

"Ship?"

"Yes, John?"

John wasn't sure about the Kdackan singer, but he thought it might be the same as the *Limbo* song. "Did Chubby Checker also do a song called *The Twist?*"

"Yes, John. Shall I play it?"

"Crank it up to eleven!"

John sprang up, grabbed hands, and forced Chuckie and Meehix to their feet.

"We're taking you down on this one, Meehix!"

"Come on baby, let's do the twist." Ship couldn't help but sing along.

Three minutes later, John and Chuckie once again sat with their backs to the wall with Meehix between them. Once again, Chuckie leaned forward past Meehix's breasts and spoke to John.

"The fuck were you thinking?"

Meehix smacked both of their heads. "Is there a trophy for me somewhere in this competition? 'Cause no one can out-dance a Dolurulodan party chick."

"John?"

John leaned his head back against the wall before responding. "Yes, Ship?"

"Before leaving Kdack 3a, I was also able to upload what looks like some type of board game that gets played on the floor. It might be related to the last song. It's called Twister. Shall I project it?"

"Not unless you want me to leave you in a recycling bin behind our hotel."

"My programming informs me it would be a career choice that is in my best interests not to pursue."

Between the jailbreak and the dancing, John's body told him that he had exhausted his physical, emotional, and mental limits for the day. He knew they *all* needed to take a short break from consciousness. He concentrated and let his mind drift back to the weekends he'd spent visiting with his grandparents when he was much younger.

"Ship? Do you have any Perry Como in your database?"

It took Shippewa a few moments. **"Yes, John. I have a recording of his greatest hits."**

"Turn the volume down to three and let it play for a while, please."

Ship complied.

After a few hours of a Como-induced coma, there was movement on the floor.

"Excuse me, boys, emphasis on *boys,* but I need to visit the little girls' room."

John and Chuckie, with a blank space between them where moments before there had been a warm blue body, stretched and made eye contact.

"Was it good for you?"

Chuckie stretched. "I've had worse dreams."

"Dear species."

"Yes, Ship," Meehix replied as she returned to the small common room, "what's up?"

"While I don't require *sleep* and can fly or dock

anywhere, have any of you considered ongoing sleeping accommodations for yourselves?"

John came out of his drowse and looked at Meehix. *I would love to see her as my first sight every morning.* Then at Chuckie. *Him, not so much.*

"We're gonna need a bigger room at the hotel, aren't we?

"That would be my suggestion. You have an hour to upgrade before they charge you for another night in the room you currently have."

Half an hour later, John was with Chuckie back in the room that he and Meehix had shared before they'd rescued Chuckie. *Man, was that one day or two days ago? Time was weird in space.* It wasn't the first time John thought that, nor would it be the last.

Meehix had left them alone, instructing John to start packing as she'd gone to the front desk to upgrade them to a suite. A *three-bedroom* suite.

John was packing his clothes while Chuckie was at the room's small desk, hitting keys on the portable IFC's keyboard faster than John could spit out a worm from an apple he'd just bit into.

"Your IFC sucks!"

"So do the Yankees lately. What the fuck is an IFC?"

Chuckie kept striking keys. "Interface computer. Don't you know nothing?"

John decided that now wasn't the time to mention Hannah. Even Chuckie would have to offer an "I'm not worthy" bow when he introduced her to him. For now, he kept packing as Chuckie kept up his frantic typing.

The room's door swept open, and Meehix swept in,

carrying a bag emblazoned with a U-CAN-2 logo. She tossed the bag at Chuckie's feet.

"Don't worry about sorting through it. I got us a suite. You can unpack it there." She then did some scurrying of her own to get her bags packed.

"You got us a suite?" John ventured, not quite happily.

"A three-bedroom suite. One bedroom for you, one for Chuckie, and one for me. Unless you two *bros* want to double up."

John would have preferred to have a two-bedroom suite with one for Chuckie and one for him and Meehix to double up in. Chuckie seemed oblivious to the conversation as he kept pounding the keyboard and Meehix scrambled to pack.

"What the fuck happened to my panties?" Meehix came back from the laundry unit in the bathroom, holding between her fingers pieces of what looked like pink dental floss.

"Beats me. Maybe the housecleaning staff?"

"That's my go-to," Chuckie chimed in as his fingers continued their flurry.

"Oh shit! Oh shit, shit, shit!"

"How expensive were those panties?" John was afraid to ask.

"Oh no! No, no, no!"

Even Chuckie's fingers heard that cry of distress and stopped their keyboard pounding.

"You do realize," Chuckie took a chance, "that we're capable of understanding polysyllabic words, right?"

"Right, right, right!"

There was only so much they could do as they watched

her open an already packed bag and scrabble through its contents until she found what she was looking for. She pulled out a one-by-three-inch electronic stick and held it up for all to see as she jumped almost high enough to bang her head on the ceiling.

"While you two were *bromancing*, Ship told me that he'd been searching through the inventory files of everything brought onboard during his fabrication. He hadn't paid any attention to it before because it was one of hundreds of inventory items and simply listed as an HLTD. Once he'd deciphered the acronym, he located its onboard compartment and said that I should find it and take it with us whenever we went left."

Chuckie leapt as high as his four-foot frame would allow and snatched it from her. He hit two buttons.

"Ship?"

"I assume that she finally remembered?" Ship's response came in loud and clear in all of their earpiece translators.

"Yes, yes, yes!"

So much for polysyllabic word choices, John silently mused.

"I don't know why they labeled it as HLTD.

"Hyperlink translator device is my best guess."

"Close enough for me!"

Chuckie's excitement inspired Meehix to take a step back and John to take a guess.

"It's a pocket translator?"

"Exactly! Our earbud translators are distance-restricted. Three clepps, max. With this baby, we, or at least I, can keep in touch with Ship for at least sixty clepps!"

"You're not gonna let anyone else touch it, are you?"

88

"Do Kdackans have three feet and two dicks?" It sounded like a rhetorical question. "Let's move our shit up and into the suite. We got some shopping to do."

After they got their shit settled into the new suite and some squabbling about who got the room with the biggest bed—six-foot-four John won that one—they hit the street.

Meehix led the way because she was more familiar with Space Station Nerth B and the shops. John and Chuckie followed in her wake.

"Does she seem a little pissed off?"

"Just a tad. You won the argument for the room with the biggest bed."

"I like a bed that's long enough not to let my feet dangle down to the floor."

"Yeah, but it's the only room with a separate bath. Don't you know nothing about women?"

John thought back about his relationship with Hannah. *The* Hannah, not the Hannah now connected to one of Ship's USB ports. The now nineteen-year-old Hannah who had cheated on his then eighteen-year-old ass and was now living with some dude, ass-age unknown. *No*, he concluded, *he didn't know nothing about women.*

Ahead of them, they looked at the pissed-off woman who was leading the way to the closest electronics store because Chuckie needed some new equipment.

The snatch-and-run thief picked the wrong Dolurulo-dan's bag to snatch. It wasn't a delicate handheld purse that some females carried by their dainty little handles in their dainty little hands. It was a bag with a shoulder strap slung over her shoulder.

The thief grabbed the bag. Meehix grabbed the strap and planted her feet. She and her purse weren't going anywhere. Neither was the thief, whose feet left the ground, his hands still firmly grasping the bag. Meehix looked down at his semi-prone body.

"This bag is a *Praga*! Not a one-off! Are you going to let go of it or do I have to rip off your arms and beat you with their bloody stumps?"

The thief let go. Meehix looked down at him without an ounce of mercy in her heart, eyes, or voice. "Don't fuck with my Praga!" She stormed off.

The females on the sidewalk who had witnessed the scene started a chant. "Praga! Praga! Praga!" and kicked the would-be thief as he scrambled off.

John and Chuckie formed fists and raised their arms, joining the chants as they hustled through the throng. They caught up with Meehix half a block later as she stood in front of an electronics store. She spun on them.

"A lot of help you two were."

The boys looked at each other before answering.

"It didn't look like you needed our assistance," John answered truthfully.

"I was ready to go all Chuck Norris on his ass if needed," Chuckie N added.

Meehix couldn't help but smile, then nodded at the store. "Can you get what you need in here, Chuckie...N?"

Chuckie did his best foot scuffle. "I don't think so."

"Why not?" Meehix looked through the window at all

of the displays. "It looks like they have a wide assortment of everything."

"Including facial-recognition surveillance cameras."

"You've been here before, bro?"

"I can neither confirm nor deny, bro."

"All right. There's another store around the corner where I once bought a necklace. It had eight different mini-cams designed to look like zimlum shells."

"Eight?" Chuckie was curious.

"Sometimes clubs get rowdy."

"What's a zimlum shell?"

"Sometimes a girl's best friend. Remember that the next time you're in a gift shop and thinking about me."

They proceeded around the corner, reached the shop, and again Chuckie did his foot scuffle. Meehix turned on him.

"Here too?"

"In a manner of speaking."

John was curious. "Five-finger discount?"

"I'm *not* a thief! Define discount."

John looked at Meeehix.

"What, did you think we were jail-breaking a saint?"

She had a point.

"There's another store just up the street that might be better." Chuckie led the way, talking softly with Ship. Meehix and John followed until they stood in front of the Max-Comp showroom window. It looked like another quiet day inside, with maybe a few dozen shoppers wandering around.

"Ship, you're into their system now?"

"Yes, Chuckie. You would think that an electronics

chain would have enough sense to change their password after the last time you hacked in."

"Arrogance. Simple arrogance. Plus the fact that I was in cryo-jail for the next five hundred years. Hang tight, I'll tell you when." He looked up at John. "You got your AEC ready, right?"

"AEC?"

"Our Abyss Exchange card." Meehix shook her head, worried about John's lack of memory retention. "We both have one. My *master* was kind enough to provide me with one linked to his account."

"Right, that whole nonentity slave thing." Chuckie had to pause. "So, help refresh my memory, because a lot's happened in the last few days. *You* no longer officially exist."

"Try telling that to the sneak thief a few blocks back."

"So the exchange account is in John's name only."

"Correct."

They looked at John for confirmation, but his attention had fixed on the glorious electronics he could see through the window.

"And he gave you a card that allows you total access to the account."

"He thought it would help me feel like less of a slave. We're partners, and partners share."

"Never trust a partner who trusts his partner. Dude is one weird Kdackan."

"That's our Jojacko. So, what's the plan?"

Chuckie explained as they headed into the store. Meehix went straight to the line at the register and kept fumbling through her Praga, seemingly looking for something. She let other customers step in front of her while maintaining her space as the next in line.

John followed Chuckie to the aisle with the most high-end portables.

"Try not to drool when you see this sucker."

John had to call on all of his reserves not to drool as Chuckie stopped in front of an LMX laptop.

"Get two down."

John did just that. Although the display model was small and sleek, the boxes they came in were much bulkier, and it was obvious that John would be the better of the two to carry them.

"Did you see the specs?"

"Know 'em by heart." Chuckie headed to the register.

John leaned down and lowered his voice. "Did you see the price? We don't have enough in our account to even afford one of them!"

"We'll see."

They reached Meehix, who then stepped up to the register, AEC at the ready, as John set the two boxes on the counter.

"Now, Ship."

The clerk scanned the items. "That comes to two hundred credits," and did a double-take. "Two hundred? These retail for five grand each!"

"Must be on sale. Scanners don't lie."

Meehix swiped her card. Chuckie grabbed the receipt as it printed out and John grabbed the boxes.

Chaos then reigned inside the Max-Comp as the digital displays on every item in the store suddenly changed to less than ten percent of the price they were seconds earlier.

The dozens of customers quickly snatched up as many items as they could carry and headed for the register.

Three of the four cashiers left their posts and hopped the counter to get in on these insane discounts. John, Meehix, and Chuckie had to fight their way *out* of the door as dozens of pedestrians were fighting to get *in*.

"We're good now, Ship."

"Returning prices to normal. Was anyone hurt?"

"Not sticking around to find out."

John and Chuckie ran the four blocks back to their suite at the hotel. Meehix took her time.

Two nerds with two souped-up laptops.

"I'll be in the hotel bar!" she hollered at them. "Come and get me when you're both orgasmed out from your new toys!"

That caused the others on the sidewalk to cast curious glances at the strange pair rushing past them, but Chuckie gave her two thumbs-up as he tried to keep up with John.

I hope the bartender can make a decent dibble-blink cocktail because I'm gonna order a pitcher.

CHAPTER SEVEN

It had been several hours, and the boys hadn't come down from the suite to fetch Meehix from the hotel bar. *Bastards.* But the bartender *did* know how to make a decent dibble-blink. *I wonder if he'll marry me?*

As she drained the last of her pitcher, John finally made an appearance.

"Jojacko-o-o!" Meehix raised her glass and was pissed when John went to the bartender first.

"Thanks, man. Add forty percent for a tip when you charge whatever she's consumed to our suite."

"My pleasure, sir. I think she may need some help getting back up there, which is why I called."

"I appreciate it."

"So, Jo-jo-jack-jack-o-o-o. Is there an echo in here?"

John leaned down and spoke softly. "We're going to go now. Do you feel the need to vomit?"

"No." She stood, wobbled, and was about to sit back down when John swept her up in his arms. She waved bye-

bye to the bartender as her partner carried her to the elevator.

"You're sho shweet...and such a gentleman." She hiccupped as the door dinged. "Will you ask the bartender to marry me?"

"You can ask him yourself once you've sobered up."

Having reached the suite, John carried her through the door.

"You're carryin' me crosh the threshold. Did we get married?"

John set her down. "Are you able to walk?"

"Maybe?"

John held onto her hand as he carefully guided her through the living room and toward the bedroom that had been his when the biggest bed had been his primary motivation. He opened the door.

"Are you finally taking me to—*hiccup*—bed?"

"No, I'm taking you to *your* room. The room with the private bath."

"My own bathroom?"

"Yes."

"Tha's wunerful. *Hiccup.* Point me in its direction."

He did, and she rushed as fast as her wobbly legs allowed.

John discreetly closed the door as Meehix made her offering to the porcelain gods. He knocked on Chuckie's door as he passed on the way to his room.

"Everything all right?"

"Oh yes...Oh yes...Oh...yes, yes, yes!"

John wasn't sure if the little man was watching porn or

if he'd discovered the Nev-stop program that came already installed on his recently acquired LMX. They truly were beautiful machines.

"See ya in the morning."

John went to the table in the small dining room. The common areas in the suite consisted of the kitchen, the dining room, and the living room. They weren't overly large, but they were clean and could serve as their home base for a while.

The boxes and protective packaging from the LMX's still lay scattered on the floor. When he and Chuckie had made it back to the suite, they'd immediately unpacked the laptops and Chuckie had hurried to his room with his. *Sometimes it's best to explore things in private.*

John had decided to leave his on the dining room table. That would allow joint use for everyone and give them enough room to move around and look over the shoulder of whoever was sitting at the keyboard. He desperately needed some sleep and glanced back at Meehix's door.

Now is not the time. Especially not now. There'll never be a time as long as we share the suite with a third wheel. At least Meehix won't walk around naked all day.

"It's not like she's an intentional tease," he spoke to his LMX as he fired it up. "She just doesn't realize that causing a guy to have a constant hard-on is less than a pleasant experience after a few days."

He played with his new toy for a little while, learning more of its ins and outs. Then, out of curiosity, did a quick search and one of the loads on his mind were lifted. There was no longer a Crec Alert out on them! No price on

Meehix's head, alive, nor on his head, in any condition. He made a note to look deeper into it tomorrow when they all got together and started scanning for jobs.

"Oh, that is beautiful!"

John was back at the dining room table, scrolling through Crec Alerts when Meehix emerged from her room and took in the room service display laid out on the kitchen counter. He smiled.

"We'll have to start buying groceries soon. These room service prices are gonna kill us. But after yesterday, I thought we should splurge. How's the head?"

"My head's fine. I don't get hangovers."

"Just asking. You look a little more purplish than blueish this morning."

"That fades fast." She fixed herself a plate and sat across from him. "Thank you for swapping rooms with me."

"Chuckie helped me get my priorities straight."

"*Our* Chuckie?"

"Took me by surprise too. Oh, he came out this morning to take a piss, then holed back up in his room."

"What have you been doing?"

"Scrolling through Crec Alerts, trying to find our next money-maker."

"Crec Alerts. Fuck. I wonder how much we're worth by now?"

"Nothing." John smiled and spun the laptop so she could see.

"Nothing? I'm not worth anything?"

"I thought that would come as good news. They canceled the alert on us!"

"Although, technically, as a nonentity, you don't exist, so being worth nothing would be an upgrade."

She spun the laptop back to John and turned to face the approaching Chuckie.

"And a good morning to you too, asshole."

"I'm not going to talk to you any more until your purple tinge fades a little."

"You're used to that?" John asked as Chuckie busied himself snatching up and eating various delicacies while standing in the kitchen.

"I've known her since we were both kids in school. You think I've never seen her purple-haze before?"

Chuckie finished his quick bites, wiped off his hands, and moved to look over John's shoulder, ignoring Meehix's angry stare. He'd seen it before and knew that distraction was the best cure.

"What'd'ya got pulled up?"

"Crec Alerts."

"Pilot's seat."

John stood, and Chuckie took the chair and control of the LMX.

"Already found you two bounty hunters' next target. I mean, we're trying to make a living right? And I'm trying to avoid another gig in a cryo-unit."

"Right." Meehix joined John in looking over Chuckie's shoulder.

Three quick keystrokes later, a Crec Alert started a slow scroll.

John and Meehix watched the scroll of names, faces,

and prices with occasional *Oohs* and *huhs,* and *that one's worth a bundle.*

Chuckie stopped the scroll and leaned back.

"That's the one we want first."

"Blip Freckson?" Meehix was more than a little confused. "He's not worth very much."

"He is to me."

"What kind of a name is Blip?"

"Blip is the name of the guy who dropped the dime on me that led to my cryo."

"He's goin' down! No one fucks with our Chuckie N! Gear up!"

They watch John rush to his room.

"*Your* Chuckie N. Does that mean you two are a couple now?"

"A couple of idiots. Nothing beyond that."

"Not yet at least, huh?"

"Don't read too much into it. It was just an expression."

"I'm not. I'm really trying not to. It's just that..." he struggled to find the words.

"It's just that you love me, yeah, yeah, I know. Half the known universe knows. But John and I are *not* a couple. Hell, I may have even married the bartender last night."

"You *may* have?"

"Things got a little fuzzy toward the end down there while you two were circle-jerking with your computers up here. But whatever John and I are, or are not, or will ever be, you are *our* Chuckie N. Does that compute?"

"Yes, it does."

"Good. Pack up the toy for John to take with us. I have to change." She headed for her room.

Chuckie waited until he was alone at the table before he responded. "It's just that I've never been a part of anyone's *our* before." He wasn't the emotional type but felt two competing tears. One tear said, *They're not a couple yet, but they should be.* The other tear countered the sad one with; *You're part of a family now.*

He took one last look at Blip's face before shutting down the laptop. *You, on the other hand, are nothing more than dust waiting for me to grind beneath my feet. How does it feel to be a dead hack walking?*

It didn't take long for Meehix and John to find the closest Galactic Safety Office, pay the five thousand credits for the bounty certificate, and be on board Ship, ready for take-off.

"I didn't know that the certificates were adjusted by how much the target was worth."

"Neither did I," Meehix answered as she strapped in. "This is how we learn. Ship, find the closest Gate that'll get us to Woohall City on..."

"Flendip II," John prompted from his notes.

"We have a job?"

"It's more of a mission," John clarified.

"Almost like a favor, for Chuckie."

"If I were capable of emotions, I would probably feel sorry for the poor bastard, whoever he is."

With that, they were off. Meehix had no trouble remembering the Gate codes while they were in her old stomping grounds and it wasn't long before they had docked in Woohall.

"What do you know about Woohall?"

"Let's just say that the city isn't known as party central. I've only been here twice, and it is the quietest city I've ever heard."

"Quiet?"

"You'll see…or hear…or in this case, not hear."

Back in the hotel room, Chuckie had been busy with Mixie, wondering if John had given his LMX a nickname yet. While he might never get to be intimate with Meehix, although he hadn't quite conceded, he could let his fingers fly all over Mixie until they were worn to stubs if he wanted.

He'd located Blip Freckson at the Fly-hi-bye and sent the directions to Ship to pass on.

Meehix and John found the Fly-hi-bye after a fifteen-minute walk through the streets of Woohall. It seemed to John to be more of a small town than what he thought of as a city, but Meehix was right. The place was quiet enough to pass for a ghost town.

"Woohall is unofficially known as hacker heaven haven. They're so addicted to their electronics that Woohall banned motorized vehicles within city limits due to too many DWOs."

"DWOs?"

"Driving While Online. The city has the highest known rate of pedestrian-on-pedestrian accidents because no one can take their eyes off their screens long enough to pay attention to where they're walking. According to Chuckie, they've got the fastest connection speeds of any city in the third arm."

"That explains the towers." John marveled at the towers encircling the town. Each one was at least half a mile high. He could barely make out the specks on top that were the satellite dishes and probably the size of hockey rinks when viewed up closer. *Beats the hell of retiring in Phoenix.*

Entering Fly-hi-bye, they found a relatively small space, furnished with a scattering of neat little tables and the most comfortable-looking chairs that John could ever remember seeing. There were maybe a dozen occupants from various planets, and all hunkered down over their computers. The only sound came from the striking of the keyboards.

"Hey all," John announced, "I'm looking for—"

"SSSSHHHHHH!" came the collective response.

"Blip Freckson," John continued. Six arms left their keyboards long enough to point at a corner with the nicest table and the ugliest occupant in the room. He looked like a pencil with three arms, and an eraser for a head would have been an improvement. John's first thought was that the three arms gave him an unfair advantage while coding, or hacking, or whatever the fucker was doing.

John approached and held out a copy of their bounty certificate. "You are Blip Freckson?"

"Fuck off."

Meehix double-checked the Crec Alert photo. "That's him. You wanna cuff him or should I?"

John tossed the certificate on top of Blip's keyboard. It took Blip three seconds to glance over it, crumple it up, and toss it toward a wall before returning to the keyboard and screen. He laughed.

"Lay one hand on me, and you'll both be broke and slaves before you get me anywhere near the door."

"I'm already broke."

"And I'm already a slave."

John shrugged. "May I suggest that in the future, you don't piss off a hacker who is better than you?"

"There's no one alive who's better than me."

Everyone's screen went dark for a moment, then came back with Chuckie's avatar.

"No...you're supposed to be on ice!"

The other dozen hackers in the room lifted their hands away from their keyboards and rolled their chairs a foot or so away from their desks.

Blip made one last frantic try to get to his keyboard, but John grabbed his arms, all three of them, and improvised with the cuffs he carried built for two arms.

Meehix yanked the power cord out from the wall socket, just in case, as John slung the skinny, ugly hacker over his shoulder and they headed for the door.

A voice came from everyone's computer. "Don't fuck with the Kdackan. We haven't fed him yet today."

John unloaded the hacker at the local Galactic Safety Station, got ten thousand more credits than they'd paid for the certificate added to their Abyss account, and returned to Ship.

"Have you two figured out how to perform a successful high five yet? Because now would seem like a very appropriate time."

"Not our most profitable gig."

"No," Meehix agreed, "but our most enjoyable one so far."

They exchanged a high five that was hard to find fault with, and Ship put himself in gear.

CHAPTER EIGHT

Damn, he missed Jojacko!

They'd seen each other nearly every damn day from the time they were five-year-olds. By the time they were thirteen, they were comparing penis sizes after Jojacko discovered the wonders of Internet porn.

By the time they turned sixteen, Jojacko had jerked off enough—*Can anyone ever jerk enough?*—and turned his hacking skills to other ventures. Gage still clearly remembered the Saturday afternoon when Jojacko had swung by, all innocent-like, to raid the fridge while Gage's dad had the tube tuned to a Liga MX *fútbol* match.

"You've been busy." Gage snatched a Montejo, and they snuck out back.

"No idea what you're talkin' about."

"Yesterday, we were wetbacks. This morning I discovered that we're all now natural-born citizens with Social Security cards and everything!"

"Really?" John took a quick sip and passed the bottle

back. "I guess the U.S. government websites must not be as secure as they should be. Do your folks know yet?"

"Nah." Gage drained the bottle and put it in the trash can they kept out back and only emptied after their monthly barbecues. "Dad's a big Pachuca fan, and they're getting their asses kicked. Thought I'd save the good news to cheer him up after the game."

"You won't tell them how it happened, will ya?"

"No, *amigo*. When you're illegals, you learn to take good fortune in stride. You never know when you're about to be blindsided by bad news, so why should we be surprised by good news?"

Damn, he missed Jojacko!

Even at five years old, John had been big for his age, and Gage was shocked when a gringo had rushed in and scattered three six-year-old bullies from doing more damage to his scrawny Mexican ass. They'd been inseparable ever since. John had no siblings and envied Gage's *familia*.

The Gonzalez' had gone on to provide three more younger siblings for Gage...no, four!

Shit, he hated it when he forgot about Jaime. The little dude was blind from birth, and the Gonzalez family was in no financial situation for any kind of special education schools, which was a constant worry.

The summer that Jaime turned three, Uncle Luciano had come up to visit for a week. Uncle Luce owned a pig farm in Mexico, but on weekends, he also played in the best mariachi band in all of Coahuila, Los Locos Grande, and Luce never traveled anywhere without his guitar.

It was early in the morning after a night of a few too many Montejo's that the Gonzalez household woke up to the sound of Luce playing in the living room. Gage's dad was less than thrilled as he came out of his bedroom.

"Damn it, Luce, not this early in the morning!"

Luciano raised his hands. "Don't blame me. He's your *hijo*."

He was sitting on the couch next to Jaime, who had the guitar and was the guilty party.

Gage's dad stood there, speechless.

His mother emerged from their bedroom, took in the scene, and made the sign of the cross.

"What have you done?"

"I was sleeping here on the couch, and he wandered in. He'd had a bad dream, so I played him a lullaby. Next thing I know, I've discovered the next Jose Feliciano."

They'd only seen Jaime once in person since then when Los Locos Grande came up to play at a fundraiser for a senator who was courting the Hispanic vote in the upcoming election. Although Gage could see Jaime any time he wanted on YouTube, he was so good that Gage had a hard time thinking of him as his little brother. His parents might have been illegal aliens when Jaime was born, but Jaime seemed like an alien from a whole other dimension.

The thought of aliens brought him back to what he was doing awake and online at three in the morning. He wondered how Jojacko and the blue chick were getting along and if he'd banged her yet.

Right, right. Save the Aliens!

Thanks to the nearly defunct PC, he still had the video. He hadn't used that machine to get online since baby Isabella was born, except for that one moment a few months ago. That was when he'd sent a copy of the mystery sender's video to an AOL email account that was still active and belonged to his mom.

The video of the USSF pilots left to die on Jupiter. Draylop swore he didn't send it, so it must've been Jojacko.

Using the old PC, Gage had managed to save the video to a USB flash drive. He'd wanted to take the flash drive to a copy center where he could safely get more copies made. The trouble was that after his experience with the anal-probing agents Bixby and Shaw, he wasn't sure where he could go that would be secure.

Yes, Agents Bixby and Shaw, bullies are just pussies with weapons. And I remember the name of every pussy I've fucked or been fucked by.

3:15 a.m. With a little luck, I got two hours of quiet time left in the Gonzalez abode. Better get my anally-probed ass in gear.

He filmed himself doing his next broadcast of Save Aliens From Assholes. It took him a few tries. The first attempt showed part of a Kirk and Spock poster in the background on the wall to his right. Not good if he wanted people to take him seriously.

He changed the camera angle. Tits intruded over his left-hand shoulder now. He changed the angle again, quite proud of himself for not spending too much time being distracted by the tits.

At 7:00 a.m., he locked and loaded his newly filmed piece, plus the original video of the USSF pilots left to die, on every platform he could find. Jojacko had taught him well.

He knew by now that he had, maybe, twenty-seven followers on his Twitch page from his first Save the Aliens broadcast. He knew that maybe twelve of them might be anxiously awaiting his next post.

After his hard night's work, and the several weeks of thinking that went into it, he took a moment to pat himself on the back for changing the name of the movement from Save The Aliens to Save Aliens From Assholes.

Acronyms were important for people to reference while doing searches. Just ask PETA or NASA or any city's PTA. Plus, SAFA was a hell of a lot more memorable than STA, which sounded too much like an STD for his liking.

He'd also decided what to call himself during his broadcast, for however many or few there might end up being. He'd even set up a separate Twitch account under his new moniker. Double-checking the camera angles, he signed into his existing Twitch account, live, while also posting the two current videos on all the various platforms and let loose.

"Yo dudes and dudettes, this is Gonzo Gage comin' at'cha with the truth! The government can't shut down Twitch, but their agents *can* delete videos.

"We prolly got thirty seconds before they get to work on that, so check out any media platform you can find and look for SAFA, Save Aliens From Assholes, and you'll find two vids that I just posted. One of my handsome self and one pirated directly from the USSF. Warning ya's, the second one ain't pretty.

"From now on, you can follow me on my new Twitch account at Gonzo Gage. I'm gonna post the two vids on Twitch right here, right now." Two more buttons pushed.

"The second one was sent to me by Jojacko, who had just rescued an actual alien from a prison base right around the corner from me. She'd been held there by a black ops branch of our very own government known as Alien Neutralization Anti-Liberation…or as those of us in the know refer to them, the ANALs.

"It'll only be moments before the ANALs—yes Agents Bixby and Shaw, I'm talkin' 'bout you—try to take all the vids down, so get 'em while they're hot! Download and share on all of your online socials! Let's get SAFA rollin'! Gonzo Gage, out and gone!"

———

Agent Bixby was leaning back in his chair, eyes closed while ignoring the ringing of a telephone.

"Can you get that, Agent Shaw?"

"No, Agent Bixby." Agent Shaw was balancing a tray of donuts and two coffees as he came through their office door. "You were late, so I went down to the cafeteria and brought up some breakfast and coffee because I figured you hadn't bothered with either before you left your tramp's room this morning."

The phone continued to ring.

"Don't call her a tramp! She's my wife's sister!"

"Sister schmister." Shaw set the tray down on the nearest surface. "Someone has to answer the goddam phone!"

Bixby left his chair, truly thankful for the coffee, both for the caffeine fix and that he could use it to multi-task and wash down a mouthful of donuts. "nffoncallear."

Shaw held up a hand as the phone continued to ring. "Chew, swallow, repeat."

Bixby did just that. "No one calls anyone at seven in the morning except telemarketers and bill collectors."

Ring. Ring. Ring.

"Persistent fucker, whoever it is," Shaw observed.

"All right, all right, I'll put it on speaker. Whoever has the least bites of donuts in their mouth at any given time can respond. Oh, and thanks for the coffee."

"You're welcome." Shaw reached for a donut as Bixby hit the button.

"Bixby and Shaw." Fuck. That made them sound like a law firm that needed one more partner.

"What in the name of Gandhi's holy cow-burger is going on?"

Shaw stuffed his whole donut in his mouth, forcing Bixby to respond.

"Good morning, boss. I'm not sure what you're asking."

"It's quarter after seven! You two haven't checked your online memos yet?"

Shaw made a "stretch it" motion with his hands as he hit the remote to turn on the sixty-inch wall-mounted monitor linked to their individual desks' PCs and fired up both of their computers.

"Yes, sir, we've been catching up on all the emails that flood in every night. You know how full they can get."

"Fuck your inboxes! I was under the impression that you two had taken care of our Gage problem!"

Bixby hit mute. "What's a Gage?"

"Anal probe down in New Mexico."

Bixby smiled at the memory. They hadn't used any lube on the fucker before they'd rolled him and his abused asshole out of the tan DeVille. They spun. Gage was on the screen, looking no worse for wear.

Then came the video of the USSF fuck-up on Jupiter on the wall monitor and both of their PCs. They scrambled to their desks, all thoughts of donuts forgotten as the video ended and Gage came back on all screens in what seemed like surround sound.

"Gonzo Gage, out and gone."

"Can either of you two asswipes tell me," the boss continued his obscenity-laced barrage, "why the fuck he's online broadcasting to the whole cock-sucking world for every man, woman, and their bastard-born baby from every bitch momma to see and hear?"

Shaw pointed at his chest and Bixby un-muted.

"We were just about to call you, boss." Shaw tried to keep the panic out of his voice. "We can't take down his Twitch account, but we're scouring all the Internet platforms to delete the videos as fast as we can."

Bixby gave Shaw a thumbs-up and chimed in. "It's only the two of us here right now. The rest of the staff doesn't show up until eight. We're doing the best we can."

"One of you call the front desk. Make it clear that anyone coming through the door has orders to go immediately to their workstations and scour the Internet. They're to delete any of this jerk-off's videos, or they'll no longer have a workstation by nine o'clock if I find one more video online!"

The boss didn't wait for a response before slamming down his phone.

"Mother fuck." Bixby went for another donut to help him fuel up.

"Piss shit." Shaw did the same. "Aw man, I wanted the Boston cream."

They took their donuts and coffee back to their desks and settled in.

"We should've stripped him naked and staked him out in the desert for the rattlers and scorpions to finish off when we had the chance," were Bixby's last words before he bit into his cream donut.

"Shoulda, coulda, woulda. Start scouring. Right now, our mission is to search and destroy."

"We're gonna do some searching and destroying of our own later on. We got some vacation time coming, right?"

"That we do, Agent Bixby. But if we don't get those fucking videos taken down in the next two hours, we won't have to worry about having any vacation time left."

"Where you wanna start?"

"Time zones. I'll take everything east of the Mississippi. They're already up, and I'm faster at this than you."

"Deal. I'll handle west of. Those coming in will have to divvy up who gets the other sides of the Atlantic and Pacific."

They'd dropped off their target and collected their credits. With Chuckie's appetite for revenge on the fucker who'd put him on ice now sated, they left their hotel suite and followed Chuckie to a restaurant that he insisted he needed to satisfy his actual appetite.

"If this is one of those dives with the three-titted

bottomless waitresses, you two are gonna be dining without me."

"Naw, nothing like that. John and me'll save for a trip to Woo-Dare-Don't-Stare while you're away on your honeymoon with the bartender."

"Oh, like you've never downed one or twelve too many."

"Is that place really real?" John couldn't help but ask.

"The building is. Can't vouch for the titties," Even as short as he was, Chuckie had to duck to avoid Meehix's head-smack. John never saw the one that was aimed his way.

"There it is! And sorry, not sorry, your blue highness, if it isn't up to your hoity-toity standards." Chuckie hustled and held the door open as Meehix, who felt that she had no alternative, held her head high and entered. Chuckie let the door go before John could follow. He was gonna grab the seat at the booth next to Meehix.

John opened the door and let himself into the Nerth B equivalent of a Waffle House. It was a little rundown with age but relatively clean. He took the seat across the booth but didn't bother looking at the menu. Nor did Chuckie. He already knew what he wanted.

When the waitress, waiter? Even with his recent experiences with aliens, he still had no clue as to this one, came to take their orders, John let Meehix decide for him.

"But please, Meehix, be merciful."

He couldn't tell if her crooked-assed smile was one of kindness or if she would take out her revenge for him asking a little too eagerly about the Woo-Dare-Don't-Stare.

Chuckie was bursting to tell them about the next job

he'd lined up but said it would have to wait until after they'd eaten. He intended to enjoy his meal thoroughly.

Meehix had been merciful. John's meal, when it came, resembled a salad but consisted of colors that Crayola had never come up with. He worked his way through the various colors one nibble at a time. There was one thing that looked like a cross between purple and green that was quite tasty.

Chuckie's meal, on the other hand, looked something like goat stew poured over a fruitcake. He held his plate out over the table.

"Try some?"

Meehix reached out and gently guided the plate back toward Chuckie.

"I don't think he's ready for that quite yet. Besides, your taste buds have been in cryo for a while, so I'm not sure they're fully functional yet."

"His loss." Chuckie dug in but continued between mouthfuls. "Meehix is right. My taste buds are still recovering. Out there on Kdack 3a, I understand that your impregnated females get food cravings, correct?"

"You're referring to the infamous middle of the night runs for ice cream and pickles?"

"There ya go!" He shoveled in another mouthful. "This food has minerals that my body is begging for right now. Because of that craving, I could be eating the innards of a Flylobian Fulax and think it was the best-tasting meal since Lankle Lancy first roasted a grindle greddit."

"Oh, who but Lankle would have ever thought of doing that?"

"Heaven, right?"

Meehix smiled at the memory of her first bite of Lancy's signature dish.

"Gotta warn ya though, John. When we get back to the suite, you might want to give the bathroom an hour or so for the air to clear after I finish in there later."

John slid his plate away. He'd suddenly lost his appetite.

Chuckie also decided that the diner was now too crowded to unveil his plans for their next job.

"Too many ears with nothing better to do than eavesdrop."

"Back to the suite?" Meehix was full.

"I'm not going anywhere near it until the Chuckster here deposits in a non-shared bathroom." John was adamant.

"How about the hotel bar? There won't be a crowd now." She also wouldn't mind another drink.

"Sounds like a plan. We can ask your new husband how his honeymoon arrangements are going."

Chuckie didn't need to duck from a forthcoming head smack. The look Meehix gave him would have turned the mortals on Kdack 3a to dust, but Chuckie was built of stronger stuff and simply smiled.

Damn, John thought. *One of these days I'm gonna have to try whatever he just ate, intestinal fortitude be damned.*

"Another pitcher of dibble-blinks?" the bartender asked as they made their way to a table. "Now that your friends are here to share it with?"

"No!"

"One to start with!" Chuckie overruled her. He'd managed to get on and off her shit list twice already today, so he was going for a trifecta.

"I hate you, Chuckie!"

"I love you, Chuckie!" John countered as he went to the bar to get the pitcher.

"Will you marry me, John?" Chuckie hollered after him.

"I think we can arrange that here, Chuckie!" John yelled back.

When John reached the bar, he leaned over and whispered to the bartender as he was mixing up the pitcher.

"Keep your voice down. Do you want another forty percent tip like the one the other night?"

The bartender leaned forward and returned the whisper while continuing the task at hand. "It would seem to be in my best financial interests to say yes."

"Okay. Then play along and refute, deny, and in every way you can, say no to whatever I'm about to ask. Feel free to raise your voice."

The bartender had the pitcher almost full. He leaned closer. "I'm only working here to pay for my acting classes and the rent. Are you three something like an improv troupe?"

John risked a glance over at the table to find Meehix and Chuckie staring at him, then turned back to the bartender and continued with his whispering.

"Something like that. So remember, refute, deny, call me an idiot."

"And project?"

"Correct. Here we go."

"What do you mean, the concierge at a hotel can't perform a wedding ceremony?"

"That is correct, sir."

The bartender's acting classes had paid off because he was projecting just fine without seeming to shout.

"But on the planet where I come from, the captain of a ship at sea has the authority to officiate at weddings."

"I'm sure that it's a fine planet, sir. But in hotels on Space Station Nerth B, the hotel concierges have no such authorization."

A lean forward and a quick whisper. "Okay so far?"

"Your middle name should be Oscar for Best Supporting Actor."

John found himself suddenly also caught up in the improv. It was like gaming. Every decision you made depended on the results of the last decision. He left the pitcher on the counter and approached the table, pointing first at Chuckie.

"So, you're telling me that my dearly beloved here and I can't bring in the concierge to marry us right here and now before we have a chance to change our minds?"

"That is correct, sir."

John circled the table and pointed at Meehix.

"And that my other beloved and I will also be bereft of the concierge services."

"Sadly, yes, sir. Even though bigamy is allowed and honored and legally recognized on Nerth B, there is no one in this hotel authorized to officiate a wedding."

"I can do it!" came a voice from the end of the bar who had obviously been there too long. "I'm licensed."

"Keep out of this, judge!" The bartender returned to his

co-improvers. "There has been no exchanging of vows in this bar while I've tended it."

John returned to the bar while still pointing at Meehix, who by now had simply lowered her head to the table and accepted her punishment.

"So that woman has never been married while in this bar?"

"No, sir."

"Not even to you?"

"She proposed to me the other night, and I accepted, but to my everlasting regret, the judge was not here that night, and we parted in tears."

John collected the pitcher. "You killed it, man."

The bartender handed him a card. "If you ever need a fourth, let me know."

John returned to the table with the pitcher. Chuckie gave him and the bartender a standing ovation. Meehix gave him four thumbs down.

Once John took his seat, Meehix picked up the pitcher and stood holding it over their glasses.

"Are you quite done, now?"

John nodded, hoping that she'd pour some of the liquid into his glass and not empty the whole thing over his head.

"And you?"

"That was John's and the bartender's show. For once, I was an innocent party."

Glasses filled and heads still dry, things got serious as Chuckie continued, "While you two were out avenging my incarceration, I found our next job."

"How much is he worth?" John cut right to the chase.

"Why do you assume it's a he? Us gals can get pretty outlaw-ish too."

"Wrong time and place," Chuckie cut in. "It's not a bounty hunting gig."

"But we're bounty hunters now," John protested. "It cost us a lot of credits to get our license. Our first bounty didn't pay as much as we'd hoped for, and the second one was your mission of revenge. You're welcome very much."

"Fuck you very much, and I'll get back to your first bounty in a minute."

Chuckie raised his hand to signal the bartender to bring another pitcher. He knew that they'd probably regret it in the morning, but he also knew that it would take some serious mental lubrication to get them to agree. They could go over the details in the morning back in their suite, but first, he had to make sure they were both on board.

"Forget, just for now, about the bounty hunting."

"Why?" John interrupted. "It's legal, and our first score would've been a big one."

"If you hadn't managed to kill him before bringing him in. I'll get back to him, I promise."

"We're trying to stay aboveboard with this. Aren't we, Meehix?"

"Trying," she agreed.

"Right. Save the Slaves or whatever the fuck you two are calling it. I came this close to hacking into the hotel's system and having them comp our suite for the next year to use as a home base because it's such a worthy cause."

"That's an idea…ouch!" Meehix kicked John's leg under the table.

"If you steal something from a thief who'd stolen it

from someone else, would you consider yourself a criminal?"

"Depends on whether or not you're going to return it to the original owners."

"Damn, Meehix, he really is just one step short of being fucking perfection personified."

"Yeah. Pisses me off too when he pulls that shit." She gently ran a foot up his leg under the table.

Beats the hell out of a shin-kick. "I'll shut up," John said out loud. "You go on."

The bartender delivered the second pitcher.

"You have my card, sir. Just in case you ever need me again." John tapped his shirt pocket, and the bartender retreated.

The bar wasn't overly crowded yet, so there was no need to shout to be heard, but something in Chuckie's voice led them all to lean over the table, then lean back as they tried to look all casual and shit as he laid it out.

"There's a private residence compound, more of a fortress, actually. I have the whole layout and specs saved on Mixie up in our suite."

"What the hell is a Mixie?" Meehix had formed an immediate suspicion.

"Have you given your LMX a nickname yet?"

John looked sheepish.

"Spill." Meehix was curious what John had come up with.

"I almost named it Hannah."

"Glad you didn't, bro. The program you created is more than that trollop of an ex-girlfriend of yours deserved as a tribute." Chuckie took another sip. "So, what'd you come up with?"

John moved his legs out of both kicking and stroking distance under the table and 'fessed up.

"Heemix."

Chuckie was glad that he'd ordered a second pitcher because Meehixiheem took the time to refill her glass and take a sip before responding.

"Hmm. Mixie and Heemix. Give me a minute while I decide whether to be flattered or kill you both."

"I hope she chooses flattered."

"You better. You're a much bigger target than me."

"Yeah, but I can run faster."

"Enough!" Heads turned, and Meehix toned it down. "I have decided that you both will survive. At least until this second pitcher is empty. So, clue us in, Chuckie N."

"Okay. There's this very bad dude who lives in a fortress. He's spent his whole life building up immense wealth, most of it illegally obtained."

"With ya so far. Is there a damsel in distress that we can also rescue while relieving the bad dude of his ill-gotten gains?" It sounded like a game John had once played. Actually, it sounded like several games he'd played.

"Might be. Don't know yet. Only one way to find out." Chuckie smiled to himself because he already had John hooked. He decided to do his bit of improv.

"There are two rooms in the fortress that no one can get into, except for the chosen few. One room is at the top of the highest tower. One room is so deep underground that you have to get beneath the level of the lowest dungeons even to begin searching for it. Rumor has it that the treasure and the damsel might even be kept in the same room because they're both treasures to the Evil Dude!"

"Cut the shit and get to the point because Jojacko is beginning to drool with excitement. At least I hope that drooling is the only mess he's making with his various body parts."

John drew a deep breath and leaned back, swiping his sleeve across his chin in case he had drooled. Chuckie went after Meehix now. This was gonna be a buzz-kill for sure.

"Does the name Victor Vikrellion ring any bells?"

"Head of the Vikrellion mob. Supposed to be some kind of big-shot gangster." Meehix was fast approaching boredom. "Lives out on Brakeb III, which I've heard is an armpit of a planet."

"Does the name Frelo Cocksman Raxmugg ring any bells?"

"The armless dude who was barely worth the effort of bringing in?" John was on the edge of boredom now too.

"Because you two brought him in dead! Did either of you two bounty hunting newbies ever wonder why someone with such a high bounty on his head was so easy to find?"

Meehix suddenly realized why Frelo's name had sounded so familiar when she'd first heard it. She turned to John.

"We fucked up big time, partner."

"You didn't mean to kill him. You gotta stop beating yourself up over that."

"Tell him, Chuckie." She refilled her glass and wondered how long they had to live.

"Frelo was the aforementioned Victor's baby brother."

"Victor, the mob boss on Bobaloopek III or something, right?" John tried to keep up. Damn, no wonder Meehix had gotten wasted after drinking a pitcher of these by herself.

"Brakeb III. And you both have a price on your precious little heads for having murdered his little brother."

"It wasn't a mudder...murder...it was a riotous kill."

Chuckie chose to ignore John and focus his attention back on Meehix.

"Victor won't put out a Crec Alert on you two. From what I know of him, he'll handle this in-house. But trust me, he will find you."

This so shook Meehix that she addressed him by her favorite nickname for him when they were still in school, and she was his only friend. "Shit, Fuck-Chuck, we're already dead. Where are we going to hide?"

"For starters, right in the belly of the beast."

"The fortress you were talking about is Victor's?"

"Uh-huh. Which pair of fools would be stupid enough to try to break into it and rob him blind? Especially while he has the best and the brightest and the most ruthless scouring three galaxies trying to find two second-rate bounty hunters?"

John chose that moment to start snoring.

Time to help get the big oaf up to their suite and resume the conversation in the morning. Which is what they did. By the time John woke up the next morning, the smell of the toxic dump from Chuckie's earlier dinner had time to dissipate, mostly.

All had survived the two pitchers of dibble-blinks and gathered as early as they could around the dining room table. Chuckie had Mixie fired up, and they watched as he scrolled and showed them everything he'd been able to find about Victor's compound.

"Don't try to focus too much this morning, okay?" Chuckie instructed. "There's too much info to take in at one sitting," He handed John a flash drive. "It's all on here."

John pocketed the drive. "That's the place we're going to try to break into?"

"We is a relative term. This is the joint that you and Meehix are going to break into. I'm gonna stay right here with Mixie and do what I do best."

"Please don't spend too much time doing what you do second best." Yep, Meehix knew him all too well.

"My best suggestion for you two to survive is to get hold of some more weaponry and head for Ship. You can review all the info there, and I'll get back in touch in a few hours."

CHAPTER NINE

After leaving Chuckie back at the hotel to keep working, their first stop was at a pawnshop to pick up some additional armaments. They spent more of their dwindling funds than would normally be considered wise, but if they succeeded in their mission, money would no longer be an issue. If they failed, well, finances would no longer be a concern for either of them.

Among the assortment of assault accouterments, there was one weapon that John insisted he needed.

"What was the name of that tickle-gun?"

"The what?" Meehix was eyeing various footwear that could be extremely useful in hand-to-hand or foot-to-foot combat.

"In the hotel that time. The thing that was deadly to everyone else but only made me laugh until I'd pissed myself."

"The Vetralaun semi-automatic?"

"What she just said." John tried to catch one of the four

ears on the dude behind the counter. "Do you have any of those?"

"Yes and no." He hesitated. "I have a couple, but because of their lethality, I have to keep them in the back." He looked the two of them over. "I'm afraid that they're only available to military personnel, law enforcement officers, and hairstylists."

"Hairstylists?"

"Ask your friend over there with the green mop of hair on top whether or not a stylist who pisses off a client that's not quite happy with her recent 'do might need a lot of self-defense on hand."

"Well, hell." John turned away.

"Oh, and bounty hunters."

John turned back. "Meehix, can you come over here and show this fine gentleman my license?"

Meehix did as requested. After verifying the veracity of the license, the *gentleman* headed to fetch the guns from the back room.

"Good memory. Those babies are lethal. Get two."

"Don't you remember? They're *not* lethal to me. They give me a shit-load of laughing for a minute. Then I become unstoppable."

"The unstoppable part *was* pretty impressive."

"I'll have to time it right, but I think they'll come in useful."

Half an hour later, weapons chosen and paid for, Meehix and John carried their cache back to Ship.

"Good old faithful Shippewa," John offered as they each lugged a duffle bag full of their pawnshop scores, two of which were the military-style duffle bags. "Pieced together from various parts as a hybrid earth-alien spacecraft. He really is one of a kind. "

"That he is." Meehix shouldered a slow-walking Nexburgian out of her way. *The Nexies really should learn to keep far to the right with their fat asses.*

"Then again," John followed his thoughts, "Frankenstein's monster was a hybrid too."

"What are you mumbling about?"

"Oh, nothing. Just a story with a sad ending." He let the subject drop.

"Welcome back aboard. Did you two have a pleasant dinner with Chuckie?"

"*Chuckie* and *pleasant* used in the same sentence," John mused aloud. "How often does that happen?"

"I can calculate the percentages if you wish."

"Nah. Whatever likely percentages you'd come up with, I'd *still* bet the under."

They unloaded their stashes and put them with their existing weapons. Quite the arsenal the Dolurulodan party girl and the Kdackan computer geek had put together lately. John opened Heemix and spoke to Ship.

"Shippewa, my good spacecraft. I need to borrow Hannah for a minute. Are you running anything from her now?"

"No, John. She's all yours. Tell her I'll miss her."

"I'll have her back to you in a jif."

He gently relieved Ship of the silver and turquoise pendant and inserted it into one of the many USB ports on

Heemix. *Inserting Hannah into Meehix. Good name for a girl-on-girl porn flick...I wish I could insert what I'd inserted into the real Hannah into the real Meehix. If wishes were horses, beggars would ride. Yeah, Mom, thanks for the advice.*

There wasn't a whole lot of room in Ship's cargo area, but Meehix was able to move a few things around and clear a ten-by-fifteen-foot space as she stacked her weapons alongside John's against a wall and took inventory. She returned to the main cabin as John was returning Hannah to Ship.

"Ahh, Hannah-banana, so good to have you back."

Meehix tossed a quizzical look at John, who returned it with a *what can you do?* shrug.

"What am I looking for, John?"

"A new file that Chuckie named U-B-Fucked."

"Found it."

"Can you put it up on the big screen?"

John took the pilot's seat with Meehix riding shotgun. Not that they were going anywhere at the moment, but it allowed them both to lean forward and touch the screen as they flipped through the hundreds of images and specs of Victor Vikrellion's humble abode.

"How does he get this shit?"

"You're the hacker, you tell me."

"I'm a hacker from Kdack 3a. Damn! I just called Earth by its name in space. I'm becoming acclimated!"

"Congratulations, John."

"You were saying?" Meehix reached out to the screen.

"I can pretty much find my way anywhere on my planet of origin. But it's a finite place. The number of places that Chuckie's hacking into is almost infinite. Don't touch it!"

"I just wanted to scroll back a screen."

"Okay. Sorry. I hadn't finished studying this one yet, so I didn't want to go forward. Going back is always good in case we missed something."

"I told you," Meehix continued about the ultimate hacker, "and he won't hesitate to tell you himself, Chuckie's the best hacker anywhere so far discovered."

"That's why we had to rescue him."

"No. We had to rescue him because he's my friend. You would have done the same for Gay-jaw."

"We really do have to work on how you pronounce his name, but yeah, I'd do anything for him."

They scrolled some more. From the outside, Victor's fortress—there was no other word for it—looked like the bastard child between the Parthenon in Greece and various Mormon temples. John had seen a few online pics of each when he was searching while bored.

It appeared to be the size of a rugby pitch. Three stories high with pillars surrounding the whole building, spaced ten feet from each other, and towers reaching up to kiss the sky on all four corners. No, they scrolled some more. The damn building had six corners, not four. Six corners and six corresponding towers.

"Maybe we should stick to bounty hunting," John suggested as Meehix continued scrolling.

"Chuckie is calling in via the hyperlink translating device. Shall I put him on speaker?"

"The what?" John had no idea what Ship was talking about. *Must go lighter on the dibble-blinks.*

"The HLTD I found in my bag, and he immediately snatched away."

"Right. Sure Ship, put him through."

"Have you had a chance to scroll through U-B-Fucked yet?"

"Only halfway through so far, shrimp-dick."

There was a cackle on the other end of the line. "Have you gotten to the underground portion yet, or are you crapping your pants at the outside so far?"

"He's your bro-ho, Jojacko. You two work it out." Meehix continued scrolling as John drew a deep breath.

"I bow to your abilities as a hacker. You're riding a Harley while I still have training wheels on a tricycle."

"Figured that out on your own, did ya?" Another cackle followed.

John pulled out and flipped his hole card face up. *Everyone needs an ace.*

"I know that complete honesty doesn't come easy for you, but can you dig deep and answer one simple question with the bottom-line truth?"

"Just one question?"

"Just one."

"Bottom-line truth?"

"If you're capable of it."

There was no cackle from the other end as Chuckie answered. "Ask away."

"With operation U-B-Fucked, I know that it won't be Meehix, but will the *fuckee* be Victor or me?"

"Victor," came the response without a moment of hesitation.

"Why is that, Chuckie N?" Meehix decided that it was time for her to chime in. Besides, she was curious herself.

There was a long pause before Chuckie responded with a few questions.

"First of all, Jojacko-bro. You risked life and limb to rescue a perfect stranger from his cryo-prison with no financial benefits expectations. True or false?"

"True."

"Meehixiheem."

"Yes, Chuckie?"

"John joined you on that suicidal endeavor simply because you asked him to?"

"True."

"John?"

"Yes, Chuckie."

"One of the *main* reasons that you joined in my *liberation* was because you were looking to score some points to help you in your unspoken effort to flip open her vaginal flap eventually. This next question requires a one-word answer, John. Is my surmise correct?"

John didn't have the courage to meet Meehix's eyes as he answered.

"Yes."

"Meehix?"

"Still here."

"You knew that your flap was part of John's motivations as you led him to his more than likely death. True or false?"

Meehix didn't have the courage to meet John's eyes as she answered.

"That would be true, too."

"Yet, you rescued me, even knowing that I'd be forever driving you crazy as I tried to figure out ways to flip that flap myself?"

"Also true."

"Glad we had this little chat." The cackle was back for a moment. Then Chuckie got serious again. "You two are really and truly dedicated to this Save The Slaves movement, right?"

Meehix and John exchanged head nods.

"I can't *hear* you."

"Yes."

"Yes."

"Good. Then the first thing you have to do is find a better name for it. Acronyms are important! Save The Slaves' acronym, STS, sounds too much like the Space Transmitted Disease's STD acronym!

Fuck, he missed Gage. Was he still on board? How was it going back there on Earth? They hadn't been able to keep in touch since he and Meehix had dropped him back home before heading off into space.

The two of them hadn't gone more than a day without seeing each other since they were both snot-nosed five-year-olds. Gage might be worrying more about how he would fund his Community College tuition than with some cockamamie assignment he'd left him to deal with.

"John?" Chuckie wondered if John had gotten lost thinking about how many diseases he could catch in space.

"John?" Meehix wasn't sure where John's head was either at the moment.

"Ship to John!"

"Huh? What?"

"He's baa-ckkk."

"Sorry. Got distracted there. Where were we?"

"Before you went all astral projecting on us," Chuckie

picked up where he'd left off. "The fortress that you're going to try to break into and rob blind? The primary profits have been built by Victor being the galactic king of slave trading. If that don't float your collective boats, I don't know what will.

"You two might wanna consider spending the rest of today and tonight onboard Ship. I've arranged to have some *acquaintances* drop by. Five's company. Two more would form a bit of a crowd. Talk again tomorrow. Chuckie N out and gone!"

Five minutes of silence followed. **"Have you both had enough time to digest that yet?"**

John turned to Meehix. "So, do we go back to our relatively safe bounty hunting gig, or do we go on a suicide mission to fund the Free The Slaves movement?"

"Do all Kdackans have a bottomless reserve of stupid questions?"

Back to scrolling through U-B-Fucked. They discovered that the pictures had their limitations. John guessed that someone, or several someones, had cribbed many of them to accompany a variety of news articles.

The interior shots were mostly from filming the Brakeb III equivalent of the TV shows John's parents watched. All of them could've had the same title: houses you'll never be able to afford, owned by imbeciles, and what wrong career move did you make, you loser?

There were also blueprints—seventy-six pages of them, including the structure's various schematics. Having reached the end, Meehix started scrolling back up. Up and down and down and up, trying to take it all in.

"What would Jojacko do?"

Meehix touched the screen and paused her scrolling.

"I don't know, Jojacko. Maybe you should ask Jojacko. He's around here somewhere."

"Look, I'm nowhere near the coder that Chuckie is, but I'm one helluva *gamer!* As Jojacko, I kicked ass in every game I ever played!"

"And?"

"If there was a game where Chuck Norris could be the avatar of choice, millions of gamers would be asking themselves, 'What would Chuck do?'"

Ship couldn't help himself. He let loose with a song that he'd downloaded from some of his Kdack 3a programming, and Dick Siegel's *What Would Brando Do?* came out loud.

Meehix listened and couldn't help but shake her blue butt a little but muted the speakers after about thirty seconds.

"What the fuck is a Brando?"

"Someone you didn't want to fuck with. Then Chuck Norris came along, and Brando got old and fat and faded into Kdackan history."

"The point, Meehix, is that there are some people you don't want to fuck with. When it comes to hacking, Chuckie N is one of them. When it comes to gaming, Jojacko is another. So let's try to look at this as a game. While we play it, Jojacko will simply be referred to as Jo while communicating with each other. Just Jo, because every split second will count."

"What will be my moniker?"

"Your choice. Just keep it to one syllable."

Mee? Too confusing if we're trying to figure out who's talking. She ran through various ways to abbreviate her name.

"Hix! I shall be Hix!"

"You go, Jo! You mix, Hix! Ship likes!"

They were all very pleased with themselves.

"Ship. Can you put all of the U-B-Fucked info into a 3D virtual setting so Hix and I can do a few run-throughs?"

"Yo, Jo. I can project it in 4D if you wish, but where?"

"Cargo, Ship. Set it up to project in Cargo. I cleared space there earlier."

"Give me five minutes, and that's where you'll find the mix, Hix."

"What's in Cargo?"

"Our weapons collection, and the only room I could find that was big enough to practice some moves on this badly pieced-together galaxy-traversing maniac of transportation."

"I heard that."

"I meant that as a compliment to you and a criticism of the assholes who threw you together in more haste than you deserved."

"Apology accepted."

They headed to Cargo.

"Whoa! Are those all ours?" John gawked at the weapons lined up along the walls.

"Been busy, haven't we?"

Meehix grabbed a long sword in one hand and two titanium throwing spears in the other. Her earlier purchases of the tanto knife, throwing stars, bolas, and the metal grappling hook with a hundred feet of retractable cord waited patiently for inclusion in the party.

She took advantage of the space she'd cleared, sliced the air four times with her sword, and did a quick spin that ended with John having two spearheads half an inch from his neck.

"Okay, okay! I apologize for anything I've ever said or done that offended you even in the slightest."

"Apology accepted." Meehix smiled and returned the weapons to their proper place against the wall.

"In three, two, one."

"What the?"

"Whoa, fuck."

"You may both need a moment or two to adjust. No virtual reality glasses necessary."

If it wasn't for the fact that he and Meehix would die if they went through with the plan and failed, John found himself in a gamer's wet dream.

"Steady there, cowboy."

"That's *Jo* to you, *Hix*. Those are our names whenever we're in this setting."

"Right. Every second counts."

Three-dimensional cubes like holograms surrounded them, each one about a foot square. They filled the entire cargo hold. They seemed to be stacked according to their location, rotating around them, waiting for the first move. Jo and Hix played statues.

"I believe that the best way to work with this is for one of you to touch a cube. Then that cube will open, and that room is where you'll be."

"Touch a cube to get in. Got it. How do we get out?"

"How about you simply say *out*? Then you'll be back in Cargo, and you can choose the next cube to enter."

John's foot chose that moment to twitch. He and Hix landed in a dungeon filled with dozens of alien species chained to the walls and screaming as a humanoid figure tortured them into submission.

"Out, out, out!" Meehix screamed, and they were back in Cargo, afraid to move a muscle.

"See how easy that was?"

"Take it all down for a minute, please."

"Done."

"That was not fun!"

"No, Hix. Nor was it a game. Those scenes were for fucking real!"

The two bipeds took a minute to get their breathing back to a relatively normal pattern.

"Ship? Is there a way to have better control of which cube we touch?"

"Your twitchy foot interrupted me before I had a chance to advise further."

"Advise now, please."

"Somewhere among the inventory list that my builders left on me before we left Kdack 3a in such a hurry...aahhh, I was such a young ship back in those long-gone days..."

"*Somewhere among* you were saying before you took a trip down memory lane?"

"I didn't know that ships could have sentimental feelings."

"*Feelings* isn't quite the correct term, Meehix, since I don't have feelings in the way that you do. But I do have memories."

"And among those memories was something about the

141

inventory aboard?" John prompted again.

"Gloves. Yes. Somewhere back in Cargo is a box that contains six pairs of mesh-metal gloves. If you can find them, I can set up the program in such a way that only the gloves will be able to access a cube."

"Back in a flash." John went one way. Meehix went the other. They needed to search the boxes that Meehix had shoved aside when she'd cleared out a practice space.

"Might be a long flash, Jo."

They started scrambling through a hundred or so boxes.

"Suggestion, John. Behind the copilot's seat in the main cabin is a metal-detecting wand that might help shorten your search."

Meehix rushed and found the wand and didn't give a moments' thought as to why they would need to check passengers for metals. Returning to Cargo, it took her two minutes to find the box with the gloves.

"Thanks, Ship."

"I live to serve."

"Aw, man, come on. I thought you and me and Meehix worked our way through that whole slave-master bullshit!"

"Just funning with you, John."

"Good one, Ship!" She turned to John. "Ready to glove-up, Jo?"

"With ya, Hix."

Gloves on, Ship put them back in Victor's virtual fortress.

"Which cube first, Jo?"

"Not sure if I wanna go with ladies first or brains before beauty."

"Either and any which way you want to slice it, you're coming in second, Jo."

"Let's get this party started."

Mix reached for one of the higher cubes. They now stood behind a parapet that protected a narrow walkway spanning Victor's entire fortress from the top of the third floor.

"Nice view." Hix was impressed. "Maybe the whole planet isn't an armpit after all."

"Yeah, nice view, unless you take into consideration the six towers covering the corners."

Hix counted them for herself and sighed.

"Six."

Jo took his time to take it all in.

"When you're standing up here, how high do you think those towers are?"

"At least ten of you. Why?"

"Ten of me would only be sixty-four feet. So even if we added another two of me," Jo did a quick mental computation. "That would still bring them in somewhere around eighty feet, give or take."

"I'll take your word for it."

"One of the weapons you chose when we started bounty hunting was a grappling hook with a retractable cord that I think went to one hundred feet. You remember that?"

"Yes! It's lined up along the wall in Cargo right now!"

"Okay. So if we find that we can't fight our way up from the inside of the towers..."

"Then we can get at them from the outside!"

Hix had never battled anything before except groping

hands, but she was starting to get into this. Jo looked around at the grounds surrounding the fortress. They were expansive and wide open. There was no way to approach it without being noticed. *Deal with that minor detail later.*

He'd seen enough from up top. "Out."

They were back in Cargo.

"That was trippier than anything I ever smoked of Daukhl's."

"The stoner who crash-landed you back on my turf?"

"Yeah, and he had some really trippy shit."

"Was there a fun factor involved while you two were in the cube?"

"Back on Kdack 3a, barrels of monkeys are green with envy."

Meehix rushed to check out her grappling hook measurements. "At least fourteen of you."

"One problem solved. Three hundred and forty-seven to go."

"That's a very specific number, Jo...I mean John. Do games have a predetermined number of problems?"

"I pulled that number from out of my ass. The games I played all had a nearly incalculable number of problems. "

"And if you don't solve them all, you lose?"

"If you don't solve them all, you die and have to start all over again from level one."

"Which you will work your way up from before dying again somewhere between level one and level, what, eighty-six?"

"Something like that."

"If you survive and make it to the toppest level, do you win anything?"

"No one *ever* makes it to the *toppest* level."

"So no one ever actually wins? Ship? Am I the only one here who thinks that sounds like insanity of the highest order?"

"Straitjackets for all."

"Winning isn't important! Reaching a higher level than anyone else has ever reached is what matters!"

"I concede the floor to you, Meehix, to address that one, but may I inject a reality check?"

"You can give it a try."

"Since this is not a game, if you die, it doesn't matter which level you die on. You will both be dead. There is no 'New Game' option unless I'm missing something?"

"You didn't miss nothing, Ship," John conceded.

"There is one main difference between this and the games you wasted your youth playing, John."

"Yeah, yeah, I'll die." John looked at Meehix, sitting there with her haystack of green hair, perfect blue body, four thumbs, and the mouth that wasn't showing off her weird-ass smile at the moment. "We'll *both* die for real in this one."

"All of that and more, John. But in this one, while you both only get one chance to die, your advantage is that you can see all or most of the levels before you begin to play."

Funk over, they stood, squared their shoulders, and faced each other.

"I'll go where you go, Jo."

John pointed to a room at random. They ended up in a closet with gaudy dresses and more shoes than your typical arachnid could wear in a year, even if they chose a new pair every day.

"Out."

Cargo.

"How many shoes does one woman need?" John was trying to recover from a claustrophobic panic attack. *Let's keep that fear of mine between Gage and me.*

"How bad can one woman's tastes be to go out in public wearing dresses five years out of date?"

Meehix had a quick flashback of her Uncle Bleenum, a widower who showed up at a family function wearing his late wife's clothes. *It helps me still feel connected to her.* He continued doing that until he no longer received invitations to family functions.

John had a flashback to rumors his dad had told him about J. Edgar Hoover. *Yeah. That looked like the kind of wardrobe J. Edgar would choose to try on when he was behind closed doors.*

Meehix pointed at a room on the second level as quickly as she could.

They spent the next several hours visiting every room available, looking for doors and windows and how they could either invade or escape. She even had Ship toss in some mean-looking dudes here and there to help them explore their virtual *freeze, fight, or flee* options.

"The trouble is," John said, as they caught their breath halfway through, "these are only the rooms Chuckie was able to find for us."

"The two dungeon rooms were enough to convince me that we need to take this fucker down! Agreed?"

"Agreed. Victor's going down, or we're going down

dying and trying."

"May your names stay etched in everyone's galactic memory."

"Thanks, Ship. Ready for another go, Jo?"

"Ready if you are, Hix." He slapped a cube.

Three hours later, they'd had enough of virtual reality experiences for one day and were sitting on the floor in Cargo.

"Where's a dibble-blink when you need one? That beat the hell out of any game I've ever gamed before."

"Back at the hotel bar?"

"You mean the hotel where Chuckie's in our suite and about to spend the night with whomever and doing whatever? I'm not getting within pissing distance of that place."

"Agreed, especially not tonight."

John glanced at the cargo bay's walls.

"Ship, can you find someone, someplace, who can deliver us something resembling water, a decent drink, and something to munch on tonight and for breakfast in the morning?"

"I'll see what I can do."

There was a worried look on John's face as he looked around.

"What's up?"

"Something that Arnold once said back on Kdack 3a when someone asked him, 'What does it take to learn how to be an action movie hero?' Arnold's answer was, 'Learn your weapons and know how to empty and unload them without having to look at them.'"

"What is an Arnold, and why is this relevant?"

"Because I can game with the best of them. Two hands

with one thumb each…damn! With your four thumbs, you could become queen of Kdack 3a's gaming community!"

"Great. Then I could die happy with my life's goal accomplished."

Sarcasm didn't need an interpreter.

"Here's why it's important. As a rugby player and as a wrestler, believe it or not, I physically rocked. I could hold my ground and more. As a gamer, I could do even better using my two thumbs and my wits. But I've never held a real weapon in my hands and used it except for the one time when my dad was drunk and took me out back to shoot some coyotes with his old shotgun. It had a killer of a kickback to it!"

"I think I know where he's going with this, Meehix."

"I'll trust your judgment, Ship. Go on, John."

"Throwing, stabbing, and piercing weapons? We got that down. At least you do. But firing, reloading, and firing weapons again? We might need a little more practice before we use them in actual combat."

"You may be right."

"Ship, are our food and beverages on their way?"

"Yes, courtesy of Chuckie, who told me to tell you not to fucking bother him again until tomorrow."

"Message received." He held out his arm. "Join me for dinner? I know a great spot."

"I thought you'd never ask."

When the food arrived, they were in the front cabin still sorting through U-B-Fucked. Several bottles of decent water and just enough liquid libations to take the edge off, but not enough to get silly on, accompanied their meals. They multitasked munching, drinking, and scrolling.

"I think I have the layout of all the rooms memorized. How about you?"

Meehix took a swig of Nerth B's Best Lager before answering. "I'm good. Wish we could see inside the towers."

"I wish we could see where Victor stashed the loot so we could narrow our focus."

"Maybe we can learn something from the blueprints."

Up came the blueprints. Neither one of them had ever seen one in their lives, so it took quite some time to get used to the diagrams and schematics. It involved a lot of squinting, and they took more than a few notes before they finally couldn't focus anymore and decided to pick it up again in the morning.

"There are a few inflatable cots in the room behind Cargo. You might find them more comfortable than sleeping upright in your chairs."

"Thanks, Ship."

It had been a long and stressful day, with more similar days ahead. They found the cots, inflated them in Cargo, and crashed, falling asleep so quickly that they didn't even have time to wonder if they'd ever share an actual bed. Although it was a thought that had crossed both of their minds more than a few times, it had never been the right time.

Just before they drifted off, they had one quick conversation.

"Goodnight, Hix."

"Goodnight, Jo."

Good night, John-boy…

CHAPTER TEN

Gage's mom came through the door promptly at 12:15. She was working a split shift today and had promised to take care of the little ones for a few hours. He'd told her he needed two hours to concentrate for one of his online classes at the New Mexico Community College of Albuquerque that had a test starting at 12:30.

She and Gage's dad were so proud of the first of their children to go to college, even if it was only online, that they wanted to do everything they could to support him. They also had two *niños pequeños* at home, and because childcare was so expensive, it worked out well for all of them if Gage could stay home as they worked. He took care of the house and kids rather than spending six hours a day making minimum wage at a job to help pay for his education.

He handed her a freshly changed and powdered Toñito and told her that both kids ate their lunches. Isabella was on the floor watching one of their many *Muppet* DVDs so his mom carried their baby brother over to join her.

Gage turned to hustle to his room because he had a *test* to take at 12:30. The doorbell chimed *La Bamba,* and he grudgingly hurried to answer it because his mom and siblings were settling in to see what Kermit and the gang were up to now.

"UPS. Got a package for Gage Gonzalez?"

"You got him. Where do I sign?"

The driver held out an electronic pad, and Gage scribbled as quickly as he could and rushed to his room with the package.

"Something good?" his mom called.

"Very good! I hoped it would come before the test started!"

"John hasn't been around for a long time. Did you two have a fight or something?"

Even if he had the time before his test started, he doubted that he could properly explain.

"No fight, Ma, we're still cool. He's out of town—*just a little out of town*—on a work-study program. Should be back soon." Gage disappeared into his room.

He now had five minutes before his next live podcast of SAFA was about to start. It would be his third one. After seeding the videos all over the Internet during his first Twitch post, the one that Jojacko and Meehix had sent him and the one he'd made of himself explaining what was going on, he'd gotten down to some serious work.

Had he signed up for classes at NMCCA like he'd told his parents he had? *Not really, but man, am I getting an education. Maybe when all this is over, I can get a job as a DJ or a TV talking head for some cable show about Encounters with UFOs or something.*

He ripped the package open. *Yes!* He'd gotten it on eBay for only eight dollars plus shipping and handling. *Fuckin' bargain!*

He'd previously rearranged his room so that Kirk and Spock and the big tits chick posters were no longer in danger of being in the background. Now he hastily managed to get his new prize hung on the wall behind him with thirty seconds to spare.

The second of his two podcasts had garnered four hundred viewers. He'd gotten a few emails asking him if he could arrange to field phone calls while he was live, and he'd figured out a way to do that. Jojacko would have been so proud of him! He reached back to turn on his new eBay prize and behind his head, in big red letters, the digital sign announced ON AIR.

He hit the button. The third podcast of Save Aliens From Assholes was now live.

"Gonzo Gage, in and on! *Whoa!*"

He wasn't sure if he was reading his screen right.

"Okay. Sorry there, believers and deceivers, I had a slight glitch that I had to correct. The last SAFA podcast a week ago had four hundred viewing and listening in. Right now, there are eight thousand, four hundred and seventy-one joining us. Eighty-four seventy-two. Eighty-four seventy-three, eighty-four seventy-four, and the numbers are rising faster than this *hombre* can count."

He risked a glance at another corner of his screen. There appeared to be two hundred waiting in the phone queue, many from his home area code.

"Sorry, again, but my producer called in sick today, so I'm handling this one all by my lonesome. But enough about me and my problems. If you were able to snatch up the videos I sent out before they were all mysteriously *disappeared*, you know that the aliens are the ones with problems much bigger than my piddly-ass whining.

"I wanna hear what you think, so I'm gonna start answering calls, and you can hear what others are thinking. I don't know who the callers are or what they're gonna say, but Gonzo Gage has his finger on the disconnect button, so let's keep it rolling."

He hit the answer button and hoped that his setup would work.

"Caller number one."

"Am I really caller number one?"

"You're the first button I pushed, so I guess, yes?"

"Oh my God! I've never won anything before!"

"You, umm, didn't win anything, now. I don't have any prizes to give away."

"But I'm the first, right?"

"I guess."

"Hey, everyone! I'm the first!"

The sound of jubilation came over the line as office coworkers in the background shouted their congratulations. He hit a button.

"Next?"

"The video you posted of our USSF leaving their pilots to die. Was that real?"

"Make some calls to the USSF and find out their names, then call their widows and ask *them* how real it was. Next."

He was getting the hang of the buttons and wanted to get as many calls in as possible.

"I stumbled on the video of the pilots, but it disappeared halfway through. Did you suddenly decide to take them all down?"

"Gonzo Gage don't post nothing that he's gonna take down! Except for a coupla dick-pics once that were supposed to be only between me and a *chica*. Next."

"I didn't know what to make of the vids. They were all over my feeds, but then they were all gone. If you didn't *gone* them, who did?"

"Good question, *amigo*. Next."

"Do you have a comfortable chair to sit your ass down on? Because you are going to need to upgrade it after the next time we see you."

"Is this Agent Bixby or Shaw?"

"Both."

"Nice of you to drop by and join us. Can you see my live video feed?"

"Yes, fuck-head." *That was definitely Bixby.*

"People, these two gentlemen are part of the government agency responsible for the deaths of the pilots. Their agency enslaved the aliens who dropped in from space to hang out and get to know us before they were taken captive and enslaved. Agents Bixby and Shaw are also a couple of potty-mouths who need their mothers to wash out their mouths with soap, so I apologize for their language. And I apologize to you all, in advance, because I'm about to give them a *visual* regarding their reference to my ass."

He stood, turned, bent over, and dropped his pants.

"Next." He hauled his chinos back into place.

"Gonzo Gage. I thought you were a third-rate loser trying to gain some kind of following that you could scam people with and ask them for money, like maybe you were also gonna raffle off a Bigfoot hide. But *that* video seemed real enough to me, so I download it. I searched for it again, and *poof*, man, it was gone from the 'net!"

"Do you still have it in your PC files?"

"Sure do."

"Then put it on a USB and hide it somewhere safe, or give it to someone you can trust with your life because they're gonna come looking for it. Next."

"Same thing as the last caller."

"Gracias!"

A glance at the screen showed there were now over ten thousand viewers! *LIVE, right fuckin' here and now!* He had a decision to make.

Announce that the whole thing was a hoax, and he'd been having some fun—he didn't realize that others would look at *Gonzo Gage* as the leader of some *movement* or something. He could apologize for getting everyone all excited and shit, go back to his normal life, and sign up for classes at NMCCA.

Or, he could trust what he'd seen with his own eyes and hope that Jojacko and Meehix, *the blue chix with the sex mix,* were also following through with the SAFA program in whatever neck of the galaxy they currently found themselves in. *What would Brando do?*

Two seconds later, he was back.

"Gonzo Gage has told a lot of lies in his nineteen years of life. Who hasn't? But I ain't gonna lie on my podcast, 'cause you *all* deserve a touch of honesty now and then. So I'll go first.

"Yes, SAFA will be hoping for donations. Not for me to

pocket, because I can live on peanut butter sandwiches and Corona's and be happy, but to help carry on with our mission to Save Aliens From Assholes, a very worthy cause. I got three hundred callers now wanting to chime in, and I wanna get to as many as I can in the next hour. So whether you're a deceiver or a believer, you're only going to have ten seconds to state your case. Next."

An hour later, shortly before he had to relieve his mom of the young ones so she could go back to work, he signed his exhausted ass off.

"That's all the time for today. Thank you everyone for joining in. I couldn't understand all of your accents because you're calling in from all over the world, but many people and I heard your voices, and we will again on my next podcast. Until then, Gonzo Gage, out and gone."

His bedroom door opened.

"I have to go back to work, sweetie. Did the test go well?"

"Yes. I think I aced it."

"Good. I'm so proud of you."

She kissed him on the cheek, and he got up to follow her to the door. He glanced at the TV that his younger siblings were still watching.

"I don't know who they like more, the frog, the pig, or the bear. I have their dinner all laid out in the kitchen whenever they're ready. Try to get them fed before your dad gets home. You know how tired he is after work."

"Almost as tired as you."

Another kiss on the cheek and she was gone. a DVD they'd already watched a gazillion times still enraptured the siblings so Gage joined them on the floor. He didn't know how many calls he'd answered after his deceiver-believer statement, but they were in the high hundreds, with at least ninety percent of them being believers.

He would check out the official numbers later when he had a little quiet time. For now, he would enjoy the movie. *Shit, I wish we were watching Shrek.* There was a song at the end of it that was now an earworm. *I'm a believer.*

"Sleep well?'"

"Slept well. Dreamt weird," Meehix answered as she deflated her cot. They returned them to their proper places before heading up front where water and breakfast munchies were available.

Meehix availed herself of the one small bathroom unit as John took his pilot's seat.

"Good morning, Ship."

"Good morning, Dave."

"Let it go, will ya?"

"I'll try. Pick up where we left off with U-B-Fucked?"

"Maybe later. Meehix and I have some weapons practice scheduled first. Any word from Chuckie today?"

"Did you really expect one this early?"

"Stupid question, huh?"

"A Kdackan specialty, from my observations," a second voice chimed in.

"Good morning, Meehix."

"Good morning, Ship."

She took her copilot's seat, grabbed a bottle, unscrewed the cap, and took a long drink of water. *Aahhh, water.* Every planet she'd visited had its version of it. Some better than others, but all good to quench a dry throat.

"Why do I always get the copilot's seat?"

"Because I'm the only one with the Kdackan DNA to fly Ship."

"Sure, when we're flying. But when we're not flying, has it ever occurred to you that I might want to sit in the power seat? Or is that too much for a slave to ask?"

"Again with the master and slave routine? Knock it off, will ya? Both of you! If either one answers with a 'yes master,' I'm gonna walk right out of here. You, Meehix, will be a nonentity left sitting in a pieced-together ship that you can't fly, and you'll both spend the rest of eternity forever docked right here! "

"Whoopsies. Looks like we struck a nerve."

John got up and stepped to the side. "I call shotgun."

Meehix threw an elbow at his ribs as she scooted past him and settled in, her hands immediately slipping into the control gloves. John sat and watched her and her goofy-ass smile.

"Vroom. Vroom. Whoosh! Ship? Optics, please!"

A second later, the screen was a rolling scene of meteors, enemy aircraft, and several random flocks of nockadoodles for her to avoid. She kept her hands in the controls and shifted her body left, right, up, and down, with an occasional head duck.

John remembered how good she was as a pilot after he'd rescued her from prison and they'd made their first escape from Kdack 3a. *Some are born for it.*

Half an hour later, she leaned back.

"Thank you, Ship." She turned. "Thank you, John. I needed that."

"I wish I'd had some popcorn while I enjoyed the show."

"Now we have to get in some practical practice. Weapons time?"

John picked up a couple of items from last night's food order that looked like fried pig's tails and headed for the bathroom.

"Meet you in Cargo."

"Why is it that men are the only ones who can eat and shit at the same time?"

"Bodily functions aren't in the range of my personal experiences, so I might be the wrong one to ask."

"So tell me, Ship. Honestly. You've seen the same data in U-B-Fucked as we have. Do we have any chance of surviving?"

"Tell me, Meehix. Honestly. Will you ever have a good night's sleep for the rest of your life if you don't try?"

"I hate you, Ship."

She grabbed her seat's armrests and held on through a brief shudder that seemed to shake the whole craft.

"What the fuck was that? Are we under attack?"

"No, no. Nothing like that! That was my way of smiling before I responded to your most recent statement with 'I love you too.'"

"What the fuck was that?" John hurried out of the bathroom. "Are we under attack?"

"No. That was Shippewa learning how to giggle."

"You can do that now?"

"I've had some free time to practice. Want to feel me frowning?"

"No!" came the simultaneous replies.

"I believe that there is a space in Cargo eagerly awaiting your arrivals."

That's where they headed. John took in all of the weapons lined up against the walls. "I'm in an Arnold wet dream."

"Don't you mean a Chuck Norris wet dream?"

"Chuck Norris doesn't need weapons. In fact, he isn't afraid of weapons. Weapons are afraid of Chuck Norris."

Chuckie N would be proud of him for coming up with that one. Meehix sighed. "Where do we start?"

"We start with inventory. Make sure all of the weapons aren't currently loaded and figure out how many ammunition reloads are available."

"Boringggg."

"So's Gay-jaw's *La Bamba* doorbell after you hear it ten times an hour when you're hanging with him. You start on the right. I'll start on the left and meet you somewhere near the middle."

Meehix wanted to argue with him but had no clear idea what her argument would be, so she decided against it.

They systematically made their way along the walls. Weapons and their corresponding ammo having been counted and separated, they met on John's side of the middle and stepped back, surveying their work.

"Do you know how to shoot all of these?"

"Only with my thumbs while gaming."

"We got some work cut out for us, don't we...Jo."

"Yes, we do, Hix."

They lost track of how many hours they spent, tossing weapons back and forth to each other with the various guns' corresponding cartridge reloads as they scrambled around the confined space in Cargo, imaginarily firing on imaginary targets.

"I'm out of ten-rods, Hix!"

"I'm out of bu-bees, Jo!"

Weapons tossed to each other, they unloaded their empty cartridges, reloaded the same empty cartridges, and continued into battle. By the time they finished practicing, Arnold would have been proud of them, and even Chuck Norris would have second thoughts about taking them on.

"Time out!" John called.

"Time out why, Jo? You need a gasp for oxygen intake already?"

"Time to be out of ammo and go hand-to-hand, Hix!"

They rushed to the walls and grabbed weapons of choice. Meehix had the advantage over him because she knew exactly what she was going for. John went for the biggest and longest.

He is such a guy. Hix reached for a long spear and grabbed hold of it simultaneously with Jo, tussling for control. Hix looked over Jo's shoulder.

"Fuck, what's that?" Jo fell for the distraction, and Hix was in sole possession of the spear.

"You are now one dead bro, Jo."

It had been too long since he'd used his rugby-playing muscles. Were his thumbs in shape? *Oh yeah.* Was the rest of his body and muscle memory in playing shape? That would be a big *oh, hell no!*

"Kick me, Hix!"

"Kick where and why?"

"Kick anywhere, or I'll flip your flap against your will!"

Her first kick aimed to hit crotch-first, but he'd turned so quickly that it only landed on his hip. She spun and would have taken off his head if he hadn't dodged under it.

"If I was wearing the boots I bought yesterday, you'd be dead now!"

"You gonna attack or stand there bitching?"

"You're gonna wake up dead!"

Game on. They kicked and swiped and ducked each other's blows. She landed a good kick to his head that left him prone.

"Hah!"

From the floor, he executed a leg swipe that ended with her perfect blue ass on the floor too.

"Hah yourself!"

An hour later, they called a truce and headed to the front cabin for some water. Meehix took the pilot's chair.

"Having fun back there, were you?"

"Just getting started, but man, I'm out of playing shape. How do you do it, Meehix?"

"Do what?" She grabbed a water bottle and took a quick swig.

"Do what we just did and not pull a muscle?"

"A decade of all-night dance parties on at least fourteen different planets keeps a girl limber."

He couldn't argue with that, but there was something he needed to verify, and he didn't know if his suggestion would go over very well.

"There's one more weapon we have to try out."

"We just went through them all," Meehix protested.

"Yeah, but with empty rounds. There's one weapon that we *have* to fire hot."

"Which is what and why?"

John could see the light come in as it dawned on her.

"I won't do it!" she sounded adamant.

"Someone has to!"

"It hurts to hear children argue. May I inquire as to what the debate is about?"

"He's about to ask me to shoot him with a *tickle gun!*"

"I'm always in the mood for a good giggle. Can you shoot me too so that you can feel my reaction and let me know if I've got it right?"

"No!" They answered together and shared an unspoken thought. *At least we agree about that!*

"This is a weapon in our arsenal that you're not aware of yet," Meehix began to explain.

"It's a Vetralaun semi-automatic," John interrupted. "What's the big deal?"

"The big deal, lumpwad, is that it's deadly!"

"But not on me! Maybe my Kdackan DNA is good for something other than flying Shippewa."

"I'm not sure if that's a compliment."

"It was meant as a compliment of the highest order, Ship!"

"Thank you, John."

"You're welcome, Ship."

"Can we get back to how John, Jojacko, Jo, or whatever the fuck name he wants to go down as in history wants me to kill him in a few minutes when we go back to the weapons in Cargo?"

"I'll need a little more information before I can answer that correctly."

"There's a weapon back there that shit-for-brains wants me to shoot him with."

"A Vetralaun semi-automatic that someone shot me with three times. Instead of killing me, I had a pissing-my-pants laughing fit and an insane burst of energy! I think that energy might come in handy in our not too distant future."

"Sure, once you finish wetting your pants."

"I was good for the first two shots. It was the third one that caused me to let loose with a yellow river."

"They're deadly for everyone, except for mister here with his Kdackan DNA."

"That's why we need to try it out! If my survival was some kind of a fluke, then I'll be dead, can hang out with my ancestors, and Meehix will be left to find another Kdackan to fly you both on a suicide mission. If I'm right, Meehix and I will at least have a sweet-smelling fart's chance of us both surviving our upcoming attack on a fortress."

"I have to side with John on this one."

"Fuck." *They've backed me into a corner that logic will not let me get out of.* She turned to John.

"Do I get to choose which body part I want to shoot?"

"You're the one sitting in the pilot's seat. Pilot's choice."

"I hate you, John."

They reached for something solid to grab onto as Ship practiced his giggle.

"He loves you too, Meehix."

"When we get our galactic divorce, I won't dispute your request for custody of Shippewa."

"Yes, you will. So, you gonna shoot me or not?"

"Can't wait. But now is not the time to ask me who I hope is right about the outcome."

They headed toward Cargo where the Vetralaun semi-automatic was waiting. Meehix picked up the gun and aimed it at John's heart. *One of us is right. I hope that I'm the one who's wrong.* Before she had a chance to fire, Ship butted in again.

"John?"

"Yes, Ship?

"I only had time for a quick search of downloaded songs. Do you want a Mr. Dylan song titled *Knocking On Heaven's Door*, or a Mr. Holly song that says, 'that'll be the day that I die?'"

"Ship's choice."

He closed his eyes, hoping for the best results from whatever Ship's song choice would end up being and the gun firing.

Knocking On Heaven's Door came on, accompanied by the scent of a fresh-from-the-oven blueberry pie over-taking his olfactory senses as warm lips gave him a kiss for the ages.

"Am I in heaven?"

"No. Ship chose the song. I chose the scent and the kiss because I may never have another chance, and I want you to die with a smile." Meehix pulled the trigger.

CHAPTER ELEVEN

Chuckie was beginning to think they'd never leave. So she'd shot him with a Vetralaun semi-automatic. He'd survived and didn't even wet his pants. Big whoop. They then spent two days alternating between spending time on Ship and *practicing* and coming back to the suite to grab a quick shower and a nap. Never, he was happy to note, in the same room at the same time.

That didn't mean he didn't have to hustle his companions du jour back into his bedroom and tell them to entertain themselves until his suitemates left. *They were on the clock. They could entertain themselves.* It just meant that Meehix, the love of his life, and his Jojacko-bro were cramping his post-cryo style with the ladies. But his *family,* however dysfunctional it was, were now on their way to Brakeb III to steal some treasure, free whoever they could find, and do their best to try to survive—a mission he'd inspired them to undertake.

They'd trusted him! That wasn't something he was used to. He had to bring them back alive! Because of the distance issue, he lost contact with Shippewa shortly after they'd taken off. *Fuck, that was one cool-drool of a ship,* but that didn't mean he couldn't try to keep track of their progress and that Chuckie N didn't have their backs.

After three, *or was it four?* days of in and out and sometimes on the clock companionship, he needed some alone time. He ran Mixie through her paces, creating a new program he would use in the future. It was so complex that no one could ever trace its origins back to him and he'd never have to worry about any future confinements.

He was running the program, checking for flaws. He'd invited hundreds to try to hack into it. At least two hundred hackers were already trying. The hacker community was always up for a new challenge, and he adjusted it each time accordingly.

It was during that alpha feedback process when he discovered it, he, her, or whatever. Someone was searching! A hired hacker was looking into his prison break and who had helped him. Although the prison didn't disclose the name of who had broken out, he knew that it was his humble self they were looking for.

That didn't worry him overly much, but it might also put Meehix and John on their radar, and *that* was not acceptable behavior.

All right, assbrains, whoever you are. You don't know it yet, but your ass is going to be in my grasp before you can blink three times, and the experience will not be a pleasurable one. At least not for you. I, on the other hand, will enjoy the hell out of it.

He reviewed what he knew of the relatively recent events. Meehix had gone off on one of Daukhl's interplanetary party trips. He'd always hated that dude and his "Ain't

I the just the coolest one in the room" attitude. Meehix did love to party, one of her very few faults.

As far as he'd been able to learn, it was her consistent insistence on partying that had eventually forced her family to declare her as a nonentity. *Her high and mighty privileged family!*

Although when he was truthful with himself and thought about it, she *had* taken full advantage of her family's privileges, not to mention her use of daddy's money to finance her *party on, girl* lifestyle.

Daukhl had been so stoned that he'd crashed his party ship on the boring blue ball known as Kdack 3a, where she wound up a prisoner, and he'd somehow managed to escape easily. Although he couldn't prove it, Chuckie suspected that he might have sold Meehix out to the authorities to save his ass.

He made a mental note that Daukhl also had a day of reckoning in his future, courtesy of the one and only Chuckie N.

He still wasn't exactly clear about the circumstances that led Jojacko to rescue her, but he did. That led to a Crec Alert placing an extraordinarily high bounty on both of their heads.

Whoever it was on Kdack 3a that had put up the bounty had made it very clear that they wanted Meehix's head still attached to her body and functional. John's head could be captured and returned in whatever manner seemed most convenient to the bounty hunters.

They had just met and already had half the galaxy looking for them. *I know the feeling.*

The two geniuses then decided to become fucking

bounty hunters themselves. Did they choose a two-bit scofflaw with a Level Four alert who would be an easy, relatively harmless catch as they learned their trade? Not those two.

They chose to go after *Frelo*, managing to accidentally kill him in the process, which led his older brother Victor Vikrellion—one of the most dangerous and powerful men alive—to go searching for them without bothering with a Crec Alert.

And if *that* wasn't enough, their next bright idea was to plan a prison break to free the notorious Jxzobbliningo-zlinxfipple, sentenced and cryo-confined for five hundred years of doing mental crossword puzzles.

If they were that stupid as adults, how did either of them manage to survive childhood?

He paused the access to his new program for a few minutes so the hackers who'd been helping him test for flaws couldn't get in until he'd made a couple of adjustments, then started running U-B-Dead again. He'd been tempted to label the new program U-B-Chuck-fucked, but had decided against it for simplicity's sake. *Sorry, Mr. Norris.*

Phllyrp threw up all eight of his arms—or legs, depending on various interpretations of appendages—in frustration, coiled up, and rolled his body back a few feet.

"Problem?"

Trexit, known galaxies-wide as the best tracker ever employed, had a reputation to keep up. For Victor, he had managed to track down the identities of Frelo's murderers. By now, he knew them both by their names, faces, and planets of origins, but someone who hadn't wanted them found had blocked their current locations and movements, no matter how many resources he'd employed.

He'd assured Victor that he would find them but needed a little more time because they were sneaky little shits and must be getting help from an unknown source. From the video he'd watched of Frelo's murder and the few credits they'd earned for it, he knew that someone else had to be financing them.

Were they a professional hit-team, new to the scene, who he wasn't aware of? Did their backer have a grudge against Frelo? If so, he wouldn't be the first.

Or did he have a score to settle with Victor, which would put him in a whole other circle of the dumb and desperate? He wouldn't waste any time wondering who was sponsoring them now, but he *would* find the duo and deliver them to Victor as requested.

He had feelers going out and was waiting for the answers to come back. While he waited, he decided that picking up a second job wouldn't take up too much of his time. He was never opposed to padding his bankroll. The cryo-prison wasn't releasing the escaped prisoner's name, which made his job a little more difficult.

Officially, they never acknowledged that they'd had a prisoner escape from their *ultra-secure* complex, which put Trexit at a bit of a disadvantage. He was chasing a ghost, which is why he'd come to Phllyrp. The round pseudopod was, to the best of his knowledge, the third-best hacker currently living and the only one who was still available.

The best was a Dolurulodan named Jxzobbliningo-zlinxfipple. *Someone should've executed his parents for combining twelve family names into one. The poor kid never had a chance.* But Jxzobbliningozlinxfipple, *I wonder what they called him for short?* had been caught and sentenced to five hundred years. The second-best known hacker, one Blip Freckson, had recently dropped off the grid.

"Sorry, Trexit." Phllyrp was agitated. He currently had three of his appendages lifting him off the floor. Three others had another crack at breaking into the program. One made an obscene gesture in the air at a random target, and one out of sight beneath his body did whatever it was doing. Trexit wasn't going to ask.

"Just tell me where we're at."

Phllyrp rolled himself back again in defeat.

"We're at the point where I refund your money for the last four hours. *Satisfaction guaranteed,* and I failed to satisfy.

"Every time I think I'm getting close to making some progress, the fucking program shuts itself down, does a reboot, and I'm back to square one. It's a program I discovered after you gave me your initial info, but it must be in its alpha stage while the creator is fucking around and setting up firewalls to prevent anyone who's trying to break in."

"So you're basically helpless?"

"Me and around three hundred others who've been trying to invade it for the last four hours. Whoever is in the process of creating it has given all us hackers a real challenge!"

"You're saying that whoever it is, is good?"

Phllyrp sighed. "Better than me, apparently. I'll refund your credits."

Trexit felt the sudden need to hurt something, but if he threw a punch at Phllyrp, his round body wouldn't even feel the blow. The only way to cause the hacker any real pain would be to rip off one of its limbs, but Trexit had a code and didn't want to prevent someone else from earning a living.

"The room above us is only for storage, right? You don't have a clerk up there somewhere stacking something?"

"I'm a one-man operation."

Trexit pulled out a gun and fired eight shots into the ceiling. A few flakes came down, but he easily avoided or dusted them off. He felt better until he had his next thought. *Oh, fuck no!*

"Your equipment and the system it runs on is top of the line, right?"

"It all has to be. My customers depend on it, and I like to eat."

"Can you give me access to it?"

Phllyrp was already out the credits he had to refund for his last four hours.

"How's about we do this? I'll eat fifty percent of the original fee, and the system is all yours for the flat fee of the remaining fifty percent."

"Deal."

"Just so you know. My entire system will shut down at three hours. I have to input my three passcodes every three hours personally and don't have time to babysit."

"I'll be in and out in an hour. Now go roll yourself off somewhere, although I suggest your location not be upstairs because I can't guarantee that more shots won't come up through the floor."

Phllyrp made himself scarce as Trexit went to work and used Phllyrp's system as quickly as he could.

Best known hackers in descending order. His fingers flew as he gathered data, some from memory, some from searches he'd already performed.

Jxzobbliningozlinxfipple: sentenced to five hundred years of cryo-freeze. Four hundred ninety-seven years yet to serve.

Who was it that he was trying to identify and track down who'd recently had a jailbreak from a cryo-prison...and his accomplices?

Blip Freckson. Brought to the authorities by a couple of bounty hunters. According to the reports, one bounty hunter was a blue Dolurulodan female. The other was a large Kdackan male. Blip was brought in two weeks or so after the cryo-prison break.

Fact: new program created earlier today that the third-best hacker couldn't crack.

Fact: a pair of bounty hunters had murdered Frelo. One a blue Dolurulodan chick and the other a large Kdackan male.

Fact: Jxzobbliningozlinxfipple was a Dolurulodan.

Fact: *What the fuck was going on here? Did he really have two targets from two different jobs, or did he have* one *target from two different jobs with the* ultimate *hacker running interference?*

Dolurulod was the one common connection between the three of them, and that's where his next stop would be. It had only taken him an hour.

"The system's all yours, Phllyrp. Keep the change." He was gone.

"I'm worried that this may not end well," Ship admitted as John removed Hannah from Ship's port and secured the turquoise and silver pendant around his neck.

They were hovering over one of the "not quite armpit" portions of Brakeb III, about to embark on storming Victor's fortress.

"You and us both, Ship," John answered.

"Can I give you both a hug?"

John and Meehix exchanged a glance and held on tight as Meehix gave her approval.

"Go for it, Ship."

"What she said."

Ship had been practicing and responded with a shudder that was neither a shake, a rattle, nor a roll.

They felt it in their feet first. A slight vibration worked its way up from their toes to the top of their heads and down again.

"That was lovely. Thank you."

"As my mom back in Albuquerque would say, back at'cha, Ship."

He turned to Meehix. "We don't have to go through with this."

"What will happen if we don't?"

"Then we'll spend the rest of our lives, living in bliss as we try to make a bounty hunting living while looking over our shoulders as Victor searches for us."

"And he will never stop until he makes sure that we're dead."

"Dead *after* torture. Yes."

John had never seen Meehix looking wistful before.

"Before I met you, I only used to wonder where the next party was. Pretty shallow of me, right? Don't answer that."

"Before I met *you,* I only used to wonder if I could slip out of an online game for a few minutes to jerk off after a hot chick's avatar showed up to play."

"I told you not to answer!"

"Are we done with our confessions now?"

"Done enough. Time to put me in the fucking box."

The fucking box was a crate they'd put together. It was large enough to hold Meehix and a plethora of weapons.

Since there was no way that the two of them could storm Victor's fortress, they decided to resort to subterfuge.

Meehix would go into the box, geared up with all of the other weapons in the box ready for use. John had already put on his bounty hunter attire, with as many weapons as he could reasonably attach to it without drawing suspicion. John also had the comm-stick that Chuckie had lifted from Meehix's bag so that he and Ship could communicate while they were inside the fortress.

Ship would settle down and land in Victor's front yard, a safe distance from the front door. That would give Victor's guards a chance to approach cautiously.

From Chuckie's U-B-Fucked files, they knew that Victor didn't have any surface-to-air missiles to do Ship any harm. All that Victor's guards could do was approach the ship that had just landed and inquire about its intentions.

Ship settled down. Not a blade of Victor's lawn was disturbed. Ship lowered the ramp.

"If you die before I do, I will be really pissed, Jo." Those were Meehix's last words to him as he wheeled her box down the ramp.

"Only bad people are going to die today." The scent of blueberry pies filled the air.

Four security guards warily approached. They weren't expecting any deliveries today, and no one had ever dropped in to ask for directions.

"Purpose?" the one whose nametag read Lexmeer asked.

John pulled out his bounty hunter's license and held it out for all to read.

"You mother-tit sucking bastard of a Flikian's turd! Let me out of here!"

"She's got quite a mouth on her, doesn't she?" It wasn't really a question as Lexmeer looked over the bounty hunter's paperwork.

"After three days of listening to her constant bitching, I would have to agree. She's one of the duo that murdered Frelo. I'm bringing her in alive, which is what Victor requested. Just tell me where to drop the bitch off so I can collect my reward and return to my ship."

The paperwork and license all seemed to be in order. The guard made his decision.

"Your ship is free to hover until you return, but it can't remain on the ground. Let's take the bitch to the front door." Lexmeer motioned to two of the other guards, who took hold of the box and wheeled it and its foul-mouthed cargo to the front door as Meehix shouted curses on them and their families to their third generations.

The front door opened and they wheeled the box in as Ship rose and hovered, hoping they would survive long enough for him to transport them both out again.

CHAPTER TWELVE

"Does she ever shut up?" Lexmeer asked.

"Not since I've known her. Look, according to Lazy Buff," *Chuckie had found the names of Victor's most trusted henchmen, and they'd decided to try his name first,* "Victor wanted to congratulate me in person when I delivered her. He hinted that there might be a little something extra for me."

"The boss and Lazy ain't in today," the one with the Vimlot nametag answered, "but we got a very special room already set up for Frelo's murderers downstairs."

"Is that one of the ones I saw on the G-Viz show? They called it something like *Dungeons for the Dangerous and Soon to be Dead?*"

"Nah." Lexmeer's smile was not one of humor. "Totally different setup. It's down on the dungeon level, but this room is one-of-a-kind. Specially designed so that her and her partner can watch each other suffer before its lights out time."

"Aw, man, I'd love to see that, especially having spent three days with her screeching at me."

"I bet you would, you mama's ass-fucking no-cock son of a Melavian whore!" Another scream came from the box. "I bet you'd love to see it, but you can go swallow a pile of your shit because I don't want you getting anywhere near it."

"You can understand my request, can't you?" John beseeched Lexmeer, who could easily see where the bounty hunter was coming from.

"After what you've suffered? Sure. Right this way."

"Hold on first." John looked around, embarrassed. "I really gotta take a dump before I go much further. Not even sure if I can hold it 'til I get back to my ship."

"Second door on the left." Vimlot pointed.

"Do any one of you whip-stones have a dick bigger than my little toe?"

It was now Lexmeer's turn to beseech John. "Just hurry, all right?"

Meehix continued with her verbal barrage from the box as John hustled to the bathroom. Once there, he pulled out his Vetralaun semi-automatic, dropped his pants, and sat on the toilet. *One shot or two?*

Remembering the scene at the hotel and his first introduction to the gun and the energy their shots gave him, he chose three. It was an awkward move to lean far enough forward and still keep his finger on the trigger, but he managed and gave himself three in the ass.

"What is he doing in there?" as hysterical laughter came from two doors down.

"I dunno, Vim. Musta found the jokes forum in the latest *Big Booties of Brakeb* I left."

"There *were* a coupla good ones in there this month."

"Like either of you two would know what to do with a booty, you scrotum-sucking simians!"

The laughing fit neared its end, and John was glad of his plan to be sitting on a toilet when he shot himself. Just like the first time, when he'd taken three to the chest, he wet himself as they took effect. The last thing he needed was to wage war with his pants soaked in urine.

"Out in a minute!" he hollered.

"Must be a hell of a dump he's taking, Lex. You sure you want to have him with us?"

"Yeah, the poor bastard deserves it after the hell he put up with. I just hope he leaves the fan on in there.

Laughing fit and pissing party over, John felt the energy burst coming on. He was going to need it.

He took an extra couple of moments to ask forgiveness from whatever gods existed for the lives he was about to take. He and Meehix had talked about this part. The death of Frelo, as accidental and probably deserved as it was, had shaken her. Other than rugby and wrestling matches, he had never drawn blood before either. Now, they were planning to not only draw blood but spill gallons of it.

They'd decided to set their weapons to stun, at least to start with, but this was about to become a literal kill or be killed situation. He left the bathroom and returned to the guards, who had already had enough of Meehix's taunts. *Atta girl, Hix!*

"Sorry for the delay. That was a big one. Now, where's

181

this special room so I can give it a look and at least visualize how much this bitch is gonna suffer."

"This bitch ain't gonna suffer nothing! You better spend the rest of your life sleeping with a gun under your pillow because the next time I see your rectum of a face, anyone in the same room with you will be sorry that their mothers ever pinched them out of their birth canals!"

The other two guards who'd greeted them had returned to their duties outside. Lexmeer and Vimlot tried to lift Meehix's box so they could carry it to the elevator to take her down but could barely raise it off the floor. Vimlot went to fetch a handcart from a nearby closet. Apparently, Meehix's wasn't the first box ever delivered with the dungeons as their destinations.

"Heavier than she sounds," Lexmeer offered. John knew better than to answer that one within earshot of Meehix. Handcart retrieved, they set her into place, wheeled her to the elevator, and hit the bottom button.

The doors opened to a hallway on the bottom level that looked nothing like any dungeon John had ever seen.

"Welcome to hell, bitch," Vimlot whispered into the box. "Enjoy your stay and pray that it ends quickly."

John was surprised to see that it all looked modern and more on the high-tech side than he'd imagined.

They were at the end of a long hallway with only one way to turn, which was left. After turning, they confronted a windowed guard station. Three guards looked up from what appeared to be a board game they were playing on a small table. They weren't expecting a delivery today either.

Lexmeer pointed at Meehix's box and motioned to have

the doors opened. One of the guards inside hit a button, and the glass door leading into their station slid open.

It looks like glass, but I bet it's like none I've ever seen.

"I will slice your fat bellies open and suck out your intestines and save them for dessert!"

Damn! When Hix gets into a part, she really gets into it!

"Got one for Frelo's cell," Lexmeer was pleased to announce.

They immediately forgot the board game they'd been playing and scooted the table out of the way. They suddenly had a special, albeit unexpected, arrival.

"You know the way," the guard with the most badges on his uniform answered.

Lexmeer followed Vimlot as he wheeled the Meehix in a box through the guard room and down the hall to where her torture and slow death awaited her.

"You go, Jo."

After all of her shouting and cursing, it almost sounded like a whisper as they wheeled her past him. John was sure that he was the only one who heard or understood it.

He slapped the box and shouted, "You're in the mix now, you fucking bitch of a Hix!"

"Fuck you too!" came the reply.

Vimlot paused. "Wanna come down and see the cell for yourself? It'd probably give ya a smile."

"No need. I just want her and her potty-mouth out of earshot a soon as possible. I'll hang here and watch from a distance. "

John watched as they wheeled Meehix down to the very end of the hallway. He offered his hand to the booth guard with the medals.

"They call me Jojacko."

"Flibbit."

John sat and glanced around the small guard station as the other two station guards returned to their game.

"Don't they need keys or something to open the door and drop her into her cell?" John asked his new best friend.

"It's all electronically controlled." He pointed at a button-filled panel on a wall. "I only been here a month, but it's the easiest job I ever had."

John surveyed the panel as Flibbit ran his minimum-wage mouth.

"This floor is all controlled by that there panel. I'm not sure, but I think that everything in the compound is tied together through the panels so they can all talk to each other if there's an intruder or something. Cool, huh?"

"Very cool." John stood and stretched out his six-foot-four frame's shoulders, back, and arms. "Been a long three days. I'm so glad to be rid of that bitch."

He stretched out his legs. Right leg. Left leg. Stretch, stretch, stretch, until he was standing in front of the control panel.

"So, everything here is connected by nothing but electronics?"

"That's the way they explained it to me. Something about cutting down on costs and not having to pay for manpower. Pretty smart, huh?"

"Very smart." John slipped Hannah into one of the three USB ports on the panel.

Hannah, do your job. Chuckie N, I'll track you down to the lowest level of the hell we'll both end up in and squish your head like a carved pumpkin four weeks after Halloween if you lied.

Before Chuckie had sent them off on this suicide mission, *for a good cause,* John had told the little hacker-fuck, *who was better than him, he had to admit,* about a program he'd created called Hannah.

"I gotta meet his chick."

It had taken the exchanging of various oaths between Chuckie and Ship. John had been the middleman, but Chuckie had his hot hacker hands on Hannah for an hour before he let John return her to Ship's care.

Chuckie had done his *Chuckie thang.*

All the electronics in Victor's compound went on the blink!

John grabbed Hannah and reattached her to the chain around his neck. Ship would never forgive him if he didn't return her to him safely.

The doors of every cell flew open.

John gave two quick stun blasts to the two game-playing guards. Then he hoisted Flibbit over his shoulder and did three quick, complete spins. That left the guard as nothing more than a useless, dizzy bag of flesh.

John held onto him as he rushed down the dungeon corridor and tossed him at Lexalot and Vlimineer, or whatever the fuck their names were, who had no choice other than to try to catch him as all hell broke loose. Three quick punts into the gonads of the three guards left them gasping and prone on the floor.

He flipped the locks on Meehix's box that were only there for show.

"About fucking time, Jo!"

"Got here as fast as I could, Hix!" He kissed her potty mouth. They looked around.

Prisoners and future slaves were slowly making their way out of the cells. *This couldn't be happening!* As they looked up and down the hallway in hesitant collective confusion, one of them focused on the only two new faces and addressed them.

"We're being freed?"

"No," John answered with his arms around Meehix. "We're trying to rob this motherfucker blind, and including everything and anybody who isn't here by choice."

"Good enough for me. What are we supposed to do next?"

John pointed toward Meehix's delivery crate.

"Weapons in the box. Have at 'em and use as necessary! Our ship is small and only has room for the two of us. You're on your own about where to go after getting out of this hellhole. Best of luck! She and I have some pillaging to do." That's what they did as all hell broke loose in the lower levels of Victor's fortress.

"You can put me down now!"

His Vetralaun shots hyped up John so much that when he'd freed her from her box and exchanged a few brief words with the recently released prisoner, he'd slung her over his shoulder and carried her up three flights of stairs until he'd reached the main floor. *Elevators be damned!*

He obeyed her request and set her down.

"That was fun."

"What? You having a potty-mouth that would make an

Irish sailor proud, or me groping your ass as I carried you up three flights of stairs?"

"Can I choose both?"

"Abso-fucking-lutely!"

"It does not seem to me that this is the proper time for romance."

"Ship?"

"You haven't quite got the hang of the HLTD commstick yet, have you, John? I heard the whole thing. Glad you're not in a dungeon, Meehix."

John checked his pockets, and sure enough, there was the stick that he hadn't taken the time to learn how to use thoroughly. *Crash course.*

"You and me with the stick, Ship. Me and Hix with our earbud thingies?"

"There ya go."

"See you soon, Ship!" Meehix shouted.

"I'll be hovering right where you left me, Hix! The DNA sweat that John left on the controls will wear off soon. Then I won't be of much use, and God help us all."

"Which way, Jo?"

"There's actual loot around here somewhere, Hix. Thanks to Chuckie, all electronic doors and electronic doors to safes will be unlocked when we find them. Where would you look first?"

"First, I'd look at the purse."

"Huh?"

"When they had me in your prison, the guards had a lot of music playing. So fuck searching high and low for some secure room. They'd have a ton of shit too heavy to carry. I'd bet my cute blue ass that he keeps the most valuable items hidden somewhere in his wife's bedroom. Where did the blueprints say it was?"

They did a mental scroll.

"Third floor." John was certain.

"Northeast corner?" Meehix wasn't sure.

"Southeast?" John wasn't sure either.

Shots rang out. Apparently, there were still a few guards left in the fortress who'd dropped their cocks and grabbed their socks in the middle of what started as a lazy afternoon. They hadn't rushed down to the disturbance in the dungeons.

"Every second counts, Jo."

"Head for the corners. Meet you on the third floor!"

They split up, each having the utmost confidence in the other after all their practice.

Meehix had taken the long-handled weapons with their pointy ends as she'd exited her box. A stun-gun shot here, a flip of a spear over her shoulder there as someone grabbed the pointy end. Toss in a rubbery leg-kick to a head now and then, and she was on the third floor in a Javovian minute.

John went up the stairs to the third floor his way. He lowered his shoulders and bum-rushed anyone who got in his way until they were all prone before they could get a shot off.

At the top of the third-floor stairs, he turned to those in his wake and brandished his weapons in case they entertained thoughts of following him. He still had most of his weapons set to stun, but they didn't know that. Jo knew that he was the one with his weapons ready as others came up the stairs chasing him. He turned and faced them down.

"I have eighty-four rounds left and nothing to live for. You can fire however many rounds you've got, and I'll end up dying, but I'll take eighty-four of you fuckers with me before I go!"

"Any problems, Jo?" Hix asked him as she met him outside of Mrs. Victor Vikrellion's bedroom. She'd been right. It was the northeast corner, but now wasn't the time to gloat.

"None so far, Hix. Where do we search first?"

John thought she'd head for the closet first. He was wrong. Well, not completely wrong.

Meehix headed for a huge-ass sliding door and slid it open. In front of them was a perfectly designed display of dresses, pantsuits, jewelry, and shoes, all set on specially designed shelves that slid back and forth to display the finest of what part of her apparel she was looking for.

"Ta-dah!"

"Ta-dah yourself. It's a big fucking closet!"

"Yeah. I had one just like it at home when I was a spoiled little rich bitch."

If John were wearing a wristwatch, he would have pointed at it.

"Time, Hix, time!"

She ignored his impatient anger as she crossed the room to a set of old-fashioned hinged double doors and flung them open.

"Double the whooping *Fuck-ta-dahs!*"

"Another fucking closet! How many does one woman need?"

She gave him her best weird-ass smile, although he'd never seen it look so self-satisfied before.

"Only one."

The sounds of chaos and battles were coming from the floors below them as the dungeon prisoners, using the weapons from Meehix's box, were apparently kicking some serious ass as they fought their way to freedom. The two of them seemed to have the upper floors all to themselves.

John held up a hand as he reached for his comm-stick. "Ship?"

"Here, John."

"You might want to hover a little higher for a bit."

"Please tell me that Meehix is safe!"

"Safe enough to be raiding a closet at the moment."

"And Hannah too? I miss her."

"She misses you too. Thanks for asking about my welfare."

"You were next on my list. Ladies first, and all that."

"Of course! Just hover a little higher! We've freed the slaves, and they're going to be running out in droves soon. You can't carry them all. I think the leader knows how to get them away safely from here on foot, but Hix and Jo will need you all to themselves shortly."

"Hovering higher. See you soon."

"Here's the thing, Jo." Hix tossed things in the second closet aside. "A woman of wealth always has two closets. One for things she might need daily, and a second closet for things she thinks might come back into style someday."

"And?"

"It could be years between second glances into her second closet. What better place to hide something?"

Hard to argue with that kind of logic.

"Found it! Let's blow this joint!"

"Meehix." John held up a finger. *Hold on a minute.* "Remember the Vetralaun giggle gun you shot me with? Back when we were practicing to make sure that it only gave me the giggles and an insane amount of energy but not kill me?"

"Yeah. Remember the blueberry kisses I gave you before I shot?"

"Blueberry kisses. I could've died happy."

She had a briefcase in her hand that she'd dug out of a recently opened safe built into the back wall of the second closet. They had to make their way to Ship while chaos of the first degree was going on.

He chooses this moment to start babbling on about blueberry kisses?

"Guns and kisses. One of my favorite combinations. Can we go now?"

"You go. Save yourself!"

On the edge of victory, he's going down for the count? What the fuck did he do?

"What the fuck did you do?"

"When you were in the box, and I was in the bathroom, and the plan was for me to shoot myself a couple of times to make me feel like I was indestructible?"

"Yeah. We'd agreed on two shots."

"I upped it one and fired three."

"Judgment call. I forgive you. Let's move!"

"It's a semi-automatic. So the three might have been six."

"But it worked! I found what we were looking for. The

prisoners are overtaking the guards. Where's the problem?"

"The higher the high, the farther the fall." He collapsed in her arms.

Big energy rise. Bigger energy drop.

Against all odds, they'd succeeded in freeing the dungeon dwellers and found the fortune hidden in a closet. Now all they had to do was rush down three flights of stairs and out to Ship, except she had to deal with a lump of Kdackan clay. *A girl can only do so much.*

She searched him and found the comm-stick.

"Heya Ship. How's it hanging?"

"Hanging good, Meehix. Awaiting your arrival."

"Need a little help. Third floor, middle of the south side. Can you hover there and lower the stairs?"

"On my way."

She never thought she'd need the grappling hook, but it was coiled in her box and was one of the things she'd grabbed when the box opened and the battle joined in earnest. Now she uncoiled the rope as she dragged John toward the nearest window. Not an easy task.

Fighting the urge to do a one-loop around his neck, she did a three-loop of the rope around his body. She looked out a window. Ship was hovering, stairs already lowered. She threw a chair through the window and cleared the glass away.

Ship moved a little closer, and she threw the grappling hook out and caught the stairs on the first try. Lifting John's deadweight body into the window, she wrapped the remaining rope around her left hand, held tight to the briefcase in her right hand that also held the comm-stick, and gave her command.

"Go, Ship! Land us a little ways away from the fray so I can drag him up the stairs. I can't haul both him and a briefcase up while we're in the air, and right now, I can't guarantee which one I would choose to drop to climb on board."

Susky hated underground compounds with every inch of his six-foot-five frame. Never enough head room and nothing to breathe but recycled air, but when the general gave him an order, well, he wasn't called *the general* for nothing.

Sure, he was the top alien species specialist, but did that mean he always had to be the first one assigned to spearhead one of the general's assignments? Maybe Susky's nickname, the Ass, was accurate after all because every time he turned, that's where the general gave it to him.

"Ooohhh. Tooo baaad fooor youuuu."

Not only did the little shit's voice sound like it came from his navel with the same tone of someone scraping rust from the bottom of a muffler, but it came out slower than cold molasses. The insurance agent was the first Munimorphian he'd met, but he already hated his entire species and any other creature he would ever meet who came from Munimorph.

"Youuu haaave tooo taaake this tooo Roooneee fooorr finaaal approoovaaaal."

"Why didn't you tell me that right up front?"

"Myyy jobbb isss toooo."

"Never mind! I'd rather not still be standing here when my pension kicks in twenty years from now. Where can I find this Rooney?"

"Left out of the door and right at the end of the hallway. Rooney's office is the third door down on the right," the insurance agent's voice came from his mouth this time.

"What the fuck?"

"We have a talent show coming up, and I'm practicing my ventriloquist act. When I perform, I draw a face on my belly with my navel as the mouth. Did I have you going there?"

"Yeah, you had me going. I've never met an insurance agent in my life who I've ever liked."

"Did I change your mind? We can be quite humorous when given a chance."

"No. My streak remains unbroken. Have a nice existence."

Susky grabbed the paperwork and stormed out of the office to find Rooney, forgetting to duck as his forehead hit the top of the doorframe.

"Fuck, that hurt!"

"Obscenities may be allowed in the halls, but I prefer that they not be used in my office."

Susky ducked and stepped into the hallway but took a moment to face his most recent tormenter one last time.

"Fuck you, you navel-picking shit-turd."

He headed down the hallway until it ended in a large circular space, maybe fifty yards side to side. He couldn't remember if it would be called the radius or the circumference and didn't care at the moment. It was a big-ass room with at least half a dozen doors.

There is no right at the end of the hallway to turn! Fucking Munimorphs and their piss-poor directions!

There was a glassed-in station in the middle of the room. He watched as one hallway door would open, and a guard or two would bring an alien, their appendages secured depending on the species.

The guards would head to the station, present paperwork. One of the doors in the large room would electronically open, and the guards would lead their prisoner through it. Another door would then open. Only one door would open at a time.

Left out of the door and right at the end of the hallway.

He realized that after head-smacking the doorway of the Munimorph's office, he'd stormed off to the right. Reversing course, he paused in front of the offending office's entrance long enough to shout to the occupant.

"Your ventriloquism sucks ostrich eggs! I thought your voice was coming from your ears because it was a shit voice and must be drivel coming from your shit brains!"

Reaching the end of the hallway, he turned right and found Rooney's door in the third office down on the right. He tried the door and found it locked. He knocked. There was a *click* as the door swung open and he entered.

"Rooney?"

"That would be me. You may enter."

Rooney sat behind his desk, stacked with paperwork.

Susky knew he was behind the paperwork somewhere because he could see the tips of his Brivian ears, as long as a ZZ Top beard above the stacks.

He approached requisition forms in hand and tried to make friends.

"Must be some really important paperwork you're doing. Yours is the only office I've been to here that has a secured door."

"I don't give two farts about the paperwork, but I am concerned about my ass. You never know when a prisoner might make a run for it from C-3, and I don't want any of them to wander in here unannounced. I also installed security cameras. What can I do for you, Mister?"

"Ass...Sorry...Susky, just call me Susky."

The Brivian stood and came out from behind the paperwork. His four eyes extended like feelers from his furry head.

Susky knew that one of the unique qualities of Brivian eyes was that each one could focus individually, which made them ideal for sorting through paperwork. He handed Rooney his acquisitions form and wondered why the desk still had so much paper stacked up.

Four eyes and he still can't get through the paperwork fast enough?

Rooney gave the forms a quick scan and shook his head.

"Sorry. One of the routing numbers is missing a digit. I'm surprised that Flidgit didn't catch it."

"Flidgit?"

"Munimorphian who probably sent you here? Ventriloquist wannabe with the most annoying navel on any given planet?"

"Flidget's his name? Yeah, we've met."

"My sympathies." He took a yellow highlighter perched behind an ear and circled the offending routing number. "I'm afraid you'll have to return and get the complete number."

"Are you fucking kidding me?"

"Sorry, I'm only a paper-pusher. I can push and pass along, but according to the Galactic Agreements, I'm not allowed to correct any mistakes myself. Flidget will have to do that. Be careful to mind your mouth when you're in his office, or he'll make you talk to his navel."

Rooney went back to the stack behind his desk and hit the button to open the door. Susky was halfway out when a voice called from behind the paper.

"You don't happen to have any maple syrup in your pockets, do you?"

"Not at the moment."

"Oh well. It never hurts to ask."

That explains the lack of focus on all the papers stacked up.

Susky headed back down the hallway. He hoped he could get the missing digit filled in before he strangled the little obscenity-hating fuck. Then he could return to Rooney before someone snuck an extra bottle of Mrs. Butterworth's to him as a bribe to push their papers to the top of his piles.

CHAPTER THIRTEEN

Ship carried Meehix with the briefcase, and John with his dead-ass-weight a short, safe distance from Victor's fortress, set down and lowered the ramp. Meehix was proud of herself for not dropping either of them during the short flight.

She rushed halfway up the ramp, tossed the briefcase inside, and hurried back to John. After a failed attempt to carry him, she let out a whiff of what she used to use with her cousin, who had often passed out when they used to party together and had also been too heavy to carry.

It revived him long enough for him to make it up the ramp on his own with minimal assistance. She guided him to the pilot's seat and managed to slide his hands into the controls before he passed out again.

"I had just enough residue left of John's DNA to be able to move with the programming Hannah provided, but it was running low."

"Nice hanging in there, Ship. I'll take it from here." She

slipped her hands over John's and guided them all back to a safe hovering distance.

Below, she could see the prisoners winning the battles with Victor's guards as they fought their way to various craft, some ground, some air, and made their escapes to freedom as best they could.

Not done yet.

"Ship? Weapons at the ready!"

"No need to shout. I'm right here."

"I'll hover us. You lay down some ground fire."

"On it, Hix."

The escaping future slaves, now having air support, suddenly found their pursuers running for their lives. The one who was leading the escapees looked up. She hadn't had time to learn his name back in the dungeons, but he waved two of her spears at her.

Ship did his version of a nod, and Meehix got them the hell out of there.

"May I inquire as to how far we are going?"

"I think we're far enough away now. Can you do one of those disguise yourself as something else things that you did back on Kdack 3a?"

"Will a small random asteroid aimlessly drifting be acceptable?"

"Works for me." She took her hands off of John's and let Ship drift as she headed back to the floor above the ramp and returned with the briefcase and took her copilot's seat.

"With all of the recent commotion, I neglected to welcome you both back on board, Meehix...are you Meehix again or still Hix?"

"Meehix again for now, Ship. Good to be back."

"**Obviously, you raided the dungeons successfully. How did your raiding of the loot go?**"

"We're about to find out."

"Muffflyflroomp," came the voice from the Kdackan occupying the pilot's seat.

"**No onboard translators available for that one, I'm afraid.**"

"Returning to the land of the conscious are we, Jojerkoff?"

"Maybe? Do I smell blueberries?"

Meehix hadn't been able to help herself, so glad that she and John had survived and he was finally coming out of his self-inflicted giggle gun haze.

"Yes, John," she admitted, "you smell blueberries."

John rubbed his eyes and stretched out his back. "I love the smell of your farts."

"For the sake of all gods anyone ever imagined," she was torn between a slap and a hug, "I don't *fart*."

"That's what you told me."

"When you asked me a stupid question," she went for a slap on his face to help bring him around a little more, "I gave you a stupid answer, and you fell for it, you moron!" She then went in for a hug.

"No farts?" John wasn't completely back yet.

"No farts. The smell comes from my pores. I guess you could call it airborne sweat."

"Well, shit in my bed and call me stinky. I fell for your farts line," he couldn't resist adding. "Feel free to sweat at me anytime."

"What are we going to do with him, Ship?"

"**We could always toss him out of the airlock. Then**

we all can drift aimlessly through space for as long as we all shall live."

"Tempting."

John was now fully back and turned to Meehix. "How'd we do, Hix?"

"All captive slaves freed and on their merry way home."

"And the safe in the closet?"

"We're about to find out." She opened the briefcase and looked inside.

John didn't know what she saw, but if pheromones were liquor, then he suddenly found himself drunk as the proverbial skunk.

"Credit certificates! Credit fucking certificates!" Meehix set the briefcase down and did a Dolurulodan version of a happy dance, at least the best version she could, considering the cabin's confined space.

"Good news?"

Meehix settled back in her seat and picked up the brief-case again, holding its contents out for all to see.

"Credit certificates." She stared in wonder with a smile she thought might break her face.

"My sire had maybe a dozen of these. He allowed me to visit him in his office one time when I wasn't even tall enough to see over the top of his desk. He showed me a few sheets of paper he was very happy about, having just gotten them before he filed them away. He said that they were a tax break investment or something like that."

"Bring your daughter to work day?" John was still working out a few kinks from his recent real-life adventures. "Inform us uninformed, please?"

"These are CC's, payable to the bearer." Meehix used all

four thumbs to flip through the certificates. "There are over a hundred of them here! Enough to buy two moderately sized planets!"

John was trying to keep up. "And he hid them in a safe in a closet?"

"Hidden in plain sight!" Meehix was so excited that she thought she might wet John's pants for him. "We only needed to know where to look, and you found it!"

"Help me out here, Ship. Do you know what she's babbling on about?"

"Congrats on successfully surviving the raid, John, but no, you're on your own."

"You're the one who found the closet back when we were practicing with the cubes! You touched one that put us in a closet with the way out of date clothes."

John's memory kicked in. "The J. Edgar Hoover closet?"

"Whatever you want to call it, it's the one place in any house that no one ever looks in except every few years to see if anything in it has come back into fashion in a retro-style way."

"I love you, Chuckie N, and your U-B-Fucked info!" John wished he could swing the little king of the hackers around in a Texas two-step, but he would settle for swinging Meehix. *Oh poor me.* "Ship?"

"Yes, John?"

"We're heading back to Cargo. Hix and Jo got some dancing to do. You be the DJ."

"May I have Hannah-banana back first? We've already put together a mix tape from the various space stations where we've docked."

John removed the pendant from around his neck and

returned her to Ship. He held out his hand. Meehix took it, and they headed to Cargo.

"We don't need no stinkin' pheromones." John couldn't help himself.

"I'm sure that makes sense to the only Kdackan on board."

"Bogart. Nice appropriation of the line, John," Ship butted in. **"Music awaits."**

John and Meehix headed to Cargo where they were greeted with *Blue Suede Shoes*, followed by a dozen other songs that Ship had thrown together. They bopped until they dropped.

FBT&A wasn't the largest interplanetary insurance firm. The fact was, they were fairly new on the scene, but the four brothers who'd started it were working their way up and making a decent living with big plans for the future. They had signed to insure a Kdackan shipment and needed ten mercenaries to assure its arrival in a safe and timely manner.

Frix, the oldest brother, was sitting in the brothers' joint office, sharing a smile with Brix, who he'd beaten out of their mother's womb by ten minutes.

"Ten mercs, five of them Crom Limeans, can't ask for a better or safer accompaniment than that."

"Can't argue with you when you're right, Frix," the younger twin agreed.

The second set of twins rushing in crashed the party.

"You're not going to believe this," Trix started.

"There is a Kdackan mercenary," Ax finished his older twin's sentence.

Frix and Brix couldn't keep from snorting out a laugh.

"Whoever heard of a merc from Kdack?" Frix aimed what he thought was a rhetorical question at his younger twin.

"Not, no never, have I," came the response.

"Well, apparently there is." Trix was the one who paid attention to details and didn't share his older brothers' sense of humor.

"And," Ax backed his older twin up and recited what they had both read before rushing to the office, "if anything ships from a planet, that planet has to have at least one person of said planet's origin hired to guard it if guards are deemed necessary."

The older twins were still laughing at the thought of there being a Kdackan mercenary.

"This is serious!" Trix turned to his younger twin, who was the best of the four when it came to verifying. He rushed to his desk to do a quick search.

"There really is." Ax looked up from his screen.

"Best way to deal with it?" Frix was the eldest after all, and had a handle on how to help his younger siblings to focus on any given problem that popped up.

Brix took his feet off his desk. "Send me an inter-company notice, Trix, and back date it, telling me that we did all due diligence before we hired the ten mercs now assigned and that no Kdackan mercenary was registered or found at that time ."

Trix got to work. He was the best of them at that kind of obfuscation.

"It's a minor detail, my younger siblings." Frix leaned back in his chair. "It's only a matter of paperwork."

"Just paperwork," Brix backed his twin up.

"Paperwork," Trix joined in with a frown, "the bane of our existence."

"Paperwork, paperwork, fucking paperwork," Ax tossed in.

Frix did his duty as the head of the firm and reminded them all. "You can't spell T-I-T without crossing the *T's* and dotting the *I.*"

Brix found himself caught up in the moment. "Are you saying, brother of mine, that what's holding up progress in hundreds of worlds is that they have to spend too much time trying to spell *tits* exactly correct?"

"Just a thought." Frix nodded.

Tits, tits, and more tits became FBT&A's new battle cry.

"A little warning would have been nice." Chuckie was sitting at their suite's dining room table in his underwear, pushing Mixie harder than he'd ever pushed a machine before when Meehix and John burst through the door.

"You're a fucking genius!" John swept him up out of his seat and into a bear hug as he spun them both around.

"And you're a fucking maniac."

John stopped the spinning but kept him in the bear hug. "We survived, slaves are free, and we're all now fucking rich thanks to fucking you!"

"If you're about to give me some kind of big wet sloppy

kiss, could you at least put me down and offer me a flower first?"

John set him down, and Meehix provided the big wet sloppy to Chuckie, whose legs were now wobbly, but the jury went out to deliberate as to whether it was the result of the spinning or the kiss.

"Hannah says hi."

"Hi back, Ship. So the Kdackadoodle managed not to lose the HLTD?"

"For simplicity's sake, we went with comm-stick."

"Fair enough." Chuckie held out his hand. "Gimme."

John was relieved to hand it over. He still hadn't mastered the buttons yet. Transaction done, and everyone now able to hear each other, they took seats around the table.

Meehix set their hard-earned briefcase on the tabletop, careful not to disturb Mixie in the process. She flipped open the lid so that Chuckie could take a good long gander at the contents.

It took twenty seconds before he could respond. One second to realize what he saw and nineteen seconds to look at each certificate's specific value. Meehix and John shared a smile as Chuckie's eyes grew wider with each passing second.

"No," Chuckie finally looked up and met their eyes as they both nodded. "None of us will ever have to work another day in our miserable lives."

They took a collective minute to enjoy the thought before Meehix was the one to bring them all back.

"We haven't finished yet...I didn't enjoy my brief time as an imprisoned alien."

"Hey, you're not the only one here who served jail time."

"Yeah, Chuckie, for a crime you'd committed and that John and I rescued you from. But have you ever been locked in a cell for no other reason other than being innocent at the wrong time and place?"

She had him there. He headed to the fridge, pulled out a partial seventeen-pack, and set it on the table to the left of Mixie and the right of the briefcase. They all reached for one and settled back in for a serious discussion.

"Do we split up the Credit Certificates now and all go our separate ways, never to meet again?" Chuckie hoped the answer would be a joint *oh, hell no.* He wasn't disappointed.

"What we need," Meehix leaned forward, "if we're going to pursue freeing captured aliens from various locations, is a new home base to work from. Nerth B is fine for what it is, but has its limitations, long term."

"You don't want to set up base on a planet, right, Ship?"

"Correct, Chuckie, and thank you for including me. The gravitation pull of a planet could present a major obstacle, depending on the planet's size. I would suggest remaining on a space station."

"L-222!" Meehix had it. "Four times the size of Nerth B and three times the class."

"Isn't L-222 where we had our first bounty hunting gig that didn't end well?" John had a brief flashback.

"Okay, so I made a mistake with the bolas."

"How's about we call that a happy accident, Meehix?" Chuckie was already hitting Mixie's keys at a pace that anyone who didn't know him would consider frantic. "No one would ever think to look for Frelo's murderers on the station he'd died on!"

For once, John beat Meehix to where Chuckie's mind was going.

"Frelo, murdered. Frelo's older brother Victor's fortress robbed blind by Frelo's murderers because no one would think to look for them there? What better place to set up a home office than another place where Victor wouldn't think to look for them again? Tell me if I'm wrong, Chuckie N."

"I can't argue with you when you're right, brother." *Fuck! I have a bro from another ho. No, wrong phrasing. Shut the fuck up, Chuck.*

"Fuck all y'all!" Meehix smiled as she gave the order and snapped up the briefcase. "Ship, leave any stragglers behind. We're heading for L-222!"

She turned. "Line us up some realtors, Chuckie. We're going house hunting!"

"Last one on board will be the last one on board. Ship, out!"

All necessities packed and all bills paid, they made it to Ship. John punched Space Station L-222 into the Galactic Location Locator and slid his hands into the controls.

"Remind me, when we get there, to figure out a way to program Ship so that someone other than me and my DNA can fly this glorious example of an intergalactic spacecraft."

CHAPTER FOURTEEN

They docked on L-222, prepaid the docking fees for a year with one of Victor's credits, and chose Meehix as the best one to find them another hotel suite as they went home base-hunting.

When she returned, she passed room keycards around. "We're good in a suite for a month. It has three bedrooms, four baths and is only a block away."

"Only four baths?"

"Don't start with me Mister Chuckie N. Weapons are on board. It's time to go house-hunting. Anyone want to argue?"

Her partners in galactic endeavors decided it was in their best interests to go along with the plan, snatched up their most valuable possessions, and followed her to their new one-month prepaid abode.

"Sweet suite. Well done, Your Blueness."

"He's right," John agreed.

The common area was composed of four rooms with only half-walls between them. Standing anywhere, you could look to the kitchen with its small dining table, to the living room with a six-by-twelve-foot G-Viz screen mounted in the wall, and to two separate work enclaves.

"It's a corporate suite." Meehix was pleased with her choice and their reactions. "All paid for courtesy of Victor the not quite victorious."

"How do we choose who gets which bedroom?" John hoped they wouldn't get into an argument.

"I get the one at the end of that hallway." Meehix pointed. "I love the view, and it gives me some sense of privacy. You two can fight it out over the two down that way." Another gesture indicated a short hallway on the other side of the common area.

"Since I know you two boys are going to want to set up your *girls* as quickly as you can, and this girl wants to take a long soak in a big tub, I'll leave you two to battle it out." She grabbed her bags and made her way to her room.

"She always did know how to take control." Chuckie watched her walk away. "Let's go figure out who's going to sleep where."

That decision ended up being easy. John got the room with a window because Chuckie wanted the room with no external lights shining in. They moved their belongings into their rooms, met each other back at the two work enclaves, and set up their *girls.*

"Want to play a game?" Chuckie had Mixie fired up.

"Sure." John had Heemix ready to go as they sat across from each other with only a half-wall between them, their girls already connected to the hotel's network.

"Find me as Norris-C."

John hit a few keys, and Gage-O popped up on Chuckie's screen.

"Gage. Your best friend back on Kdack, right?"

"Yeah. I miss him. I don't know how or what he's doing now, but if it weren't for him, we three would have never met. He's sort of our silent partner in all this."

"Any friend of yours is a friend of mine. I look forward to meeting him some day, but now I'm gonna send a code, and I'll own Gage-O if you can't break it."

"Bring it. Your ass is grass!"

Two hours later of mutual code sending and breaking, they called a truce for a piss-break, relieved themselves, and headed back into battle.

"Beats the hell out of five hundred years of doing crossword puzzles."

"Crossword this!" John sent another code Chuckie's way.

Two hours later, when John had held his own against the best, he called for another truce.

"I need some sleep."

"Sure, you Kdackans don't want to miss your beauty rest."

"See ya in the morning, piss-pot."

"I'll be waiting, shit-breath."

They shut their girls down, and Chuckie watched John head off to his room. He'd gone easy and let him win a few early coding battles but had then lost a few that he hadn't planned on losing. *The big fuck knew how to code.*

Chuckie made his way to his room, eventually drifting off to a well-earned dreamlessness.

Chuckie was already up and working something on Mixie when John got to the kitchen the next morning.

"The fridge has enough stocked for the first week," Chuckie greeted him. "Courtesy of U-Buy We Fly delivery service. I took the liberty of ordering and used my best guess as to the consumables."

John chose a roll that looked relatively harmless. "What'cha got going?"

"Just a new program I'm fiddling with. Nothing important." He exited the program as John came to look over his shoulder.

"Aw, come on man, I just wanted to see the coding."

"It's still too early in the development stage for anyone else to read yet."

John held up his hands and backed away. "All right. If you need any help, let me know." He headed for Heemix.

Meehixiheem emerged from the bedroom down the hall and made her appearance. John thought she had the best bed-hair he'd ever seen but decided not to compliment her on it in case she'd just spent half an hour working on it.

"Good morning, boys," eyeing Mixie and Heemix, "and girls."

"Chuckie N here was kind enough to stock the fridge for us."

"At least he's good for something." She helped herself to a bottle of water and headed to make herself comfortable on the sofa. "Weren't you supposed to find us a realtor?"

"Already done. She has three places lined up, and we're

supposed to meet her in an hour at the first one. I arranged for an auto-guide driver, and he'll be here in forty-five minutes."

"We're splurging on an auto-guided?" Meehix wondered how fast it would take them to burn through Victor's money if they were going to hire an electronic chauffeur for even the simplest tasks.

"I don't drive. John has never driven on a different planet before, not to mention a space station, and I've seen you drive. I'd prefer going back to five hundred years in cryo to death by madwoman behind the wheel."

"I flew Ship just fine, even using John's hands."

"Yes, but there's a lot of room between planets in outer space. It's a lot harder to avoid moving objects on L-222."

"I concede."

An hour later they met a three-legged realtor who carried a nice briefcase and held out her hand.

"Brezlew Anlin. Please, call me Brez."

"Nice bag." Meehix was the first to shake. "Is that a real Nipian briefcase?"

"I wish. Maybe one day." She shook the others' hands. With the how do you do's completed, she turned her focus back to Meehix, sensing that all final decisions would ultimately be hers.

They followed her up a short walk to the door of a storefront on the bottom of a two-story building.

"The street's a little busy," she reached for the keys, "but I understand that you wanted a commercial office space with living accommodations, so I thought this would be a good place to start."

On entering, they found the storefront to be acceptable.

Nothing fancy, but functional. There was a space behind the main room that was large enough to set up three desks and store a weapon or thirty-seven, depending on the sizes.

John liked it. The street and the neighborhood behind the store were a long way from being considered upscale, but their auto-guide had no trouble finding it, and easy access was desirable if they were going to go into business.

It was a little meh for Meehix's tastes, but she held off commenting until they'd had a chance to go upstairs and check out the living quarters.

"I'll wait down here," Chuckie had Mixie fired up and was checking out the network connection speeds. "I can sleep anywhere that's a room of my own. I'm not going to bunk up with John."

"Would you be willing to bunk up with me if you had to?" Meehix smiled as she turned to follow Brez up the stairs.

"You've been hanging out with the Kdackan too long," he hollered at her. "The need to ask stupid questions appears to be contagious."

Maybe his lifelong crush on me is evolving if he can joke about that.

John decided that it was in everyone's best interests if he didn't add anything about who he'd be willing to bunk with.

Three bedrooms, one with a bath, and two others with a shared bathroom in the hall. Again, John thought it was fine. Again, Meehix went with *meh*.

"Can you give us a minute?" she turned to Brez. "The first floor is fine,"

"If you're worried about the neighborhood," Brez interrupted her, " it's on the rise, not on a downslide. Two years from now this place will have tripled in value."

"I'm sure it will, and I'm not saying we'll rule it out. I just want to talk a few things over, and Chuckie may have a few questions regarding network connections and upgrade availabilities."

Brez took the hint. She knew a squabble coming on when she saw one. It was Realtors 101.

John was looking out the bedroom window facing the street. It was quite a scene, unlike anything he'd ever seen back in Albuquerque. He took it all in, realizing that this was the first time since he'd met Meehix that he was simply able to stand and take a moment to realize that he was in outer space.

No jail breaks to plan. No bounty hunting *targets*. No fortress to storm. Just him, standing at a window taking in the view of everyday life on a space station in outer-goddam-space.

"I don't like it." Meehix brought him out of his reverie.

"Why?" he continued his gazing without turning around. "You'd get the room with the private bath, we can make a few minor stylistic changes to the storefront, and there's plenty of storage room. What's not to like?"

"The neighborhood may be up and coming, but it's not quite there yet. What if our new enterprise results in clients who might want to take out their frustrations on the building?"

"As opposed to on us?" John turned.

"Like that, yes."

"Then we won't have to worry about paying for any

damages because there's not a lot here that hasn't already seen harder days."

"All insurance policies I've ever heard of say that if others do the damage, we wouldn't be liable for it." Meehix wanted to phrase this next part just right. "This is probably close to perfect for our working needs. I just wanted a somewhere a little…"

"Nicer?"

"Nicer, yeah. Not rich-bitch nice. Just…"

"A little nicer than this?"

"Like that, yeah."

"Fair enough. We still have two more properties to look at, so there's no yea-nay required quite yet." A smile rewarded him. "Shall we go downstairs and see how many ways Chuckie N has managed to offend the nice saleslady so far?"

"The speeds are adequate. Not great, but I can work with it. Did you know that Brez here passed her Realtor's License Test on her first try? We're in good hands here."

Brez blushed and shuffled her three heels together in an *aw, shucks* kind of way.

"It really wasn't that hard, as long as you'd studied enough."

"Smart *and* humble. Such an attractive combination."

"Why, thank you, Chuckie N. I'm flattered."

"I try."

I gag. Meehix kept that thought to herself. "Nothing really wrong with the place, Brez, but you have two other properties to show us?"

"Sure, yes, sure," Brez was going to make it as a professional realtor yet. "Meehix, I think you'll like the next one."

Meehix and John followed Brez and Chuckie N out front to their vehicles. Chuckie handed John the address to their next stop. "I'll ride with Brez. Meet you two there."

They watched Chuckie accompany Brez to her car, where he held her door open for her and circled to the passenger seat.

"Did we just see what we think we just saw?"

"The Chuckster making a move?" John smiled in response. "The little dude can be smooth when required."

"We better hurry over there. I don't want to arrive and find them testing out a mattress that goes along with a fully furnished house."

Brez and Chuckie were waiting out front when the other two caught up to them and auto-parked in a not quite legal space.

"I'm in love." The ten-minute drive brought them to a whole different neighborhood and vibe. Meehix was not displeased.

"Not much foot traffic." John surveyed the block.

"Anyone who hires us isn't going to be walking." Chuckie and Brez were already leading the way to the estate. "We better catch up before they have a chance to test out the mattresses."

The front door opened to reveal a parlor that took up most of the first floor.

"Isn't this just to die for?" Brez asked when they'd all gathered. "Sitting spaces along the walls and room in the middle for whatever other furniture you might need."

"It's lovely." Meehix wandered around, greeting imaginary future clients. "If you'll take a seat over there, sir, one of my assistants will be with you shortly."

"So," John whispered to Chuckie, "she's now relegated us to being her *assistants?*"

"What the girl wants." Chuckie kept his voice low too, as Brez led Meehix on a grand tour.

"We're good down here!" John called. The ladies thoroughly ignored him.

"I think she's got a fever for this one." Chuckie found a seat and pulled out Mixie again.

"Come on, Chuckie N." John found a seat of his own. "You're not even going to give me a sneak peek?"

"Just testing for connection availability."

"That's probably true." John accepted the explanation as a half-truth but was still a little pissed that Chuckie wouldn't share what he'd been working on with him. He knew when to bide his time.

"It's classic!" Meehix rushed down the stairs twenty minutes later with Brez trailing in her wake and sensing her first sale *ever*. "There's a full kitchen up there, and we can convert two spare rooms into full baths so everyone will be happy. Then we can turn this parlor into a fully functioning work space. We've got everything we need!"

She was about to lead them all in a dance she'd learned somewhere during her travels but Chuckie's frown curtailed that.

"What?"

"It's abysmal."

"You haven't even seen it!"

"Nor will I ever." He handed Mixie over to John. "Try reaching Q-vex and tell me how long it takes."

Chuckie's trying to make a big-fuck point here if he's giving me Mixie. John tried to reach Q-vex.

"What is the matter with you?" Meehix was pissed.

"It's a great joint, but the network connections are two levels below abysmal." Chuckie was equally pissed.

"The connections are fine." Brez wasn't letting go of the sale *that* easily.

"Fine for Trogpupples, maybe."

"I'm on Q-vex now," John was happy to report.

"There you go." Brez held out her hands, signaling *how simple was that?*

"That," Chuckie answered, "took all of five seconds."

"I've never been able to get to Q-vex in less than ten seconds." Brez was getting defensive. "Eight seconds is good enough for almost everyone."

"We're not everyone." He squared around to face off with Meehix now. "It just. Won't. Do."

"John! Can you please knock some sense into my fellow Dolurulodan?"

"It's not high on my list of priorities at the moment. You two are going to have to work it out." John had never seen a site like Q-vex before and was fascinated by what he was finding.

"If you want this place, go for it. I'll find another place for Mixie and me." Chuckie slapped Mixie closed and headed for the door, leaving John open-mouthed because he hadn't finished exploring the wonders of Q-vex.

"Sorry." Meehix turned back to Brez, "I should have warned you about the drama queen. I think we should put this place down as a maybe."

Meehix headed for the door and without a glance back at anyone called over her shoulder, "Meet me in the vehicle, John. Brez? You can either bring him along or leave him behind, your choice."

Thanks for the realtor advice, Mom. Brez and her Nipean knock-off headed outside. Chuckie, having made his stand, was waiting for her and followed to her ride, doing his best to apologize.

"I didn't mean to make such a scene." Apologies were not Chuckie's forte.

"Could have fooled me." Brez wasn't sure if she wanted him along anymore.

"It really wasn't about the network speeds." Chuckie tried his best to look sheepish as he improvised. "I just wanted to spend more time with you."

"You could have asked me for my number." Brez was not a happy realtor at the moment.

"Look at me, then look at you. I already have your work number. Would you have given me your personal number? You probably have a line of suitors three blocks long leaving messages and hoping they'll be the first one whose message you return."

That took her by surprise. Not that she was interested in the little man, but flattery was always nice, and at the moment, sadly, there was no queue lining up for her to return their calls. She let him in the car and drove off, Meehix and John following behind with their auto-guide.

"There's the Tri-2-Beatum Casino," Brez pointed out a few minutes later. "Ever been inside? It's really something."

"Nope, never been there, but my partners have, and they didn't come away with the happiest of experiences. I hope the next place isn't anywhere in this neighborhood because I don't think they'd like to have to pass it and the reminder every day."

"Oh, I'm sorry. Gambling problem?"

"Something like that."

"We're headed to a much less commercial area and a very nice neighborhood."

"Good," he grumped. "*Nice* is something that one of us is now insisting on."

"It's a shame about their gambling problem because there's a cute little house around the corner that just came on the market and could be useful to have if any of you three ever needed some alone time."

"Our first bounty." Meehix nudged John as they passed the casino moments later. They exchanged a look and said nothing more.

CHAPTER FIFTEEN

They followed Chuckie and Brez down the boulevard, and the housing changed dramatically a few minutes later as they gazed out toward the side streets.

Houses. Real honest-to-God houses. "They're not mansions, but they sure do all look roomy enough. Definitely upscale back in Albuquerque."

"I'm not displeased."

Brez turned into a neighborhood, Kabanek Woods, with a welcome notice that read **Welcome home, assuming you live here. If not, turn around and get the fuck out right now.**

"They're a lot friendlier than the sign would suggest," Brez explained to Chuckie. "They just want to discourage drifters and pamphlet-pushing whatevers."

She pulled into a driveway a block down, giving her clients a few minutes to stand outside the vehicles and take a good look around at their surroundings. The house itself was a rambling one-story affair. From the front, it looked like one main portion flanked by a wing branching out on each side.

"I like the neighborhood." Meehix turned to her partners when they'd gathered together. "Will the residential aspect be a detriment to business?"

"It's not like the last house was on a major thoroughfare, and if it weren't for the practically non-existent network speeds, it would have been just fine for you."

Brez took Meehix by the elbow and guided her toward the house, away from the boys who trailed behind.

"He doesn't let things go very easily, does he?"

"Never has. Never will. So, tell me what you know about the upside here."

They reached the door, and Meehix turned to the boys. "Stay! Or something. Brez and I are going to do a walk and talk by ourselves. I'm sure you bros can find enough things to bitch about as you do your tours."

Brez led the way through the front door, where they stepped into a good-sized foyer with a large living room to the right, a nice-sized dining room to the left, and a hallway that led farther in.

"All the furniture comes with the house, but as you can see, the living room is large enough to accommodate three desks comfortably, so if you're thinking of your business venture, you could use it as a shared office."

"Or throw one hell of a party, which would be preferable to sharing space with either of those two morons any more than necessary. But yes, you're right, this would make a good office space."

"The foyer is large enough to serve as a waiting room during business hours. And if," she corrected herself, "I mean *when* your business takes off, you can always convert the dining room to accommodate the overflow."

"Show me more." She followed Brez down the main hallway that deposited them into a very spacious kitchen, with two more hallways branching off to its perpendicular sides.

"Are any of you into cooking? Because, as you can see, the kitchen is laid out in such a way to make any gourmet chef happy."

"I'm more worried about us all having access to the knives and cleavers when we have coinciding bad days."

"Moving on." Brez headed for the hallway on the right. "The funny thing is that the former owner passed away recently under mysterious circumstances."

"I don't see the humor."

"Maybe funny was the wrong word. There is also a small house two blocks from the Tri-2 Casino that the same guy owned, and that house was a real dump. Oh, dumb, dumb, dumb, Brez," she paused and faced Meehix. "Chuckie may have let slip about yours and John's little," she went to a whisper, "gambling problem back at the Tri-2. No judgment on my part."

It took Meehix a moment to realize how Chuckie had spun the incident with Frelo. "We *did* have a little problem, but we've moved past that now, so it's all good. You were saying?"

"I'm so glad to hear that. I have an uncle who once lost everything. It took him several years of meetings with a support group, but he finally beat his addiction and worked his way back up to solvency. He stopped gambling and drinking and put all his energy into exercise programs."

"You must have been very proud of him."

"We were, all of us! That's why we thought it was such a shame when he forgot to look both ways before running his daily route and hurrying across a street against a light. We had him sun-bursted and scattered his ashes in the fountain in front of the Try-2 because we wanted him to remember that he'd finally beat the house." She stopped her rambling. "I forget. Where was I?"

Beats the flotsam out of me. "Something about the house, or two houses, or *this* house?"

"He was a quiet guy. That's what I was getting at. Kept to himself. No wild parties. No troubles whatsoever. I asked around, and the neighbors couldn't remember what he looked like. The master bedroom here? To die for."

"Lead the way."

The boys hadn't made it past the living room yet.

"Think it'll work for a front office?"

Chuckie was eyeing the various connection sockets around the room and held up a *gimme a minute finger.* There were built-in shelves along one wall with a monitor screen that, if laid flat, could carry entrees for a dinner party of six. Chuckie opened a cupboard at the end of the cabinet.

"Go find Meehix and...and..."

"Her name is Brez, or didn't you take the time to remember it while fantasizing about how many of her three legs could wrap around your face at one time?"

"Never crossed my mind," Chuckie lied.

"Nor mine," John lied back.

"I could die happy here," Chuckie took in the equipment in the cupboard. Routers and switches and boosters, half of which were illegal for a private citizen to own.

"Just see what you can find. All I need is for you to assure me that there is a bedroom somewhere with no windows...windows are nothing more than nature's way of distracting me while trying to focus on important things."

John decided not to pursue the matter. If pupil size categorized nirvana, Chuckie's eyes would be the picture that went along with the description. He wandered off to do some exploring on his own.

He made it to the kitchen and could hear the girls talking from somewhere down the hallway to the right. He decided to take the hallway to the left when he was distracted by a ceiling-to-floor four-foot-wide framed painting on the wall hanging on the backside of the kitchen.

Art on Earth often left him confused. Some he got, easy-peasy-puddin'-pie. Some he never would. He wasn't interested in how he would critique the painting. *Not that anyone would ever ask a dumb old Kdackan's opinion, but it looked out of place.*

The painting was soft and colorful and stood in stark contrast to the gleaming white and silver themes of the kitchen's design. It was also in an intricate wooden frame. *Another incongruity.*

He could spot something *off* in a code faster than Gage could even *think* about jerking off. *Fuck, he missed his amigo.* But if something was off, Jojacko was genetically incapable of not trying to figure out why. He approached the painting.

A still life with apples and pears and shit would make sense, what with it being in a kitchen and all. Something like a Picasso or a Salvador Dali-Llama-Parton would have also fit in, but this was nothing like that. It was a simple skyscape—blue skies and clouds and specks of what were probably birds in the background.

It's a window, looking out at something beyond...or something behind.

He took hold of the frame to try to lift it off its hanging hook. No go. It wasn't wall-mounted. *Must be a part of it.* He tried lifting it, then twisting it. The damn thing didn't budge.

Getting seriously pissed off, he tried brute force to yank it down. Finding himself defeated and short of breath, he took a step back and decided that maybe he was wrong and the painting wasn't worth the effort. He was going to head down the hallway on the left, but not before giving the frame a quick kick on its shit-for-frame bottom.

The door swung inward. *No fucking way!*

He pulled the painting-slash-door back into place. The kitchen returned to an undisturbed state. He set his foot on the bottom of the frame and gave a gentle push. *Hello, something!*

A glance around told him that he was alone with his discovery and made a quick decision not to share it...*At least not quite yet.* Checking out the back of the door, he found a push bar. He hoped that meant he wouldn't get locked in and left to decay. *Time to explore.*

He entered and closed the door behind him. As a test, he pushed the bar, and the door opened again. Satisfied, he found a light switch, closed the painting, and moved on to find a short hallway with one door on the left and a door opposite on the right. Almost scared of what he would find, he tried the right-hand door first.

There were no windows. Magnificent lighting, but no windows. The room was longer than it was wide and its most prominent furnishing was a desk set near the back. If you sat behind the desk, you would have a clear view of anyone who entered without any worries about someone sneaking up behind you. It was one serious office! *Time to try door number two.*

"It's funny," Meehix and Brez were making their way back to the kitchen from the hallway on the right. "There are no windows in the hallway."

"I wondered about that too," Brez agreed. "But it's just a hallway and when was the last time you were in a hallway with windows?"

Meehix could think of a dozen hallways with windows in Tagbedden Castle, her childhood home, but decided that this wasn't the time to go strolling down memory lane. *What did memories matter when your family declared you a non-sentient property and you now officially existed as a slave?*

"Good question. Silly me."

They entered the kitchen on their way to checking out the rooms in the left wing.

Meehix paused long enough to holler, "Chuckie?"

"Busy! Fuck off!"

"Is that good or bad?" Brez had her hands full trying to deal with this threesome.

"Where's John?"

"Not my day to watch him!"

"That's good." Meehix tried to clue Brez in. "They're both back to normal."

"That's normal? You and I have very different definitions of good or bad."

"We all have our burdens to carry. I call dibs on the right wing. Let's see what awaits the children on their side of the house."

Brez could smell a sale in her not too distant future and led Meehix to explore the left wing.

Never judge a client. Get them to sign on the dotted line and get the hell out. Thank you, Mom.

Holy mother of Gage. John took in what was behind door number two. He'd only seen bondage dungeons in a few games, and maybe a few S&M's in XXX-rated games and a few porn sites he'd visited when he was bad. *Gutter, calling John. Get your mind out of me and focus on what you see.*

After he blinked a few times, he saw benches and treadmills and weights stacked along the walls. The pull-up bars were just that, not something to chain someone to and whip them until blood dripped from their backs.

It's a fucking home gym! He couldn't help himself from trying it out. Practicing with the cubes and the raid on Victor's fortress had reminded him of how out of shape he'd gotten after Hannah had cheated on him. He'd buried his now fat ass in his parents' basement, his main exercises consisting of working out his thumbs while playing games and his right wrist when he needed a moment of release.

Ten minutes of working up a minor sweat later, he was sold and left the gym, but not before looking back at the various equipment. Whoever owned this place was either really cut or seriously kinky. Either way, he wanted it and headed back down the secret passageway, snuck a peek into the kitchen, and finding the coast clear, entered.

"Hello?" he tried as he found himself alone and wondered where the others were.

"Hello and keep fucking the fuck off!"

At least he'd located Chuckie's location, obviously still in the living room.

"Down here!" Meehix called from the left wing. He headed that way and met her and Brez in the hallway as they returned to the kitchen. He followed them back, thankful that neither of them noticed his slight perspiration.

Chuckie was even kind enough to join them.

"So, now that you've all had a chance to view the property, what do you think?"

"We'll take it!" all voices answered in unison, surprised that no one made a fuss.

Weirdest threesome I've ever seen.

"About the price."

"Yes, Meehix?" Brez was so close to having her first sale that her middle leg started twitching.

"I know it lists at five hundred thousand credits."

"I might be able to knock a little off, but not much."

"It's not the price." She looked at her partners. They all knew they could afford it with their remaining plunder from Victor's, but Brez didn't know that. "It's the commitment. We've never done anything like this together before, and if it doesn't work out, well, we'd be stuck for a long time of antagonizing each other."

"If it would ease your mind," Brez shuffled her left foot. "We could start with a six-month lease with an option to buy, for thirty-k per. That way, I can take it off the market, and you'll have enough time to sort out the survivors. Would that work?"

"Sounds good to me," John put in, and Chuckie nodded his assent.

"Well, there we go." Brez opened her briefcase on a kitchen counter and started pulling out contracts. "All I need is the first and last months upfront."

"I got this." John brought out his Abyss Exchange card. *Don't leave Earth without it.* "Since it will be in my name, just show me where to sign."

"You don't want to have all of your names on it? Because it will all be on you, John, if things blow up."

Meehix was still listed as non-sentient property and was technically his slave. *Let's not give that ugly subject time to rear its head.* Chuckie still had four hundred ninety-seven years of imprisonment to serve. It seemed most expeditious for him to be the only one to put pen to paper or finger to tablet as the case may be.

Contracts signed, they headed to the cars. Chuckie joined John and Meehix in theirs. Brez never did give him her private number, and as she watched them drive off, she wondered if maybe she should have taken a chance. *Probably best to keep business and personal separate.*

Even though it was rent-to-own and not technically a sale yet, it was still the first contract she'd gotten anyone to sign for one of her properties. She headed for a spa to treat herself to some well-deserved pampering.

Meehix used all the wiles she had, including a few pheromones, to get them out of their one-month lease of the suite. They took up residence in their new headquarters the next day. Meehix took the right wing all for herself and let the boys battle over the bedrooms in the left wing.

She hadn't noticed before, but the wall facing the back of the house had no windows. Instead, it had a sixty-foot mural in the same style as the kitchen painting with an overly ornamental frame. *The kitchen painting has to go, but that's a battle for another day.*

The boys settled into their rooms in the left wing, and they met up in the living room-slash-future office.

"We need some new furniture," John pointed out the obvious.

"We also need to watch our expenditures," Meehix pointed out the practical. "We're going through Victor's money way too fast."

"Yeah, one-point-two mil doesn't go as far as it used to." Chuckie led John to the cabinet and showed him the electronics.

"Oh my," was all John could manage to say.

"Uh-huh. Beautiful, ain't it? Mixie and Heemix have never had it so good."

"About the cash flow?" Meehix tried to bring them back to pragmatism.

"Yeah, yeah, I'm already on it."

"More bounty hunting jobs?" John was hopeful.

"Not quite." Chuckie was evasive. "I thought we could branch out in a slightly different direction. It'll be fun."

"You didn't think to bring this *new direction* up earlier?"

"Don't you and John have some office furniture to buy?"

They spent the next week getting used to the new digs. Chuckie insisted that the business he was setting up would be a money-maker *and* exciting but wouldn't give out the details until he had it a little further along.

A week later, as they were all sitting in the front office, wishing they were somewhere else because there was nothing to do other than die from boredom, the doorbell rang.

"Either of you two expecting anyone?"

John shook his head.

Chuckie ignored both the question and the bell.

Meehix sighed and went to the door, ready to give hell to whoever was bothering them. Opening the door, she found *hell* already waiting for her.

"Sorry, no one ordered any demons today." She was about to slam the door to avoid any hissy-fit the demon was about to throw, but his suddenly sad face made her pause.

She didn't hold the fact that he was red against him. It would be pretty hypocritical for a bluesy to look down on anyone for their genetically colored skin. Nor would she judge him for his height. Standing all of five feet tall, he was two inches taller than her oldest friend, who happened to be sitting one room away.

Knowing that demon tradition required certain dress codes, she also wouldn't hold his fashion in contempt. She simply didn't like the way they always seemed to throw a temper tantrum for the tiniest of reasons, which is why she paused in mid-slam and stood in the doorway as the little red beast looked like he was about to cry.

Deep breath. "May I help you?"

"I seek the NutBusters."

"The what?"

"The NutBusters." He removed his horns and held them as he would hold a hat while talking to a lady.

"You might have the wrong place."

He checked his notes. "No, miss. This is the right address. I have an appointment to meet with a Mr. Chuckie N. He's part of the NutBusters, one of whom once told a Blavarian dreadnought captain to, and I quote, bust a nut. Hence, NutBusters.

"That story traveled through the third arm faster than a Noatian could chug a glass of warm maple syrup." Introductions made, the demon replaced his horns.

"Who was at the door? Fuck the piss outta me!" John leapt back.

"I thought you said you weren't expecting anyone?" So much for the friendly competition in the gym. She had won and shouldn't have any reason to look at him like that.

"The devil?" John was rooted to the floor, not trusting his legs to carry him in flight.

"Who? Deville?" He held out one of his claws. "No. My name's Phil."

John wasn't going to move a muscle, let alone stick out a hand he had no guarantee of ever getting back.

"Says he's looking for the NutBusters."

"Aaannnddd," the new business that Chuckie had been so elusive about suddenly came into focus. "That would be us," although John still wouldn't hold out his hand to be shaken or bitten off.

"Great!" Phil removed his horns and stepped inside.

Meehix held out an arm, blocking his way. "No one invited you in yet."

"This must be Phil, our newest client." Chuckie came up from behind his partners and reached out to take Phil's claw. "Chuckie N, pleased to meet you. Right this way." Chuckie turned to lead Phil to the office.

Phil followed. Meehix and John remained behind.

"So it wasn't you with the whole NutBusters thing? It was all Chuckie-the-soon-to-be-dead-N?"

"Seems so. Let's go see what kind of trouble he's getting us into."

Phil was already seated in front of Chuckie's desk, but jumped up to offer a bow, sweeping his horns off his head while doing so.

"Chuckie tells me that you're the one who told off the Blavarian captain. Well done, sir."

"Oookaayyy. If Chuckie says it, then it must be true."

"We've had so many adventures that it's hard to keep track of every detail, so please, excuse his confusion, Phil."

Chuckie gave his partners a shooing motion as he sat back down to do business. John wasn't quite ready to shoo yet, because he had a few questions for their guest. He sat behind his desk so he could dive under it if the conversation took a wrong turn. He was determined to ask as many questions as necessary to determine whether or not his soul was up for bargaining purposes.

"Please, anyone, feel free to clue this stupid Kdackan in as to why I'm now sitting in the same room with a demon!"

"He's from Kdack?" Chuckie and Meehix both nodded.

"Well, that certainly explains a lot." Phil turned back to face John. "I'm only a simple, humble demon. Our dedication is to do a little mischief and a fair amount of good along the way.

"Several millennia ago—we lost track of the exact date —a splinter group broke off. They were young ones and wanted to form something that you would probably call a gang. A rebellious bunch of turds, if you want my honest opinion."

John made eye contact with Meehix, who he trusted, and Chuckie, who he hoped was enough of a bro by now. They both nodded, and Phil picked up the story.

"They weren't happy being simple demons, like the old folks, so they called themselves and their gang The Dee-mons and went out hunting for mischief. That's when they stumbled onto Kdack 3a, which was still a young planet at the time."

"So," John was trying, "demons and dee-mons are not the same?"

"Originally, yes," Phil was ashamed to admit. "But they caused so much trouble on Kdack 3a that the Demon Council decided that they should stay there for a while so they wouldn't cause havoc on other planets."

"You're telling me that the dee-mons on Kdack have basically been sent to the corner until they learn to behave?"

Applause all around. John, while pleased with the applause, still needed a few minutes to take this all in.

Meehix took mercy on him. "Chuckie. How about you

MICHAEL TODD

and Phil carry on with business and I'll sit over there and help John adjust."

"Have him check Heemix for an old Kdackan transmission that I tracked down and sent him."

Meehix pulled a chair around to John's side of the desk as he pulled up and downloaded Chuckie's message. *Damn, that took less than a second. Chuckie's right. This place is really wired.*

They watched what Chuckie had sent them together. John recognized it immediately as an old Kdack commercial. It took Meehix watching it three times before she understood why Chuckie had sent it.

Pardon me sir, do you have any Grey Poupon?

"Got it! John, it's time for a diction lesson."

Nothing else had made any sense that day, so why should he expect Meehix not to join in with the insanity?

"Listen to me carefully. If you shit on something... No, that's wrong. Repeat after me. *I'm going to poop on you.*"

"I'm going to poop on you." John obeyed because the day was already shot to hell, *as proven by the demon sitting with Chuckie.*

"Again."

"I'm going to poop on you."

"Now finish this sentence: *Pardon me sir, do you have any Grey...*"

"Poupon. So?"

"Poop on, Poupon."

"Wax on, wax off. Big fucking deal." That earned him a smack on the head.

"Focus! Poop on as opposed to Poupon."

Maybe it was the head-smack that did it.

"Poop on. Poupon. Demon. Dee-mon."

"Again!"

"Poop on. Poupon. Demon. Dee-mon."

They joined hands and circled the desk repeating their new chant.

"Excuse me, Mr. N. Are you sure they're quite sane?"

"Perfectly *insane,* actually," Chuckie leaned forward. "Who else would agree to what you're asking us to do?"

Happy dance over, Meehix and John pulled chairs up around Chuckie's desk. John stood and reached out his hand.

"I'm sorry, Phil. Slight misunderstanding there when we first met."

Phil stood and shook the offered hand. "Quite all right, sir. Considering your planet of origin, I can understand the confusion. Would you like to wear my horns for a while?"

"Not quite yet." John took his seat. "So, where are we?"

"I was explaining to Chuckie N why I needed to hire the NutBusters."

"Chuckie N." Meehix was curious. "The NutBusters?"

"It sounded very Chuck Norris to me." Chuckie pantomimed a crotch kick. "Kick 'em in the nuts. Gives us a very macho image. Where's the problem?"

"The *problem* is in the origins of the phrase." Meehix's eyes bored into Chuckie's, and he turned to John for help.

John pantomimed the universal sign for a male jerking off. Chuckie caught on immediately, and John had just enough time to stop the motion before Meehix turned and caught him in the act.

"What I came here for, and was explaining to Chuckie

N, hoping you could help me out, is that my cousin has gone missing."

John didn't have much experience with demons, but if they were all as polite as this guy, he could understand why they would all want to clearly separate themselves and their reputations from those of the dee-mons.

"Does your cousin have a name?"

"Already got it, Meehix." Chuckie verified his info. "Vixaleen. Vix for short."

"She's a *succubus?*"

"It's not her fault." Phil was quick to defend her. "That's the side of the family she was born into."

"A succubus?"

John had run into a few of them in the games he'd played. More than once, he'd taken an intentional wrong turn into an unmarked cave, away from the action with a succubus tagging along for some momentary pleasure before they went back into battle.

"Terrific. Now we've lost John."

"I'm right here!"

"You weren't a moment ago, were you, perv?"

"Point taken. I'm here now."

"Tell them more, Phil." Chuckie became the voice of reason and focus, although he wouldn't mind rescuing a succubus and letting her thank him, up close and personal.

Phil suddenly found himself the center of attention. *I sought them out. They didn't come looking for me.* They really were crazy enough to try to bring his niece back to him safely.

"Someone kidnapped her," Chuckie tossed in before heading to the kitchen because he'd heard this part before and decided to try his hand at mixing up a pitcher of dibble-blinks to pass around once their client left.

"Kidnapped?" John's save the damsel in distress instincts took over.

"Kidnapped, yes," Phil nodded, "and now held prisoner."

Meehix finally found some empathy for the poor Vix. "Do you know where she's being held?"

"I know exactly where, and I could probably rescue her myself."

"Then why do you need us?" John was curious.

Phil pulled a cloth out of a shirt pocket and raised it to his nose.

"Excuse me for a minute, please."

He sneezed into the cloth and vanished.

"I wish it was that easy."

"Wish what was that easy?" Meehix needed an explanation.

"Think about it." John hoped he could explain without drawing another head-smack. "You find yourself in an uncomfortable social situation, with no polite means of escape. So you pull out a hanky and say, 'excuse me, I feel a sneeze coming on,' and *poof*, you're gone."

Meehix had to admit it to herself. John had a point. Before any more contemplations about the benefits of being able to disappear with the help of a sneeze, Phil was back, sitting in the same chair and looking around in a slight daze.

"Oh, thank God. I'm back where I left, and you're still here."

"Right where you left us." Even Meehix had never seen that trick before.

"And that, my kind people, is why I can't rescue the niece of my heart. If I sneeze, I could be gone for a second. Or days… What if I've just broken into where she's being held captive. *Oh, Uncle Phil, you saved me! Yes, Vix, you're free. I just have to get you past a few guards…*I sneeze and am *poof* gone, leaving her alone to fend for herself as an escapee."

Meehix and John were beginning to understand where the hyperallergic demon was coming from.

"Chuckie has all the info on her, right?" John was starting to negotiate the contract price Meehix stomped on his foot under the table.

"What John was trying to say," Meehix took her foot off John's because she realized that time was of the essence here. "It will be a hundred thousand credits. That will cover our daily fees for three months and incidentals. It might only take one month, but it might take five. Either way, flat fee. One hundred thousand."

Phil pulled out his pocket tablet. "Will transfer right now…Excuse me," as he pulled out his cloth again to sneeze… *poof!*

"Shit! Easy come, easy go, I guess." John sighed.

"Lighten up." Meehix was checking their account. "Whatever dimension he's in is one with bank communications. He deposited the money."

"Dibble-blinks anyone?" Chuckie returned from the kitchen a few minutes later with a pitcher and three glasses.

CHAPTER SIXTEEN

In the past, Gage had only used the dark web to search for porn that was beyond anything you could find in a magazine, regardless of the mag's title or promises. It also put the commoners' Internet porn sites to shame. For the last several weeks, he'd been spending his time on it, well, not *all* of his time, tracking down ways to help promote his Save Aliens From Assholes.

He needed information, as much as he could gather, and money, *as much as I can gather*, which was not very much so far. He looked at his screen. Thirty thousand people already signed in to view his broadcast. Two hundred of them were also waiting in his phone queue. He lit up his *On Air* sign. The host was about to join the party.

"Gonzo Gage, coming at'cha with the truth. I'd like to personally welcome my two favorite viewers, agents Bixby and Shaw. Found a therapist yet to help you deal with your mommy issues?"

He knew that he would probably one day pay for his taunting of them in front of thirty thousand viewers, but he'd survived his anal probe with no major damage done. Egos were a lot more fragile than assholes, so he wanted to get his licks in while he could.

"First things first, and I hate to ask, but SAFA is far below their fund-raising goal this quarter." *Something like only having fifty dollars in his account right now.*

"There's thirty thousand of you viewing right now, so obviously, you're interested in SAFA and its mission. We're bringing the truth of what happened to our off-planet visitors at the hands of our dark government forces to light.

"If you listen to the official reports, we do not now, nor have we *ever* had alien visitors. Do you really need Gonzo Gage to tell you that our government's fed us enough bullshit to fill the Grand Canyon?"

He had become more confident in his approach and spiels. A handful of scribbled notes to refer to when necessary and otherwise just let it rip.

"Of course, you don't need me. You've seen the evidence for yourselves. Here's the thing. SAFA is a nonprofit organization." He had been quite proud of himself for having taken the time to set it up that way. Filling out forms to make it all official and shit. "We keep the staff to a minimum so that ninety-eight percent of every penny goes into the fund to finance our operatives saving the aliens."

Give the pitch and move on.

"Like I said, there are thirty thousand viewers right now. The average cost of the operation to find an alien and rescue it is ten thousand dollars. So if each of you would pitch in just one dollar, we could rescue three of our friendly visitors from where they're being held against their will and set them free!

"You won't have to support them for the rest of your lives. Once they're free, they book out off Earth and plan never to return...and I can't blame them after the treatment our government has given them."

He pushed a button and a chyron scrolled across the bottom of his screen. *Support SAFA at Pay.com/SAFA.*

"Ten grand to free an alien? Where'd he come up with that amount?"

"Probably pulled it out of his soon to be anally probed ass, Agent Bixby." Shaw kept his focus on the broadcast. *Gonna get this prick.*

On the lower quarter of his screen, Gage started a slide show he'd put together of videos and photos others had sent him. These were basically harmless, often blurry, and not deserving of any anal probes for the people who'd sent them.

"The videos you're watching have all been sent in by The Gonzo Gang. Keep 'em coming. I've screened them, but need to warn you to be careful what you send.

"There could be unwanted and unpleasant consequences if you send something that the *you know who's* decide is too dangerous to be shared. Trust me on that! For those of you who want to send videos that might put you in danger, pay attention, and you'll know how to contact me."

The chyron kept scrolling, reminding his fans to continue to help the funding. It also included enough letters in a code that Jojacko had once taught him to do and had all the info needed for the code-breakers to find him on the dark web.

"Let's go to the phones." Button pushed. "Caller number one, what'chu got for the Gonzo?"

"Am I really the first caller?"

"Yes, Albert. You're the first caller for the third broadcast in a row."

In the background, thirty thousand viewers heard Albert's co-workers starting the chant. *We're number one! We're number one!*

"But I still don't have any prizes to give away to the first caller."

"Fuck the prizes, Gonzo Gage. We're talking international bragging rights here!" He hung up with the chanting getting louder in the background.

"Caller number two."

"We wanna have your babies!" three women shouted. *Groupies?*

"Who wouldn't? My mix of good looks and charm would set the children up for a long and happy life." There was happy screeching in the background as he hit the button and moved on.

"Next?"

"My Uncle Chester has one."

"One of what?"

"One of the aliens!"

"Really?"

"He says it's my cousin, but he don't look nothin' like anyone else on either side of the family."

"Next."

Ten calls later of various levels of silliness and stupidity later, it was Shaw, yes, *definitely Shaw*, on the line.

"The doctor may have slapped your ass when you came

out of your mother's womb to make you cry, but you'll be crying a lot harder the next time we finish with your ass."

"Here we go, folks. Agents Bixby and Shaw calling in, so concerned with covering their asses that they're trying to divert the focus onto mine. Your tax dollars hard at work. You all know the drill by now."

He stood, dropped his chinos, and mooned them again for all thirty thousand viewers to see. Hiking his pants back up to where they belonged, he went back to trying to squeeze as many callers as he could into the next hours before he had to take care of Toñito and Isabella while his mom went back to work.

Some callers were simply whack-jobs.

"No. Bigfoot may be real, but he's not an alien," Gage tried to explain.

"Can you prove that? If we caught him, we could test his DNA."

"Next."

Some callers contributed some intelligent thoughts. He had five minutes before his mom had to leave.

"Gotta wrap this up. Until next time, Gonzo Gage, out and gone!"

He ended his part of the broadcast but left the screen running as he went to take care of the little ones and helped his mom to gather her belongings as she headed for her second shift.

"All changed, fed, and fresh."

"And another Muppet movie to keep them entertained? I'm tired of watching the Muppets."

"You loved them yourself when you were their age. Dinner is in the fridge."

Quick cheek kisses and she was gone.

He looked at them sitting and fixated on another Muppet movie. *I'm so fucking sick of the Muppets. What did I ever see in them?* He was still so wound up from his latest broadcast that maybe taking a few minutes to sit and cuddle with his flesh and blood might give him some time to chill.

He sat, pulled Toñito onto his lap, and drew Isabella close.

"What Muppet adventures am I being forced to watch now?"

"*Muppets From Space,*" Isabella answered on behalf of her and her little brother, who hadn't learned to talk yet. *Muppets ain't the only thing in space, lemme tell ya, little sister.*

Five minutes later his mother's words came back to him of how he'd loved them when he was much younger.

"Oh…" he stopped himself just in time to not add *fuck.* There on the screen was *Gonzo the Great! AKA The Great Gonzo!*

He set Toñito down next to his sister. "I'll be right back." He headed to his room.

Muppets. Space. The Great Gonzo. Fuck! Maybe Jim Henson had been an alien who'd avoided detection all along!

Back in front of his screen, the *Pay.com/SAFA* account now had four thousand, nine hundred and twenty-seven dollars in it and counting. He unplugged his *On Air* sign, which he'd forgotten to do after he signed off, and shut everything else down, not sure he could trust his eyes. He returned to the living room and hoisted Toñito back onto his lap. Remembering what he'd once told Jojacko. *When you're an illegal, you learn to take good news and bad news in stride.* He would check back online tomorrow, but for now, he was going to trust the good news and pull Toñito back onto his lap and watch the DVD, searching for hidden messages.

"Teething rings and Pampers for life, little brother. What are the *fuck*-Muppets up to now?"

"You said fuck."

"That's a word only *hombres* are allowed to say. *Niñitas* say *sweet.*"

"Sweet fuck?"

"No! Just *sweet.*..Like what we're watching the Muppets do is *sweet.*"

"So fuck isn't the same as sweet?"

"Sometimes yes. Sometimes no...Shit!" *What am I teaching them?*

"Is shit like sweet or like fuck?"

"Sweet is sweet. Those other words are not nice words to use."

"Fuck is shit and shit is fuck, and I should never say them?"

"Exactly. Can we go back to the *Muppets From Space* now?"

"Yes, please. The Great Gonzo just got himself into a lot of trouble and doesn't know what will happen to him next."

From the mouths of children comes wisdom.

With a new client to focus on, and while Chuckie was obsessed with finding her, John decided it was the right time to take Meehix into the kitchen and explain why the painting that annoyed her couldn't simply be moved into storage and replaced.

"Why is that?" she stared at it, crossed arms and body language expressing displeasure.

"It's sort of built into the wall."

"We can't just remove it?"

"You can try."

She tried pulling, shoving, sliding. "You knew that wouldn't work, didn't you?"

"Not for sure. I thought maybe you had some super-powers that I didn't."

"Aren't we pleased with ourselves?"

"If you want to take out some frustration, I suggest you kick the bottom frame."

"What? Like this?" She gave it a half-hearted kick, and John enjoyed her surprise when the door swung open. "You knew about this all along." She was ready to kick John in his lower regions also, if only to knock the smug smile off his face.

"Want the tour?"

"Lead on."

He led her first to the spacious room they could use for either an extra office or for weapons storage.

"So this is why the hallway walls inside the wings don't have any windows to the outside."

"Because there *is* no outside. Wait 'til you see the other room." He led the way.

"Is this a sex dungeon or a gym?" Meehix hoped the answer would be *gym*. "Is this where you've been disappearing to a couple of times each day?"

"The raid on Victor's made me realize how out of shape I'd gotten."

"And you didn't tell us about this room why?"

"Chuckie's not going to start exercising suddenly, and you're already in great shape. I mean, all of you is."

She took the flattery for what it was and smiled. "Thank you. Glad you noticed." Looking around at the equipment, she added, "You can beat me on the weights, but I bet I'd kick your ass on the cardio."

They joined Chuckie in the front office an hour later. "Where have you two been? And why are you both sweating like a flignut?"

"We had a bet, and I won." Meehix took the seat behind her desk with a very satisfied smile.

"There's a hidden gym on the other side of the kitchen." John wanted to reassure Chuckie that the sweating had nothing to do with an afternoon romp. *Although he wouldn't be opposed to one. Someday? Maybe?*

"I found her!"

"The love of your life? About time. When will you introduce her to us?" Meehix was still on an adrenaline high from having kicked John's ass on the cardio.

"The demon's niece. The demon, our *client's* niece. You remember our client, right?"

"The scary red dude with an allergy problem?" John remembered him well. "I'll grab a couple of bottles of water from the kitchen and be right back."

Bottles of water retrieved, he handed one to Meehix, who chugged half of it down in one gulp as she looked over Chuckie's shoulder.

"The report says she's already packed, stacked, and racked, and ready for shipment."

John had gotten used to acknowledging his ignorance. This seemed like a good time to put it on display again.

"Packed?"

"Go for it, Chuckie." Meehix stepped back.

"Packed means they caught her. Stacked means that she's in a box just large enough to ship her and any other objects of a similar size."

Chuckie was simplifying things very well so far. Meehix decided to continue not to butt in.

"And racked?"

"Racked means they've got her so doped up that they won't have to worry about feeding her during her shipment.

"So they won't have to feed her. That probably cuts down on food costs."

"Are you playing ignorant again?" Meehix had to know. "Are you really that clueless?"

"My money's on clueless."

"Shut the fuck up, Chuck. Go on, John."

"I'm trying to look at it from her captors' viewpoint. The more money you can save on feeding a captive means more money they can put in their pockets. I don't know how much she could eat, but it makes financial sense."

Chuckie stood, walked around his desk, and gave John a head-slap, saving Meehix the trouble.

"That was very satisfying, Meehix." He returned to his chair. "Thank you for giving me the honors."

"The pleasure was all yours, Chuckie N."

"What?" John was getting a little tired of the head-slap

routine, especially since it seemed like his was the only head slapped on what seemed like a daily basis. "All I asked was how much it would cost to feed her. Does she have special dietary needs that are expensive?"

"She's a succubus, John." Chuckie leaned back in his chair, happy to let Meehix handle this while he massaged the pain out of his head-smacking hand. *Well worth the pain for the pleasure it brought.*

"In the games you played before we met," Meehix decided to be patient and help him work his way through. "Between all of the blowing shit up and trying to survive to the next level, what does a succubus need to eat and survive on?"

"Sex. Every gamer knows that."

"Aaannd?" She needed an answer.

"No way. That's real?"

"Really real in the real world."

John's response was total silence. While gaming, if you ran into a succubus, it could be a lot of fun for a few minutes of distraction, even though he knew damn well that it was probably just Slim-Slam-Sam from Sonoma yanking everyone's chains so he could beat them to the next level.

A real-life succubus? No. He had no interest in meeting one. They only had one thing on their minds. His mind and other organs were already committed to the blue chick, but now wasn't the time to declare that in front of Meehix, Chuckie, God, and everyone.

"No." He shook his head. "Not interested."

Meehix sighed. She'd fallen in love with the big oaf. Now wasn't the time to discuss it in front of John, Chuckie,

God, and everyone. She leaned back in her chair as casually as she could.

"So, the slut niece is now being held captive at Point A and will be delivered to Point B. To fulfill our contract with her demon uncle, we have to find two undisclosed points and intercept her and her carriers at either A or B or somewhere in between. Do I have that right?"

"Close enough." Chuckie was digging for more info as fast as he could.

"Let us know when you find it. I'm going to grab a snack and retire to my room for the night. See you in the morning. And I mean, *morning*."

They watched her storm off, grab something from the kitchen, and disappear down her wing.

"You've known her longer than I have. Is she pissed?"

"Your guess is as good as mine. Now let me go to work and stop dripping sweat on my shoulder."

John took a step back. "Sorry about that."

He left Chuckie alone to do his job and headed back down the hallway. Reaching the kitchen, he paused to spare a glance down the right wing, wondering how Meehix was going to spend the night in her room.

He decided to kick the painting and head for the gym. He half-hoped he would find Meehix there ahead of him. He was disappointed. *Not for the first time when it came to females.*

"Hello, cardio bastards," he addressed the machines in the gym. "I've got some pent-up sexual energy built up, and I'm about to take it out on you before I go to my room and exercise the one part of my body that you can't help me with."

An hour of heavy cardio sweat later, he toweled off and headed to his room needing a long hot shower, followed by a short cold one.

Ten minutes later, the door to the gym opened again.

"Hello, cardio bitches." Meehix had some pent-up energy of her own to burn off.

CHAPTER SEVENTEEN

John and Meehix were on the same cycle because they met up again the next morning in the kitchen. A recently brewed pot of cafamee greeted them.

"Sleep well?" John poured her a cup.

"Always," she lied.

"Me too." He matched her lie as he filled his cup. They tracked down Chuckie, who must already be in the office and was the guilty party when it came to the cafamee.

"Shut the fuck up," was their greeting before they had a chance to say a word. Meehix and John knew enough to take seats behind their respective desks and enjoy a sip. After that, Meehix decided to be the first to approach the dragon in the room.

"Sleep well?"

"Sleep is for the weak." Chuckie looked up with a way-too-satisfied smile for anyone this early in the morning. "Enjoy your cafamees, and at the risk of sounding redundant, shut the fuck up." He went back to what he was working on.

Chuckie's partners raised their cups at each other in a silent toast and let Chuckie do what Chuckie did. Ten minutes later, Chuckie gave his Mixie time to breathe and leaned back in his chair with a smile that might be either friendly or evil, depending on which side of it you were on.

"We get to double-dip! I gotta piss," he announced as he hustled himself out of the office, leaving his partners to converse among themselves.

"He's your *friend*."

"He's your *bro*."

Having said everything that needed to be said, they enjoyed their cafamees while waiting for him to return.

"Here's the deal." Chuckie settled back in after his piss-break, looking at Meehix while nodding at John. "He's going to become useful."

"What was I back at Victor's, canned Spam? That's the food, not the Internet version."

"I'm not familiar with Spam as a food item, but for your ego's sake, I'll give you credit for probably being at least one rung up the ladder from it." Chuckie leaned back and addressed them both. "Vix is on a cargo ship docked on Space Station Frommix I, one galactic Gate away from here. I don't have their whole itinerary, but one of its destined stops is good old Kdack 3a, and that's where you come in, my lumbering friend."

"They need a tour guide on Kdack for some R-and-R during their stopover?"

"Funny, but wrong. They need mercenaries to guard the various shipments from pirates." Chuckie seemed quite pleased with himself as he brought his partners into the loop.

"There are pirates in space?" John tried to keep up.

"Yes, John. There are pirates in space." Meehix had more patience than he did, so Chuckie left it to her to explain.

"Aren't pirates sort of the same as mercenaries?"

"No, John. *Mercs* do what they do as a *paying gig.* Pirates do what they do so they can enjoy their plundering." She let that settle in for a few seconds before continuing his education. "Mercs are hired to prevent the pirates from plundering."

"Oh."

"Oh, he says." She tossed it back to Chuckie.

"Among the items they're transporting is something a firm on Kdack is insuring, and that, my friends, is our ticket in."

"Clarification, please." Meehix was now drawn in and wanted to hear more.

"Because," Chuckie delivered his coup de grâce, "any insured shipment that hires mercenaries to guard it has to, by galactic decree, have at least one mercenary from the insurer's planet of origin. Do you have any idea how rare galactically licensed mercenaries from Kdack are?"

Head shakes seemed to be the collective response.

"There is a grand total of one!"

"I never dreamed that Earth had galactic mercenaries, even if there's only one." John was stunned and wondered what kind of badass dude he must be. "Gotta be honest, I'm kind of glad I've never met him."

"You'll see him soon. The next time you look in a mirror."

John pointed at himself. Meehix pointed at John. Chuckie enjoyed the looks on their faces.

"I'm the merc?"

"As of an hour ago. Gotta piss again. Too many cafamees." He vanished almost as quickly as the sneezing demon.

"Maybe I should go back to bed. I'm not sure I like the direction this day is taking."

"Two cups of cafamee and you think you're going to be able to take a nap? Good luck with that."

"Let me get this straight," John began when Chuckie returned with a relieved look on his face. "I'm a mercenary now?"

"Yes. You *and* Meehix. Signed and licensed through the auspices of the NutBusters."

Meehix leaned back in her chair and let the boys duke it out.

"You didn't think to ask us first?"

"We have a demon of a client to satisfy, and I didn't want to disturb your beauty rest. Trust me. This is a plum gig. Phil has already paid us to rescue his niece. His niece is captive and waiting for transport on a cargo ship.

"Said ship has other insured cargo, needs mercenaries to protect that cargo, and is paying the NutBusters to provide two of the ten mercenaries they need. Oingo-boingo, you're suddenly on board! How perfect is that?"

"You left out the part about the space pirates."

Chuckie waved that off and turned to Meehix.

"Explain to your fellow *merc* how insurance works in space."

"How long do I have?"

"As long as you need. Might want to try using small words." Chuckie went back to Mixie to do some more research. Meehix turned to John.

"Cargo on a ship. Cargo is insured. Mercs get hired to protect cargo."

"See Spot run. So far, I'm somehow managing to keep up."

She smiled. Although the Spot reference eluded her, she could appreciate sarcasm.

"Insurance in space works like this. Mercs, in this case, you and I, would be part of a crew of ten." She turned to Chuckie. "Ten, right?"

"Ten, twenty, whatever. You both are officially welcome on board. Now fuck off."

Back to John. "We are hired as mercs for *this* particular job, specifically because you are the only known Kdackan merc. Take that one in. Jojacko, the Kdackan merko."

"Has a nice ring to it." He couldn't help but smile. "Then what? Pirates invade, and we put some whup on their asses?"

"Hopefully, no pirates show up, and it ends up being a bum ride with no threatened cargo, no battles fought, everyone gets paid, and the mercs go on their merry way, cargo protected and delivered. A happy ending for all."

"Sounds a little anticlimactic if you ask me."

"Yes, no battles or bloodshed. It does sound boring, doesn't it?"

Sarcasm is a two-way street. They both thought it. Neither of them said it.

"Then battles only come into play if pirates show up?"

"No. Bargaining first. Battles second."

"Bargaining?"

"Bargaining. Mercs, by definition, sell their services to the highest bidder. If the pirates bargain with the mercs to pay them more than the insurer who hired them, well, the insurer should have paid more."

"So the mercs let the cargo go to the highest bidder and tell the insurance company who originally hired them 'Whoops?'"

"Something like that, yeah."

John realized that he was new to this whole mercs in space thing, but that didn't sit right. He drew a deep breath.

"You're telling me that the tradition of space mercs is to give up what they've been assigned to protect? If someone accepts a job, they're obligated to fulfill their obligations!"

"He's going to start stamping his feet soon." Chuckie chose that moment to chime in while not taking his eyes off Mixie and what he was searching for.

"Ignore him, John. Continue."

He couldn't continue without standing and pacing and waving his arms. He looked like one of those promotional tubes in front of a used-car lot with a fan blowing up its ass, causing the tube and its smiling face to bend and flail in every direction to draw everyone's attention.

"If someone hires you to do a job, you see that job through! Is *that* too complicated a concept? Even in space?"

"If a fast-food joint hires me to flip burgers, I'm not gonna quit my shift halfway through a burger-flip because the joint down the block suddenly offered me more money to flip theirs! If someone hires me to wash down a parking lot, the next one who wants me to wash *their* parking lot will have to wait until I finish with the first one!"

Afraid of ranting more and breaking something with his flailing arms, he returned to the chair behind his desk to give his heart rate a chance to settle down.

"Bravo." Chuckie was almost done with his research and didn't bother to look up. "I'll let our client, Phil the demon, know that the NutBusters will find his niece, whatever it takes."

"Phil?" Meehix had a reality check.

"Yeah, Phil and his niece, Vix the succubus. Ring any bells?"

Meehix took in the view. At one desk was Chuckie, working every angle to bring in some mostly honest pay. He knew damn well that he could do better if he returned to his pre-cryo occupation of seeing how much he could get away with before the authorities caught him.

At the other desk was the Kdackan who'd rescued her, not caring what the consequences might be if he'd failed. He set out to do something and seemed willing to stand barefoot on the edge of a spreading fire with nothing at his disposal other than to piss on it to put it out before he lost the battle and was burned alive. He was willing to go down fighting, or pissing, whichever seemed more appropriate when he had a job to do.

She loved them both but also knew she'd be sleeping alone that night. The Universe had a strange sense of humor. *Batteries. Must make sure to recharge the batteries in her A Girl's Best Friend before she went to bed.*

"Got it! Headed your way, Shippewa."

"Huh?" That brought Meehix out of her thoughts.

"What?" John joined her back in the moment.

"I'll be right where you left me, Chuckie N."

He faced his yet-to-catch-up work partners. "Ship will be multitasking today. Our carriage awaits." He flipped Mixie shut and carried her with him as he headed for the door. "Our auto-driver will be here in five minutes. Grab what you need but don't dawdle. We're about to get down to some serious NutBusters business."

An hour later, since even auto-drivers made a wrong choice now and then to avoid construction zones, the NutBusters, two of them still semi-clueless, were welcomed by Ship as they came up the ramp.

"Please check your weapons before boarding. Your flight will leave in two, maybe three days from now, depending on Chuckie's mood...I, myself, am incapable of moods."

Meehix and John knew enough to grab hold of something solid because Ship was about to cut loose with a chuckle.

"Good chuckle, Ship."

"Thank you, Meehix. I've been practicing."

"You succeeded."

"Thank you, John. I've been working on it. Chuckie N?"

"Mixie's ready. Look for We-Be-Fucking." He connected a cord between Mixie and Ship.

"Got it...oh my!"

"Big fucker, ain't it?"

Meehix and John both knew how to back off when they were late to a party.

"It's a Bargeflat 489. There are only three of them still flying because the companies who keep them airborne are too cheap to upgrade."

"We need to learn everything we can about this transportation ship?"

"Exactly! Set up the cubes back in Cargo so Jo and Hix can start to learn their way around it, up one side and down the other. You and I have to figure out how me and you can go along for the ride until we're needed."

"No weapons practice today?" Meehix wanted to be clear on their task for the next couple of hours.

"No. Just the two of you toddling off into Cargo and getting acquainted with every inch of the ship. Every storeroom, hallway, and cubby-hole.

"You're going to have a demon's niece to rescue, possible pirates to fight off, and whiny insurance agents to explain your actions to. Ship and I have our work to do to make sure we can save your sorry asses when the time comes."

The NutBusters' mercs knew a dismissal when they heard it and headed to Cargo.

"That's one big-fuck ship," John offered when he and Meehix reached the cargo space and found three times as many cubes floating around than they'd practiced with for their attack on Victor's fortress.

"Don't forget the gloves."

"Thanks, Ship." Meehix found the gloves right where they'd left them after their last session with the cubes. She handed John his. "Time to glove up again, Jo."

"Bet your cute blue ass, Hix. Did I just say that out loud?"

"**I believe you did, John.**"

Hix had to turn away to hide her smile at the compliment. *Maybe there's hope for us yet.*

Chuckie hoped that there was a soon to be rescued succubus in his not-too-distant future but joined the conversation.

"Learn every in and out and battle point. We have a demon's niece to rescue and maybe a little bit of another semi-precious part of the manifest that no one will miss until it's too late."

"What do ya think, Hix? Top to bottom or bottom to top?"

"Let's start at the top, Jo. Front to back, swap sides and double back to the front in case we missed something. Then the same on the next level down until we hit bottom and back up again?"

A gloved-up high five moment later, Hix reached up, hit the first cube, and they were off, scoping out their next adventure.

Ship muted the voices coming from Cargo and Chuckie disabled the two in Cargo from hearing the voices in the front cabin.

"**This is going to be somewhere between a cakewalk and a disaster.**"

"That's the way I see it," Chuckie agreed. "We have to figure out a way to be there, but there are at least two galactic Gates to get through, and we can't simply follow. We have to be there the whole way."

"**While remaining undetected?**"

"That's the plan."

"**This isn't just about the money. Is it, Chuckie?**"

"I've never been opposed to a money opportunity."

"There are easier ways to make money."

"Alone, yes. But what good is money if you can't drag friends along with you on the ride?"

"Wise words."

Shit! Did I just sound wise and philosophical at the same time? What have they done to me?

"I've been looking over the schematics of the Bargeflat 489 cargo carrier. So far, I can't figure out any way to tag along."

"That's because you've never taken the time to learn about my construction."

As focused on the NutBusters as he was, sitting in the pilot's seat and imagining how it must feel to be at the controls, that brought Chuckie up short. *I've always been short but never been short this way.*

"What did I miss?"

"When I was assembled back on Kdack, a piece here and a piece there, they welded a plate of metal on my underside."

"To protect you from missiles coming from below?"

"That's my best guess. The metal slows me down, but I suspect that they didn't build me for speed. Proficiency was more likely."

Empathy wasn't a word in Chuckie's vocabulary, but he felt it now.

"Sorry that I never took the time to ask."

"You never had a reason to ask. Now, how is a Bargeflat 489 powered?"

It took Chuckie only a minute to find the answer.

"Got it. A magno-flow generator. Very old-fashioned

and probably why they're not in use anymore. Very energy inefficient."

"Why is that?"

Chuckie kept reading, gathering information, and found more than one review. He read the most relevant one out loud.

"The magno-flow provides consistent, steady power but creates a magnetic field that will attract metal objects to it, sometimes causing a slightly slower speed as metallic objects are drawn to it during travel. It is recommended to inspect any ship powered by the magno-flow, once safely docked, to check for debris it may have gathered and remove the debris before its next flight to save on travel time to its next destination."

"Thoughts?"

"No fucking way! It can't be that easy."

"Fucking way! It appears that it is that easy! In Kdackan phraseology, we would be like a remora attached to a shark. "

"So all we have to do is flip you belly-up and let the magno-flow do all the work for us."

"No guarantees of whether we could pass through the Gates still attached, but it seems like our best bet. I also have enough power to push off the magnetic draw should the need arise."

"Did the reprogramming work so that anyone can fly you whether they had Kdackan DNA or not?"

"Better to find out now rather than later, captain. I'm in a dock, and no engines are on. Put your hands in the controls and give me a quick turn or two."

Chuckie did as suggested and felt a vibration like

none he'd ever experienced before. He was familiar with the power he could exert with a few strokes on a keyboard and bring his enemies to their knees, but this power was something different. Something *other.* It was visceral.

"Easy now. Keep it short, or your partners back in Cargo will crash into each other and wonder what the fuck was that."

Chuckie moved his hands to the left and back to the right for no more than a moment.

"What the fuck was that?" Meehix was there a few moments later.

"Are we under attack?" John was right behind her.

"Grab hold of the floor!"

They had neither a chance nor choice.

"Chuckie N is in the house!" He rocked them up and down and sideways and backward.

Chuckie jerked his hands out of the controls when he saw his partners rolling helplessly on the floor, looking for something to grab.

"Whoa! Sorry!"

"I'm guessing that my DNA is no longer needed to fly this hap-trap?" John was prone behind the copilot's seat.

"It seems that my reprogramming was successful."

"We'll never reprogram you again!" Meehix's head was on the floor with her feet above her ass and resting halfway up on the entrance door.

"Problem?" Chuckie asked from the comfort of the pilot's seat.

"You could have warned us." Meehix righted herself.

"Where would the fun in *that* be? Besides, you two need

to learn how to go with the flow because you never know when something unexpected might happen."

"Everything that's happened to me since I left off on a game to hook up with Gage for a quick scope-out of a seemingly harmless building has been unexpected."

"Whining is not very becoming, bro. Ship and I have a few more logistics to work out, so why don't you two toddle off and go play with your cubes?"

The members of NutBusters, Inc. made good use of their time while waiting to dispatch. John and Meehix spent a few hours each day in Cargo learning every cube of the Bargeflat 489 with Ship getting creative about inserting pirates, other mercs, and an occasional officious jerk-prick with a paper that needed to be signed.

They also hit the home base gym for an hour or two each day. John would never beat Meehix on the cardio machines, but he was lasting longer before calling *"No mas."*

Chuckie had also been splitting his time between Ship and the base. The auto-driver company had assigned one driver to be at their every beck and call. Chuckie was working every angle.

He had the demon's niece to rescue as their main mission—*can't wait to meet her!*—the merc-work, which should be a laidback easy affair, and one other small item in the shipment that might be worth the effort to snatch up along the way.

He hadn't been able to find out what the item was, but he recognized the shipper's name, Flitzbart. The item wasn't insured. Insurance would throw up red flags that whatever Flitzbart was shipping was of extraordinary worth and needed to be stolen at any cost. It would be a small electronic item that they were probably sending to one of their other facilities for testing and refinement before marketing.

Whatever it was, *Chuckie wants!*

Between the workouts in the cubes and the gym, Meehix and John had done more sweating together than newlyweds on a tropical honeymoon spending five days in bed, but neither of them was confident enough to make the first pass.

Meehix kept the batteries charged but was afraid she might wear out her vag-vibe, pussy-pleaser, and girl's best friend.

John had gone from cold showers to ice baths.

To be fair, they both thought but never shared, *if they weren't sharing a house with Chuckie, things might be a little less complicated if they wanted to have conversations about copulating.*

CHAPTER EIGHTEEN

"In my next life, I want to be a mercenary."

"Why is that, Krock?" Zloe had a lot of notices on his desk to work through, and Krock had given him another one.

"You get hired, do a lot of nothing, and retire after a few star-circles." He pointed at the form he'd laid on Zloe's desk.

"Nice work if you can get it." Zloe hated it when Krock started sharing fantasies about his next life. In this life, all he knew was that he was stuck pushing papers with a coworker who would rather dream of anything other than his next twenty star-circles before he could collect his retirement pay.

"The Kdackan shipment." Krock stared at a crack in a wall wishing, not for the first time, that they had a window in the office. "They need ten mercs. One of them has to be from Kdack. A company calling themselves the NutBusters just sent us two. One a Kdackan USSF member and one who's registered as a slave."

"Two mercs down, eight to go." Zloe put his digital stamp on it, hoping that Krock had other mercs applying to complete the request for ten. Krock continued contemplating the crack in the wall.

"This crack started at the bottom of the wall and is working its way up. A little zig here, a little zag there, but always up. Never sideways. Do you ever wonder if that's the way life should go? Always up with a few misdirections here and there but never turning sideways and leveling off as a simple flat line?"

"*You* are a flat line. *I* am a flat line. Our *jobs* are a flat line. Steady and straight. If you want to explore other directions, bend over to examine the origins of the crack. I'll do you the courtesy of kicking your crack, and we'll see in which direction you'll fly."

"Are you upset with me? I didn't mean to upset you."

"I'm not as upset as I will be if you don't find me eight more mercs by the end of the day. They've scheduled the transport ship to take off tomorrow, and we don't want to be the ones responsible for keeping it docked, do we?"

"No. I suppose not. I'll go and see if I can find another eight." Krock sighed and headed off to find eight other merc applications. Now that they'd filled the Kdackan stipulation, it shouldn't be too hard of a job.

"Onward and upward are dangerous directions," Zloe mumbled after Krock had left. "Sideways has always been the safest path to follow."

Their home base was secured and protected by a safeguard shield that wouldn't let anyone get within thirty feet of it without lasering off parts of their anatomy. The NutBusters headed for Ship.

They were heading for Space Station Frommix I, where a fully packed Bargeflat 489 awaited the arrival of two mercs, one of them a Kdackan and an unexpected remora.

"This is your captain speaking. Passengers have arrived. Shippewa ready for takeoff as soon as all baggage is stored."

Storing the baggage turned out to be the easy part. The hard part started when Chuckie, Meehix, and John returned to the cabin and John headed for the pilot's seat.

"Fuck you and your DNA. I can fly this ship now too, lard-ass!" Chuckie elbowed John out of the way.

"Fuck the both of you!" Meehix threw two elbows, each one making a solid connection, and took her seat. Slipping her hands into the controls felt like she'd downed a pitcher of dibble-blinks without having to worry about the consequences that might follow.

"Buckle up, boys! Next stop, Frommix I!"

She didn't bother to wait for any replies. *Let the big boys fend for themselves.*

The boys held onto each other and whatever else they could grab as the wild woman put her metal boots to the pedal.

"A Gate is coming up. I do hope you remember the code."

"I could recite it in my sleep! Chill out, Ship!"

"I'll try."

Into the gate. Out of the gate. She was a woman on a

mission and also in control. *I'm one dangerous fuck of a combination.*

John found himself with Chuckie on his lap in the copilot's seat, having somehow managed to get them both buckled in after the pre-takeoff tussle.

"I'm comfy. How are you, big guy?"

"I'm good, but there's room enough in this seat for two. How's about you scooch over a little bit to your left?"

Scooching mission accomplished, they settled in for the rest of the ride.

Meehix found a docking bay on Frommix I and burned up a few NutBusters credits to get the most convenient one. It was only a one-minute walk up a flight of stairs to the next level where a monstrosity of a Bargeflat 489 had docked as it was being loaded and readied for take-off the next day.

Her crooked-ass self-satisfied smile would look the same no matter which direction you were viewing it from. It was a combination of *I Love you* and *fuck you if you don't love me too.*

"Are we there yet?"

"Bet your Kdackan ass! We are there! All yours to explain, Ship. Thank you for the pleasure of letting me take everyone for a ride."

"Ship?" John was almost afraid to ask.

"I am docked one level below the Bargeflat 489. Once you and Meehix make your mercenary appearance, Chuckie N will guide me to do a flip and attach my humble self onto its bottom."

"That was the plan, right boys?" Her grin seemed like a permanent part of her face.

Neither of them could argue. So far, the first part of the plan had gone like clockwork. Other than who was going to fly Ship, but the boys knew who had won *that* battle, and they were now safely docked for the night.

"Next step?" Captain-merc-slave Meehix asked.

"Weapons check." John dug deep and recalled both his gaming lessons and his real-life game lessons when he was still an athlete.

"One last run-through. Jojacko and Meehix board the cargo ship because we are mercs and the NutBusters have a demon's niece to rescue."

"They might have one other item to collect along the way." Chuckie chose that moment to remind them.

"Meanwhile, you and Ship can skip away any time you please." Meehix chose that moment to remind Chuckie N.

"Chuck Norris never skipped away from anything! Especially when it involved friends!" Chuckie reminded Meehix.

"Have those of you who have actual emotions, or friends, gotten those emotions out of your systems yet?"

"No!"

There was an intensity in John's tone that silenced them all.

"I have a friend. His name is Gage Gonzalez. It's because of him that I'm even here now! I would bet my first earned dollar that he's in Albuquerque, right now, working on how to save the aliens on planet Earth, or Kdack 3a, whatever you want to call it."

"Gay-jaw is a Kdackan male. I doubt he's even given a moment's thought to us after I tossed a pheromone his way."

"Shut the fuck up!"

They did.

"His name is Gage! It rhymes with cage! Anyone ever been in a cage before?"

Resounding silence because it seemed like a rhetorical question.

"Well, I've been in a cage. It was one of my making. I was so wrapped up in my world that I never gave two shits about the world around me. I was Jojacko, the kick-ass king of the gaming world. In my spare time, I created Hannah, who is now Ship's nearest and dearest."

"Hannah-banana is something special, John."

"You shut the fuck up too, Ship! Where was I?"

"Gay-jaw?" Meehix dared to chime in. *When he gets passionate, he really gets passionate. I'm going to get me some of that eventually.*

"Gage, right. Right now, back on Kdack, or Earth, or whatever the fuck you want to call it, my best friend is working to help free the aliens on Earth. Not because he can make millions of profit from it, but because I asked him to, and as a friend, he will do his damnedest to follow through. Chuckie."

"Umm, yes?"

"Have you ever had a friend like that? One who you could trust from the highest of heavens to the deepest pits of hell?"

Chuckie N looked around.

"Yes. I believe that I now might have a few."

"Good. I hope I'm one of them." Rant ended, John took the time to smile at his partners. "Here's the thing about friends. There will be times that you hate them because they can get themselves, and you, into trouble that you never asked for.

"There will also be times that you hate them because they know more about you than you wish they knew. They'll know all of your faults, all of the times you've failed at something, and just how much of a loser you can be. Show of hands of how many in this cabin have ever felt like a loser?"

Hands of the two Dolurulodans went up.

"You know what? Your friends won't fucking care! How cool is that?"

Chuckie leaned into John and smiled up at him. "Are you saying you love me?"

Realizing that he and Chuckie were still belted together in the copilot's seat, John released the buckle and shoved the little smartass to the floor.

Chuckie landed on his feet and leaned back against the front console. "You two run along now and get us a room for the night, someplace with a bar. I'll catch up as soon as Ship and I run through a few contingency plans."

A couple of hours later, Chuckie found them at the hotel bar. There would be no dibble-blinks tonight since they had a nine o'clock mercenary check-in the next morning. The food was buffet-style. Chuckie loaded up his plate and joined them.

"Any more info on the barge's itinerary?" John asked as Chuckie scooted up into his seat and started to dig in.

"One galactic Gate, it's a short one, so Ship and I should

be able to stay attached. If we don't, the first stop is Station Xenon, so we can always catch up to you there. It's a simple traveler's stop. Refuel, drop off some cargo for other carriers to pick up, and off again. The next Gate is more difficult to get to."

"Is it far?" Meehix wasn't familiar with this part of the galaxy.

"It's not the distance that's the issue. There's an asteroid belt to navigate. Nothing too dangerous, but it will be a slow-go to get through. I haven't been able to track the first destination after they make the second Gate."

"If Operation Remora works during the first Gate, does that mean it'll hold through the second?" John didn't know if the size or lengths of the Gates would make a difference.

"One way to find out. Whoa, their flibblub doesn't totally suck." He held out a forkful of it to John, who passed.

"Thanks, but no. Anything more on Vix?"

"I think, but can't guarantee, that she's on the third deck, Section C, Bay 12."

"And the other item you want us to look for? Can you give us more of a clue?" Since this might be their last chance to talk face-to-face, Meehix wanted to know more about this item that Chuckie had been insistent on stealing but elusive about.

"You wanna try the flibblub?" He held a forkful out to her. She aimed a sharp kick under the table at where his ankle should be but had forgotten to adjust for his shortness.

"Oww! What did I do?" John yelped as Meehix's boot connected with his ankle.

"Nothing this time, John. I was practicing for the future." Meehix smiled, never wanting to let the warning of a potential ankle kick go to waste.

"Chuckie? The item?"

Seeing the pain on John's face and not wanting to have the same look on his, Chuckie did his best to come clean.

"It'll be something small, probably small enough to stick in your pocket, but might be packed in a crate large enough to hold a full-grown Grimler."

"That certainly narrows it down." Meehix rubbed a foot gently across John's ankle to apologize for her misdirected kick.

"What you need to look for is a crate that has Flitzbart stamped on it. It won't be in a section with a freezing unit or one with a heating unit."

"Okay. So it's not food or flowers." John always enjoyed the game of Twenty Questions and wondered if his last statement would qualify as a question.

"Neither food nor flowers. Next question?"

Nineteen to go. "Probably small enough to fit in a pocket. So, under five pounds?"

"That's my guess."

Focus, John. He kicked himself under the table because he wanted to win with fifteen questions still left to go and felt like he'd missed something. Ten seconds later, he thought he had it.

"What is Flitzbart?"

"The cognitive ability of Kdackans has been vastly underrated."

John had him, and Chuckie knew it. He was also glad to have made a friend who wasn't four levels below his intellect.

"It's an electronics firm."

"They're working on a prototype of something. Probably still in its beta stage."

Chuckie nodded as John worked it out.

"And one of them is packed on board...a disc or a chip or a drive of some kind."

"Go ahead and try to lie by telling me that you don't want to get your hands on it."

John stuck out a fork and stabbed one of the two pieces of the flibblub left on Chuckie's plate.

"Bon Appetit."

John chewed and swallowed. "Tastes like chicken."

With Chuckie back on board Ship the next morning, Hix and Jo found themselves standing in a long corded line. Both had dressed like mercenaries ready to kill before taking the time to ask any questions and carried bags that wouldn't pass through any metal detectors anywhere without being totally emptied.

The line snaked back and forth as hundreds of people took one slow step forward in unison.

"I'm seeing people."

"Of course you're seeing people. It's a long-fuck line, John, and we're stuck in it. We should've gotten here earlier, but I guess it's one of the contingencies we didn't see coming."

"No, Meehix." He scooted his bag one step forward on the floor as the line continued its slow crawl. "I'm not seeing aliens. I'm seeing people!"

Meehix used a foot to nudge her bag a few inches further.

"Are we having an epiphany moment?" Meehix knew that one of them was. *About fucking time.*

She gave him all the time he needed to take the scene in because she'd been waiting quite a while for this moment.

"I'm there." John smiled at her. "I'm finally there."

"Welcome to galactic reality, John from Kdack 3a." Meehix smiled back at him. There was no need to say anything more because she could see it in his eyes, and they still had half an hour of scooting bags ahead of them before they reached the end of the roped corridor.

"Yesterday, you were talking about Gage."

"You've been practicing."

"Yes, names are important to learn how to say properly. Just ask Jxzobbliningozlinxfipple. I'm sorry that I didn't give your friend's name the same respect. It's just that my short experiences with Kdackan males led me to the conclusion that their attention span only lasted until the next cute ass walked by."

"Yellow chick bending over to pick up and move her luggage two rows behind us. I wouldn't mind rear-ending her caboose."

"Yo! Clitipian! Bend with the knees!"

The males waiting in line with spouses or children in tow diverted their eyes quickly and hoped they looked innocent. The other males in line would have stared daggers at Meehix, but the fact that she had already dressed for battle gave no one any desire to get into a tussle with her.

She looked back at John, unsure if she wanted to head-smack, shin-kick, or kiss him. He looked down and scooted both of their bags a foot farther along.

"Hix and Jo, taking care of business," was all he said.

At the end of the corded line, they faced five different counters, without a clue about which one they should head for. Fortunately, there was an animitron waiting for them.

"Purpose of travel?"

"Mercenaries looking to board the Bargeflat 489." John offered the authorization papers.

"Expendable Resources. Counter C."

"Expendable resources?"

Meehix grabbed his arm. "You can't argue with an animitron. Counter C is our next stop." She moved him along.

"I'm an expendable resource?" John had no choice but to follow his dragged arm.

"All mercenaries are." Meehix was trying not to draw any more attention to them than necessary. "Being an expendable resource is several steps higher than being a *non-sentient being* slash *slave!* Welcome to my world." She kissed his cheek. "Onward?"

"Onward." The partners made their way to Counter C.

The line at Counter C was much shorter, and they passed through to a waiting area with benches built into the walls and a couple of tables with stools that swung out bolted to the floor.

They found a space to sit and looked around at the other occupants. It was an odd assortment, maybe a couple of dozen, and Meehix and John played the game of trying to pick out which ones would be their fellow mercs.

"The table across the way." Meehix nodded. John followed her gaze.

"Why them?"

"They're playing bones-down. It's a simple game that doesn't require much brain capacity and is more of a time killer than anything else. Plus, they're all dressed in similar clothes."

"Not totally unlike us. Probably a team?"

"A team with a 'been there, done that, another boring job to collect a paycheck' attitude."

John leaned back against the wall, trying to match their demeanor. *Just another day at the office.*

"Mercs for the Bargeflat 489?" a man who'd entered from a side door called. His uniform suggested a low-level security-type guard. The bones-down table stood, as did four separate others of various sizes and outfits.

None of them looked anywhere near being dangerous and certainly not as well-armed as him and Hix.

"I guess that's our cue." He stood and shouldered his bag. Meehix did the same, and they joined the group following their guide.

Fifteen minutes later, having traversed several ramps, two moving walkways, and an elevator, they beheld the ship. It was a big bastard of a carrier.

"Virtual reality didn't do the size justice," Meehix whispered as the guard led them in and down more ramps and hallways and more twists and turns as they made their way to merc quarters.

"We should have brought a map."

"Or a family-sized bag of bread crumbs," John agreed.

CHAPTER NINETEEN

Captain Richnot Johenimeihn, known to his crew as RJ, was scouring manifest reports. Half the trick of being a space pirate was figuring out which transport ship to attack. His crew didn't mind spilling a little blood during a raid. In fact, for many of them, it was the favorite part of their career choice, but piracy was still a business, and businesses ran on profit and loss.

He could have worked his way up corporate ladders and made a great CEO or the emperor of a small planet, but the adventure stories he'd heard of being a pirate had captured his attention from a very early age. The part that the exciting pirate stories had always left out was all the goddam planning that went into a raid. Tedious, thorough, and dare he say, *boooring!*

"We ever hit a 489 before?"

One of the other parts of being a pirate, especially for a captain, was knowing who he could trust. Pirates weren't notorious for being loyal, but his two lieutenants, Ice and

Spid, would follow him to hell and back, with hell eventually being all of their final destinations.

"A Bargeflat?" Ice, a Cyclopian with one eye in the middle of his forehead, looked up from sharpening a short-sword. "Are any of them still in service?"

"At least one, and it's headed in our direction."

"I thought you'd notice that." Spid looked up from his keyboard.

Ice had earned his nickname by having once sliced through ten mercenaries, three robo-guards, and two Crom Limeans without working up a sweat. Spid had earned his nickname by having four arms, four legs, and a brain that never slept when he spun out webs to search for potential plunder possibilities. RJ was RJ because *Richnot* wasn't something to aspire to.

"The Kdackan goods caught my eye too, which is why I sent it along to you." Spid was glad it had caught the captain's eye.

"Do we know what the goods are?"

"No, sir." Spid referred to the information on his screen. "All I have is that the shipper insured them for three hundred fifty thousand credits with a declared value of half a mil. Current open market value estimated at six hundred fifty thousand."

"Kdackan's are not famous for correctly evaluating products."

"Correct. It's always a crapshoot with them. But let's say that they're right this time. We hit the shipment, and there are only ten mercs assigned to protect the Kdack goods, and that's all we're going in for.

"We sell the goods for six hundred fifty thousand, pay

off the insurance company their three hundred fifty thousand, plus another thirty-five thousand to cover their paper-burying fees, and we're over two hundred thousand in profit."

"I like it." RJ nodded. "Sounds like it might be worth the effort. How much extra will it cost us to pay off the mercenaries? Every credit counts."

"It's hard to factor in that cost when we don't know if the mercs are dedicated to their protection mission or out to collect a paycheck. You know how unpredictable they can be."

RJ sighed. "It was so much simpler when we could plunder at will before insurance companies, and *bargaining* and paper-fucking-work got involved."

"I agree." Spid agreed because it wasn't a good idea to argue with the captain at any given time, especially when he was right.

"How the hell did Kdackans get involved in this?

"I don't know. When it comes to negotiating with the mercs, it would probably be better for our profit margin if we killed them."

Someone had said the magic word, causing Ice to leave off his blade sharpening for a moment as he looked up and joined the conversation for the first time.

"Let's hit it!" He went back to his blades.

"Toñito, my Tito, my little bro." Gage leaned over the stroller he'd splurged on as the CEO of SAFA to make sure he'd adjusted the shade protector properly. "When we get to Lieb's, if you don't tell Mom, I will buy you the first item you point to at the candy counter as a special treat."

Tito giggled up at him, not understanding a single word that Gage said. Words were not one of Tito's specialties, especially considering that he'd yet to utter one, but he knew a smile when he saw one. His big brother had a killer smile.

It was a rare day off for the Gonzalez's. Gage had decided to take his little brother up to the corner store, where he planned to pick up a twelve-pack for his dad to help ease his pain after watching tomorrow's loss to the Planos.

He'd splurged on the stroller from the SAFA funds and explained to his parents that the money had come from Jojacko, who was still off on his work-study but sent some money back to buy birthday presents for Toñito and Isabella.

Their neighborhood in Albuquerque didn't have a large Jewish population, but the Lieb's represented them well. They'd run the corner store since before Gage had been born. Hershel and Hilga, the children of immigrants themselves, had a special empathy for those who held onto their family traditions no matter how far away their physical or spiritual homeland was, and Gage had always enjoyed heading up there to buy something.

He'd even managed to learn a few words in Yiddish along the way. He had "Oy vey" down pat.

It wasn't a tan DeVille he spotted that distracted him from his pleasant reverie. It was a black sedan with darkened windows parked half a block down with potentially ominous intentions.

"Fuuuuuck."

"Fuck," repeated Tito, his baby brother's very first spoken word. Gage quickly leaned into the stroller and faced his brother down.

"Oy vey! Oy vey! Oy vey! Not *fuck* as your first word!"

"Oy fuck," came the response.

"Shit! Mom is going to kill us both!"

"Oy fuck shit."

Toñito wasn't helpful at all! Gage decided that his dad's beer and little brother's treat could wait and spun the stroller back toward home, hearing the sedan's engine coming to life behind him and hoping he could make it back to his front door before the agents could catch up to him.

"Oh my God, it's Gonzo Gage!"

"No way!"

"Way!"

Three thirteen-year-old girls ran across the street, screeching in a way that only thirteen-year-old girls could do, and practically accosted him while jumping up and down in delight and pulling out their cell phones.

"You're the Gage Master, right?" The leader of them managed to get in the first question mid-jump and squeal.

He saw the black sedan pause, pull off, and park again, leaving the engine running.

"I'm nobody's *master,* but I am a Gage."

"I knew it, I knew it, I knew it!" the leader turned to the others. "Told'ja's!" She turned back to Gage.

"I'm Becka." She pointed at her friends. "That's Yolanda and Tam, Tamie for short."

"Hi, girls." *Maybe Gonzo Gage did have groupies. If Jojacko could see me now.* "The cute little guy in the stroller is Toñito, Tito for short."

"He *is* cute!" Yolanda snatched Tito up, spun him around, and handed him off to Tam.

"And short!" Tam continued the spin.

"Short and cute won't clean your clothes when he pukes on you," Gage advised. "Putting him back in his stroller would be my best advice right now."

Tam stopped her spinning and gently put Tito back into place. The black sedan revved its engine.

Probably not the best time to stop-drop-and-moon Agents Bixby and Shaw.

"Anyone up for some selfies?" Gage decided it was in his best interests to keep the young groupies around for a while. *The price of fame.*

"Here's the deal," he stepped back and gave them his best *serious* stare. It seemed to work because the squealers stopped squealing. The sedan hadn't moved. He fussed with the stroller as casually as he could and spoke to the three teen girls who were no more than five years older than his little sister Isabella.

"Yes, I'm Gonzo Gage, in real life and off the air."

"You're not gonna hook up with the sluts who want to have your babies are you?"

Gage wanted to take another step back, but the sedan was still hovering.

"No, *chicas.* SAFA is a serious organization with a very serious mission. I'm just the face of it, speaking the truth to anyone with ears to hear."

He fussed with the stroller a little more, not wanting to get the girls involved and yet needing them. He suddenly realized that the sedan's occupants could hear anything he might say with some kind of listening device aimed in his direction, and he might have already said too much.

"It's hot out here. Anyone want ice cream?" he spun the stroller back around. "Tito has money to burn and wants to spend it at Lieb's."

"Cool!" Tam grabbed for the stroller handle. "I get to drive!"

"Oy fuck," came the response from the passenger, and off to Lieb's they went. The black sedan pulled away, its occupants deciding to wait for a less crowded sidewalk to snatch the fucking Gonzo Gage up from.

A twelve-pack secured on the bottom of the stroller later, Gage led his groupies outside Lieb's, ice creams in hand. Hilga had given him a sheet of cardboard and a Sharpie, smiling at the young children who seemed to be enjoying themselves. She knew that the beer was for Gage's dad because it wasn't the first time that Papa Gonzalez had sent his young son up there with a note to let him bring one home.

Gage suddenly realized that the girls might become targets of the agents. They might be in danger if they started posting selfies all over their social media pages.

"Here's the deal, *chicas*." Gage tried his best to explain as his groupies enjoyed their ice cream back on the sidewalk. "I am *not* Gonzo Gage."

"You told us you were!" Tam was crestfallen.

"I lied. I happen to look a lot like him. You three aren't the first ones who've got us confused with each other. To be honest, I'm tired of him and his *crap*. Really. Aliens from outer space held as slaves on Earth? What kind of shit has that dude been smoking?"

"You're not Gonzo Gage?" Becka looked like the ground had fallen out from beneath her feet.

"No, kid. My name is Inigo Montoya, the man who just bought you ice cream. Prepare to eat."

With that parting line, Gage left the girls on the sidewalk and wheeled his Tito home, trying to make him repeat *Oy vey, Oy vey.*

Oy fuck vey was the response from the stroller.

Throwing his arms up and explaining to his mom that Tito's first words must have come from a Muppet movie seemed like his best defense when he got home.

Putting the beer in the fridge, and handing one to his dad as he watched his favorite team lose another match was his second strategic move.

How's that for knowing how to game, Jojacko?

"Are we actually going to get into a fight this time, or will we stand there looking all scary and shit as the captain negotiates?"

RJ had guided his ship into the asteroid field and set it down on one of the larger ones where they could chill and wait for their prey to pass through. They had two sleep cycles to kill before there would be any action or non-action, and Ice was running his men through their paces with weapons and hand-to-hand combat practice.

"What are you saying, Blat? You'd rather fight and risk

your life than be a bones-down clown for a couple of hours?"

"Bet your fuckin' ass, sir."

Ice loved his crew. It did get three shades of boring when bloodlust was flowing, only to have to sit back as the standard negotiations went on, and everyone knew that the deal would go down and there would be no actual fighting.

"There might be some actual action on this one, boys. RJ has decided that he's not going to negotiate with the mercs hired to protect the cargo. If they decide to surrender and slink away, all we can do is taunt them as they run. Those are the rules. But if the ten mercs discover that they have two pairs of balls between them, it's party time."

"Party! Party! Party!" rose the chant. Ice let the chant rise and come back down to rest. He knew how to inspire his men.

"Will there be any Crom Limeans?" someone called. "I wanna face some down like you once did."

"What's your name, boy?"

"Brittig, sir." He stepped forward and faced the lieutenant. "They're mean fuckers, but ain't near as bad as they think they are and I wanna prove it."

"Up close and personal, or from a safe distance with a flitgun while hiding behind a pillar?"

"Up close and personal, sir."

"Then bring it!"

Brittig brought it. Ice engaged him in battle. Short swords and knives flashed in a furious flurry. Bloodlust was in the air. Ice's soldier was holding his own and thought he had the notorious Ice at his mercy when he suddenly found a four-foot-long sword under his crotch about to slice its way up to his chin.

"You forgot about the Crom's stinging tail, didn't you?"

"And you forgot about vlotters." Brittig had pulled one out of a boot and had it aimed to do some serious damage.

Ice was impressed. He sheathed his long sword and shoved the feisty one back, feeling proud of himself for teaching the lesson. Of course, he knew Brittig had the vlotter strapped and ready to use. He hadn't been sure if Brittig would remember he had it during the heat of battle.

"That's how you do it, gentlemen. You've never won a battle until your opponent is dead. It's either him or you. Which shall it be?"

"Him!" came the unanimous response.

"Then live it, prove it or die!"

Ice stepped back and watched them have at each other. Such a glorious sight. Sure, there were a few flesh wounds, and he almost lost someone when a gun actually fired, but that's how you kept the troops fresh and on their toes.

Please, mercs, grow a pair and give us a fight.

CHAPTER TWENTY

Operation Remora went off as planned. Ship and Chuckie made it through the first Gate, attached to the Bargeflat tighter than a tick on a nipple.

The massive barge was docked for the night on Space Station Xenon as the crew unloaded some cargo and brought new loads on board. There was only one more piece of freight not listed on any manifest that needed to be loaded.

"Ship?"

"Yes, John?"

"You're still attached?"

"Would I be answering if I wasn't?"

"Give me the comm-stick!" After a little static, Meehix took control of the conversation.

"Where do we find you?"

"Hello, Meehix. Pleasant flight so far?"

"No time for shit, Ship. Where are you?"

"Bottom level. Find Door 4-B."

Meehix and John headed that way.

"Okay." They'd reached it. "Now what?"

"I would suggest opening it."

They did. Chuckie made his entrance, carrying a small bag that they all knew held his Mixie. Not wanting to spend time with greetings or being discovered, they left the immediate area, huddled between a stack of crates, and waited for an alarm to go off for a door opening.

Resounding silence filled the air.

"What a fuck-piece of security system they have." Chuckie looked around. "Where do I bunk?"

"You're now an additional merc. You bunk with the rest of us." It took John all the effort he had not to grab him up in another bear hug and spin him around.

Meehix looked him straight in his eyes. "Welcome aboard, Chuckie N."

They made their way back to merc quarters, and Chuckie claimed a spare bed. Ten mercs, eleven mercs, who was counting.

The Chuckster had joined the party. John treated himself to a smile.

The next morning the mercs strapped in as the Barge-flat took off to make its slow way through the asteroid field and to the next Gate. Once away from the station, they unbuckled and were free to roam. As big as the 489 was, its design meant a minimum crew could run it, so there wasn't a lot of activity or workers to avoid.

The group of mercenaries had been given a tour before undocking so they knew the location of the cargo they were protecting. John and Meehix gave Chuckie the same tour. There was a large crate, roughly six-by-eight feet, located on the third deck with red, white, and blue Kdack

3a stickers pasted all over it. Alongside were several smaller boxes with the same stickers, six in all, and neatly stacked.

Fortunately, if Chuckie's guess was right, that was the same level Vix was on, which meant they wouldn't seem out of place as they wandered around trying to locate her.

Chuckie carried Mixie in a shoulder bag. He'd made major improvements in his new U-B-Dead program and was anxious to try it out. Having Shippewa attached over a cargo door made it easier to find the demon's niece, let her and Chuckie escape back to ship, and Meehix and John could slip out after the next Gate.

If Ship's magnetic attachment held through the Gate, all was good. If it didn't, Meehix and John would remain on board, and Chuckie could pilot Ship to the 489's next docking location, which Chuckie now knew was Space Station Tryon 2.

"Any luck on locating the Flitzbart crate?"

"It's a big fuck ship, Chuckie. Your guess is as good as mine." John's focus now was getting a fix on Vixaleen. They paused at a Cargo Logistics workstation. With no one around, Chuckie slipped Mixie out of her bag, attached her to a spare port, ran his U-B-Dead, and had them both located ten seconds later. John was impressed.

"Is that what you've been working on?"

Chuckie nodded as he slipped Mixie back into her bag.

"Sweet." Even sweeter, the succubus and the Flitzbart container were both on the same level.

"Are you sure the Flitzbart is worth stealing?" John wasn't sure if they'd have enough time to both rescue and steal.

"Is life worth living?" was Chuckie's answer.

"So far."

"It'll be a lot more worth living if Flitzbart is shipping what I think they are."

"Not that anyone asked me," Meehix interjected, "but if they had, I'd say fuck the succubus and go for the big prize."

"I hope to do both." Chuckie headed for the Flitzbart first.

It ended up being a very small package, and Chuckie slipped it into his bag with Mixie without taking the time to open it, which annoyed John because his curiosity was killing him.

"Don't be a whiner. We got a demon's niece to rescue."

The pilot of the big barge was guiding his ship carefully through the asteroid field, but a dodge here and duck there caused a little wobbliness for those who hadn't remained strapped in. Nonetheless, they managed to find the niece right where expected.

Her crate was laid flat on the floor, with a few grommeted air holes for breathing purposes. The container had an electronic lock, but Chuckie had it open within seconds. Still undetected, it should be easy for them all to make their way to the bottom level and Door 4-B where Ship was waiting, and they could get their mercenary and thieving asses to safety with both prizes.

John only knew succubi from various games, and each one offered a different representation. Big tits and long legs were usually their most prominent features. John wasn't opposed to either or both options, so it took him by surprise when the crate door opened and they found a little waif of a sleeping young woman.

Vix had her uncle's side of the family's bright red skin and straight pitch-black hair that passed her waist. Several layers of what seemed to be thin diaphanous sheets wrapped her body.

"She looks so innocent."

"She's heavily medicated." Meehix didn't want to give John any more time to admire the innocent-looking creature. "She's had thousands of years of nearly fucking men to death to feed her appetite, so now is *not* the time to get all sentimental."

Chuckie wanted to snatch, grab, and run before anyone discovered them and other difficulties presented themselves.

"You two might be ready for battle, but I'm a lover, not a fighter, and if any pirates *do* attack us, I'd rather not be part of the welcoming committee. Can we pick up the pace here?"

John snatched the sleeping niece up into his arms, but she was heavier than she looked. He wasn't sure how far he could carry her as they headed for the three flights of stairs and the back cargo area, where Ship waited on the other side of Door 4-B to get them all the fuck out and away as fast as possible.

Against her better judgment, Meehix gave the drugged-up succubus a shot that would wake her up so she could walk instead of being carried the whole way.

She soon regretted her decision as the tramp came to in

John's arms and had her tongue in his ear and a hand reaching for his crotch before he'd had a chance to set her gently down. He did manage to toss and drop her, though thankfully not in Chuckie's direction because the bitch was hungry.

Meehix grabbed one of her arms and held on tight as she dragged her along.

"I'm hungry. Can I have the big one first and the little one for dessert?"

"No, Vix." Meehix, having once been a prisoner herself, almost felt sorry for her. "Your Uncle Phil sent us to rescue you, and escaping comes before sex."

"But I want sex and I want it now!"

"I hear ya. Believe me, I hear you! Now focus!" *You whiny little slut.*

That's when the first alarm sounded.

"Shit!" John turned to Meehix. "That's the alarm for the mercs!"

"The pirates chose *now* to invade?"

A sudden flurry of activity made it impossible for them to get to the bottom level so they headed for the mercenaries' room to grab their weapons and stash Chuckie and their recently rescued succubus.

The other mercs had already rushed out. They left Vix in Chuckie's care.

"Don't!" Meehix pointed first at Chuckie as she was gearing up.

"Don't what?" Chuckie was the model of innocence.

"Just don't! And you!" she pointed at Vix. "You're looking a little chunky. It wouldn't hurt you to miss a meal."

"Just make sure you stay hidden and out of the way and out of *harm's* way." John felt the heat of a battle coming on. "Hopefully, we can keep the fighting away from you two, and you can make a run to the bottom level and the door. Stay here for now and make sure the coast is clear before you do anything stupid."

John strapped on his second ankle holster.

"Ready, Hix."

"Right with you, Jo." The two badass mercs went looking for trouble or to at least find the other mercs who should be near the Kdackan shipments they were here to protect.

"This is Captain RJ, of the good ship *Whoozaloo*. To whom do I have the pleasure of speaking?"

"Admiral Angiere." The admiral took the mic. "In charge of the Bargeflat 489 whose progress you are impeding. Please move your ship out of our way so we may proceed without causing your craft any damage."

"Come now, Admiral. You know it doesn't work like that. We both know that we on the *Whoozaloo* are more than capable of doing much more damage with me not even needing to leave my cockpit than you're able to do to us. Bargeflats are for transport, not battle."

For appearance's sake, Admiral Angiere had to pause the communication, letting the pirates know that he was giving the current situation some serious thought before making a decision.

"That is, indeed, the *Whoozaloo*, Admiral." The pilot, Lackmere, spoke up.

"And RJ?" the second mate, Knockabee, chimed in. "We're dealing with first-rate pirates here, Admiral, not some newbie who thinks he needs some scary-sounding name like that last loser who attacked us. What did he call himself?"

"Dickbeard the Deadly, I think." Lackmere chuckled. "Whooo, he had us sooo scared."

"Dickbeard." Even the admiral had to smile at the visual image that name conjured up.

"He could have used Penis Nose the Protruding," Lackmere suggested.

"Or maybe Genital the Gargantuan," Knockabee joined the fun.

"Enough." The admiral turned the comm back on. "Captain RJ, your reputation and that of your crew precede you. We would be honored if you would inform us of your intentions so we can make the best accommodations for your needs."

Ice was with Spid and the captain in the main cabin, and he wasn't happy. His fired-up troops were ready to go with dreams of mercenary blood. He didn't relish having to tell them that it looked like the admiral of the Bargeflat was going to give up without any intention of putting up a fuss.

"We are primarily here to relieve you of your Kdackan shipment. You are much too large a carrier for us to search through every nook and cranny trying to find anything else of value."

"You realize that the Kdackan goods are insured and have ten mercenaries ready to protect them."

"We are aware of that."

"This group looks like they might be taking their jobs seriously. I can't guarantee that they'll give up the shipment without putting up a fight."

"Yes!" The admiral heard an as yet unidentified voice coming from the background from the pirates' end of the conversation.

"Yes, we're aware of that." RJ aimed a shushing motion at Ice. "We are quite willing to deal with the mercenaries. They often put up a brave front but are also often willing to negotiate. Don't worry about the mercs. We will negotiate with them separately."

Ice left the cabin to give his troops the good news.

"The Kdackan goods are on Level Three, but to open the bay doors for you to enter and dock would require more people than I currently have assigned on that level. If you wish to dock there, I'll have to pull crews from another level.

"That means paying them extra because Level Three is a pay upgrade from where they're currently assigned. You can dock on Level Two, but it's a lot of stairs and a fair distance from the Kdackan goods."

"How much extra, Admiral?" RJ had run into this ploy before. The reality was that the admiral was blowing smoke about the extra pay and would simply pocket the additional fee. *Gotta give him credit for trying, but a few flights of stairs wouldn't do Ice's troops any harm. They've gotten a little lazy lately.*

"I'm looking at ten thousand in extra credits to have to pay out."

"Open the docking doors on Level Two. A little exercise won't do us any harm."

"Agreement reached." The admiral was disappointed that he wouldn't get the extra ten thousand, but he knew that sometimes discretion was the better part of greed. "The docking bay is on the starboard side, two-thirds of the way down to the stern."

"Thank you, Admiral. We shall arrive shortly," RJ confirmed.

"But RJ, I mean Captain RJ." The admiral still had a little pride and didn't want to appear too weak if news of his easy capitulation made its way to other pirates. "The bay you will be docking in is magno-pressurized. So if you and your crew deviate overly much from our agreement, I can turn off the magno. That will leave you to track down *Whoozaloo* after it has drifted off into the middle of the asteroid field we are currently in."

"Tsk, tsk, now, Admiral. We have both bargained in good faith. I see no reason for men such as ourselves to risk our agreement. That would be bad form, not to mention impolite, wouldn't you say?"

"I would say. Pleasure doing business with you."

"Likewise."

The admiral turned to Lackmere and Knockabee. "See how easy that was?"

They nodded, impressed with the admiral's handling of the situation as he hit the button to blast a second warning signal that echoed around the vast Bargeflat for a couple of seconds.

"This is Admiral Angiere speaking," he announced to all over the loudspeakers once the warning had finished its echo.

"We are being attacked by pirates but have negotiated for them only to take the Kdackan shipment, which is somewhere on Level Three. Anyone who is not a mercenary assigned to protect that specific shipment should report to a higher level, either Four or the main deck.

"Anyone on Level Two is also advised to reposition themselves up to Level Four or the main deck. The pirates will enter through Dock 5-C near the stern and then make their way to the Kdackan shipment. You might not want to find yourselves mistaken for one of the mercenaries."

He turned to Lackmere. "Did I leave anything out?"

"The Level Two crew have to open the door at Dock 5-C before they make a run for a higher deck."

The admiral added that with another short announcement.

"Anything else, Lackmere?"

"You could have wished the mercs *good luck.*"

The admiral waved him off. "If the mercs don't know how to either fight or negotiate, they made a poor career choice somewhere along the way."

It took a little maneuvering, but RJ found the door open and waiting for them right where the admiral had told him it would be. *Admiral, my ass. He's nothing more than a barge-bumper.* RJ guided *Whoozaloo* in to dock.

Whooz was a magnificent ship and designed for nothing other than speed and weaponry. The crew's accommodations weren't as nice as RJ's and the lieutenants'. Still, they were spacious enough to hold twenty-five. That was more than any halfway competent pirate needed, especially when they had the Iceman leading them.

RJ shut down the engines and confirmed that *Whooz* wasn't going anywhere. The 489's magno-pressure held it firmly in place. Not that he had any intention of leaving the cabin. He and Spid had more work to figure out what the Kdackan goods might be and where would be the closest and most profitable place to sell them.

Ice was the one in charge of the raid now. Thinking about it, RJ couldn't remember the last time he'd set foot inside a craft he was raiding. He used to be pretty fearsome with weapons in his hands.

He'd earned his honorific title of captain and the reputation of fear that his name evoked, but over time, he'd learned that his voice held such a tone of menace that little else was needed these days.

Having settled in and making sure that *Whooz* was secure, he lowered the ramp. If he hadn't, Ice's men would have probably broken down the door and leapt out, so hungry for battle they now were.

Through the out-view cameras, he and Spid watched Ice's men cascading down the ramp, with Ice casually trailing behind, saving his energy for when the fighting started.

"Think they'll find any mercs waiting for them?" Spid looked up from his screen.

"If they don't, we're gonna have a bunch of really pissed pirates coming back on board."

"Got it covered. Remember Daukhl? From Dolurulod?"

It took RJ a few minutes. "The space-case cadet?"

"That's the one. After the last time we bailed him out of a jam, he gave me a sample case as a way of thanks."

"Was that anywhere near around the time when we couldn't find you for two days until someone opened a vent that seemed to be blocking our airflow, and you tumbled out still half-stoned and barely coherent?"

"Not one of my proudest moments." Spid had hoped that everyone else had relegated the episode to a memory closet they seldom opened. "I haven't touched it since, so there's enough left to keep Ice's whole gang chilled out long enough to forget all about the raid of boredom that might await them."

They looked at the out-view screen. Three of the crew, wanting immediate action, had just sliced an innocent-looking crate into six pieces, out of which fell forty pounds of harmless Gottagetas. *Gottagetas, the snack that tastes better than any meal your mother ever served.*

"Once the coast is clear," Spid eyed the bags strewn all over the floor, "I might venture down and get me some Gottagetas."

"Get enough for both of us and a few for Ice. Hell, grab as many as you can. If the raid ends up being a pissing contest, the crew might need them after Daukhl's shit kicks in."

A few minutes later, Spid hurried down the ramp and used all four arms and two of his legs to haul back enough Gottagetas to feed a hungry twenty-five man crew for a week, with enough left over for him, the captain, and Ice to keep them satisfied for a month.

CHAPTER TWENTY-ONE

Jo and Hix found their fellow mercenaries right where they were supposed to be after the alarms summoned them, set up on Level Three in front of the Kdackan crate, ready to... ready to...ready to either wet themselves or start another game of bones-down.

"Relax, guys and hot chick. You act like you've never been a merc before." This came from the one who seemed to be the leader of the bones-down group.

John had shown enough interest in them to learn their names when they'd had a little time to kill. *You needed to know the names of your teammates when battles were raging. Gamer 101.*

The one who had spoken up was named Gidge, and John had taken a liking to him. Gidge and Gage were close enough to start with, but he also had Gage's attitude of *What's the worst that could happen? Chill, Jojacko.*

The day before, when he'd introduced himself as Jo between rounds of bones, Gidge had replied, "Yo, Jo with the hot chick. How's it hangin'?" John knew full well that

Gidge was using a double-entendre as he smiled at Meehix. Gidge had style.

He knelt so he could face the foursome as they kept rolling the bones on the floor, there being no convenient table.

"Here's the deal, guys." He looked at each one as earnestly as he could. "Brack, Fluesome, and Jetty, right?"

"Fluesome. Rhymes with gruesome. Thanks for remembering," Fluesome gave him a short smile, then turned back to the game. "Whose roll?"

John shifted position and gave the bones a vicious kick, scattering them so that the others couldn't track them down between the crates and use them in another game.

"Have I got your attention yet?"

"Yo, Jo, you've got our attention." Gidge leaned back. "You also have my undying vengeance in your future because I was up three paychecks to one and now will never be able to collect." He even had Gage's *fuck us both* smile.

Meehix kept her place, leaning against a stack of crates a few feet away. She watched Jojacko take control of the situation and liked what she saw. Her Jo had the bones throwers' full attention. Even though she kept her distance, she was still close enough to hear what he said.

John looked around at the four other mercenaries that weren't either him or Hix or the players. They huddled together, obviously scared out of their wits but not making a run for it to save their asses. *They're showing moxie, the poor fools.*

"Look, Gidge." John knew enough to know how to identify a leader and focus on him. Because where a leader goes, others will follow. "You four are obviously a team and have probably done the merc gig a dozen times. All of them successful, am I right?" John also knew when to throw in a compliment to the gamers on his team.

"A time or two." Gidge saw the intensity in John's eyes and suddenly understood that this might not be their run-of-the-mill merc job.

"I have some inside information on this job."

"Big whoop." Fluesome wasn't quite as quick as Gidge to catch on. "Everyone claims to have inside information on every job we've ever been on, and it's usually bullshit rumors. Why should yours be any different?"

John stared him down with his best Clint Eastwood glare. "Are you willing to bet your life on that assumption?"

"I'd advise against it, Flue," Gidge added. "Let's hear the crazy man out. Either he's right, in which case we're about to get our asses kicked, or he's wrong, in which case we'll kick *his* ass before we make the next station."

Fluesome leaned back with a smile. "All right. Either way, someone's gonna get their ass kicked, and I'm first in line for his."

John smiled back. "That's a deal, Flue. My ass will be all yours to kick if I'm wrong, and the first round of whatever you want to drink will be on me when we make it to the next station with a bar. I really hope that I'm wrong because if I'm right, there won't be a pretty picture left of any of us to take."

"Me too," Flue found himself suddenly trying to keep the panic out of his voice because he had also caught on to the intensity in the merc named Jo's eyes.

Not a lot of time to spare, John. Make your case and make it now!

"You four are obvious partners, so you've probably already talked between yourselves, speculating about my partner." John motioned for Meehix to join the conversation.

About fucking time. Meehix joined them, sitting on the floor because that's where they were all sitting and this didn't seem to be the time to posture for the physical position of dominance.

"This is my partner, Hix. *The* Hix, and if you've never heard her name before, it's because we both like to fly under the radar." John winked at his partner. His partner winked back. "Are any of you familiar with the name Frelo Cocksman Raxmugg?"

"Yeah," Brack finally joined in because he'd followed that story. "Victor Vikrellion's youngest brother who some blue chick bounty hunter was stupid enough to kill, not caring what wrath she'd have to face to earn a buck."

"Hix? Care to take a quick bow?"

Meehix stood in all her blue glory and curtsied before retaking her seat on the floor and felt that this was a good time to join the conversation.

"Have any of you heard the tale of someone who once told a Blavarian dreadnought captain to suck eggs?"

"That's not what I told him, Hix."

"I cleaned up the language for family-friendly audiences." Hix smiled. "Time for your bow, Jo."

"No." Gidge was having a hard time believing but was scared not to.

John nodded. "Yeah, that was me. I'd had a hard day and

might have raised my voice and used some words that I'd never say in front of my mother."

Time to bring it home.

"We all signed on to protect a Kdackan shipment, right?" Four heads nodded, and John continued. "Insurance agreements state that the planet insuring the items must hire at least one merc from that planet to protect the goods unless none exist."

Gidge and his boys were all well aware of those contractual stipulations and again nodded in unison, true fear finally raising its ugly head concerning what they'd signed on for.

"Gentlemen," Meehix picked up the story, and John would have fucked her right there on the spot if circumstances had been different. "May I introduce you to my partner Jo, the *only* Kdackan with enough balls to become an intergalactic mercenary...*ever!* He's not someone you want to fuck with!" *Although I'm looking forward to the day.*

"So here's the deal, guys." He and Meehix had their full attention now.

"I'm the Kdackan merc who once told the Bavarian cream donut captain to suck his own cream-filled eggs! Hix here is the one who killed the worthless shit-for-fuck Frelo! And the pirates who have already boarded this Good Ship Lollipop? *Where the hell did that name come from?* Have no intention of *bargaining* with us!"

John was only guessing at that last part but suspected he was right. He hoped he was wrong, but he didn't want the four professional mercs and the four other quivering but seemingly ready to stand their ground mercs to be left for the slaughter. *At least, not without a fighting chance to be prepared for what they might face.*

As large as the Bargeflat was, sounds had a way of working their way between floors. A gun blast here and there, pounding footsteps, and shouts of anger from the deck below were audible to all.

"You all heard the admiral's announcement." John was channeling his inner Jojacko. "These four here are used to this gig and being able to bargain with the pirates."

He turned to Gidge and trusted him to come up with the right answer.

"Do those pirates coming our way sound like they're in any mood to bargain with anything other than blood?"

Gidge rose to his feet. He looked down at his three partners still rooted to the floor, then at the other four mercs who he hadn't paid any attention to as they'd settled in for another easy-play-easy-pay job a couple of days ago.

"Now, my friends is the time to cut and run."

John and Meehix stood and flanked him, hoisting a few of their weapons.

Gidge hoisted a couple of his as he continued. "Cut and run, or stand and do your job. No one will shoot you in the back if you decide to choose safety instead of honor. But now is the time to make that choice."

One of the four new mercs stood.

"Permission to cut and run, sir. I have three children who need a dad more than their dad needs a paycheck."

"Permission granted. When you signed up, you didn't know this would happen. You honor your family more than you honor a job. Your children should be proud of you."

The merc laid his weapons at Gidge's feet. "Thank you." He was gone.

"Now is the time, gentlemen, to make your intentions known."

Fluesome, Brack, and Jetty rose to their feet, weapons at the ready, and stood alongside the fearsome threesome.

"Better to die in battle," Brack whispered to Jetty.

"Than to die of boredom," Jetty whispered back, finishing the line from the Mercenary Code.

John flinched and spun as he got a kick with serious intent behind it to his ass.

"Just in case you're right, and I won't have another chance to deliver one." Fluesome smiled.

There were now nine mercs left, not all of them privy to the earlier conversations.

"These two are Jo and Hix." Gidge took a step back. "Listen to them as if your lives depend on it because they do."

"What have we gotten this gang into?" John faced his partner.

"The more important question, Jojacko, is how do we get them out of it?" She smiled and delivered a kick to his ass.

"Look, guys." John stepped forward before Meehix could deliver another kick. That sounded like a weak opening line, so he started again.

"Pirates are making their way up here. You can hear them for yourselves. Do they sound like a gang that wants to sit and work out a bargain over a game of bones-down?"

He had their undivided attention.

"For those of you whose names we haven't learned

yet…" He did some quick math and turned to Gidge. "Which of you is the best shooter from a distance?"

"Jetty. It's not even close."

"Jetty!"

"Yes, Jo."

"Set yourself up. You're the sniper who will also be laying down ground fire when needed."

"Yes, sir." He was gone.

John faced the three new mercs. "No time to waste now. Which of you is the best?"

Two of them raised their hands.

"Brack, step forward." Brack did.

"Point." Brack did, and just like that, he partnered up.

"Fluesome."

"Yes, sir."

"You now have your new partner."

Fluesome stepped forward and shook the other merc's hand.

"You." John pointed at the third merc and motioned him forward. "What's your name, sir?"

"Lisby, sir."

"Do you have any skills that would be useful as a mercenary?"

"I was a fisherman, sir. I can toss a mean harpoon and skin and debone a flark faster than your mother could cook it."

"Meehix?"

She threw two spears and a short blade from her backpack at the fisherman, and he caught them all without a flinch or a scratch.

"This is Gidge. Keep an eye on his back and don't let him die." He turned to Gidge. "Will that work for you?"

"As long as he doesn't totally suck at his job, sir." *Gidge and Gage, twins at heart.*

"Hix!"

"Yes, sir!"

John held out his hand. She stepped forward and took it, hoping that the dampness in her vag flap wasn't showing.

"For those who don't know us, I'm Jo. This is my partner Hix. The both of us would rather be anywhere else right now, as I'm sure the rest of you would. But here we all are. Hix and I will stand guard as the first line of defense against the fucking pirates. The rest of you cover our flanks and each others'. Before this day is over, there will be blood! May more of theirs be spilled than ours!"

Everyone took up the most strategic positions they could find, and John took her hand and held it hard, forcing her to look at him.

"Listen to me carefully now."

Her ears were wide open.

"If worst comes to worst, which it probably will, you know where Chuckie and the suckusall are. You get yourself to safety, then go and guide them to the bottom level and onto Ship.

"Me and the merc gang will hold off the pirates for as long as we can. Chuckie will make sure that if I live, you'll get out of your being my slave designation, and if I die, the whole slave issue will be a moot point."

"So, if you live, I won't be a slave?"

"Yes, that's what I'm saying."

"And if you die, I won't be a slave?"

"Did I stutter or something?"

"No. You just said the sweetest words I've ever heard anyone say to me." She reached out to touch his face and draw it closer.

"Are you two gonna get a room or fight pirates?"

"Fuck you too, Gidge!"

"Raincheck, Jo?"

"Bet your cute blue ass, Hix."

All eyes being on them, they both realized that this was a moment to prepare for battle, not romance.

Can't catch a fucking break.

Can't catch a break for fucking.

They'd reached the point where they could hear each other's thoughts but couldn't tell who thought what first.

"I could run from one end of Klimsy and back, and it would be a shorter run than this."

"And it wouldn't have any stairs either."

"Bet ya ten glicks that RJ could have bargained to get us a closer landing dock."

"RJ. Is that short for Rectal Jerk?"

"On my planet, it's short for cheap bastard."

Ice kept his steady pace behind and let them rant against his captain. The more they bitched, the angrier they would get. Once they found the mercenaries who were guarding the precious cargo, they would feel less mercy about slaughtering them all.

RJ and Spid and he had already agreed that would be

more financially beneficial than bargaining to pay off the mercs.

They hit another flight of stairs. It was a tall flight, and they had a traditional mantra to chant as they climbed them. "One, two, three, next. Reach the top and cut off necks. Five, six, seven, eight. We're killing those who stay to wait." Then the chant started again because any higher number wasn't worth the effort.

"No! No! No!" Chuckie never thought he'd ever say those three words to a sex maniac who wanted him. He'd found a broom in the merc quarters and ripped up a bunk's bedding to form a makeshift holder to keep the uncle's niece at a safe distance. Meanwhile, he had Mixie connected into the 489's video system to enable him to keep track of Meehix and John.

The good news was that they'd somehow not gotten themselves killed yet. The bad news was that they still hadn't met the pirate crew, and they looked like a really pissed-off gang. Chuckie's stock in trade was staying three steps ahead.

With one hand, he was keeping the succubus at bay, and with the other hand he'd pulled out the comm-stick to talk to Ship.

"Help me here, Ship! Meehix and John are in a shitload of trouble, and I can't help them because I'm spending all of my energy trying to keep our client's niece at bay."

"Fingers in her ears."

"The fuck you say?"

"Stick a finger in each ear simultaneously, and she will be gentle as a lamb for an unspecified period. Some last for minutes, and others might be docile for a day. Of

course, you'll have to repeat the process whenever necessary to keep her acting relatively manageable."

"Why didn't you tell us this before?"

"**No one ever asked. Kdack 3a has a long history of succubi. You only need to know which hieroglyphics to consult.**"

"Look," he was hesitant to free Vixaleen but also didn't know if the fingers in the ear trick would simply dampen her hunger or make her nearly catatonic. They needed to be able to run. "I'm going to unleash you now, but you've gotta promise to behave because we're going to make a run for it."

"Okaaay." She wasn't happy but also didn't quite promise to behave either.

Chuckie unhooked her from the broom and went to check the door to see how clear the coast was. The hallway was empty, but before he could turn to motion her to follow him, her tongue was already in his ear.

One tongue in his ear or two fingers in hers? Reluctantly, he chose safety over sex and plugged her up.

"You're no fun." She dropped off his back and onto her feet.

"Can you run?"

"Yeah, sure. You're one of those all run, no fun, guys aren't you?" She pouted.

"Run now, fun later. We have to get to safety first."

The hallway was clear so they made a break for the stairs. They'd reached Level Three when the sounds of pounding feet and shouting pirates roared up from the stairs below. Chuckie grabbed Vixaleen and rushed through the door and onto the vast space of stacked cargo, hurrying to hide behind some crates.

Seconds later, the pirates were in the room and heading for the Kdack shipments. The first shots rang out moments after. Now would be the time for Chuckie to get both their asses down to Shippewa.

He started to do just that, but more shots quickly followed, and he froze. Not out of fear, because the fighting was a safe distance away, but because Chuck Norris never ran from a fight in his life. *Fights run from Chuck Norris!*

Physical fighting wasn't in Chuckie N's genetic makeup, but there had to be something he could do to help his partners. He did what he did best. He thought and schemed. When he remembered a small office in the front corner, he led Vix that way, staying as close to the wall and behind as many boxes as possible.

CHAPTER TWENTY-TWO

The pirates burst through the doors and were firing before they even had a target to fire at.

"Spread out!" Ice commanded. "Find the Kdackan shit and kill anyone or anything that stands in your way!"

Gidge made eye contact with John and nodded *thanks*. John nodded *you're welcome*. Because of Jo's and Hix's warning, they had all found strategic locations and at least had a fighting chance.

John and Meehix had taken up a position, lying flat on top of the large Kdack crate.

"I don't think they want to buy us off, Hix. I'm not setting anything to stun."

"I don't think you're wrong, Jo."

He scanned the hundreds of shipping containers and their various heights and flashed back to a game he'd mastered when he was twelve.

"It's *Rambo* time."

"The fuck is a Rambo?"

"On the Brando to Chuck Norris scale, he's closer to Chuck."

"Found it!" One of the pirates had turned a corner and spotted the Kdack goods.

Dozens of other feet were now pounding their way with shouts and shots freely distributed. Jo saw one pirate fall and knew that Jetty the sniper had drawn first blood. The pirates turned to where the bullet had come from and let loose with a barrage.

"Stay flat, stay low, and never give up the higher ground."

Jo used the distraction to leap up. "Say hello to my little friend!" He let loose with a barrage before he jumped and rolled on the top of another container.

He knew he'd taken down at least two. More importantly, he'd drawn the pirates' attention his way, which was his plan. Keep the focus on him and away from Hix and the others.

"I love the smell of alien blood in the morning!" That brought a burst of gunfire his way, answered a split second later with a blast from Jo as he leapt to another container. He misjudged his momentum, rolled across the top of it, and landed on the floor, finding himself with Fluesome and his novice merc partner.

"I got one so far, Jo," Fluesome was proud to announce as shots continued to ring out around them.

"My gun won't fire." The novice sounded panicked.

Jo grabbed the gun, which happened to be the same model as his. *The safety was still on, for fuck's sake!* He checked the ammo cartridge, found it fully loaded as opposed to his, which was nearly empty. He swapped guns.

"If you survive, you can tell your boss that this gun took out at least two pirates. Then find another line of work." He looked at Fluesome. "You good with that?"

"He don't tell, and we won't tell."

Jo scanned the next crates in line. "Cover me!"

Fluesome laid down some good cover while Jo used the crates as stepping stones leading to higher ground.

Jo did a quick scan. The pirates still outnumbered the mercs three-to-one, but the latter were holding their own, especially considering that they'd never done any real fighting before. He suspected that the bones-down foursome had probably done some practice training together before. If they were Earthlings, it would have probably been at a paintball range, but at least they knew to take the safety off.

Gidge was between two crates, leaning out to take a few shots and back in. Jo had a freak-out moment when he saw a pirate working his way behind the containers to Gidge's position, ready to take him out from behind. Gidge would never know he was coming.

The pirate also didn't know what was coming.

The fisherman merc leapt up from the top of the crate. One of Meehix's spears hit the pirate so hard that the tip passed right through and stuck in the side of the next crate, leaving the lifeless body dangling like a catfish head on the outside of a bayou shack.

———

The fingers in the ear trick hadn't worked out as well as it could have. It had ended up making the demon's niece sluggish and slow-moving. It took Chuckie longer than he was happy about to half-carry, half-drag her along the wall to the small corner office.

Shots and shouting intensified out in the huge cargo bay. He wasn't sure what he could do to help, but he knew he needed access to the 489's automated system, and he could only get that once they were inside the office.

They finally made it. Chuckie plunked the succubus into a chair, pulled Mixie from her bag, and plugged her in. Using the comm-stick, he made sure that Shippewa would come in on cue. All fighting on Level Three halted as the loudspeakers emitted an ear-shattering *screech*. Chuckie adjusted the volume down a couple of notches.

"To the pirates on Level Three. This is Chuck Norris speaking."

Jo and Hix were on the same level of boxes, above the fray, and had a clear view as they smiled at each other. Both threw up their hands. Sometimes you didn't need to hear someone talking to know what they were thinking.

What the fuck?

Your guess is as good as mine. He's your friend!

He's your bro!

By mutual agreement, they both ducked and laid flat to see how this played out.

"Admiral Angiere has been relieved of his command, having failed to tell the pirates to fuck off and instead entered into negotiations. I and my crew, fifty strong, have been posing as the maintenance crew on this ship because the admiral had capitulated to pirates' demands more often than was acceptable to management."

Shots peppered the ceiling where the loudspeakers were, and Ice stepped out front and center.

"Who the fuck is Chuck Norris, and why have I never heard of him?"

"You've never heard of me because anyone who has fucked with Chuck never lived to tell the tale." Chuckie N was on a roll now.

"Because your captain operated in good faith with the admiral, you will be allowed ten minutes to vacate to your ship. If you don't comply, the only thing you will have left to vacate are your bowels."

"He's fucking bluffing, men!" Ice remained in control of his crew. "It's all a bluff!"

"Grab hold of something and tell me if this feels like a bluff."

Shippewa's timing was impeccable as he let go with a sonic blast. As massive as the 489 was, with Ship physically attached to it, the sonics reverberated through its walls and floor, vibrating every surface from the bottom level to the top deck.

"You now have eight minutes to vacate or die. Choose wisely."

A tongue was suddenly in his ear, and a whispered, "I want you now."

Apparently, the fingers in the ears trick had worn off.

"I need you. *Now*, or else you'll have to drug me again and carry me like a lump of coal to wherever we have to get."

Chuckie covered the 489's comm-mic.

"I-I give you what you need, then you'll be able to run with serious intent to where our transport is waiting?"

"Just a little nibble, no more than an appetizer, and I'll be good to go."

Time to take one for the team.

Four pirates had already deserted back to *Whooz*, leaving Ice with a dozen and only three minutes to make a decision when another announcement from Chuck Norris came out over the loudspeakers.

"Oh. My. *Gawd!*" followed by some clattering that knocked the comm-mic out of commission.

Ice had been able to gather and hold his men together a row down from their targeted cargo. He'd lost a few to death. That wasn't common but wasn't unheard of during a raid. He'd deal with the few who had deserted because of Chuck fucking Norris later.

They still had the mercenaries outnumbered and Kdack cargo to bring in.

"If you run now, I will kill you myself. I'd rather kill deserters than brainless mercs who at least have the balls to stand and fight."

He had to give the mercs credit. They were a feisty bunch, but that didn't mean they weren't already dead in his mind.

"What about Chuck Norris?"

"Brettig, right? Begging the other day to take on a Crom Limean and prove how fearless you were?"

In your face time.

"Now you're shitting yourself, afraid of facing someone who, the last time we heard from him, was begging *Oh My*

Gawd? Does that sound like someone you should run from?"

Brettig pulled up his emotional bootstraps. "No, sir. Sounds more like something a Grivadivian would say."

"That vibration was nothing more than a cheap parlor trick. We came here to take the Kdack shit and spill some blood, and none of us are leaving until we get some of each, are we?"

"No, sir," Brettig was back on board. "Kdack shit and blood sound good to me!"

"Kdack shit and blood!" was the new battle cry. *Do I know how to inspire or what?*

Meehix, inspired by John's actions and knowing that Chuckie was still onboard doing *gawd* knew what with the succuslut, decided to take a more active role. *Never give up the higher ground.*

She spotted some higher ground and ran for it. Following John's lead, she leapt from crate top to crate top, three rows over and two rows down until she was at a pulley hanging from the ceiling.

She would need both of her feet to climb it. Her bare feet.

No way am I giving up these boots!

She slipped out of her boots, strapped their laces together and slung them over her shoulder, leapt, and grabbed hold as she shimmied her way up. The tricky part about climbing pulleys was that you had to hold both ropes together. Otherwise, it would keep looping you down to the bottom.

Two minutes later and five feet below the ceiling, she wrapped the ropes between her feet and took in the view.

Chuckie and the Fuckie were coming out of an office in the far corner. Chuckie still had half of his shirt untucked. *Oh, fuck!* They couldn't see that ahead of them were two pirates who were trying to circle back to the Kdack crate.

She watched as they ran into each other, taking all of them by surprise. The pirates already had guns drawn. They were about to shoot when the succubus grabbed the bag from Chuckie's shoulder and swung it faster than the pirates could pull their triggers. The girl had good aim, and both pirates staggered back a few steps after having their heads hammered.

Of course, she'd lost hold of the bag in the process, and it landed several feet away.

"Run!" Hix hollered. "Run, Chuckie, run!"

Chuckie was more than a little distracted, but he recognized that voice and knew a command when he heard it, especially when two well-armed pirates had gotten over the unexpected blows to their heads and were coming back at them.

"My bag with Mixie is on the floor somewhere! We need it!"

Hix fired, hitting one pirate and giving Chuckie time to grab the suckallofus's hand, head for the stairs, and down to Shippewa as she fired some more to cover them.

"We'll find it!"

"Overhead, overhead, overhead!" Ice hollered.

All of the pirates' attention was drawn to Meehix, hanging high and in plain view with clear sightlines to her. Shots rang out. Fortunately for her, no matter how many practices and paces Ice had put his crew through, much

334

like the mercs, they'd seldom had to fire with real-life action going on.

They'd also never had to fire with mercenaries doing their damnedest to save Hix the blue chick who, with her partner Jo, had saved all of their asses from certain death.

The fisherman was throwing knives. Jetty was still firing from his sniper's perch. Gidge, Brack, and Fluesome were also coming to her defense. *They had no idea who Chuck Norris was, but they were now honest to Gawd mercenaries earning their honest to Gawd pay!*

Jojacko had mastered this particular game when he was twelve and knew how to keep four levels ahead of everyone else. A laser bolt here, an explosion there, chaos everywhere didn't distract him because he wasn't the focus of attention. Hix was the focus, and she was firing back. She may or may not have hit anyone, but she certainly threw off their aim.

It was a lucky shot that did her in. It was always a lucky shot. You aim for one thing, miss badly, and somehow end up on the next level.

Not today, buckos!

The shot that dropped Hix didn't hit her. It hit the pulley ropes, slicing through both of them and leaving her hanging by little more than a thread, forty feet above the floor.

It took only a few seconds before the remaining strands gave out, and Hix plummeted toward the floor faster than a booger leaving a nose after a good sneeze. Jo was waiting to catch her, his last thought being one of his mom's favorite songs by the ancient folkie Bob Dylan, titled *Tangled Up In Blue.*

Hix hadn't died from the fall and gone to either heaven or hell. However, her breasts had buried Jo's face. When she shifted away, his smile made her think that he believed he'd died and gone to heaven. She rolled off.

"Dammit, Jo, if a little cleavage sends you off to dreamland, we're gonna have some serious problems."

He was out cold.

"Jo? John? Jojacko?"

Two frantic shoulder shakes followed by a slap on the face brought him back.

"I was having the nicest dream."

"Save it! You can dream when you're dead!"

Jo gave his head a waking-up shake and sprang to his feet.

"How are the good guys doing, Hix?"

"Holding their own and doing their best not to die."

"Well then, how's about we help them to achieve their goals, shall we?"

"We shall." They rushed back into battle, only to discover that there wasn't much of a fight going on, and paused behind a crate during the silence.

"Chuckie lost Mixie."

"What?"

"I saw it while I was hanging out up there. The slut-bucket grabbed his shoulder bag. She did some serious damage to a couple of pirates' heads but lost control of it, and it slid behind some crates. We need to find it!"

John felt torn. He no longer cared about the Kdackan shipment but an obligation to the mercs he'd inspired and led into battle tugged at him. Meehix grabbed his chin and forced him to look her in the eye.

"Strangers who signed up to do a job and you helped them to do it, or Chuckie and Mixie?"

Even hard decisions can be easy to make.

"Where was he when he lost her?"

"Fuck it, Ice!"

"RJ?"

"You know anyone else on this ear-comm?"

RJ had never chimed in when Ice was in battle, but this was the first time they'd ever been on the losing end. RJ had been watching the whole way through Ice's head-mount cam.

"No, sir. Your call." Ice was well aware of what RJ saw, and they both knew that things hadn't gone as planned.

"All we have so far is part of your crew dead, another part in here begging for mercy for having deserted, and a month's supply of Gottagetas. Does that sound like a successful raid?"

"Can't say that it does, RJ."

"The insured Kdackan goods must be worth something. Grab what you can of them and get the fuck out of there before we have to find an entirely new replacement crew!"

"On it!"

His crew, not having been successful, had found their way back to him to regroup.

"We're now on a snatch-and-grab mission, boys."

They couldn't argue with his logic. The dead and deserting had seriously depleted their numbers, but they still had their pride and wanted to come away with some reputation intact.

"The Kdackan goods. I saw one large crate and several stacked boxes beside it. Fuck the big crate. We're going for the smaller boxes. Me and A Company will go for it. B Company will lay down covering fire, and C Company will clear the way for the long haul back to *Whooz*. Any questions?"

No questions that anyone was willing to ask.

None of the mercs had lost their lives, although several were wounded. Gidge had gathered them all back to his location during the pause in the action.

"I don't know what to tell you guys. You saw Hix fall, and Jo was probably killed in action while saving most of our lives."

The pain in his fellow mercs' eyes reflected the pain he felt in his heart. "We've done Jo and Hix proud. The pirates haven't taken anything so far, and there's not enough left of them to take the big crate."

Shots suddenly rang out, and three pirates rushed in and took the top two boxes of the smaller Kdackan shipment. They would have taken more, but the mercs opened fire. The pirates ran off after snatching up as much as they could without any more of them getting killed.

Other than the sound of scurrying pirate feet, silence settled back in.

"Have we lost anyone?"

"No one other than Jo and Hix." Gidge had never heard Fluesome sound like he was on the edge of tears before.

"To Jo and Hix." Gidge held his right hand high, fingers and thumbs together, palm up. The Mercenaries Code way of honoring those who had fallen in battle. None of them had ever had a cause to do it before, and all of them hoped they'd never have to do it again.

After a moment of silence to honor their fallen comrades, Gidge brought them back.

"Okay. Who's wounded?"

"Scratches here and there, nothing that a few wrapped bandages won't help," Jetty spoke up. "I took one in my arm, but I think I broke a leg when the shot knocked me out of my perch." He looked around and smiled. "Does anyone know how to make a splint?" He passed out.

CHAPTER TWENTY-THREE

"There it is!" Meehix pointed.

There it was. They were both on the floor, looking under pallets because Chuckie's bag hadn't fallen anywhere in plain sight. *That would have been too easy.*

The bag had slid several feet under a stack of pallets. Jo couldn't reach it, but Hix did her rubbery leg thing and was able to snatch it up with her toes. A brief flurry of gunfire distracted them, but it was over seconds later. The only sound now was running feet storming for the stairs.

Hix took a moment to get her boots back on and laced up, but by then the footsteps were already out the door and halfway down to the next level.

"Pirates on the run?" she guessed.

"Sounded like that to me."

"Fuck the pirates!" Hix heard Chuckie in her ear.

"Fuck the pirates. Is that similar to fuck the succubus?"

"Not fair."

"Where the fuck are you?"

"We're on Ship. Your magical comm-stick is in the bag with Mixie, which is why I'm able to talk to you."

"They made it onto Ship." She reached into the bag and pulled out the comm-stick.

"Great, ask him how to adjust that damn stick so we can all hear each other."

"There's a small knob that has a light above it and is now lit up red." Chuckie had anticipated the question. "Turn the knob until the light is purple, and it will connect anyone within ten feet of the stick."

Meehix did as instructed, and Chuckie came in loud and clear in both of their ears.

"Not dead yet?"

"We had a little help from Chuck Norris, so nope, Hix and I are still upright. The niece is safe?"

"And satisfied?" Hix tossed in.

"I have to stick my fingers in her ears every half-hour, but yeah, she's fine."

"Your fingers in her ears?" Hix hadn't heard that one before but decided that the explanation could wait for another time. "So we can head back to Ship now?"

"Not until I go check on our mercs and make sure they're okay." John wasn't leaving the men behind without knowing if he could do something to help.

"You've got to get over this 'too noble for your own good' shit, but first, I can tell you that once I got back to Ship, I've been able to follow all of the action through the overhead cameras. I had help from a little program modification I made to their system while I was in the office. Let me reassure you that none of your precious mercs are dead."

Hix and Jo did high fives proud.

"Before you go back to them and exchange big, wet, sloppy goodbye kisses, you need to get to the pirates' ship."

"Why?" Hix looked at John, who appeared to be as confused as she was. "We won, and the pirates are booking out. Why would we want to join them?"

"Because they managed to make off with three small Kdack goods. Two crates and a tube-like container about twenty inches long and six inches across."

"It's vital that we steal it back?" Hix wanted to be able to revert to Meehix as soon as possible, and this seemed like an extra complication to that happening any time soon.

"Ship and I believe it is, and we want it on board with us and not left behind with the other Kdack shit."

"So we're going to steal something for ourselves after being hired to protect it from being stolen?" That didn't sit right with Jo.

"Ship says you should do exactly that."

"If Ship says it, we'll give it a try." Hix sighed.

"If I say it, you question, but if Ship says it, you're all like, okay?"

"Ship is Ship. You are and will always remain Chuckie. Which one would you trust if you weren't you?"

"You got me there, Hix. Try not to die—oh shit, I've got some ears to poke." He was gone.

"Any idea where the pirate ship is?

"We know it's one level down." John remembered the admiral's earlier announcement-slash-warning. "How many pirate ships can there be down there?"

They hit the stairs running and discovered that the ship wouldn't be too hard to find. All they had to do was follow a light trail of blood that one or two of the pirates had left behind. They became more cautious when they reached Level Two, knowing that the numbers were now heavily against them. Stealth seemed to be their best strategy.

The blood trail led the way to where the pirate ship had docked. They checked their weapons and swapped in a couple of new cartridges.

"Surprised they haven't taken off yet." He and Hix had moved to within striking distance and took shelter behind a crate as they scoped it out.

"Why is the ramp still down?"

"Probably for the same reason that two pirates are still guarding it."

"That reason is?"

"Beats the hell outta me."

"I got an idea."

Hix laid out her plan, and two minutes later, they walked toward the ramp in plain sight, their hands held high and looking more than a little pissed.

"One more step and you're dead!" one of the pirate guards shouted. Both of them had their guns aimed and ready to fire at the approaching duo.

"Those are two of the mercs, Flibby." Tronk recognized the blue chick immediately. She hadn't killed any of them with her high-wire act, but she had certainly gotten all of their attention.

"Isn't the big one the one who ran all over the top of the crates like a madman?" Tronk nodded in agreement. Flibby continued, "If you're coming for battle, now would be a good time to turn right around and walk the other way."

"If you're coming to surrender," Gronk added, "my advice would be the same. We don't take prisoners alive."

Flibby and Gronk were blustering as best they could. Neither of them wanted to have anything to do with the two who'd fought so hard and still managed to survive without a visible scratch.

"Attack?" Jo called. "Why would we want to attack?"

"Surrender?" Hix followed. "Never in this lifetime."

"We've come to join and get the fuck off this barge."

Three pirates appeared at the top of the ramp and made their way slowly down it. Very slowly down it. It was hard to walk with their legs manacled together and hands tied behind their backs.

"Do they look like prisoners, Hix?"

"They look more like they're about to face an execution squad."

The execution squad appeared at the top of the ramp. He was the biggest and baddest-looking Cyclops Jo had ever seen. Granted, he'd never seen one in real life, *who has?*, but this one looked like he would be hard to get past and reach the next level in any game Jojacko had ever played.

The three prisoners reached the floor and shuffled off to the side with both guards flanking them as Ice made his patient way down, keeping the pirates in his peripheral vision. His eye's main focus was on the two strangers standing with their arms raised.

"What the fuck are you two mercs doing here and why shouldn't I kill you before waiting for an answer?"

"I was about to call you down, sir," Flibby tried. "They say they want to join us."

"Did I ask you?"

"No, sir."

"Then shut the fuck up." He motioned the mercs forward. Jo and Hix kept their arms raised and approached slowly.

"You want to join us. Us, who you were trying to kill a few minutes ago. May I inquire as to why?"

"My name is Jo. This is my partner, Hix." Hix nodded her greeting. "We're tired of getting teamed up with a bunch of mercs we've never met and when it comes to an actual battle, don't know if they should run or shit their pants."

"We apologize for any of your crew we may have harmed or killed." Hix stood her ground, trying to keep her legs from shaking. "We were doing our jobs."

"Just another day at the office for you two, was it?"

"At least it was more exciting than the usual sitting around waiting to work out bargains."

"You're the one who was dangling from the ceiling?"

"That would have been me, yes."

"The fall didn't kill you?"

"Obviously not, or I wouldn't be standing here looking to join a band that fights rather than dies of boredom."

"And you and your crew evidently prefer fighting over waiting for rust and dust to gather on your weapons."

Ice snorted. They talked a good game, and he was down several crew members already from today's fighting, so two more capable hands would be good to have. He'd seen them in action, even recognized the big one as the crate-runner.

"Sad to say, pirates are also capable of running, as these

three can testify before they die." He motioned to the prisoners then slowly circled the new applicants who still had their arms raised. They were certainly well-armed, and other than the blue chick's slight leg quiver while facing him, they appeared brave enough.

"You have ten seconds," he'd completed his circle and was facing them again, "to convince me how to decide whether to trust you or kill you."

Hix's plan was working to perfection because that was a question they'd hoped he'd ask.

"On my back is a Vetralaun semi-automatic. I don't want to reach for it, but I ask that you take it. I'll keep my arms raised while you do, but please don't dawdle. They're beginning to get tired."

Ice had seen pretty much every trick in the book and survived them all by not being a fool. His short sword was at Hix's neck, the point ready to slice.

"She pulls it out. I'm not going to get my hand blown off by a booby-trapped holster. One hand, little sister. Lift it out and hold it up."

Hix did. Safely out of its holster and with her hand still intact, she held it up. Ice took hold of it, sheathed his short sword, and stepped back. The Vetralaun was a beautiful weapon, not easily attained, especially by civilians. He took a step back.

"So, you're offering me this as a bribe to let you join?"

"No, sir. May I lower my arms now?" Jo hadn't been lying. It had been a busy day, and his arms really *were* getting tired.

"You may."

Jo lowered his arms and stepped away from Hix.

"It's not a bribe. It's my weapon, and I will want it back."

This is a gambit I haven't seen before. Ice liked it.

"If not a bribe, what, exactly, is it?"

"It's one of the deadliest weapons known, but you already knew that. May I take more steps away from my partner? I don't want any ricochet to hurt her accidentally."

Ice didn't know if the big guy knew how a Cyclopian's eye worked. He hoped the merc didn't think that drawing attention to himself would mean that Ice couldn't keep his partner in view at the same time. More than one opponent had tried to pull a weapon when they thought he couldn't see them, and he was bored with that routine.

"One more step."

Jo took it. "You gave me ten seconds to convince you to trust us. Those ten seconds are now up."

"Not to quibble over a minor technicality," Hix couldn't help herself, "but it's now been twenty-seven seconds, and my arms are getting tired too. So please get on with whatever you're going to get on with, boys."

Damn, that is one feisty bluesy. Ice had to admire her spirit. *Not to mention a body to kill for.*

"Trust is letting you take my weapon and putting my life in your hands. You can either shoot me now or give me back my gun and take us on as part of your crew."

"There is a third option," Ice countered and faced Hix. "You're determined enough to join us that you're willing to let your partner die if I call his bluff?"

"It's not a bluff." Hix met his eye. "You kill him and me, and the galaxy is down two mercs, and you're out two damn good fighters."

"The third option is that I kill him, the galaxy is down

one merc, you come on board, and I'm up one damn good fighter." He shot Jo in the chest.

The force of the blow knocked Jo back a step. Ice expected him to collapse, dead before he hit the deck. What he didn't expect was that the merc-slash-wannabe pirate would remain standing. He also didn't expect that the merc he'd shot with the Vetralaun would start giggling.

"He's one tough son of a bitch, ain't he?" Hix smiled at the Cyclops, who was having a hard time believing his eye.

"Dummy rounds," Ice decided. He'd had enough of whatever game these two were playing and fired three more rounds at the three pirates who were about to be executed as deserters.

The three deserters *were* dead before their bodies hit the floor. *What the fuck? The merc must be wearing some new kind of chest protector.* Ice shot Jo in the leg.

"Ow!" Jo hopped. "That was annoying!"

"You going to take us on or keep executing at random? My partner is damn near indestructible." They'd decided in advance to let Hix take over the conversation after the pirates shot Jo and before he started giggling too much. Pissing himself also wouldn't have been the best look.

Although Ice had hoped to kill the big one and have the bluesy on board so he could form his own "partnership," he'd run out of ways to test them further. He handed Jo's gun back to him and led the two new crewmates up the ramp onto the good ship *Whooz*.

The first thing Hix did was hide the small transponder from Chuckie's bag in an out-of-the-way nook, as requested. Chuckie had been vague on why they needed to keep track of the pirate ship, but it seemed like a harmless enough request, and it was easier to go along with it than to argue.

She then tagged along in line and spotted the tubular container right next to two other crates of the Kdack shipment. Snatching it up, she quickly stuffed it into one of her packs. Fucker wasn't light.

"Time to go, Jo."

Jo had been fussing with the Vetralaun as if it had been hard to put back into place and now spun with it and got everyone's immediate attention.

Ice suddenly found a short blade against his neck, courtesy of the blue chick whose legs were no longer quivering and whose hand felt like it had done this before.

"Gentlemen!" Jo addressed them as he moved to ensure that the Cyclops would be the first one taken down. *Cut off the head, and the snake dies.*

"My partner and I are simple mercenaries, hired to do a job. Our job was to protect some goods, not kill pirates. That's just what sometimes happens when others attack our cargo."

There would be no gentlemen's agreements here so Jo needed to stress his next point as all ears and eyes were on him and his Vetralaun.

"I don't know the value of what was in the Kdack crates and really don't fucking care. We only signed on to the job to protect one specific item that has sentimental value to *her* aunt and *my* uncle. Cousins have to stick together when the family is involved."

Hix wasn't the only one on board who experienced a *what the fuck is the big fuck talking about* moment.

"It was one of the last things you grabbed, and now we have it back."

"You going to try to make a stupid move if I back off?" Hix whispered into the Cyclops' ear.

"As much as I would like to, with the Vetralaun aimed at my chest, I'll choose not to."

Hix sheathed her blade and backed toward the ramp with Jo at her side.

"We were doing our jobs." Jo kept the gun aimed at center-mass, squarely on the Cyclops' chest. "In our next lives, we might all be friends, but how's about we not find out right this minute?"

The two mercs backed down the ramp, Hix having also pulled out a fearsome-looking gun.

"We'll be leaving now. I suggest you do the same," was Jo's last bit of advice.

Ice made his way to the top of the ramp, memorizing their faces.

"There will be nothing left of you two to have a *next* life when I'm done with you the next time we meet in *this* life!"

The ramp drew up, and the door closed.

"I've heard better parting shots."

"Speaking of parting, Jo, perhaps we should?"

"Get the container to Chuckie. I really do have to check on the mercs before we head off."

"We'll be waiting, but don't get involved in any bones-down games, okay?"

She handed him the comm-stick. "Keep in touch." She headed for Shippewa.

Jo hung back, covering Hix's cute blue butt until she'd made it to the stairway and headed down two levels. He then hit the stairs himself and headed up to Level Three. All seemed silent after the recent battles. He wasn't sure where to go, so he used the oldest form of communication he knew.

"Gidge! Brack! Fluesome! Jetty! Where the fuck are you guys?"

The guys were still in front of the Kdack goods, being reamed out by Admiral fucking Angiere. Jetty still hadn't gotten attention from any medical personnel for his broken leg other than a makeshift splint his partners had thrown together from a shattered pallet and some packing tape they'd found.

The mercs' eyes lit up.

"Jo? Is that you?" Gidge would have shouted even he was standing right in front of Jo. Suddenly, they all were happy.

"Who the fuck else knows you all by name? Now where the fuck are you?"

"At the shipment!"

Jo ran. It wasn't very often that a crew of mercs shared a group hug, but they did their best, with Jetty sitting against a crate and giving two thumbs-up.

"No casualties?" Jo hoped that Chuckie's report still held.

"No, sir," Gidge answered with a quick summary. "Jetty's got a broken leg, Brack lost a little toe on his right foot, and a few other cuts and scrapes, but we all survived."

"Tell that to my little toe." Brack smiled.

"And Hix?" Gidge was afraid to ask.

"Fine as frog's hair. She sends her regards."

That silenced them all and Jo didn't understand why.

"All hail the blue chick!" Fluesome cried, and cheers went out from everyone. Jo was a little confused.

"We thought we lost you both," Gidge explained. "We even gave you a mercenary salute."

That shook Jo. He and Hix knew they were both still alive but had been out of touch with their fellow mercs for over an hour, so how could they know? He surveyed the troops, then noticed an officious-looking prick in a uniform who was frowning at them all, not pleased with Jo's sudden appearance and interruption.

"You must be the admiral."

"Admiral Angiere. Are you the leader of these men who chose to engage in combat when I already had an agreement with Captain RJ to let his men board and peacefully remove a few items?"

"I would be proud to have them consider me their leader, so I'll just say, yes."

"So all of the damage down here—the communication speakers shot to hell, the pulley needing to be restrung, bullet holes everywhere that now need to be plugged and patched. That would be your doing?"

"Again, yes," John surveyed the still unattended-to wounded and took a step forward toward the admiral. "Are you the one who invited pirates to board and take whatever they wanted, knowing that these men were here to protect some of those items?"

The admiral took a step back. "It was an insurance issue, a common practice."

Jo advanced another step.

"Matters beyond my scope. Is it also a common practice to ignore workers who are hurt and bleeding because you're more concerned with property damage that I'm sure *your* insurance will cover?" Jo took another step forward, forcing the admiral to take another one back before he'd had time to reply with more hems and haws.

"Do you or do you not have some medical staff on board?"

"Of course we do."

"Then why the fuck aren't they down here tending to these men?"

The admiral looked around and realized that he had been negligent regarding what should have been his first priority. "I'll head to the office and summon them down right now."

He headed for the small corner office to summon the medics but turned briefly back for one last question.

"Does anyone know why the office is in such shambles?"

"Put out an APB for one Chuck Norris. I believe that he is the one responsible, but he wasn't part of our crew. He's a rogue operator, and I have no idea how or why you allowed him onto your ship."

The admiral scurried off. Jo faced the troops. His men.

"Look, guys. I'm not really a mercenary."

"I knew it!" Fluesome stood.

"I had my suspicions, too." Brack stood.

Gidge was already standing, leaning back against a crate and enjoying watching Jo do his thing. "So, you gonna clue us in? What with you saving our asses and shit, please don't let the suspense kill us."

Jo leveled with them as best he could.

"Hix and I were hired to rescue someone who'd been kidnapped and shipped as a slave. Posing as mercenaries was the only way we could get on board."

"So this was all about the two of you," Jetty propped himself up as much as he could, "trying to save a damsel in distress? For true and honest?"

I don't know about the damsel part, but close enough.

"For true and honest. Chuck Norris was one of us. He rescued the damsel while Hix and I helped draw attention away from her and onto what the pirates were after."

"Saving our mercenary asses along the way."

Jo shrugged. "Call it collateral non-damage."

"Hix and this Chuck Norris dude and the damsel are all now safe?"

"Yes. Hix will be back soon, and you can see for yourself."

Abracadabra.

"Hi, guys. Did I miss anything?"

"Attention all on board," the admiral's voice came over the loudspeakers. "This is Admiral Angiere. The pirates have disembarked with minimum damage done. We will now proceed to the next station. We will be entering a galactic Gate in about thirty minutes. Please secure yourselves."

Medics arrived, quickly tended to the slightly wounded, and carried Jetty off to have his leg put in a cast. The other mercs headed for their quarters to buckle in.

They finally made it to Space Station Erba where the mercs filed out because that was the destination stipulated in their contracts. Fond farewells given, Meehix and John hung out in the Level Three cargo space for a few minutes, watching the ship's crew patching and repairing the damage.

"Fucking mercenaries," they heard one worker gripe. "Shooting this and blowing up that and us to clean up the mess."

Shouldering their bags, they disembarked and headed to the station check-in office. Being mercenaries, they were required to give an official report to the Head of Station Security detailing which weapons they'd fired and if they planned to fire them while on Erba.

"We try to run a clean station here," Troot, an officer with three stripes on his shoulders informed them after he'd walked them through a list of questions.

"Erba isn't the largest station, but it's one of the safest, and we like to keep it that way."

"Rest assured, sir," John tried his best to look harmless so they could finish with the self-important jerk. "We're stopping off for the night after a long hard fight, I mean *flight,* and want nothing more than to find a couple of drinks and a place to bed down for the day."

"That would be a good plan." He scanned the rest of their documentation. "Ah, I see you have a slave." He gave Meehix a good look-over. "Did you inherit her or buy her outright, or were the rights to her signed over by someone who had to pay off a gambling debt? I've always wondered how one went about getting a slave."

"It's funny." John gave him a cold smile. "I've been asked

that question a couple of times before. I can give you their names, and you could consult with them about my answer. But you'll have to put your questions in writing because *she* ripped the tongues out of their mouths."

Meehix's smile at the officer was even colder than John's, and she made a quick grabbing motion. That caused Troot to trip and fall backward while trying to put some space between his tongue and the not-quite-tame slave.

"Can we go now?"

"Yeah. We're finished." Troot wasn't getting off the floor until the two of them left.

"Other than being really sick of this whole *slave* thing," Meehix led the way out of the office, "that was kind of fun. Did you see his eyes?"

"Ya-huh. I think he might have wet himself."

"Yo, Chuckster." John engaged the comm-stick, making sure that it was lit up purple. "Still there, and where is your there?"

"We detached from the Bargeflat, and I'm pleased to say that I managed to fly Ship without crashing. We're docked five bays down."

"Everyone's safe?"

"For now."

"Okay. We're gonna grab a quick meal and join you in about an hour. Turning off the comm now."

"Why'd you do that?"

John held out his arm. "Because I need a decent meal, something that resembles a beer, and a little time with Meehix, now that we've left that Hix bitch behind for a while." Meehix smiled and took his elbow as they found the closest non-fast food restaurant and relaxed for an hour, enjoying having a "mission accomplished" meal and drink.

***

"You'll never guess who's here," Chuckie greeted them as they boarded Shippewa.

"What, no 'nice to see you both still alive?'"

"Oh, did I hurt the poor little Kdackan's feelings?"

"I missed you too."

"Welcome back aboard, you two."

"Thanks, Ship. Good to be back." Meehix went to the copilot's seat as Chuckie remained in the pilot's and pulled up information on the main screen. John stepped back and watched the info come up.

It seemed to be a diagram of Space Station Erba, with a blue dot where they'd docked and a red dot a quarter of the station away.

"We're the blue dot."

John nodded, glad that he'd figured it out. "And the red dot?"

"That would be the good ship *Whooz*."

"The pirates are here?" John felt a slight panic. "They followed us?"

"Just a happy coincidence. They were already here when we arrived. We're looking at the transponder Meehix planted."

"Could they have followed the barge?" Meehix was curious. "Maybe looking to plunder it while docked?"

Chuckie shook his head. "It's nearly impossible to follow anyone through a galactic Gate, too many variables.

Besides, no one plunders anything while on a space station. It's bad form."

"So we should probably head out before they somehow discover us. I'd prefer not to run into the Cyclops again."

"Am I talking to Jo, Jojacko, or some wuss from Kdack named John?"

"You're up to something, Chuckie." Meehix liked having John back and needed to know where this was going. "Spill and spill right now, or we're taking off without bothering to borrow any more troubles."

Chuckie drew a deep breath. This was going to be another hard sell, easy sale conversation.

"The pirate ship is currently unmanned. No one plunders anything while on a space station."

"Because that would be bad form." Meehix was waiting for the other shoe to drop.

"After who knows how many days in space they've just spent in the company of men, the pirates have left the ship, probably to find some other company for the night, leaving their ship unprotected."

"Because no one plunders while on a space station, yeah, we got it." Meehix rolled her hand. "Move on."

"There are still two Kdack crates on board. As mercenaries under the auspices of the NutBusters, you two are fully authorized to go after those goods. Station Erba was where your contract ended, but we're still on it."

"Technically, he has a point." John divided his focus between the screen and Meehix. "Do we know what's in those crates?"

"Well, not specifically, but they *were* insured, so they must be holding something of value."

"So," John wanted to be clear. "We stroll on up to a mostly unguarded ship, a pirate ship, and take back what we have every right to take?"

"And maybe, just maybe, anything else that looks to be of value," Chuckie was close to sealing the deal. "You'll only be stealing from pirates who have already stolen whatever you grab. What authority is anyone going to report a theft of previously stolen items to?"

"But isn't plundering while docked on a station considered bad form?"

"Has anyone ever accused the NutBusters of having *good* form?"

Before the conversation could go any further, Vixaleen was on John's back with her tongue aimed for his ear.

"Shit, has it been half an hour already? Fingers in her ears, John. Fingers in her ears."

Enough with the fucking around with fucking fingers in her fucking ears! Meehix grabbed the succuslut by the hair and yanked her off John. "Excuse us for a moment." She started to drag the succubus back toward the cargo area.

"Can I at least have the little one?"

"You've already *had* the little one."

"Says who?" Chuckie came to his own defense.

"Says *Oh My Gawd!*"

Chuckie turned to John. "Help me out here."

"Sorry, bro." John couldn't help but laugh at the memory. "The almighty and infamous Chuck Norris saved our asses but forgot to turn the mic off."

"Sorry, Meehix." He hoped she would accept his plea. "I was trying to help you two out and keep *her* at bay at the same time."

Meehix smiled at her favorite Chuckie N. "Well, at least you were half-successful. Carry on, boys. I'm taking her to Cargo for a little woman-to-woman talk."

"If there's any girl-on-girl action, please get it on video."

"Smack him for me, will you, John?"

Reaching the cargo area, Meehix twisted the succubus's hair leaving her lying flat on her back on the floor, straddled her, and held the short-sword, point down, its sharp point already making contact with the bitch's stomach.

"Flat on your back with legs spread. Must be a very familiar position for you." She put a little pressure on the blade, ready to slice the bitch stem to stern. "Do I have your undivided attention now?"

The demon's niece nodded.

"Seriously, girlfriend, you are getting a little chubby."

"No, I'm not!"

"Looked in a mirror lately? Had to loosen up any of your wraps recently because they felt tighter than they used to feel?"

If Meehix knew nothing else, she knew how to cut without needing a blade.

"Hands off the little one, I get it. And hands off the big one because he's yours, right?"

"You're halfway there, but the *big one* isn't up for any kind of negotiations from anyone, any time, or anywhere. If he tells me to slice your fat belly open so that it will always remain empty no matter how much you try to feed it, that is exactly what I will do."

Meehix pulled back her blade and stood, keeping the succubus's long black hair still wrapped in her fist, holding her just high enough that her feet could keep some tenuous contact with the deck.

"The three of us have been through too much to rescue you and have better things to do than spend our next few days figuring out a schedule of who has the fingers in the ears duty until we can deliver you to your uncle. Am I making myself clear, little girl?"

Another nod.

"Sorry, I couldn't hear you."

"Yeah, yeah. Look but don't touch."

"Don't even fucking look. I don't want to see you until we get you back to your uncle, so I can find a crate to nail you into, or you can find a corner somewhere and whimper to yourself about how the mean blue chick sent you to bed without your dinner."

"Okay, okay. Point made. I'll make myself scarce."

"Glad we had this little chat."

Meehix released her grip on her hair, and the little slut-a-butt scurried off.

"We've figured out a plan." Chuckie was excited as Meehix rejoined them up front.

"*Oh. My. Gawd!* Really? Does it include keeping your hands to yourself and her hands off you?"

Chuckie decided to let John handle this one.

"You and I are going to get dressed in our finest going out on the town clothes. We'll have to pass through the ritziest part of the station to get to the *Whooz* and won't want to draw any attention to ourselves by being dressed as mercs."

"Outfits where a couple of weapons can discreetly hide if I hear you right?"

"Exactly."

"Meet you back here in thirty minutes, maybe forty, depending on my hair."

Forty-five minutes later, they were strolling down what passed for a scenic boulevard, not hand-in-hand, but close enough to be taken for a couple who were comfortable with each other.

"I might have gone for one of your pantsuits rather than the green dress."

"What's wrong with the dress?"

"Nothing. It's one of my favorites and accents your hair."

It was one of John's favorites. He'd only seen her wear it once. It was tight-fitting, with slits on both sides reaching to the tops of her thighs. He just didn't know how practical it would be while pilfering from pirates. And how the hell could she carry any weapons in case they needed them?

"Seriously, Meehix, you look dressed to kill."

"I am." She spun her partner against a wall. As discreetly as she could, not wanting to draw any attention from passersby, she showed John the short blade and two holsters strapped to her thighs, easily accessed through the slits.

She lifted John's jaw back into place, hoping it had dropped more from the look of her legs than from the weaponry concealed there.

"You look very nice yourself. Did you go shopping back on L-222 when I wasn't looking?"

"I might have slipped out a time or two. When in space, dress as the spacers do."

"I'm impressed." She motioned for him to do a quick

fashion twirl. Holding his arms out, he performed a slow spin. "Weapons?"

"Wristband with a ten-inch retractable blade, belt holster with the gun in the back ready for a quick release, and not that my ankles can compete with yours for their attractiveness, but I have small guns attached to each."

"Very impressive."

John held his arm out. Meehix took his elbow. It was a movement that they had become very comfortable with. They hadn't run into any pirates out for an evening stroll, and they reached *Whooz* without any complications.

"We need a rent-a-bot." Meehix spoke as soon as the thought crossed her mind.

"A what?"

"Hold on. We passed a stand of them across the street a minute ago. Stay here. I'll be right back."

Not knowing what she was talking about, John decided that the best way to not draw any attention to themselves would be by not chasing after her.

Meehix returned with something that looked like a flat-shelled turtle on wheels with its head stuck on the neck of a turkey.

"*You got, we bot.*" Meehix hit the *mute* button on a remote control. "They're chatty little things."

"And their use is?" John had no idea what he was looking at.

"Think of them as a cross between a butler and a suit-case." She took John's arm again and strolled toward the pirate ship as casual as could be and explained along the way as the rent-a-bot followed.

"Whatever crates we're going to *un-steal* from the pirate's ship, our objective while getting *our* stolen items back is to appear as normal as possible as we make our way back to Shippewa, or did I miss something?"

"No, I think that sums it up pretty accurately."

"Nothing says *normal* as well as a finely dressed couple with a rent-a-bot carrying their luggage behind them."

John kept walking but glanced back and gained a whole new appreciation of the turkey-necked turtle rolling along.

"And here we are…Stay," she commanded. "Not you, John. I was talking to the bot."

"Oh." He followed her to *Whooz*'s hatch and rapped.

She stood, ready to unleash the weapons strapped to her thighs, and hoped that John was ready to unleash his and back her play.

No answer came from inside the ship, and no shots came at them from any pirate who might've been hiding to the side.

"Time to put the Kdackan bitch who broke your heart to use again."

John didn't see that command coming, but he held the turquoise and silver pendant in one hand and touched his other hand to the door's screen pad. To the surprise of both of them, the door slid open.

Chuckie had been right. The ship was completely unoccupied. They rushed to the back, where they'd last seen the Kdackan goods, and found them right where they'd left them. Pressing their luck, which had been with them so far, they opened the ramp.

"Bot. Come." A moment later, the turkey-turtle was waiting.

They grabbed the two Kdackan crates and a couple of smaller items, not caring what was in them, loaded them all on the bot, and strolled as casually as any other good-looking, well-dressed couple with a bot following behind would.

"Did we leave the ramp down, my dear?"

"I believe we did. Oh, look." Meehix pointed as any tourist would. "The lights on that building are so pretty."

"Yes, they are. So many sights here to see." John stared at where she was pointing, which looked like any other high-rise office building with lights on for the night shift.

"Come, bot."

After reaching Shippewa, unloading the goods, and returning the rent-a-bot to the closest drop-off point, she slipped in her Exchange Card and paid for the time they'd used him. When she returned to Ship, Meehix stared at Chuckie, who was still sitting in the pilot's seat.

"You've got three seconds to vacate that seat and strap in next to John."

Two seconds later, Meehix had her hands in the controls.

"Drop your cocks and grab your socks, boys. Next stop, home."

"I won't drop yours if you won't grab mine." John strapped them both in.

Meehix reversed Shippewa gently out of the docking bay and guided them to open skies.

"Good to have you piloting again, Meehix. You have a nice gentle touch that makes me feel secure."

"Well then, Ship, I hope you can hold yourself together because I'm about to floor it."

"I'm bored." The succubus was back and started for John and Chuckie.

"You're floored."

Meehix tore out so fast that the succubuttikiss didn't have time to grab anything before she was thrown ass-over-toenails to the back of the cargo area, crashing into a wall and looking for anything to hold for protection as unsecured boxes tumbled down around her.

"Home sweet L-222 home." Meehix docked.

It hadn't been a short ride, nor a peaceful one. Meehix had to handle all of the piloting because John and Chuckie had to trade off fingers in ears duty the whole way. No one had gotten any sleep.

John was on ear patrol, so Chuckie hopped out, hurried to the street, and flagged down the first auto-driver that was large enough to carry four passengers. They would worry about unloading the weapons later.

After making their weary way into their home base, the first order of business was to lock their client's niece in the closest closet. Then they headed to their separate bedrooms where they couldn't hear her whining, and all could have a good night's worth of well-earned peaceful dreamland pursuit.

Uncle Phil showed up the next morning to retrieve his niece. Meehix went to let her out of the closet and brought her to the front office to hand off. Phil was about to congratulate and thank them for a job well done when he suddenly pulled out his handkerchief.

They all yelled *"No!"* at the same time, startling him enough that the need to sneeze passed without him disappearing.

"Just get her gone," Meehix implored.

Phil took his niece's arm and led her to the door. She shook free long enough for a lingering goodbye smooch with Chuckie.

"Just a quick energy snack," before her uncle pulled her off. The last thing they heard was her pleading with her uncle to make a quick stop at the casino. "It's like an all-you-can-eat buffet, and I'm absolutely staaarving."

"I think I'd rather face the pirates again than be stuck with her for another day." John sat and relaxed for the first time in a long time.

"Look, guys, I can explain about the *Oh My Gawd*."

"Don't try, Mr. Chuck 'Notorious' Norris."

Chuckie managed to look sheepish.

"Other than the first day," John stood and stretched, "I never took a close look at all the equipment." He headed for the data cabinet.

"That really is a butt-load of routers and switches and," he did a quick count, "four different firewalls?" He stepped back to take it all in. "I've been in corporate offices that had less than this." He turned to Chuckie. "Why would *one* individual need this much?"

Time to come clean, Chuckie-boy. "Well, he wasn't quite your average person."

"And you know this because?" Meehix felt her skin

tingle and suspected that she wasn't going to like the answer.

Chuckie took a seat, not because he was tired, so much as he wanted to keep his desk between him and Meehix. "You remember Brez?"

Meehix nodded. "The three-legged realtor."

"That's the one. When I was riding with her, a small property had just come on the market close to the casino that she didn't show us because I told her it wouldn't be large enough for our needs. That was on our way over to this one."

"What does that have to do with this one?"

"It seems that they were both owned by the same guy. They both came on the market at the same time because their owner had suddenly died of *unnatural causes.*"

"Ewww." Meehix suddenly remembered the gym-slash-sex dungeon hidden behind the painting in the kitchen.

"Don't worry. He didn't die here."

"Did he die in the other house? The small one near the casino?"

"No. He died *in* the casino when a couple of bounty hunters ripped off his arms."

It was Meehix's and John's turn to take their seats.

"This belonged to Frelo?" Meehix now understood why she'd gotten the skin tingles.

"He was a mobster." John followed. "So he probably used all the electronics and the firewalls for *family* business."

"That would be my guess."

John leapt up. "We gotta go."

"Time to find a new headquarters?" Meehix agreed but

didn't think it was something that had to happen right that second.

"No, time to search the office across from the gym. There's no way a weasel like him wouldn't have some hidden loot somewhere."

"Like a safe!" Meehix was on her feet now too, and they rushed toward the painting in the kitchen.

Chuckie got up and followed. "You told me about the hidden gym, but you two geniuses didn't think to mention a hidden office?"

CHAPTER TWENTY-FOUR

The brothers who ran FBT&A Insurance, Inc. were trying to decide if they were happy or not. The earlier Kdackan shipment they'd insured with ten mercenaries, five of them Crom Limeans, had gone off without a hitch. The Croms never bargained with pirates, and pirates tried never to fight with the Croms, so they generally avoided each other.

They had covered their asses with back-dated paper-work on that one after they'd discovered there *was* a Kdackan mercenary, but their crew was already assigned. They did use him for another Kdackan shipment, and that one hadn't exactly gone as planned.

Pirates had attacked the Bargeflat 489 carrying several crates of Kdack goods and had managed to come away with three boxes. The reports coming in were that the mercenaries hired to protect the goods chose to fight the pirates rather than negotiate to surrender them. Commendable, but not common.

"Apparently," Frix was reading, "it was the Kdackan who inspired the mercs to stand their ground."

"So not only is there only one registered merc from Kdack, but he also happens to be a badass." Brix was shaking his head as he read from another report.

"This one is from the *Spaced Cadet Gazette*," Trix chimed in. The other brothers were always surprised when the most fastidious one about numbers and details turned to the weekly tabloid that featured more accounts of the drunken exploits of big-titted actresses than actual news.

"After the 489 landed on Space Station Erba," Trix read out loud, "a handful of mercs who had been on board's first stop was at the Lop & Bop, a nearby watering hole. They seemed determined to get quite sloshed while celebrating their defeat of Captain RJ and the notorious gang of pirates of *Whoozaloo*.

"When our reporter, who was there hoping to get an interview with the up-and-coming galactic all-girl band Frenzy, asked for details, they went on about two mercenaries. They called them Jo and Hix, one a Kdackan and one probably from Dolurulod, judging by her magnificent skin tones. The pair nearly single-handedly defeated the deadly bandits before sending them scurrying back to their ship."

"And none of the mercenaries were killed," Ax looked up from his report with a touch of a frown. "That means we'll have to pay them."

"It's nice that they lived, right?" Brix wasn't sure.

"For them, yeah," Ax reminded him. "But we'd subbed out their death insurance policy to Franly-Xemin. They would've had to pay up if they'd died, and we'd be off the hook for their actual pay."

"Oh. I'd forgotten."

"So now," Ax went on, "We have to divvy up the payments to all ten mercs."

"We're still up in the profit margin," Frix was feeling better, "because the mercs saved most of the shipment. We don't have to pay off on that, and that is a major benefit."

"I think we should hang onto the Kdackan's folder," Ax suggested, "and keep it as a possible re-hire when a shipment comes along that absolutely needs to be guarded."

They all agreed.

"Trix," Frix wrapped the meeting up. "Keep the payment money in our Diversion Division as long as possible and wait for the mercs to request it before we pay out. No sense in letting a few weeks of interest-gathering leeway go to waste."

"Will do." Trix was still reading the *Spaced Cadet Gazette*. "Listen to this. It says that the mercenaries also reported that the Kdackan is the same one who once told a Blavarian dreadnought captain to suck eggs and lived to tell about."

"Definitely keep in the re-hire folder." Ax nodded.

Victor Vikrellion was one pissed-off crime boss. His wife had gone out of town for a toe-realignment week at a spa with a couple of girlfriends, so he'd taken his four most faithful and trusted associates, Lazy Buff, Crabbo, Proggetti, and Jex, off-planet for two days of rest and relaxation. Two days! *Just two fucking days!*

It was supposed to be a quiet few days at the old homestead. Lazy had Trexit, the best-known tracker in anyone's memory, chasing down the two bounty hunters who'd killed poor Frelo. Trexit didn't come cheap, and he'd reported that he was making progress. He had also had a specially designed cell waiting for them down on the dungeon level.

All was right with the world. It was all *so right* that he'd left instructions with the guards to deal with whatever came up because he and the boys were taking a well-earned two-day break from day-to-day worries.

Two days! *Two fucking days!*

What did he find when he returned?

His house, his fortress of a home, had been shot up to hell and back. All of the commodities in the dungeons were free. The perpetrator had stolen his credit certificates from his secret safe in his wife's second closet.

His wife was bitching because someone rummaged through both of her closets, and she had to start from scratch to reorganize them, and…and…*and*, one of Frelo's murderers had been caught and returned, only to escape again while managing to free the dungeon's commodities.

It was tempting to send the four main guards he'd left in charge to the dungeons, but Lazy had talked him out of it.

"Sending them to the dungeons would be satisfying," Lazy had explained in an earlier meeting between the two of them.

"Very satisfying."

"It would also be a waste of resources. They were doing their jobs—"

"And failed miserably."

"Yes, sir. Fail they did."

Lazy knew the guards. They were good men. The only problem was that a couple of professionals had duped them. He'd had the chance to review what few tapes there were from the video feeds before they went dark. That alone convinced Lazy of how good the two were. Victor's security system was the best money could buy, and Lazy had personally overseen its installation.

What he'd seen was guards wheeling in a captive in a box, and a badass-looking Kdackan was his best guess. He'd seen a couple around on space stations but dismissed them as non-players, new to the galactic scene. They'd gotten them down to the dungeons, and everything went black. Definitely professionals.

"You have a warehouse out on Kribbit," he picked up the conversation with Victor where he'd left off, "where four guards are on rotation for two cycles before they're brought back and replaced by four others who would rather be anywhere other than there."

"Kribbit." Victor smiled. "Nasty little moon, but the price is right."

"Exactly. Rather than sentence the four guards to the dungeons, where they'll have to be kept and attended to—"

"Or executed." Victor loved executions.

"Or executed, good point. But it might make more sense to assign them to Kribbit for four cycles. That way, the guards coming back will be willing to do anything to stay here, and the ones we send will be punished and useful at the same time. "

Lazy had won that discussion through sheer financial logic, but in the meeting he was now engaged in, *logic* was not on the table. He, Crabbo, Proggetti, and Jex were seated in chairs arranged in a half-circle in front of Victor's desk, and the boss was out for blood.

"Jex, have we—"

The sounds of hammering and what sounded like a bone-cutting saw came from the floor directly above. Victor pulled a gun out of his top left drawer and fired three shots into the ceiling.

"Work somewhere else, you fluktig fools!" he shouted at the repairmen on the floor above.

Voices didn't carry very well between floors, but the repairmen must have taken the gunshot hints because all noise stopped. Lazy wondered if blood on the floor above them would now be another item on the list of things to repair and restore.

A little plaster dropped on their heads, but the four of them casually brushed it off. Lazy made a mental note to have the boss' ceiling repaired too.

"All right." Victor thought about putting the gun back in its drawer but decided to leave it in plain sight. It would be handy if someone gave him an answer that he wasn't happy with. Usually that was a good intimidation action to dominate a room, but he knew that none of the answers would cause him to do a happy dance, so he decided to at least *try* to keep his finger off the trigger.

"Crabbo."

"Yes, sir."

"Commodities report."

Crabbo hoped that the boss's aim would be off as he answered.

"Seventeen escapees. None returned...Yet."

"Value?"

No one ever dared to bring a notepad into meetings. They knew that they'd better have the facts and numbers already memorized. Victor wasn't famous for his patience.

"As a whole, on the open market, three million, nine hundred thousand, eight hundred thirty-seven credits. Unless a bidding war breaks out. Then the numbers would rise."

"Let's just round it up to an even four mil." Victor sighed, put the gun back in its drawer, and locked it. Otherwise, his four most trusted advisors wouldn't live long enough to finish the meeting, and he'd be left alone and end up talking to himself.

"Of the seventeen assets, do we have any further reports as to their whereabouts?"

"We believe that five of them have managed to leave the planet." Now that the gun was back in the drawer, Proggetti felt it safe to answer.

"Five?"

"Just a rough guess, Boss. The day after the escape, a Morracron transport ship had five new enlistees who signed onto the crew. It's a miserable ship with low-level, bottom-wage help. Most of its crew are chosen at the end of a long night of drinking, half of them preferring to sign up for a six-month shit job rather than go home to face their spouses and try to explain that they just blew a week's paycheck."

Nods all around. Even Victor could appreciate that kind of logic.

"The last five signed up in the middle of the afternoon."

"So they're probably lost." *Reality is what reality is.* "What about the other twelve?"

"No other authorized people have left." It was Crabbo's turn to hope the gun stayed in the drawer.

"Brakeb III has very strict controls as to who can enter or leave. Any passenger departing would need identification, but the commodities wouldn't have any."

"And no way to get them." Lazy backed Crabbo up.

None of the four had ever lied to Victor, which is why they were still alive and sitting in his office. He addressed the rest of his answers to Lazy, letting the others off the hook. The gun routine had worked, and they'd trembled in their boots enough for one meeting.

"Just to be clear, Lazy Buff, while we were gone, we had the bitch who killed little Frelo right here."

"Correct, boss. Probably her partner as well. The big one who claimed to have captured her and brought her in."

"Your tracker, whozitsname?"

"Trexit."

"Is he still working on finding them?"

"Yessir. I haven't heard from him lately, but I expect good news any day."

Victor wished he had a poof-pipe to suck on, but he'd somehow managed to leave his with the Zrillion twins during his two-day getaway. He had to pull himself together and remain calm while issuing his next summary, better known as a combined command and threat.

"I want Frelo's murderers caught yesterday or the day before whatever yesterday was. Please make that clear to Trexit. As for you four. I still have the dungeon cell ready for Frelos's murderers when I get them back. I also have seventeen other empty dungeon cells, with twelve of their former occupants still on Brakeb III?"

"To the best of our knowledge, yes."

"Then let me be clear, gentlemen," Victor lowered his voice so that they all had to lean closer to hear what he was about to say. *They hated it when that happened.*

"I want twelve of those cells filled by the time I call you four back in for a meeting. Your bodies, or theirs, but twelve cells *will* be full."

The four of them nodded and stood to head for the door. Victor pulled his gun back out and fired four more shots over their heads and into the ceiling. They all froze as more plaster dust came down on their shoulders. It was Victor's way of giving them a gentle send-off and a serious reminder.

"I've never seen the boss this pissed before." Proggetti broke the silence after they'd gotten themselves out of Victor's office and a safe distance away from further shots.

Lazy led the way to the kitchen, where they all helped themselves to well-earned bottles of Blatz's.

"Think about it." Jex passed the opener around. "Frelo's dead. Has been for a while now, and his murderers are still out there. Now, one or maybe both of them have invaded Victor's house and got away scot-free while releasing all the other prisoners."

"Do you think it was really them?" Crabbo took his first sip. "I think it's more likely that the two of them were part of that radical Save Slaves and Free Yourself movement."

They were all aware of the SSFY group, who'd been getting a lot of broadcast attention lately, but none of them had taken it very seriously until their intruders had looted the dungeon and freed the merchandise.

"I don't know, guys." Lazy was trying to fit all the pieces

together. "I'm leaning toward the SSFY. I mean, if I had killed Victor Vikrellion's little brother, I'd want to stay as far away from Victor as possible and not come knocking on his doorstep to rub it in his face."

"So, what's the plan?" Jex had no idea of what they might come up with, but he would do anything to avoid becoming a resident of the dungeons.

"I'm going to try to get in contact with Trexit to see if he's made any progress." Lazy hadn't heard from the tracker for a while and was becoming a little concerned. "You three scope out any information you can find about the whereabouts of the escapees. Whether it's fact, fiction, fantasy, or a fly-by-night rumor, we have to track them all down, or it's the dungeons for us. Victor was serious about that. Agreed?"

They *clicked* their bottles.

"The house has eighteen guards." Lazy was doing the configurations in his head. "No one's had the balls to attack us before, and since there's nothing left here now to attack for, I think we can leave ten guards to guard it safely. That sound about right?"

No one argued with his math or logic, so he went on.

"We're gonna split up into four teams. Each of us will take two guards with us, and we'll split up and scour every inch of Brakeb to find them and return them to their proper places. We've all rested on Victor's reputation for a while now, but we also know where we came from."

He had their attention because they were all once nobodies but dangerous men who had fought their way up in the organization to become Victor's four top dogs.

"So, you guys go and figure out which two guards you

want on your teams. Then decide where the teams will go because we don't want to end up meeting each other while tracking down the same fucking piece of property."

"Because that would be embarrassing." Crabbo tried to toss a little levity into the conversation and succeeded in getting a few chuckles.

"All right. You three get busy. I'll get back together with you in the morning, and we'll divvy up the assignments and who goes where…eight guards and four directions. I've gotta go and track down a tracker."

One last *clink* of bottles, and Lazy headed to his room.

Booting up his CommPu, he found a message from Trexit.

Return to Space Station L-222. Found them. Bring support.

Lazy was about to respond, *About fucking time!* but thought twice. Trexit was being well paid and could afford to wait a few more days since Victor was footing the bills, and there was no need to insult the man.

Hang loose. Don't lose track of targets. Might be fourteen days minimum. Twenty days max. Other business at the moment. Will bring with me six of the best. Keep in touch if situation changes on your end.

He re-read his message, decided that he'd worded it clearly enough, and hit "Send."

The two who had killed poor little Frelo were now on the edge of being captured. They just didn't know it yet.

They had a painful, drawn-out, forever death ahead of them. For now, Lazy had some escapees to track and avoid some dungeon time, so he needed to gather as much information as he could before meeting with the others the next morning to put their plans into action.

CHAPTER TWENTY-FIVE

Once again, Susky found himself back in the general's office. He did his duck and dance routine so that his head was never above the other man's as he made his way to the sawed-off chair in front of the great but short man's desk. *Where to begin, and how do I keep it simple?*

"Some of the goods from our latest shipment were stolen by pirates during a raid, sir."

"Fucking pirates."

The general hated to sound like he didn't understand the various complications involved, but sometimes he had to ask a question in such a way as to put the onus on the other to explain.

"I already know the answer to my next question, but I need to hear it from you."

Here it comes. Soothe the ego. Susky leaned forward, all ears.

"Financially speaking, is that a good thing or a bad thing?"

"It's not a bad thing." The Ass leaned back. *He had this.*

"The goods were insured way higher than their market value, so the insurance company will have to reimburse us for the loss, which means our cash flow will get a nice chunk of change for future expenditures."

"That was the answer I hoped you'd come up with." The general smiled.

"But it won't be tomorrow."

The general lost his smile. "Why is that?"

"Because the insurance on this one went through two different companies. One of them ours, who farmed it out to an interplanetary firm called FBT&A. They will try to bury each other in paperwork as to who owes what to whom.

"It's all nothing more than a scheme so they can both hold onto the payouts as long as possible. The money will eventually come, but not before they dick each other around for a while."

The general stood in all of his five-foot-four glory and stormed around the office looking for something to throw. Susky hunched further in the chair and let the little man rant.

"Insurance companies! Here, there, on-planet or off, they're all the same!" He plucked a twelve-inch plastic globe off its stand and drop-kicked it into a bookshelf. The books survived. The plastic world did not. He stepped around the pieces and returned to his chair.

"What else?"

"On this particular shipment," the general wasn't going to be pleased with this bit of news either, "because Earth was the shipment's planet of origin, due to regulations, they had to have someone from Earth assigned to the protection delegation."

"They're called mercenaries, so let's drop the goop-goggle and call them what they are! But there are no known intergalactic human mercs."

"Apparently, there's at least one, and he was on board when the pirates hit the cargo ship."

"The pirates were able to make off with half of the goods that one of ours was assigned to protect? Whose side was he on?"

"We're still trying to determine that."

"Well, determine it pretty shit-drop fast because the last thing I need is some kind of rogue spy within our ranks!"

Keep it simple and let the general feel like he's still in control of the situation.

"The bottom line, sir, is that he let the pirates get away and made us some money along the way." Susky let that sink in. "It's not money that we'll see until the insurance companies quit fucking everyone around and actually pay out. But our bottom line is better off for him having been there."

The general gave this some serious thought before responding.

"He could be rogue, or he could be deep-cover. It's impossible to keep track of all divisions and who's assigned where, but I want to know who this guy is."

"I'm curious myself, sir."

"Do that thing you do with your research, but keep it between the two of us, and keep any prying eyes out of it."

"On it."

Susky was about to leave his chair when a *ding* sounded

on the general's PC. He remained seated until the general dismissed him properly. He waited while the general read through whatever the notice was. Susky tried hard not to laugh as he watched his boss's lips move as he read. Having finished reading, the general looked up.

"Are you familiar with a group called SAFA?"

So the general knows about the Twitcher calling himself Gonzo Gage.

"Yes, sir. Save Aliens From Assholes. The leader is a teenager still living with his mom and dad. Just a pissant troublemaker, trying to convince the world that we're holding space aliens captive or some such bullshit."

"Does anyone take the little twerp seriously?"

"He's gathered a small following. Nothing to worry about. Two of our agents are keeping an eye on him and have already given him one anal probe."

"Have the agents pick him up again, and this time make the probe a double-wide."

"I know the agents, and they'll be more than happy to do exactly that."

"Anything else to report?"

"Not at the moment."

"Dismissed. And find a janitor to clean up the globe."

Susky did his duck and dance and escaped out the door.

The NutBusters were collectively disappointed that they hadn't found a hidden stash in the concealed office. They'd torn it apart, with more than a little minor damage done to the walls, but had come up empty.

Chuckie had also used every trick he could think of to open one of the boxes he'd sent Meehix and John to steal back from the pirates. The crate remained closed and now sat in the middle of their front office floor. He looked up. "Anyone got a blowtorch handy?"

"I'm not in a humorous mood." Meehix wasn't. "We risked our lives, *again*, because you insisted that it was worth it."

"How do you spell shit list, Jxzobbliningozlinxfipple? Because you are now on hers." John had worked hard, in a little spare time, to learn how to pronounce Chuckie N's given name and hoped he'd come close.

Chuckie looked up, touched by the effort John had made.

"My friends used to call me J-fipple." Trying to get back in Meehix's good graces, he nodded in her direction. "Except for her, who used to call me Fuck-Chuck."

"Better than Up-Chuck where I come from." John smiled. "So, going forward, you want J-fipple or Chuckie N?"

"*Chuckie* works better for day-to-day use."

Meehix smiled her crooked-ass smile at the both of them. *Can't kill 'em, can't fuck 'em.*

Chuckie had wanted to get out of Meehix's dog house without having to resort to bribes. He'd had a hard time trying to explain it to himself, but it boiled down to them having risked life and limb more than a few times for his sake and on his say-so. They'd done it because they were his partners and *friends,* two things that he'd never really had before.

Chuck Norris isn't afraid of friends. Friends are afraid of

387

Chuck Norris. He looked at them both, smiled as he pulled out the nondescript envelope labeled "Flitzbart" that he'd insisted they snatch and set it on his desk."

"John, does the name Flitzbart ring any bells?"

John had completely forgotten about the name and the envelope until now.

"The electronics firm trying to ship something totally under the radar. Not insuring it or anything, right?"

"That's the one." Chuckie had sliced the envelope open the day before and knew what was inside it.

"So, is it a beta-test prototype?"

"Not even close. We're going to play Twenty Questions again. That was your first. Meehix, feel free to join."

"So, it's not a program?" John *sooo* loved this game.

"No. Next?" Chuck enjoyed the game too.

Two quick steps and Meehix had snatched up the envelope and dumped the contents onto Chuckie's desk. She'd always been too impatient to be much of a game player. She'd only wanted to know who won and who lost and fuck all the middle shit between the beginning and the end.

Three coded data cards tumbled out. Meehix recognized the colored markings and managed to make her way back to her desk and find her chair before her ass hit the floor.

"They aren't?" she asked after the shock had passed.

"They are." Chuckie smiled.

"They aren't, or are, *what?*" John was totally out of the loop on this one.

"These, my friend," Chuckie held up the three cards, "are identities."

"They're valuable?" John remained in his state of cluelessness as Chuckie laid them out on his desk as smooth as a Flip-row dealer and faced him.

"How many digits are in a million?"

"Seven."

"Each of these cards is worth seven digits each." Chuckie leaned back in his chair and watched John gulp for air.

"Are they real?" Meehix needed to know.

"Top-tier. They're the best I've ever seen."

While John was still gulping, Meehix rose, walked slowly across the room, and looked at the cards.

"This is me, being able to be me again." She hoped that she wasn't dreaming. Chuckie nodded.

"Can I touch one?"

"Touch it, taste it, nail it to your forehead."

"Have mercy on the poor Kdackan, please. What do you two know that I don't?"

"Come over here, John," Meehix motioned to him, "and have a look." She turned to Chuckie. "Thank you, my friend."

"Yeah, yeah, you're welcome," Chuckie snatched up one of the cards. "I'll be in my room auctioning this off to the highest bidder. If you two hear me shouting any *oh my gawd, Oh My Gawd, Oohh My Gaawwdds*, stay the fuck away because I will have started a bidding war!"

Chuckie took his card and Mixie and disappeared toward his room as quickly as his legs would carry him.

After watching Chuckie hurry off, leaving his NutBuster partners with the two remaining cards, John was still nearly clueless. Meehix still held one card in her hand and lifted it.

"This card," she looked at it, "means that I have a choice to make. I can either auction it off, like Chuckie's about to do, and party-hardy for the rest of my life, or I can use it to create a new identity and never be a slave or non-sentient being again. A new name and a few credits left over to live on for a year or two."

John picked up the third card. "This one means that I can also auction it off and become a galactic millionaire like you other two?"

"Yes! How cool is that after all we've been through?"

John thought back to his bedroom in his parents' basement, and all the time he spent gaming there before Gage had texted him about some USSF base he wanted to check out. He was nineteen years old at the time. He was still nineteen years old—*I think*—but had gained a lifetime of experience since then.

He handed Meehix his card.

"One card to establish a new identity. One card to auction off to the highest bidder. Shippewa will get me back to Earth, and I'll be no worse for the wear. But now? I've got a few kinks to work out, and the gym is calling."

John headed for the gym, leaving Meehix with two million credits' worth of cards in her hands.

Two mil and a party girl for life! Yeah, right, you silly girl.

She hid the two cards somewhere that Chuckie couldn't find them.

The next party wouldn't be the same without you, Jojacko.

Hoping that she hadn't said that last thought out loud for him to hear, she rushed to the hallway and toward the kitchen painting that John had toed open.

"Hold the door! I'm about to kick your ass again on the cardio!"

John held the door and watched as she rushed by him. "So says you, you green-haired blue chick!"

GAME ON!

The story continues with book three, *That SHIP Has a Phat Ass,* available at Amazon and through Kindle Unlimited.

Claim your copy today

AUTHOR NOTES
JULY 16, 2021

Thank you for not only reading this story but these author notes as well!

I am back in Cabo San Lucas at the Sunset Beach Resort. For those who know my past, you are aware that my wife and I started this...

Um...

'Journey' some five years ago (getting closer to six) to purchase property here in Pueblo Bonito.

At the time (Nov 2015), I had finished my second ever book, and we were down here for a friend's wedding where my wife (friends of both the groom and bride) was going to officiate their wedding as she speaks both English and Spanish.

The groom's family knows English, but many of the bride's family (especially immediate members) only know Spanish.

So she and I were staying at the Pacifica Resort and making a very long story short, we put money down on a condo here in Pueblo Bonito. The next year (or two, the year is vague), we moved the money to a house, and then another year or so we move THAT money to yet another house.

That house was supposed to be finished in 2020... And Covid hit.

So, here we are about to take possession (I hope!) in a few days, and I swear on all that is holy, I don't wish to buy any more homes the rest of my life.

I'm good doing multi-month rentals in foreign countries, I think.

But, I am looking out at the Sea of Cortez, the ocean fading into a blue-grey in the distance (some thirty miles away) and merging with the sky. The sun is setting off somewhere to my right, and the waves are crashing a few hundred yards away, the noise powering up the cliff to the patio I am sitting in as I write this.

And I am content.

It has been a hard run to be at this point... almost six years later. I am not a patient person, and frankly, if you had told me it would take this long before I could close on a property, I would have declined the opportunity.

Which, frankly, would have been a shame. Yes, it took over half a decade to get this residence. But the chance to live here, alongside the vast amount of water, is a subtle pleasure I believe I will only learn to enjoy as I go through my fifties and into my sixties. There is a peace here that comforts me in my anxiety.

I started with just one book. With providence, effort, some great people, and support from you, the readers, I have been blessed.

So thank you. I may not totally understand why my

stories resonate, but I am forever grateful that they do. Your support of our stories allows us the chance to write more.

LMBPN (my company) is a thousand books strong.
Here is to the next 1,000!

Ad Aeternitatem,

Michael Anderle.

CONNECT WITH MICHAEL

Connect with Michael Anderle

Website: http://lmbpn.com

Email List: http://lmbpn.com/email/

Social Media:

https://www.facebook.com/LMBPNPublishing

https://twitter.com/MichaelAnderle

https://www.instagram.com/lmbpn_publishing/

https://www.bookbub.com/authors/michael-anderle